SEASON
OF
WONDER

❄ ❄ ❄

SEASON
OF
WONDER

❄ ❄ ❄

Edited by Paula Guran

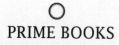
PRIME BOOKS

To Mark & Allyson
(and Malcolm & Dewie)
who are now back "home" for Christmas
(and everything else.)

Contents

Introduction

❄

Paula Guran

In the earliest days of human civilization, life itself was dependent on the seasons—especially in the northern hemisphere. The sowing and harvesting of crops, the mating of animals, the necessity of storing provisions for the lean months—all were governed by what we now recognize as the yearly rotation of the Earth around the sun and the tilt of the Earth's axis.

The most identifiable seasonal markers are the northerly and southerly migration points of the sun: the solstices. At winter solstice in the northern hemisphere, the sun appears at noon at its lowest altitude above the horizon, making it the shortest day and longest night of the year.

For our ancient ancestors, the growing darkness that preceded the winter solstice was a fearful time. What assurance was there that the sun would return? Without the sun they could not survive. Rituals began in prehistoric times with the aim of pleasing the sun or frightening the forces of darkness away or appeasing the gods or making powerful magic to assure that the world would survive this darkest time and that the light and warmth would again return.

Once satisfied the light would triumph, the celebrations could begin, joyful thanks could be offered. In Europe, midwinter was a perfect time to feast and make merry. Excess swine, cattle, and other livestock—animals that could not be efficiently fed during the upcoming coldest months—were slaughtered, so there was plenty of fresh meat. Grains and fruits made into beer and wine after the work of harvest had been completed had time to ferment by solstice.

Customs, rites, and traditions that became seasonal festivals and holidays also grew from other points of the cycle of the year. Humans have been adapting and reinventing them ever since to meet whatever our psychological and cultural needs may be.

But the winter holidays have always had more of an element of wonder to them than other observances. The concepts of magic and faith, even "good" (the life-giving light) and "evil" (the killing dark) may well have arisen in connection with the winter solstice. We seem to possess a primal need to seek light within the darkness, to find literal and metaphorical warmth, to celebrate humanity's survival, to seek hope and joy and renewal and love—and, yes, miracles and magic—in order to continue to be human.

It should come as no surprise that since Charles Dickens (at least), writers of speculative fiction have employed this season of wonder in many imaginative stories.

Until fairly recently, we could not determine the exact moment—or even the precise day—of the winter (or summer) solstice, but some of our ancestors devised relatively accurate astronomical methods to determine when solstice occurred. In simple societies, observance of the weather, animal behavior, and the appearance of plants provided appropriate dates for the rituals and customs associated with the solstices.

Even in cultures where winter's cold was not a threat, the winter solstice was noted and considered of great significance. In ancient Egypt the annual flooding of the Nile occurred near summer solstice, but the winter solstice was important in marking the birth of the sun god and the renewal of the year. Even the Great Zimbabwe in sub-Saharan Africa was evidently used to astronomically determine the winter solstice. The Sun Dagger of Chaco Canyon in New Mexico, the Calçoene megalithic observatory in Brazil, sites in Peru, and many other ancient sites constructed for astronomical tracking bear witness to the importance of the winter solstice outside of Europe.

In our western culture, the most notable winter celebrations are Christmas (with or without its religious association) and New Year's. In some predominately Christian regions, Twelfth Night/Epiphany (January 6) and its eve are also celebratory dates. Chanukah, although it is not really a solstice holiday, has been adapted into a winter holiday. Thanks primarily to the influence of neopagans, there's been a return to celebrating Winter Solstice itself.

Kwanzaa is not religious or attached to the solstice, but it is the most recently introduced (1966-67) winter holiday. So far, the fiction inspired by this cultural celebration of African-American heritage has been primarily in the field of children's literature. I could find no professional short genre fiction with a Kwanzaa theme.

There are numerous other winter festivals—from the Shinto Ameratsu marking the reemergence of the sun goddess from her cave to Ziemassvētki (celebrating the birth of Dievas, the supreme god of Baltic mythology)—that are still celebrated or that have customs and traditions that have been assimilated into current holidays.

This multitude of winter observances are, however, left mostly unexplored in this anthology of science fiction and fantasy. Perhaps such fictions will, in time, evolve.

But, fear not: the ingenuity, personal viewpoints, and creative powers of these writers still provide us with stories as diverse and wonderous as the season itself.

Happy Holidays!
Paula Guran

❄   ❄   ❄

Winter holidays mark the end of one year and the beginning of another. It may be a time of darkness, but it is also a time for rebirth, renewal, and the promise that spring will come again. In this Hugo-nominated story, we are reminded that, no matter what, there are reasons to celebrate life and continue to live.

The Best Christmas Ever
❄
James Patrick Kelly

Aunty Em's man was not doing well at all. He had been droopy and gray ever since the neighbor Mr. Kimura had died, shuffling around the house in nothing but socks and bathrobe. He had even lost interest in the model train layout that he and the neighbor were building in the garage. Sometimes he stayed in bed until eleven in the morning and had ancient Twinkies for lunch. He had a sour, vinegary smell. By midafternoon he'd be asking her to mix strange ethanol concoctions like Brave Little Toasters and Tin Honeymoons. After he had drunk five or six, he would stagger around the house mumbling about the big fires he'd fought with Ladder Company No. 3 or the wife he had lost in the Boston plague. Sometimes he would just cry.

BEGIN INTERACTION 4022932

"Do you want to watch *Annie Hall?*" Aunty Em asked.

The man perched on the edge of the Tyvola sofa in the living room, elbows propped on knees, head sunk into hands.

"*The General? Monty Python and the Holy Grail? Spaced Out?*"

"I hate that robot." He tugged at his thinning hair and snarled. "I hate robots."

Aunty Em did not take this personally—she was a biop, not a robot. "I could call Lola. She's been asking after you."

"I'll bet." Still, he looked up from damp hands. "I'd rather have Kathy."

This was a bad sign. Kathy was the lost wife. The girlfriend biop could certainly assume that body; she could look like anyone the man wanted. But while the girlfriend biop could pretend, she could never be the wife that the man missed. His reactions to the Kathy body were always erratic and sometimes dangerous.

"I'll nose around town," said Aunty Em. "I heard Kathy was off on a business trip, but maybe she's back."

"Nose around," he said and then reached for the glass on the original Noguchi coffee table with spread fingers, as if he thought it might try to leap from his grasp. "You do that." He captured it on the second attempt.

End Interaction 4022932

The man was fifty-six years old and in good health, considering. His name was Albert Paul Hopkins, but none of the biops called him that. Aunty Em called him Bertie. The girlfriend called him sweetie or Al. The pal biops called him Al or Hoppy or Sport. The stranger biops called him Mr. Hopkins or sir. The animal biops didn't speak much, but the dog called him Buddy and the cat called him Mario.

When Aunty Em beamed a summary of the interaction to the girlfriend biop, the girlfriend immediately volunteered to try the Kathy body again. The girlfriend had been desperate of late, since the man didn't want anything to do with her. His slump had been hard on her, hard on Aunty Em too. Taking care of the man had changed the biops. They were all so much more emotional than they had been when they were first budded.

But Aunty Em told the girlfriend to hold off. Instead she decided to throw a Christmas. She hadn't done Christmas in almost eight months. She'd given him a *Gone With the Wind* Halloween and a Fourth of July with whistling busters, panoramas, phantom balls, and double-break shells, but those were only stopgaps. The man needed cookies, he needed presents, he was absolutely aching for a sleigh filled with Christmas cheer. So she beamed an alert to all of her biops and assigned roles. She warned them that if this wasn't the best Christmas ever, they might lose the last man on earth.

Aunty Em spent three days baking cookies. She dumped eight sticks of fatty acid triglycerides, four cups of $C_{12}H_{22}O_{11}$, four vat-grown ova, four teaspoons of flavor potentiator, twelve cups of milled grain endosperm, and five teaspoons each of $NaHCO_3$ and $KHC_4H_4O_6$ into the bathtub and then trod on the mixture with her best baking boots. She rolled the dough and then pulled cookie cutters off the top shelf of the pantry: the mitten and the dollar sign and the snake and the double-bladed ax. She dusted the cookies with red nutriceutical sprinkles, baked them at 190°C, and brought a plate to the man while they were still warm.

The poor thing was melting into the recliner in the television room. He clutched a half-full tumbler of Sins-of-the-Mother, as if it were the anchor that was keeping him from floating out of the window. He had done nothing but watch classic commercials with the sound off since he had fallen out of bed. The cat was curled on the man's lap, pretending to be asleep.

BEGIN INTERACTION 4022947

"Cookies, Bertie," said Aunty Em. "Fresh from the oven, oven fresh." She set the plate down on the end table next to the Waterford lead crystal vase filled with silk daffodils.

"Not hungry," he said. On the mint-condition 34-inch Sony Hi-Scan television Ronald McDonald was dancing with some kids.

Aunty Em stepped in front of the screen, blocking his view. "Have you decided what you want for Christmas, dear?"

"It isn't Christmas." He waved her away from the set, but she didn't budge. He did succeed in disturbing the cat, which stood, arched its back, and then dropped to the floor.

"No, of course it isn't." She laughed. "Christmas isn't until next week."

He aimed the remote at the set and turned up the sound. A man was talking very fast. "Two all-beef patties, special sauce, lettuce, cheese . . . "

Aunty Em pressed the off button with her knee. "I'm talking to you, Bertie."

The man lowered the remote. "What's today?"

"Today is Friday." She considered. "Yes, Friday."

"No, I mean the date."

"The date is . . . let me see. The twenty-first."

His skin temperature had risen from 33°C to 37°. "The twenty-first of what?" he said.

She stepped away from the screen. "Have another cookie, Bertie."

"All right." He turned the television on and muted it. "You win." A morose Maytag repairman slouched at his desk, waiting for the phone to ring. "I know what I want," said the man. "I want a Glock 17."

"And what is that, dear?"

"It's a nine millimeter handgun."

"A handgun, oh my." Aunty Em was so flustered that she ate one of her own cookies, even though she had extinguished her digestive track for the day. "For shooting? What would you shoot?"

"I don't know." He broke the head off a gingerbread man. "A reindeer. The TV. Maybe one of you."

"Us? Oh, Bertie—one of us?"

He made a gun out of his thumb and forefinger and aimed. "Maybe just the cat." His thumb came down.

The cat twitched. "Mario," it said and nudged the man's bare foot with its head. "No, Mario."

On the screen the Jolly Green Giant rained peas down on capering elves.

End Interaction 4022947

Begin Interaction 4023013

The man stepped onto the front porch of his house and squinted at the sky, blinking. It was late spring and the daffodils were nodding in a warm breeze. Aunty Em pulled the sleigh to the bottom of the steps and honked the horn. It played the first three notes of "Jingle Bells." The man turned to go back into the house but the girlfriend biop took him by the arm. "Come on now, sweetie," she said and steered him toward the steps.

The girlfriend had assumed the Donna Reed body the day before, but unlike previous Christmases, the man had taken no sexual interest in her. She was wearing the severe black dress with the white lace collar from the last scene of *It's A Wonderful Life*. The girlfriend looked as worried about the man as Mary had been about despairing George Bailey. All the biops were worried, thought Aunty Em. They would be just devastated if anything happened to him. She waved gaily and hit the horn again. *Beep-beep-BEEP!*

The dog and the cat had transformed themselves into reindeer for the outing. The cat got the red nose. Three of the animal biops had assumed reindeer bodies too. They were all harnessed to the sleigh, which hovered about a foot off the ground. As the man stumped down the steps, Aunty Em discouraged the antigrav, and the runners crunched against gravel. The girlfriend bundled the man aboard.

"Do you see who we have guiding the way?" said Aunty Em. She beamed the cat and it lit up its nose. "See?"

"Is that the fake cop?" The man coughed. "Or the fake pizza guy? I can't keep them straight."

"On Dasher, now Dancer, now Comet and Nixon," cried Aunty Em as she encouraged the antigrav. "To the mall, Rudolf, and don't bother to slow down for yellow lights!" She cracked the whip and away they went, down the driveway and out into the world.

The man lived at the edge of the biop compound, away from the bustle of the spaceport and the accumulatorium with its bulging galleries of authentic human artifacts and the vat where new biops were budded off the master template. They drove along the perimeter road. The biops were letting the forest take over here, and saplings of birch and hemlock sprouted from the ruins of the town.

The sleigh floated across a bridge and Aunty Em started to sing. "Over the river and through the woods . . . " But when she glanced over her shoulder and saw the look on the man's face, she stopped. "Is something wrong, Bertie dear?"

"Where are you taking me?" he said. "I don't recognize this road."

"It's a secret," said Aunty Em. "A Christmas secret."

His blood pressure had dropped to 93/60. "Have I been there before?"

"I wouldn't think so. No."

The girlfriend clutched the man's shoulder. "Look," she said. "Sheep."

Four ewes had gathered at the river's edge to drink, their stumpy tails twitching. They were big animals; their long, tawny fleeces made them look like walking couches. A brown man on a dromedary camel watched over them. He was wearing a satin robe in royal purple with gold trim at the neck. When Aunty Em beamed him the signal, he tapped the line attached to the camel's nose peg and the animal turned to face the road.

"One of the wise men," said Aunty Em.

"The king of the shepherds," said the girlfriend.

As the sleigh drove by, the wise man tipped his crown to them. The sheep looked up from the river and bleated, "Happy holidays."

"They're so cute," said the girlfriend. "I wish we had sheep."

The man sighed. "I could use a drink."

"Not just yet, Bertie," said Aunty Em. "But I bet Mary packed your candy."

The girlfriend pulled a plastic pumpkin from underneath the seat. It was filled with leftovers from the Easter they'd had last month. She held it out to the man and shook it. It was filled with peeps and candy corn and squirtgum and chocolate crosses. He pulled a peep from the pumpkin and sniffed it suspiciously.

"It's safe, sweetie," said the girlfriend. "I irradiated everything just before we left."

There were no cars parked in the crumbling lot of the Wal-Mart. They pulled up to the entrance where a Salvation Army Santa stood over a black plastic pot holding a bell. The man didn't move.

"We're here, Al." The girlfriend nudged him. "Let's go."

"What is this?" said the man.

"Christmas shopping," said Aunty Em. "Time to shop."

"Who the hell am I supposed to shop for?"

"Whoever you want," said Aunty Em. "You could shop for us. You could shop for yourself. You could shop for Kathy."

"Aunty Em!" said the girlfriend.

"No," said the man. "Not Kathy."

"Then how about Mrs. Marelli?"

The man froze. "Is that what this is about?"

"It's about Christmas, Al," said the girlfriend. "It's about getting out of the god-damned sleigh and going into the store." She climbed over him and jumped down to the pavement before Aunty Em could discourage the antigrav. She stalked by the Santa and through the entrance without looking back. Aunty Em beamed her a request to come back but she went dark.

"All right," said the man. "You win."

The Santa rang his bell at them as they approached. The man stopped and grasped Aunty Em's arm. "Just a minute," he said and ran back to the sleigh to fetch the plastic pumpkin. He emptied the candy into the Santa's pot.

"God bless you, young man." The Santa knelt and sifted the candy through his red suede gloves as if it were gold.

"Yeah," said the man. "Merry Christmas."

Aunty Em twinkled at the two of them. She thought the man might finally be getting into the spirit of the season.

The store was full of biops, transformed into shoppers. They had stocked the shelves with artifacts authenticated by the accumulatorium: Barbies and Sonys and Goodyears and Dockers; patio furniture and towels and microwave ovens and watches. At the front of the store was an array of polyvinyl chloride spruce trees predecorated with bubble lights and topped with glass penguins. Some of the merchandise was new, some used, some broken. The man paid attention to none of it, not even the array of genuine Lionel "O" Scale locomotives and freight cars Aunty Em had ordered specially for this interaction. He passed methodically down the aisles, eyes bright, searching. He strode right by the girlfriend, who was sulking in Cosmetics.

Aunty Em paused to touch her shoulder and beam an encouragement, but the girlfriend shook her off. Aunty Em thought she would have to do something about the girlfriend, but she didn't know what exactly. If she sent her back to the vat and replaced her with a new biop, the man would surely notice. The girlfriend and the man had been quite close before the man had slipped into his funk. She knew things about him that even Aunty Em didn't know.

The man found Mrs. Marelli sitting on the floor in the hardware section. She was opening packages of GE Soft White 100-watt light bulbs and then smashing them with a Stanley Workmaster claw hammer. The biop shoppers paid no attention. Only the lead biop of her team, Dr. Watson, seemed to worry about her. He waited with a broom, and whenever she tore into a new box of light bulbs he swept the shards of glass away.

Aunty Em was shocked at the waste. How many pre-extinction light bulbs were left on this world? Twenty thousand? Ten? She wanted to beam a rebuke to Dr. Watson, but she knew he was doing a difficult job as best he could.

"Hello, Ellen." The man knelt next to the woman. "How are you doing?"

She glanced at him, hammer raised. "Dad?" She blinked. "Is that you, Dad?"

"No, it's Albert Hopkins. Al—you know, your neighbor. We've met before. These . . . people introduced us. Remember the picnic? The trip to the spaceport?"

"Picnic?" She shook her head as if to clear it. Ellen Theresa Marelli was eleven years older than the man. She was wearing Bruno Magli black leather flats and a crinkly light blue Land's End dress with a pattern of small dark blue and white flowers. Her hair was gray and a little thin but was nicely cut and permed into tight curls. She was much better groomed than the man, but that was because she couldn't take care of herself anymore and so her biops did everything for her. "I like picnics."

"What are you doing here, Ellen?"

She stared at the hammer as if she were surprised to see it. "Practicing."

"Practicing for what?" He held out his hand for the hammer and she gave it to him.

"Just practicing." She gave him a sly look. "What are you doing here?"

"I was hoping to do a little Christmas shopping."

"Oh, is it Christmas?" Her eyes went wide.

"In a couple of days," said the man. "Do you want to tag along?"

She turned to Dr. Watson. "Can I?"

"By all means." Dr. Watson swept the space in front of her.

"Oh goody!" She clapped her hands. "This is just the best." She tried to get up but couldn't until the man and Dr. Watson helped her to her feet. "We'll need a shopping cart," she said.

She tottered to the fashion aisles and tried on sweaters. The man helped her pick out a Ralph Lauren blue cable cardigan that matched her dress. In the housewares section, she decided that she needed a Zyliss garlic press. She spent the most time in the toy aisle, lingering at the Barbies. She didn't care much for the late models, still in their packaging. Instead she made straight for the vintage Barbies and Kens and Francies and Skippers posed around the Barbie Dream House and the Barbie Motor Home. Dr. Watson watched her nervously.

"Look, they even have talking Barbies," she said, picking up a doll in an orange flowered dress. "I had one just like this. With all the blond hair and everything. See the little necklace? You press the button and . . . "

But the Barbie didn't speak. The woman's mouth set in a grim line and she smashed it against the shelf.

"Ellie," said Dr. Watson. "I wish you wouldn't . . . "

The woman threw the doll at him and picked up another. This was a brunette that was wearing only the top of her hot pink bathing suit. The woman jabbed at the button.

"It's time to get ready for my date with Ken," said the doll in a raspy voice.

"That's better," said the woman.

She pressed the button again and the doll said, "Let's invite the gang over!"

The woman turned to the man and the two biops, clearly excited. "Here." She thrust the doll at Aunty Em, who was nearest to her. "You try." Aunty Em pressed the button.

"I can't wait to meet my friends," said the doll.

"What a lovely toy!" Aunty Em smiled. "She certainly has the Christmas spirit, don't you think, Bertie?"

The man frowned and Aunty Em could tell from the slump of his shoulders that his good mood was slipping away. His heart rate jumped and his eyes were distant, a little misty. The woman must have noticed the change too, because she pointed a finger at Aunty Em.

"You," she said. "You ruin everything."

"Now Mrs. Marelli," she said, "I . . . "

"You're following us." The woman snatched the Barbie away from her. "Who are you?"

"You know me, Mrs. Marelli. I'm Aunty Em."

"That's crazy." The woman's laugh was like a growl. "I'm not crazy."

Dr. Watson beamed a general warning that he was terminating the interaction; seeing the man always upset the woman. "That's enough, Ellen." He grasped her forearm, and Aunty Em was relieved to see him paint relaxant onto her skin with his med finger. "I think it's time to go."

The woman shivered. "Wait," she said. "He said it was Christmas." She pointed at the man. "Daddy said."

"We'll talk about that when we get home, Ellen."

"Daddy." She shook herself free and flung herself at the man.

The man shook his head. "This isn't . . . "

"Ssh. It's okay." The woman hugged him. "Just pretend. That's all we can do, isn't it?" Reluctantly, he returned her embrace. "Daddy." She spoke into his chest. "What are you getting me for Christmas?"

"Can't tell," he said. "It's a secret."

"A Barbie?" She giggled and pulled away from him.

"You'll just have to wait."

"I already know that's what it is."

"But you might forget." The man held out his hand and she gave him the doll. "Now close your eyes."

She shut them so tight that Aunty Em could see her orbicularis oculi muscles tremble.

The man touched her forehead. "Daddy says forget." He handed the doll to Dr. Watson, who mouthed *Thank you*. Dr. Watson beamed a request for Aunty Em to hide, and she sidled behind the bicycles where the woman couldn't see her. "Okay, Ellen," said the man. "Daddy says open your eyes."

She blinked at him. "Daddy," she said softly, "when are you coming home?"

The man was clearly taken aback; there was a beta wave spike in his EEG. "I . . . ah . . . " He scratched the back of his neck. "I don't know," he said. "Our friends here keep me pretty busy."

"I'm so lonely, Daddy." The last woman on earth began to cry.

The man opened his arms to her and they clung to each other, rocking back and forth. "I know," said the man, over and over. "I know."

END INTERACTION 4023013

■ ■ ■

Aunty Em, the dog, and the cat gathered in the living room of the house, waiting for the man to wake up. She had scheduled the pals, Jeff and Bill, to drop by around noon for sugar cookies and eggnog. The girlfriend was upstairs fuming. She had been Katie Couric, Anna Kournikova, and Jacqueline Kennedy since the Wal-Mart trip but the man had never even blinked at her.

The music box was playing "Blue Christmas." The tree was decorated with strings of pinlights and colored packing peanuts. Baseball cards and silver glass balls and plastic army men hung from the branches. Beneath the tree was a modest pile of presents. Aunty Em had picked out one each for the inner circle of biops and signed the man's name to the cards. The rest were gifts for him from them.

BEGIN INTERACTION 4023064

" 'Morning, Mario," said the cat.

Aunty Em was surprised; it was only eight-thirty. But there was the man propped in the doorway, yawning.

"Merry Christmas, Bertie!" she said.

The dog scrabbled across the room to him. "Buddy, open now, Buddy, open, Buddy, open, open!" It went up on hind legs and pawed his knee.

"Later." The man pushed it away. "What's for breakfast?" he said. "I feel like waffles."

"You want waffles?" said Aunty Em. "Waffles you get."

END INTERACTION 4023064

She bustled into the kitchen as the man closed the bathroom door behind him. A few minutes later she heard the pipes clang as he turned on the shower. She beamed a revised schedule to the pals, calling for them to arrive within the hour.

Aunty Em could not help but be pleased. This Christmas was already a great success. The man's attitude had changed dramatically after the shopping trip. He was keeping regular hours and drinking much less. He had stopped by the train layout in the garage, although all he had done was look at it. Instead he had taken an interest in the garden in the backyard and had spent yesterday weeding the flowerbeds and digging a new vegetable patch. He had sent the pal Jeff to find seeds he could plant.

The biops reported that they had found some peas and corn and string beans—but they were possibly contaminated and might not germinate. She had already warned some of the lesser animal biops that they might have to assume the form of corn stalks and pea vines if the crop failed.

Now if only he would pay attention to the girlfriend.

BEGIN INTERACTION 4023066

The doorbell gonged the first eight notes of "Silent Night." "Would you get that, Bertie dear?" Aunty Em was pouring freshly-budded ova into a pitcher filled with Pet Evaporated Milk.

"It's the pals," the man called from the front hall. "Jeff and . . . I'm sorry, I've forgotten your name."

"Bill."

"Bill, of course. Come in, come in."

A few minutes later, Aunty Em found them sitting on the sofa in the living room. Each of the pals balanced a present on his lap, wrapped in identical green and red paper. They were listening uncomfortably as the cat recited " 'Twas the Night Before Christmas." The man was busy playing *Madden NFL 2007* on his Game Boy.

"It's time for sweets and presents, Bertie." Aunty Em set the pitcher of eggnog next to the platter of cookies. She was disturbed that the girlfriend hadn't joined the party yet. She beamed a query but the girlfriend was dark. "Presents and sweets."

The man opened Jeff's present first. It was filled with hand tools for his new garden: a dibbler and a trowel and a claw hoe and a genuine Felco10 Professional Pruner. The dog gave the man a chewable rubber fire hydrant that squeaked when squeezed. The cat gave him an "O" Scale Western Pacific Steam Locomotive that had belonged to the dead neighbor, Mr. Kimura. The man and the cat exchanged looks briefly and then the cat yawned. The dog nudged his head under all the discarded wrapping paper and the man reached down with the claw hoe and scratched its back. Everyone but the cat laughed.

Next came Bill's present. In keeping with the garden theme of this Christmas, it was a painting of a balding old farmer and a middle-aged woman standing in front of a white house with an odd Gothic window. Aunty Em could tell the man was a farmer because he was holding a pitchfork. The farmer stared out of the painting with a glum intensity; the woman looked at him askance. The curator biop claimed that it was one of the most copied images in the inventory, so Aunty Em was not surprised that the man seemed to recognize it.

"This looks like real paint," he said.

"Yes," said Bill. "Oil on beaverboard."

"What's beaverboard?" said the cat.

"A light, semirigid building material of compressed wood pulp," Bill said. "I looked it up."

The man turned the painting over and brushed his finger across the back. "Where did you get this?" His face was pale.

"From the accumulatorium."

"No, I mean where before then?"

Aunty Em eavesdropped as the pal beamed the query. "It was salvaged from the Chicago Art Institute."

"You're giving me the original *American Gothic*?" His voice fell into a hole.

"Is something the matter, Bertie?"

He fell silent for a moment. "No, I suppose not." He shook his head. "It's a very thoughtful gift." He propped the painting on the mantle, next to his scuffed leather fireman's helmet that the biops had retrieved from the ruins of the Ladder Company No. 3 Firehouse two Christmases ago.

Aunty Em wanted the man to open his big present, but the girlfriend had yet to make her entrance. So instead, she gave the pals their presents from the man. Jeff got the October 1937 issue of *Spicy Adventure Stories*. On the cover a brutish sailor carried a terrified woman in a shredded red dress out of the surf as their ship sank in the background. Aunty Em pretended to be shocked and the man actually chuckled. Bill got a chrome Model 1B14 Toastmaster two-slice toaster. The man took it from him and traced the triple loop logo etched in the side. "My mom had one of these."

Finally there was nothing left to open but the present wrapped in the blue paper with the Santa-in-space print. The man took the Glock 17 out of the box cautiously, as if he were afraid it might go off. It was black with a polymer grip and a four-and-a-half-inch steel barrel. Aunty Em had taken a calculated risk with the pistol. She always tried to give him whatever he asked for, as long as it wasn't too dangerous. He wasn't their captive after all. He was their master.

"Don't worry," she said. "It's not loaded. I looked but couldn't find the right bullets."

"But I did," said the girlfriend, sweeping into the room in the Kathy body. "I looked harder and found hundreds of thousands of bullets."

"Kathy," said Aunty Em, as she beamed a request for her to terminate this unauthorized interaction. "What a nice surprise."

"Nine-millimeter Parabellum," said the girlfriend. Ten rounds clattered onto the glass top of the Noguchi coffee table. "115 grain. Full metal jacket."

"What are you doing?" said the man.

"You want to shoot someone?" The girlfriend glared at the man and swung her arms wide.

"Kathy," said Aunty Em. "You sound upset, dear. Maybe you should go lie down."

The man returned the girlfriend's stare. "You're not Kathy."

"No," said the girlfriend. "I'm nobody you know."

"Kathy's dead," said the man. "Everybody's dead except for me and poor Ellen Marelli. That's right, isn't it?"

The girlfriend sank to her knees, rested her head on the coffee table, and began to cry. Only biops didn't cry, or at least no biop that Aunty Em had ever heard of. The man glanced around the room for an answer. The pals looked at their shoes and said nothing. "Jingle Bell Rock" tinkled on the music box. Aunty Em felt something swell inside of her and climb her throat until she thought she might burst. If this was what the man felt all the time, it was no wonder he was tempted to drink himself into insensibility.

"Well?" he said.

"Yes," Aunty Em blurted. "Yes, dead, Bertie. All dead."

The man took a deep breath. "Thank you," he said. "Sometimes I can't believe that it really happened. Or else I forget. You make it easy to forget. Maybe you think that's good for me. But I need to know who I am."

"Buddy," said the dog, brushing against him. "Buddy, my Buddy."

The man patted the dog absently. "I could give up. But I won't. I've had a bad spell the last couple of weeks, I know. That's not your fault." He heaved himself off the couch, came around the coffee table and knelt beside the girlfriend. "I really appreciate that you trust me with this gun. And these bullets too. That's got to be scary, after what I said." The girlfriend watched him scoop up the bullets. "Kathy, I don't need these just now. Would you please keep them for me?"

She nodded.

"Do you know the movie, *Miracle On 34th Street?*" He poured the bullets into her cupped hands. "Not the remakes. The first one, with Maureen O'Hara?"

She nodded again.

He leaned close and whispered into her ear. His pulse soared to 93.

She sniffed and then giggled.

"You go ahead," he said to her. "I'll come up in a little while." He gave her a pat on the rear and stood up. The other biops watched him nervously.

"What's with all the long faces?" He tucked the Glock into the waistband of his pants. "You look like them." He waved at the painting of the somber farm folk, whose mood would never, ever change. "It's Christmas Day, people. Let's live it up!"

END INTERACTION 4023066

Over the years, Aunty Em gave the man many more Christmases, not to mention Thanksgivings, Easters, Halloweens, April Fools, and Valentine Days. But she always said—and no one contradicted her: not the man, not even the girlfriend—that this Christmas was the best ever.

❄   ❄   ❄

Chanukah is also known as the Festival of Lights. Unlike most winter holidays or festivals, it has nothing to do with the changing of seasons or solstice. Instead, it commemorates the rededication of the Temple in Jerusalem in 164 BCE after the Maccabees defeated their Syrian-Greek rulers. But, similar to other holidays, it also represents a triumph of light over darkness.

Go Toward the Light
❄
Harlan Ellison

It was a time of miracles. Time, itself, was the first miracle. That we had learned how to drift backward through it, that we had been able to achieve it at all: another miracle. And the most remarkably miraculous miracle of all: that of the one hundred and sixty-five physicists, linguists, philologists, archaeologists, engineers, technicians, programmers of large-scale numerical simulations, and historians who worked on the Timedrift Project, only two were Jews. Me, myself, Matty Simon, a timedrifter, what is technically referred to on my monthly paycheck as an authentic "chronocircumnavigator"—euphemistically called a "fugitive" by the one hundred and sixty-three Gentile techno-freaks and computer jockeys— short-speak for *Tempus Fugit*—"Time Flies"—broken-backed Latin, just a "fugitive." That's me, young Matty, and the other Jew is Barry Levin. Not Le*vine* and not Le*veen*, but Levin, as if to rhyme with "let me in." Mr. Barry R. Levin, Fields Medal nominee, post-adolescent genius and wiseguy, the young man who Stephen Hawking (yeah, courtesy of the over-the-counter anti-agathic drugs, still alive, and breaking a hundred on the links) says has made the greatest contributions to quantum gravity, the guy who, if you ask him a simple question you get a pageant, endless lectures on chrono-string theory, complexity theory, algebraic number theory, how many pepperonis can dance on the point of a pizza. Also, Barry Levin, orthodox Jew. Did I say orthodox? Beyond, galactically *beyond* orthodox. So damned orthodox that, by comparison, Moses was a *fresser* of barbequed pork sandwiches with Texas hot links. Levin, who was *frum*, Chassid, a reader and quoter of the Talmud, and also the biggest pain in the . . . I am a scientist, I am not allowed to use that kind of language. A pain in the nadir, the fundament, the buttocks, the *tuchis*!

A man who drove everyone crazy on Project Timedrift by continuing to insist: while it is all well and good to be going back to record at first hand every aspect of the Greek Culture, the Hellenic World was enriched and enlightened by the Israelites and so, by rights, we ought to be making book on the parallel history of the Jews.

With one hundred and sixty-three *goyim* on the Project, you can imagine with what admiration and glee this unending assertion was received. Gratefully, we were working out of the University of Chicago, and not Pinsk, so at least I didn't have to worry about pogroms.

What I *did* worry about was Levin's characterization of me as a "pretend Jew."

"You're not a Good Jew," he said to me yesterday. We were lying side by side in the REM sleep room, relaxing after a three-hour hypnosleep session learning the idiomatics of Ptolemaic Egyptian, all ninety-seven dialects. He in his sling, me in mine. "I *beg* your sanctimonious pardon," I said angrily. "And you, I suppose, are a Good Jew, by comparison to my being a Bad Jew!"

"Res ipsa loquitur," he replied, not even opening his eyes. It was Latin, and it meant *the thing speaks for itself*: it was self-evident.

"When I was fourteen years old," I said, propping myself on one elbow and looking across at him lying there with his eyes shut, "a kid named Jack Wheeldon, sitting behind me in an assembly at my junior high school, kicked my seat and called me a kike. I turned around and hit him in the head with my geography book. He was on the football team, and he broke my jaw. Don't tell me I'm a Bad Jew. I ate through a straw for three months."

He turned his head and gave me that green-eyed lizard-on-a-rock stare. "This is a Good Jew, eh? Chanukah is in three days. You'll be lighting the candles, am I correct? You'll be reciting the prayers? You'll observe *yontiff* using nothing but virgin olive oil in your *menorah*, to celebrate the miracle?"

Oh, how I wanted to pop him one. "I gotcher miracle," I said, rudely. I lay back in the sling and closed my eyes.

I didn't believe in miracles. How Yehudah of the Maccabees had fielded a mere ten thousand Jews against Syrian King Antiochus's mercenary army of 60,000 infantry and 5,000 cavalry; and how he had whipped them like a tub of butter. How the victors had then marched on Jerusalem and retaken the Second Temple; and how they found that in the three years of Hellenist and Syrian domination and looting the Temple had grown desolate and overgrown with vegetation, the gates burned, and the Altar desecrated. But worst of all, the sacred vessels, including the *menorah*, had been stolen. So the priests, the *Kohanim*, took seven iron spits, covered them with wood, and crafted them into a makeshift *menorah*. But where could they find uncontaminated oil required for the lighting of the candelabrum?

It was a time of miracles. They found one flask of oil. A *cruse* of oil, whatever a cruse was. And when they lit it, a miracle transpired, or so I was told in Sunday School, which was a weird name for it because Friday sundown to Saturday sundown is the Sabbath for Jews, except we were Reform, and that meant Saturday afternoon was football and maybe a movie matinee, so I went on Sundays. And, miracle of miracles, I forgot most of those football games, but I remembered what I'd been taught about the "miracle" of the oil, if you believe that sort of mythology they tell to kids. The oil, just barely enough for one day, burned for eight days, giving the *Kohanim* sufficient time to prepare and receive fresh uncontaminated oil that was fit for the *menorah*.

A time of miracles. Like, for instance, you're on the Interstate, seventy-five miles from the nearest gas station, and your tank is empty. But you ride the fumes seventy-five miles to a fill-up. Sure. And one day's oil burns for eight. Not in this universe, it doesn't.

"I don't believe in old wives' tales that there's a 'miracle' in one day's oil burning for eight," I said.

And *he* said: "That wasn't the miracle."

And *I* said: "Seems pretty miraculous to me. If you believe."

And *he* said: "The miracle was that they knew the oil was uncontaminated. Otherwise they couldn't use it for the ceremony."

"So how did they know?" I asked.

"They found one cruse, buried in the dirt of the looted and defiled Temple of the Mount. One cruse that had been sealed with the seal of the high rabbi, the *Kohane Gadol*, the Great Priest."

"Yeah, so what's the big deal? It had the rabbi's seal on it. What did they expect, the Good Housekeeping Seal of Approval?"

"It was never done. It wasn't required that oil flasks be sealed. And rules were rigid in those days. No exceptions. No variations. Certainly the personal involvement of the *Kohane Gadol* in what was almost an act of housekeeping . . . well . . . it was unheard of. Unthinkable. Not that the High Priest would consider the task beneath him," he rushed to interject, "but it would never fall to his office. It would be considered *unworthy* of his attention."

"Heaven forfend," I said, wishing he'd get to the punchline.

Which he did. "Not only was the flask found, its seal was unbroken, indicating that the contents had not been tampered with. One miraculous cruse, clearly marked for use in defiance of all logic, tradition, random chance. And that was the miracle."

I chuckled. "Mystery, maybe. Miracle? I don't think so."

"Naturally you don't think so. You're a Bad Jew."

And *that*, because he was an arrogant little creep, because *his* subjective world-view was the *only* world-view, because he fried my frijoles, ranked me, dissed me, ground my gears, and in general cheesed me off . . . I decided to go "fugitive" and solve his damned mystery, just to slap him in his snotty face with a dead fish! When they ask you why any great and momentous event in history took place, tell 'em that all the theories are stuffed full of wild blueberry muffins. Tell 'em the only reason that makes *any* sense is this: *it seemed like a good idea at the time.*

Launch the Spanish Armada? Seemed like a good idea at the time.

Invent the wheel? Seemed like a good idea at the time.

Drift back in time to 165 Before the Common Era and find out how one day's oil burns for eight? Seemed like a good idea at the time. Because Barry R. Levin was a smartass!

It was all contained in the suit of lights.

All of time, and the ability to drift backward, all of it built into the refined mechanism the academics called a *driftsuit*, but which we "fugitives" called our suit of lights. Like a toreador's elegant costume, it was a glittering, gleaming, shining second-skin. All the circuits were built in, printed deep in the ceramic metal garment. It was a specially-developed cermet, *pliable* ceramic metal, not like the armor worn by our astronauts mining the Asteroid Belt. Silver and reflective, crosstar flares at a million points of arm and torso and hooded skull.

We had learned, in this time of miracles, that matter and energy are interchangeable; and that a person can be broken down into energy waves; and those waves can be fired off into the timestream, toward the light. Time did, indeed, sweep backward, and one could drift backward, going ever toward that ultimate light that we feared to enter. Not because of superstition, but because we all understood on a level we could not explain, that the light was the start of it all, perhaps the Big Bang itself.

But we *could* go fugitive, drift back and back, even to the dawn of life on this planet. And we could return, but only to the moment we had left. We could not go forward, which was just as well. Literally, the information that was us could be fired out backward through the timestream as wave data.

And the miracle was that it was all contained in the suit of lights. Calibrate it on the wrist-cuff, thumb the "activate" readout that was coded to the DNA of only the three of us who were timedrifters, and no matter where we stood, we turned to smoke, turned to light, imploded into a scintillant point, and vanished, to be fired away, and to reassemble as ourselves at the shore of the Sea of Reeds as the Egyptians were drowned, in the garden of Gethsemane on the night of Jesus's betrayal, in the crowd as Chicago's Mayor Cermak was assassinated by a demented immigrant trying to get a shot at Franklin D. Roosevelt, in the right field bleachers as the '69 Mets won the World Series.

I thumbed the readout and saw only light, nothing but light, golden as a dream, eternal as a last breath, and I hurtled back toward the light that was *greater* than this light that filled me . . .

. . . and in a moment I stood in the year 165 Before the Common Era, within the burned gates of the Second Temple, on the Mount in Jerusalem. It was the 24th day of the Hebrew month *Kislev*. 165 BCE. The slaughtered dead of the Greco-Syrian army of Antiochus lay ten deep outside. The swordsmen of the Yovan, who had stabled pigs in the *Beis Ha Mikdosh*, even in the holiest of holies, who had defiled the sanctuary which housed the *menorah*, who had had sex on the stones of the sacred altar, and profaned those stones with urine and swine . . . they lay with new, crimson mouths opened in their necks, with iron protruding from their bellies and backs.

Ex-college boy from Chicago, timedrifter, fugitive. It had seemed like a good idea at the time. I never dreamed this kind of death could be . . . with bodies that had not been decently straightened for display in rectangular boxes . . . with hands that reached for the bodies that had once worn them. Faces without eyes.

I stood in the rubble of the most legendary structure in the history of my people, and realized this had not been, in any way, a good idea. Sick to my stomach, I started to thumb my wrist-cuff, to return *now* to the Project labs.

And I heard the scream.

And I turned my head.

And I saw the *Kohane*, who had been sent on ahead to assess the desecration—a son of Mattisyahu—I saw him flung backward and pinned to the floor of dirt and pig excrement, impaled by the spear of a Syrian pikeman who had been hiding in the shadows. Deserter of the citadel's garrison, a coward hiding in the shadows. And as he strode forward to finish the death of the writhing priest, I charged, grabbed up one of the desecrated stones of the altar and, as he turned to stare at me, frozen in an instant at the sight of this creature of light bearing down on him . . . I raised the jagged rock and crushed his face to pulp.

Dying, the *Kohane* looked upon me with wonder. He murmured prayers and my suit of lights shone in his eyes. I spoke to him in Greek, but he could not understand me. And then in Latin, both formal and vulgate, but his whispered responses were incomprehensible to me. *I could not speak his language!*

I tried Parthian, Samarian, Median, Cuthian, even Chaldean and Sumerian . . . but he faded slowly, only staring up at me in dying wonder. Then I understood one word of his lamentation, and I summoned up the hypnosleep learning that applied. I spoke to him in Aramaic of the Hasmonean brotherhood. And I begged him to tell me where the flasks of oil were kept. But there were none. He had brought nothing with him, in advance of his priest brothers and the return of Shimon from his battle with the citadel garrison.

It was a time of miracles, and I knew what to do.

I thumbed the readout on my wrist-cuff and watched as my light became a mere pinpoint in his dying eyes.

I went back to Chicago. This was wrong, I knew this was wrong: timedrifters are forbidden to alter the past. The three of us who were trained to go fugitive, we understood above all else . . . *change nothing, alter nothing,* or risk a tainted future. I knew what I was doing was wrong.

But, oh, it seemed like a good idea at the time.

I went to Rosenbloom's, still in business on Devon Avenue, still in Rogers Park, even this well into the twenty-first century. I had to buy some trustworthy oil.

I told the little balding clerk I wanted virgin olive oil so pure it could be used in the holiest of ceremonies. He said, "How holy does it have to be for Chanukah in Chicago?" I told him it was going to be used in Israel. He laughed. "All oil today is '*tomei*'—you know what that is?" I said no, I didn't. (Because, you see, I *didn't* say, I'm not a Good Jew, and I don't know such things.) He said, "It means impure. And you know what *virgin* means! It means every olive was squeezed, but only the first drop was used." I asked him if the oil he sold was acceptable. He said, "Absolutely."

I knew how much I needed, I'd read the piece on Chanukah history. Half a log, the Talmud had said. Two *riv-ee-eas*. I had to look it up: about eight ounces, the equivalent of a pony bottle of Budweiser. He sold it to me in a bottle of dark brown, opaque glass.

And I took the oil to one of the one hundred and sixty-three Gentiles on Project Timedrift, a chemist named Bethany Sherward, and I asked her to perform a small miracle. She said, "Matty, this is hardly a miracle you're asking for. You know the alleged 'burning bush' that spoke to Moses? They still exist. Burning bushes. In the Sinai, Saudi Arabia, Iraq. Mostly over the oil fields. They just burn and burn and . . . "

While she did what she had to do, I went fugitive and found myself, a creature of light once again, in the *Beis Ha Mikdosh*, in the fragile hours after midnight, in the Hebrew month of *Cheshvan*, in the year 125 BCE; and I stole a cruse of oil and took it back to Chicago and poured it into a sink, and realized what an idiot I'd been. I needn't have gone to Rosenbloom's. I could have used this oil, which was pure. But it was too late now. There was a lot we all had to learn about traveling in time.

I got the altered oil from Bethany Sherward, and when I hefted the small container I almost felt as if I could detect a heaviness that had not been there before. This oil was denser than ordinary olive oil, virgin or otherwise.

I poured the new oil into the cruse. It sloshed at the bottom of the vessel. This was a dark red, rough-surfaced clay jar, tapering almost into the shape of the traditional Roman amphora, but it had a narrow base, and a fitted lid without a stopper. It now contained enough oil for exactly one day, half a log. I returned to the Timedrift lab, put on the suit of lights—it was wonderful to have one of only three triple-A clearances—and set myself to return to the Temple of the Mount, five minutes earlier than I'd appeared the first time. I didn't know if I'd see myself coalesce into existence five minutes later, but I *did* know that I could save the *Kohane*'s life.

I went toward the light. I *became* a creature of the light yet again, and found myself standing inside the gates once more. I started inside the Great Temple . . .

And heard the scream.

Time had adjusted itself. He was falling backward, the spear having ripped open his chest. I charged the Syrian, hit him with the cruse of oil, knocked him to the dirt, and crushed his windpipe with one full force stomp of my booted foot.

I stood staring down at him for perhaps a minute. I had killed a man. With hardly the effort I would have expended to wipe sweat from my face, I had smashed the life out of him. I started to shake, and then I heard myself whimper. And then I made a stop to it. I had come here to do a thing, and I knew it would now be done because . . . nowhere in sight did another creature of shimmering light appear. We had much to learn about traveling in time.

I went to the priest where he lay in his dirt-caked blood, and I raised his head. He stared at me in wonder, as he had the first time.

"Who are you?" he asked, coughing blood.

"Matty Simon," I said. It seemed like a good idea at the time.

He smiled. "Mattisyahu's son, Shimon?"

I started to say no, Matty, not Mattisyahu; Simon, not Shimon. But I didn't say that. I had thought he was one of the sons, but I was wrong. Had I been a more knowledgeable Jew, I would have known: he wasn't the *Kohane Gadol.* He was a Levite from Moses's tribe; one of the priestly class; sent ahead as point man for the redemption of the Temple; like Seabees sent in ahead of an invasion to clear out trees and clean up the area. But now he would die, and not do the job.

"Put your seal on this cruse," I said. "Did the *Kohane Gadol* give you that authority, can you do that?"

He looked at the clay vessel, and even in his overwhelming pain he was frightened and repelled by the command I had made. "No . . . I cannot . . ."

I held him by the shoulders with as much force as I could muster, and I looked into his eyes and I found a voice I'd never known was in me, and I demanded, *"Can you do this?"*

He nodded slightly, in terror and awe, and he hesitated a moment and then asked, "Who are you? Are you a Messenger of God?" I was all light, brighter than the sun, and holding him in my arms.

"Yes," I lied. "Yes, I am a Messenger of God. Let me help you seal the flask."

That he did. He did what was forbidden, what was not possible, what he should not have done. He put the seal of pure oil on the vessel containing half a log, two *riv-ee-eas,* of long-chain hydrocarbon oil from a place that did not even exist yet in the world, oil from a time unborn, from the future. The longer the chain, the greater the binding energy. The greater the binding energy, the longer it would burn. One day's oil, from the future; one day's oil that would burn brightly for eight days.

He died in my arms, smiling up into the face of God's Messenger. He went toward the light, a prayer on his lips.

Today, at lunch in the Commissary, Barry R. Levin slapped his tray down on the table across from me, slid into the seat, and said, "Well, Mr. Pretend Jew, tomorrow is Chanukah. Are you ready to light the candles?"

"Beat it, Levin."

"Would you like me to render the prayers phonetically for you?"

"Get away from me, Levin, or I'll lay you out. I'm in no mood for your scab-picking today."

"Hard night, Mr. Simon?"

"You'll never know." I gave him the look that said *get in the wind, you pain in the ass.* He stood up, lifted his tray, took a step, then turned back to me.

"You're a Bad Jew, remember that."

I shook my head ruefully and couldn't hold back the mean little laugh.

"Yeah, right. I'm a Bad Jew. I'm also the Messenger of God."

He just looked at me. Not a clue why I'd said that. All scores evened, I didn't have the heart to tell him . . .

It just seemed like a helluva good idea at the time. The time of miracles.

❄   ❄   ❄

Considering the modern concept of Santa began only in 1822 with Clement Clarke Moore's poem A Visit from Saint Nicholas *(now known as* 'Twas the Night Before Christmas*), then further refined with seventy-six (1862-1885) Christmas engravings by Thomas Nast—Santa, although based on older traditions, is really very new. Ken Scholes provides us with a glimpse of what new, very different, mythology/theologies might arise . . . given time . . . while still providing a touching story evocative of the season.*

If Dragon's Mass Eve Be Cold and Clear
❄
Ken Scholes

Muscles tire. Words fail. Faith fades. Fear falls. In the Sixteenth Year of the Sixteen Princes the world came to an end when the dragon's back gave out. Poetry died first, followed by faith. One by one the world-strands burst and bled until ash snowed down on huddled masses whimpering in the cold.

The Santaman came reeking of love into this place and we did not know him.

This is his story.

This is our story, too.

Prelude The Santaman Cycle,
Authorized Standard Version
Verity Press, 2453 YD

I buried my father on Dragon's Mass Eve. I dug the grave myself, there on the hill overlooking our homestead, beside the grave he dug for my mother some thirty-five years earlier.

As I worked the shovel, I tried not to cry. I failed. And I recited the Cycle, just the way he taught me, as I cut the sod and turned the dirt out into a pile.

Muscles tire. It was as if he stood with me. I could hear his voice grumbling on the wind that rose as the sun dropped and the air cooled. "Pause, Melody Constance," he said. "Feel what the writer intended with the words."

I felt my foot upon the shovel, my shoulders as I bent and lifted dirt. I felt the hollow empty place inside that tried to swallow me whenever my eyes wandered to the wagon and the red-wrapped body laying there.

Words fail. Again, a hesitation, a waiting. Silence to honor the moments no words can carry.

Like this one.

Only, it didn't feel like a moment—it felt like a year, in the cold, working the shovel. Alone. Orphanhood settled onto my back and shoulders with a weight I'd never felt before. I had no memory of my mother; she'd died the morning I was born. So it was a loss I assumed and grew into, never really knowing what I'd missed out on, other than those times I stayed with neighboring families when my father needed to travel. But even then, it was only the slightest taste of someone else's life. Working the mine and farm with my father was my life. And so was Dragon's Mass Eve—his favorite and only holiday—spent quietly at home in our red paper hats with our fruit salad and rice stew while the faithful gathered at church.

Faith fades. Fear falls.

My mind blurred with my eyes as the tears overpowered me. The questions began to rise even as the fear fell upon me. What will I do now? Where will I go? How will I ever learn to live around this vast hole in my heart?

They were all things we'd talked about in passing when he talked in the midst of his illness about not getting better. And I knew that I would find the desk in his office perfectly organized with carefully written instructions for everything that needed to be done and everyone that had to be contacted. He'd learned to be meticulous during forty years working in the Bureaucracy's supply chain, and he'd instilled it into me. I think I was six when he put the first of many carefully scripted lists into my hands and sent me off to do my chores.

But having a plan and executing said plan were not the same thing.

My eye wandered to the wagon again and I tried to tell myself it was because I was measuring how much further I had to dig. But I knew better. It was because I was close to finished. And when I was done digging, when I eased my father into that hole, he would be gone. I would only ever see him again in memory and dreams, in the half-dozen photographs tucked into our leatherbound copy of the Cycle.

This would be our last Dragon's Mass Eve together. My last time reciting the words with him. Our conversation earlier that morning would be the last we ever had, and it broke my heart open even further.

I went through the Cycle three times before I finished digging, from muscles tire to upon his back, a world, quoting from the Authorized Standard Version that my father had studied during the single year he spent in seminary. It was the version he'd memorized as a part of his training, and though he'd set aside his faith years before, he still felt it had enough merit that his daughter should know it. So now I said the words, felt none of them, and gentled my father into his grave.

The night was clear and cold but I paid it no mind. The hymn might've promised that the Santaman's grace would find us here, but the reality was I'd already seen at least a half-dozen clear and cold Dragon's Mass Eves and the Santaman had yet to come back, reeking of anything, much less love. There had been, according to my father, over two hundred and thirty-seven cold, clear Dragon's Mass Eves to be exact, to the great consternation of the few remaining theologians.

We were on our own.

I was on my own.

I shoveled the earth over him and went through the Cycle another three times for good measure. But even as I did, I knew it wouldn't be enough. It was my first lesson in grief—that there never, ever was enough when it came to those we lost.

On my last Dragon's Mass Eve with Father, the rice stew grew cold upon the stove and I did not kneel and pray to the north. Instead, I cried myself to sleep, still covered in the dirt and drying sweat of digging my father's grave.

> *If Dragon's Mass Eve be cold and clear*
> *The Santaman's grace may find us here.*
> *But if Dragon's Mass Eve be clouded sky*
> *The Santaman's grace may pass us by.*
> Hymn #475, "If Dragon's Mass Eve Be Cold and Clear"
> *Hymns of the Dragon and his Avenger,*
> *Contemporary Edition*
> Verity Music, 2623 YD

"Like this," my father told me, unfolding the red paper and then folding it again in a different place, pressing the new crease into it with his massive thumb.

I watched, then took it from him and folded it again. It was my tenth Dragon's Mass Eve and it had gone like all of the others I could remember. First, he pulled out the jars and cans he'd collected over the year, separating the fruit from the vegetables and the cans of potted meat. The fruit came to me along with a notation on my morning chores list and I mixed it into a fruit salad. His own list called for preparing the rice stew, and while it simmered, we moved on to the hats.

"I can never get it right," I said.

He chuckled, and it was a low rumble in the brightly lit kitchen. "Getting it right isn't always required."

I watched his hands as they moved over his own sheet of paper, a fold here and a fold there, followed by a dab of paste and a cotton ball. I looked at mine and sighed. "Yours is better."

Lifting the hat, he placed it on my head and then pushed up his glasses. Then, he swept my paper and cottonball away with a giant hand and started over with them. "Mine is a wreck," he said with a toothy grin. He nodded to the hat I wore. "Yours looks pretty good, actually."

We laughed and after, he put the battered hat onto his head. "Now," he said, "we are ready."

We stood and went outside into the night. We climbed the hill out behind the homestead and faced north, kneeling at my mother's grave. The stone that marked it was plain, dark granite.

Harmony Angelique Sheffleton-Farrelly, it read. Then, after the date of her birth and the date of her death: *Public servant, beloved wife and mother.*

My knees were cold. "I don't understand why we do this," I said. Ten was the year that I mastered the art of the subtle complaint.

"We do this," he said, "because it's important to remember where we come from."

Of course, I'd heard the story of how he and mother had met, and about their first Dragon's Mass Eve together in the supply basement of the Bureaucracy. He'd been one of a small number of trolls in public service to the Bureaucracy, his trollishness coming in handy for safeguarding their supplies. My mother had been his replacement after thirty years in the supply chain, but meeting her had caught some part of him on fire and he'd decided to forgo retirement. They spent another decade improving efficiencies, easing the government back to some semblance of functionality. Then they'd ridden west with some of the world's last hope lining the bottom of an old coffee can to seed a mine that had long before gone dry. They raised a litter of love, selling off each pup that survived, and made do on their pensions.

Somewhere in the midst of it, they decided to have me, and that choice changed everything.

I put my hand on the stone. "But we don't believe in the Santaman," I said.

"No," he said, and winked. "We don't have to."

We said our prayer quickly as the wind rose to threaten our hats. When we finished, I looked up. "Clouded sky," I said.

Father chuckled again. "Yes."

"Last year was clear, though."

"Yes," he said again. "There have been quite a few clear, cold Dragon's Mass Eves."

I kicked the dirt. "The song got it wrong."

I felt his hand settle onto my shoulder. "Getting it right," he said again, "isn't required." We went back into the house and I pulled the door closed. He went to the stove and ladled the rice stew into simple wooden bowls that came out each year just for this tradition. He didn't speak again until we were seated at the table, the fire crackling nearby.

"Besides," he said as he tucked his napkin into his open-collared shirt, "they changed the song a long time ago. While I was in seminary there were a lot of people wanting to update the Cycle and the Hymnal. The song used to say 'will,' which implied a guarantee that the clergy couldn't afford to underwrite once the cold, clear nights started showing up again."

I'd heard this one before and I nodded. "So they changed it to 'may.'"

He grinned, his broad face lighting up. "Yes."

I tried to imitate his deep, gruff voice. "So when we sing it, we sing it as it was written—"

He joined in and we finished in unison. "— just as the writer intended it to be sung."

I paused, my spoon paused above the rim of the bowl. "But it isn't true."

He paused, too. "No, it doesn't appear to be."

"So aren't the new words more . . . accurate?"

He took a bite, swallowed, and thought for a moment. "Only if the underlying premise is accurate. I can sing about flying fish that might bring little girls vast wealth for Dragon's Mass Eve, but if there are no flying fish. . . . " Here, he shrugged.

I smiled and mimicked his shrug. "And so we return to my initial question. Why do we do it?"

My father sighed. "Someday, when you have a child, you'll understand it better, I think."

I shook my head. "I don't think I will." Then, I wrinkled my nose. "And I don't want a child."

"Ah," he said, "but do you want your present?"

I nodded. "But let me get yours first."

That was the year that I'd written him a story about the two of us fighting Black Drawlers in the north while we searched for the Santaman's fabled sword. I'd written it out in my best penmanship, and Miss Marplesbee, the sole teacher at the small one-room school in town, helped me bind it between pieces of cardboard with bright red yarn. I was particularly pleased with the cover—one of my better drawings of Father lopping the head off a Black Drawler, with me poised carefully on his back, a dagger clenched in my teeth.

And it was the year that he gave me the picture of Mother, wearing the dress she wore when she met my father, leaning against a desk in the drab cubicle wasteland of the Bureaucracy's fifth floor. He'd built the frame himself.

I was pulling the paper aside when I woke up. I lay in bed for a minute and blinked the dream away. It was a good Dragon's Mass Eve. But it was twenty-five years behind me now, and the truth I swallowed made my stomach hurt.

I looked up to the picture of my mother that had hung above my bed since the night he'd first given it to me.

I forced myself up and drew a bath. When I walked past my father's open door I did not let myself look in upon his empty bed, upon the spectacles that lay on his nightstand, folded closed and never to be opened again by his large, clumsy fingers.

Muscles tire. It's all we really knew. The dragon's back held up the world. The poetry and faith of the Singing Literocrats held up the dragon by the will of the Sixteen Princes. One Literocrat fell to the sword, another to plague, a third to famine. Halved in this way, the choir faltered in its song and the dragon caved in on its spindly legs. The Sixteen Princes had no time to act, to change the course of this sudden, sweeping end.

They drank wine and spoke of lemon trees instead.

We sat in the cold until the Santaman came.

The Breaking of the Dragon's Back
The Santaman Cycle,
Authorized Standard Version
Verity Press, 2453 YD

■ ■ ■

The first week crept by with varied weather. Storms of sorrow blew in at the slightest provocation—the smell of him on his clothes, his pen laid carefully to the left side of his desk blotter, the notes he'd written and organized for me. And on the heels of the sadness, a calm and foreboding hollowness that I didn't know I could feel. Followed suddenly by inconsolable rage that had no place to go but inward, or else it might burn down the world.

I went through the pile of papers, mailing what needed mailed and making the calls on Father's list. I loaded the granite marker he'd kept in the mine all these years onto the wagon and drove it into town. He'd had his name and birthdate carved onto it when he had mother's made. *The rest is up to you*, his note told me. And so I dropped it with Anderson, Bauer and Sons' Stonework, picked it up a week later, and planted it at the head of the fresh grave.

Drummond Angus Farrelly, it said, along with his dates of birth and death. *Public servant, cherished father, beloved husband.*

The government men showed up about a month after, briefcases in hands.

"Miss Farrelly?" the man in the suit asked when I opened the door.

"Ms. Sheffleton-Farrelly," I corrected him. "Melody. Call me Mel."

The man looked uncomfortable and his partner looked away, clearing his throat. Their pinstriped trousers and jackets looked out of place here on the edge of the world and I wasn't sure how they kept their shoes so shiny. "Is there someplace we can talk?"

I nodded toward my father's office—a shack near the gated entrance of the mine. I dried my hands and laid my dish towel over a wooden chair. "Across the way," I said.

I led us across the hard-packed yard and used the key to open the door. There had been little to do in the office, and I'd spent most of my time here arranging and rearranging the items on his desk.

I sat behind it now, still feeling dwarfed by its size, and waited until my guests sat. They each placed their cases across their knees and opened them. "First," the spokesman said as he lifted out an accordion file of papers, "let me say how sorry we all were to hear about Drum's—your father's—passing. I worked with him on several procurements and had a lot of respect for him."

"Thank you." My father, in addition to his contract for the mine, had also entered into consulting contracts with the Bureaucracy from time to time, leaving me with either the Gustavsons or the Graves—sometimes for months at a time—to ride east and do his part to help put the world right. I'd always hoped to go with him, but for one reason or another, we never made it happen. But I'd write my stories as if I'd gone, weaving tales of our derring-do and heroics on secret missions for the Bureaucracy.

"That said," the government man continued, "there are uncomfortable matters to discuss."

I nodded. I knew of at least one matter—the pension. Father thought he'd found a loophole that would allow it to pass to me—something about a Board Order from the past century regarding widows and orphans. But I'd read the order and didn't think it was likely to work in my case. "The pension, right?"

He nodded. "Yes. I'm afraid you do not meet the age requirements for survivorship to apply."

"Understood," I said.

"And then there is the matter of the mining contract."

My eyes came up to his. "The mining contract?"

His smile was apologetic as he drew a letter out of the file. "Unfortunately, amendment six removed the assignment clause from the Bureaucracy's standard terms and conditions. Which means that with the passing of your father—the contractor in this regard—this contract is null and void. I've a letter of cancellation for you, notarized by the Board clerk."

I felt anger rising in my face. "Amendment six?" I rolled my chair to the file cabinet to my left and pulled open the second drawer. "When was this amendment issued? I don't recall seeing it. Do you have an executed copy?"

He shook his head. "It's just been issued in the last fortnight. But unfortunately, Mr. Farrelly is no longer in a position to . . . " Here he cleared his voice and looked away. "To sign it."

Red tape. My father had created his share of it in the Bureaucracy's basement.

I smiled. "Surely you can re-compete it." The first ten years, father had operated the mine on a no-bid contract. It was the only operating hope mine in the western provinces and that made it eligible for a sole source exemption. But the last two and a half decades, he'd competed for it. No one else had, so of course he was awarded the contract.

Red tape.

The government man shook his head. "We are not going to re-procure in this case, Ms. Sheffleton-Farrelly. As you know, the Drawler threat in the north is taking more and more resources. The Bureaucracy is cutting expenses wherever it can."

I leaned forward. "Are you giving up on hope altogether then?"

"No," he said. "We'll fund mining efforts elsewhere—certainly where it makes sense."

"Just not here."

"Not here," he agreed. Then, he leaned forward. "Ms. Sheffleton-Farrelly, do you have any idea when the last time was that this mine produced a single flake of hope?"

I rolled back to the file cabinet, this time opening the top drawer to pull out the production journals. "Late autumn," I said. "Twenty-six-fifty-three, Year of the Dragon."

It was the same year my father had gone to seminary.

"Eighty years," the man said. "And thirty-five of them subsidized by tax dollars with nothing to show for it."

There was little to say after that. They left me with a stack of papers less than an hour later, climbing into their jeep and driving back to the town's single inn.

I went over those papers that afternoon, filing them carefully like he would have, and afterward, I adjusted father's financial projections less his ongoing pension payments and the contract revenue. I checked his notations in the savings ledger one last time before folding it up and tucking it back into the file cabinet. If I were frugal, I had maybe two years left here. And after that?

There was a form in the paperwork from the Bureaucracy—an application for the civil service exam with a box already marked and initialed on it, authorizing me to take the test in any satellite branch where it was offered and extending bonus points based on my relationship to one Drummond Angus Farrelly, a decorated procurement officer.

I filed it separately from the other papers and snuffed out the lamp. I looked over everything, neatly in its place, before locking the office door. After today, I really wasn't sure when I'd be back.

Then I went up to father's grave for the first time since digging it. I sat heavily upon the ground and leaned against his marker. "You were wrong about the pension," I told him. "The mining contract, too."

And in that moment, I was certain I heard his voice. First, he chuckled. Then, he told me what he'd told me so many times before.

"Being right," my father reminded me "is not always required."

Myth became life. No one really believed in the Santaman until he came with his tattered red robe and his dripping red sword. No one really believed in his undying love until he burst into our direst need to carve us a new home from the bones of the world.

We looked up at the whistle of his wolf-stallion. "Why do you weep and whimper?" the Santaman asked from the back of his mount.

"We whimper for the end of our world," one of us said. "We weep for the fall of the Singing Literocrats and the breaking of the Dragon's Back."

The Santaman grinned and shook his sword. Blood rained down from it, mixing with the ashes. "Weep also for the Sixteen Princes who have failed you."

"Why, Lord?" someone asked.

The Santaman spun his mount. "For I have avenged you in the Name Above All, and they are no more."

We did not waver in our weeping. There was no lull in our lament.

The Coming of the Santaman
The Santaman Cycle,
Authorized Standard Version
Verity Press, 2453 YD

In grief, time moves at inconsistent pace and the bereaved adjust and shuffle forward accordingly. I did not return to my father's grave again for nearly two years, though I watched it often from the kitchen window or from the yard.

Each month, I hitched the wagon and went into town to resupply. And on each trip, I endured the sympathy of the closest thing we had to a community, so far removed from the rest of the world.

"What will you do now?" was the most popular question, and I never had a real answer. I took their offered condolences and tucked them away. And I watched the numbers on the savings ledger shrink.

I pulled the pictures from the Cycle and tucked the book away out of sight, moving the photographs into the treasure box I kept beneath my bed. But after that, I left the box where it lay for a long time and let it find its dust.

I wouldn't have known the season but for news of the fighting in the north: more Black Drawlers leaking into the world through the ether, moving further south in their hunger. When I knew the day approached, I went into town to collect what jars and cans I could.

The mercantile even had red paper, and I bought a sheet.

But as Dragon's Mass Eve drew near, the knot in my stomach grew tighter and my eyes went more often to the hill. Finally, I surrendered and found the best dress that still fit me and rode into town.

Father had never taken me to the church for Dragon's Mass Eve, but we'd visited one Dragonsday for weekly services. On the ride in, I sat beside him on the bench and we talked about what we were going to see.

"There won't be many, I'll wager," he said. "But there will be some. Parson Brown will pray and Emily Hopewell will play a few hymns on the organ that we will all sing too. Then the parson will preach about the Santaman and take a collection."

When we arrived, the parson's eyes lit up. "Drum Farrelly," he said, "you're just about the last person I expected to show up this morning."

I remember my father's strained smile as he shook the parson's hand. "Melody was curious," he said.

I'd seen Parson Brown around town, but never in the dark robes of his priesthood. It made the short, round man look almost comical. He'd shaken my hand, looking up at me with a smile. "Welcome," he said.

We took our seat on the back row.

Then, just as father said, we prayed and sang and listened and sang again, and, as we did, father slipped a small wad of the most recently authorized currency into the plate that passed up and down the pews of scattered faithful.

On the ride home, we'd had our discussion, and father dissected the components of the service.

"At the end," I told him, "they prayed for the Santaman's return. Do they do it every Dragonsday?"

He nodded. "Some of them do it *every* day."

"Not just on Dragon's Mass Eve?"

"No."

"But they believe one day it will work?"

"Yes."

"They really *really* believe?"

He nodded again. "They really *really* believe. And *I* used to, too. Even your mother, in some ways, believed. Only she believed that if there was a Santaman, he expected us to work while we waited and make things as good as we could." He looked thoughtful for a moment.

"But we don't believe now," I said.

He smiled at me. "I don't believe now. Do you?"

I smiled back. "No, I really don't. I think . . . " I tried to find something to hitch my thought to. I remembered the growing stack of bound cardboard covers he kept in the drawer beside his bed, each containing my carefully written pages of our fictional misadventures spread out over a half-dozen Dragon's Mass Eves. "I think it's a good story but I don't think it's true." Then, I said what I knew he was going to say next. "But I suppose being true isn't always required."

He smiled. "Exactly so."

I blinked tears away at the memory as I turned the corner onto Main Street and saw the brightly lit building that waited.

Parson Brown stood at the door and smiled at me. "Mel Farrelly," he said. "You're just about the last person I expected to show up tonight."

I climbed down and hitched my horse. "Happy Dragon's Mass Eve, Parson," I said as I took his hand.

"And to you," he said.

The church was full, with men and women crowded onto the pews in their Dragonsday best. I spotted the Gustavsons and the Graces near the middle of the overflowing congregation, and though both families waved me over, I took a spot in the last row in the back corner. My nervous hands picked up the worn hymnal and thumbed through the pages until the parson took to the pulpit and offered the invocation.

After, there was a small choir that sang a medley of hymns. The room joined in and it was nothing like the scattered voices I'd heard in this very room as a child—it was one voice made of many, booming out into the night in a cry for help that I could nearly give myself over to. But I did not want help from some mysterious red-cloaked and red-bladed avenger. I wanted my father, and the power of that longing flooded my eyes with tears. Still, when we reached "If Dragon's Mass Eve Be Cold and Clear," I sang the original words—the writer's words—and not the softer *maybe* his hymn had been neutered into.

"Now tonight," Parson Brown intoned after the singing, "we have a special treat."

My first thought was that he meant to introduce me, point me out to the crowd, and I found myself suddenly wanting to flee. But it didn't happen. Instead, he nodded to a young man who sat to the side. "Tonight," Parson Brown said, "Brother Simon will bring the homily. His first sermon, I might add."

A wave of murmurs rolled over the congregation and I pressed my mouth together, studying the young man.

His robes were ill-fitting and his eyebrows and cheekbones bore a hint of the fey. He took the pulpit, thumbing through the leather-bound copy of the Cycle that he carried to it, and he smiled out at us. "Good evening," he said as Parson Brown took a seat behind him. "Tonight's message is taken from the Coming of the Santaman, verses one through three."

As he read the scripture, I mouthed the words with him. "Myth became life," he read. "No one really believed in the Santaman until he came with his tattered red robe and his dripping red sword. No one really believed in his undying love until he burst into our direst need to carve us a new home from the bones of the world."

Brother Simon closed the book and looked upon us all. When his eyes moved over the back pew, they met mine and I felt the measurement in his level gaze. "I submit to you, brothers and sisters, that like those before us, we do not really believe in the Santaman."

From there, he launched into his sermon and I found his words fading and blurring, taking a seat behind him like the parson, as he filled the room with his presence. His hands moved like a magician, illustrating this or that point, indicating this or that observation, as he moved across the platform. His voice was hypnotic, rising and falling in passion and pitch and his eyes continued wandering the crowded room, finding mine on more than one occasion. Those eyes, I knew, were unsafe. They held too many contradicting views—hope and fear, anger and grace, and something more I'd never been comfortable with: conviction.

When he finished, he sat down abruptly and Parson Brown took over. After singing "The Santman Shall Rise Again" as the plate migrated up and down the rows, he dismissed us to the fellowship hall for cookies and tea.

I was moving toward the door when Brother Simon caught up to me and shook my hand. The hand was rough and calloused; it caught me off guard. "You're not leaving, are you?"

I blushed and stammered but didn't know why. "I have . . . things to do."

"Come have a cookie at least." Then, as an afterthought: "I'm Simon, by the way." And somehow, the voice compelled me and I let him guide me by the elbow into the fellowship hall before he vanished into the crowd.

A cup of tea was pushed into one of my hands, a molasses cookie into the other, and I blessed both because it meant I need not shake any more hands.

I stood quietly in the corner and suffered the kindness and curiosity of a town that had seen little of me and little of my father before me.

I'd finished the tea and moved for the door when the parson came by with the young man in tow. "And this," he said, "is Melody Farrelly. She owns the old hope mine out past the Gustavson's farm."

"We've met," I said and forced a smile. But I shook his offered hand again, noticing once more how rough it was.

"Brother Simon is our new acolyte. He's in his last year at the Middleton Seminary. I expect he'll be taking my place when I retire next year." He turned to the young man. "Melody's father, Drummond, spent a year at Middleton."

His face lit up. "Is he here with you?"

I looked away. "He passed away last Dragon's Mass Eve."

The light dimmed and his smile faded. "I'm sorry."

"I've been meaning to ask," the Parson said. "Do you know what you will do now? Will you sell the mine?"

I shrugged. "It hasn't produced in over eighty years. Not much demand for a hope mine without hope."

And then, the conversation folded in on itself and the two of them moved on. I excused myself and slipped out under a cloudy night to find my horse.

I rode home and tried to eat at least some of the fruit salad I'd made earlier that day. It tasted empty without my father. And I knew better than to recite the Cycle. Instead, I braved his room—something I rarely brought myself to do—and curled up on his large bed. Then, I pulled open the drawer and pulled out the stack of stories I'd written for him through the years.

As I read them, I found myself laughing and crying and when I felt sleep pulling at me, I gathered them up and took them to my own room. I pulled out the cardboard box beneath my bed and laid them carefully in it.

My eyes caught the wadded up piece of paper I'd also tucked into the box and I forced them away. That ball of paper was the first to go into my treasure box though I couldn't bring myself to open it up and smooth it out. It made me too angry and too afraid.

But now, a strange fancy struck me and I lifted it carefully as a butterfly from a flower. I sat on my bed and held it, remembering my last conversation with my father. Then, I smoothed it out upon my lap.

It was a requisition slip, filled out and in triplicate. He'd completed most of it, leaving the order date blank along with the boxes used to select gender.

Then, I remembered the words I'd said to him—off and on for years— and the quiet way he smiled when I said them.

"I don't want a child," I told the empty room.

Then, I placed the smoothed-out form in the box and lowered the lid over it like a casket before laying it to rest again in the dusty grave beneath my bed.

■ ■ ■

Dust rose from the West as the Santaman approached. The wolf-stallion growled and tore sod, and the last of the Literocrats laid down their lyres by the Murmuring Stream as the dragon's eye faltered above them.

"Take up your tools and lift your song," the Santaman cried.

"We are halved," the Fourth Literocrat said. "Our song is lost. The world ends. The dragon's back is already broken."

The sword licked out, then pointed North. The Murmuring Stream ran pink. "Sing a new home," the Santaman cried again. "Beyond the ether at the Edge of the World."

Two voices rose and fell in song. A third burbled in the stream. Scooping the golden-haired head from the water, the Santaman came seeking us to tell us of our new-carved home.

The Last of the Literocrats
The Santaman Cycle,
Authorized Standard Version
Verity Press, 2453 YD

The next year moved faster. I learned that loss is like a hole in the middle of your living room floor. Your rearrange the furniture around it and you visit it once in a while, but less and less often with every month. Eventually, you grow accustomed to walking around the hole, living around it as it just becomes a part of your life.

I started writing again though I'd long ago outgrown the adventure stories I used to tell. Instead, I wrote about my father and about my memories of him. I tended the garden and stretched the savings as far as I could. And in the weeks before Dragon's Mass Eve, as the news turned somber in the north, I didn't even try to find the canned fruits and vegetables and meat. But I did slip into his office to fill out the civil service exam application. I put it into an envelope and took it into the house.

I still wasn't certain if I would mail it.

When Dragon's Mass Eve arrived, I rode into town again and like the year before, I slipped onto the back pew. The church was less crowded this year, and when Parson Brown's invocation included a blessing upon the men and women serving in the local militia, I made the connection with why.

The singing was more subdued, and when Brother Simon took the pulpit, there was something quiet about him that felt disconnected from the young man I'd seen prowling the platform a year before. "Tonight's message," he said, "is taken from the Last of the Literocrats, verses one through five."

We made eye contact as he read and the light I'd seen before was dark now. There was something of sorrow or anger in them now that resonated with me and I couldn't look away.

"Take up your tools and lift your song," he said. "That is what I want to talk about with you tonight."

What followed were brief but heartfelt comments but nothing like the lively performance I knew he was capable of. When we shook hands later, in the fellowship hall, I could even feel the difference in his grip. And the hands were less rough here in the second year of his apprenticeship.

"I enjoyed your message," I told him, even more uncomfortable with his eyes in such close proximity. "My mother used to believe that the Santaman wouldn't return until we'd done our very best with our own hands."

He nodded and smiled, but I saw the falseness in it. "Yes," he said. There were clouds behind those eyes now, too.

I leaned close to him and lowered my voice. "Are you okay, Brother Simon?"

He looked at me and I think he was surprised that I noticed though it was as obvious as his nose to me. His cheeks grew red and he looked around, panic on his face.

Finally, he pulled me aside and his words were fast and jumbled together. "We lost Fallowston and Reinburg this morning," he said. "The diocese sent a rider. The crier will be announcing it tomorrow. Parson Brown didn't want to dampen spirits tonight with the news."

I knew the towns though I'd never visited them. "Did you have people there?"

He shook his head. "No. But our militia is engaged at Candletoss." I imagined the points on the map, saw how close it all was.

Simon looked out the window and I saw the firmness in his jawline and the anger in his eyes. Outside, it was a clear night and I understood his anger better.

"Something," he said, "has to happen soon."

I nodded but didn't know what to say. Finally, I found my voice. "Maybe," I said, "it's like you said earlier—maybe we're called upon to take up our tools and lift our song. Especially when we're faced with the end of our world . . . just like the Last of the Literocrats."

"Yes. Maybe."

Then he was moving off into the crowd, shaking hands and patting shoulders. I slipped out beneath a star-scattered sky and rode home in the light of the moons.

When I reached the homestead, I stabled my horse and slipped into the house. I found the envelope first, and then I went to the box beneath my bed and pulled out the wadded-up requisition slip. Taking both, I let myself back out into the night and climbed the hill behind the house.

I sat quietly for a while, prayerless and facing north. "I don't know if it's the right thing to do," I told my father, "but I'm going to do it. I know you were right about most things—all the important things, really—and I think you were right about this. But I'm still afraid."

I paused in that moment and knew I would have given everything I owned to have this one final conversation with him, to hear his words and see his eyes as he formed them. But in thirty-five years with the old troll, I knew what he would ask next and I blushed.

"No," I said. "I don't know who yet." Still, I knew who I'd thought about the few times I'd let myself imagine it. "Regardless of who, I'm going to do it and I wanted you to know. But I'm going to have to leave you to make it happen. Because I'm also going to take the test."

I reached out then to touch the gravestone. The granite felt wrong to my fingertips and I rubbed them into the stone, feeling something powdery flaking off as I did.

My first thought was that it was ash or dust. But my second thought was the one that brought my fingers tentatively to my mouth. I'd never tasted hope before but my father had described it many times before.

Bitter and sweet at the same time.

I looked above me at the clear night and stood on shaking legs. I went into the house and lit the lantern, grabbed my knife, and lifted the keys to the mine off the hook where my father had last hung them.

I walked down into the mine and I hadn't gone very far when the dark walls started to glisten white. I paused along the way to scrape here or there, each time coming away with a handful of white flaky residue.

I went all the way to the bottom and when I reached it, I sat down and laughed until my sides hurt and then I cried until my eyes had no more tears in them.

Two days later, I phoned in my requisition at the town's single phone, dialing the number my father gave me. And when I finished with central stores, I had the operator transfer me to the contracts division.

■ ■ ■

"North of the faraway beyond the ether at the Edge of the World" the head sang and died. The Santaman cast it aside.

"The way is too hard," we told the Santaman. "And we are afraid."

He sheathed his sword and climbed down among us. He cast open his arms, his red robes hung like bleeding meat. "Do not be afraid. I walk with you."

North, he walked his wolf-stallion and we followed after. In twilight, we walked and as the ruined cities fell behind us, others joined our ragged band.

Lost also behind us, the last of the literocrats sang sunrise and sunset, sang muscles and sinew, sang bones and teeth.

Death crabs scuttled and scavenged. Snick-snack went the sword.

Black Drawlers shrieked and savaged. Snick-snack went the sword.

Some of us fell. Some of us faltered. All of us hoped.

The faraway wrapped us and the ash snows fell away.

Sunlight bathed us and we swam out into the ether at the Edge of the World.

Swam towards our new-carved home.

The Ether at the Edge of the World
The Santaman Cycle,
Authorized Standard Version
Verity Press, 2453 YD

The Bureaucracy was faster this time. Within two weeks, the suits were back. They offered twenty years but I declined, much to their surprise. "One year is about as far ahead as I can see for now," I said.

They looked nervous when I said that. "Do you have other plans for the mine?"

I shrugged. "I might sell it. And I would certainly want to entertain a bid from the Bureaucracy if it comes to that."

My reassurance helped and when they left, I went to my father's savings ledger and readjusted the figures to account for the contract income. Tomorrow, I'd ride into town and hire a small crew.

A knock at the office door brought my head up. Brother Simon stood framed in the late morning light. "Miss Farrelly," he said with a nod.

"Ms. Sheffleton-Farrelly," I corrected him. "Call me Mel."

"Mel," he said. "May I come in?"

I nodded. "Please," I said pointing to a chair. "Sit. I didn't know parsons still made house calls."

He blushed. "I'm not a parson."

"You will be soon enough."

Simon shook his head. "No, I've stepped down. I don't think I'm made for the priesthood."

I'd seen him just two weeks before and even in that short time, whatever crisis he'd been working through seemed more settled and calm. I knew it was none of my business, and it was a question that I hated but I asked it anyway. "Then what will you do now?"

He looked around the room and then our eyes met. "What I used to do. I was apprenticed to a blacksmith before."

I nodded and looked at his hands. "So you're traveling the parish and letting everyone know?"

He shook his head. "No. Just you for now."

My breath caught and for a moment, I wondered if he somehow knew about some of the thoughts I'd thought about him on cold nights beneath my quilt. But I quickly kicked my imagination back to quiet; it was an awkward quiet.

Simon filled it. "I heard you struck hope."

I laughed. "I didn't strike it; it struck me. My father seeded this place for three seasons and got nothing. Then, decades later . . . " I snapped my fingers in the air. "Hope."

"Hope," he said. "I need some, actually."

I studied him. "I have some. How much do you need?"

"A pound," he said. "I . . . I don't have any money."

A pound was a lot. Not for me at the moment, but a pound of hope in a world that had for too long gone without . . . its value was staggering. "What are you going to do with it?"

"I'm borrowing Jansen's shop at night," he said. His face went red again and he looked around the empty room as if to make sure no one could hear him. "I'm re-forging the Santaman's sword."

I sat back, surprised. "You're what?"

He nodded. "I'm re-forging the sword based on its description in the Doctrines and Affirmations. I'm going to take it north."

I raised my eyebrows. "Why would you do that?"

"Because maybe if he sees we've tried . . . really tried . . . maybe then he'll hear."

I shook my head. "Simon," I said, "I don't think the Santaman's listening."

But when our eyes met this time, I knew it didn't matter. His conviction was back and now it bent him away from words and motions, moved him toward deeds and demonstrations now, but it was still the same drive for miracles and wonders to flow into and out of his life. "Please," he said. "I can't do it without hope."

I sighed and measured him. "Okay. But I want something for it."

"Anything I have that I can give you," he said.

I smiled. "Come back tonight for dinner, Simon, and we'll talk about it. I'll have the hope ready for you."

After he left, I weighed out two pounds from the hope I'd scraped these past two weeks. I filled a small sack with it and locked up. Then, I went inside to get ready.

I put a chicken on to roast and took a long bath. I brushed out my hair and when none of my dresses fit right, I put on trousers and a cotton button-up shirt. I smiled at myself in the tiny mirror, grateful that I couldn't see my entire body in its reflection. I'd gotten many of my mother's features but I had my father's broad shoulders and thickness along with his towering height.

When Simon knocked at the door, the house smelled of chicken and fresh baked bread. Clouds had wandered in and blotted out the starlight but the temperature was still down and he was shivering. I let him in and took his coat. "Did you walk?"

He nodded. "I don't have a horse."

I hefted the bag of hope. "I'll just put this with your coat."

"Thank you."

Nothing I did felt right and my father's words—right was not required—brought little comfort. I wasn't sure what to say or what to do and it was obvious to me that I was the only one who comprehended the potential of this night. I set the table while we made small talk and then I opened the bottle of bumbleberry wine I'd kept for such a night as this. I poured out small glassfuls and dished up our plates.

We ate quickly and I watched him. He talked throughout and I finished easily ahead of him because of it. I think somewhere in the midst of it he must've noticed how I looked at him and it made him talk all the more, his nervous words bumping into each other in their rush to get out.

Finally, I took his plate to the sink along with my own. We moved to the battered old sofa in the living room and sat before the fire. I refilled our wine glasses.

"So you wanted to talk about price," he said.

I sipped the wine, set it down and nodded. "I do. And it's okay to say no. You can have the hope either way."

His brow furrowed. "Say no to what?"

I held my breath and leaned my face toward him. "This."

Then, I kissed him.

At first, he did nothing. Then, he kissed me back. And after a moment, he broke away. "I'm sorry," he said. "I don't know . . . I can't—"

I withdrew and felt the sting of the panic on his face. "No," I said. "I'm sorry." I stood, feeling small for the first time in my life. "Like I said—it's okay to say no."

He stood, too, his face and ears bright red. "No, that's not what I mean." He swallowed, stepped closer to me and stretched up on tippy-toes to kiss my mouth. "It's just that I've never done this before."

Relief flooded me. "Oh," I said. Now it was my turn to blush. "I haven't either."

"Really?"

I nodded. "Really." Then, I bent down and kissed him back.

Taking his hand, I led him to my fresh-made bed and we spent the night teaching each other how.

I never told him why. I couldn't see how it would help him at all and I could count a dozen ways that it might hurt him. Instead, I just enjoyed him and helped him to enjoy me.

In the morning, after breakfast, he walked back into town with a smile on his face and a bag of hope slung over his shoulder.

> *And in the north, he'll hear our cry*
> *Ride forth in wrath, his sword raised high*
> *To carve our home in violent grace*
> *And lead us to that promised place*
> Hymn #316, "The Santaman Shall Rise Again"
> *Hymns of the Dragon and his Avenger,*
> *Contemporary Edition*
> Verity Music, 2623 YD

It was only after that night with Simon that I allowed myself to think about my last conversation with Father. I'm not sure why but I don't need the whys nearly as much as I used to when I was younger.

It was morning when he called me to his room. He'd soiled himself again and after nearly a month in bed, I was just beginning to realize that I might not have even another year with him.

I pretended I wasn't angry and tried to find my patience but it waned. He knew me well enough to know I was frustrated and I suspected he even knew why—it wasn't the mess in his bed. It was the mess my life would become when he left it and I couldn't bear to face that.

I spent the morning cleaning him up and then cleaning his sheets. When I went into the kitchen and saw the cans and jars laid out, preparing for Dragon's Mass Eve was the last thing I wanted to be doing.

"Come in here, Mel," my father rumbled from his bedroom.

I sighed and felt my pulse rising. "What do you need, Dad?"

His laugh was more of a bark. "I need you."

I wanted to snap at him but I didn't. Instead, I closed my eyes, counted to five and then went to his doorway. "Yes?"

He sat up in bed, his lap covered with open books—not real books but bits of cardboard bound together with yarn. "You should write more of these someday," he said. "They're good."

I shrugged. "Is that what you needed?"

He shook his head. "No. Come here." He patted the bed beside him.

I went to the side of the bed but didn't sit. "I have a meal to cook," I said.

Our eyes met. "Sit," he said. "I'm not hungry."

"It's Dragon's Mass Eve and—"

"Sit down, Mel." He looked old then but truth be told, I couldn't remember a time when my father didn't. He was in his sixties when I was born.

I sat and felt the bed creak beneath our combined weight. "What?"

He smiled. "I wanted to give you your Dragon's Mass Eve present."

"Let's wait until tonight," I said. "I don't have yours ready yet."

Father shook his head and a fit of coughing took his words for a minute. "I don't want to wait," he said. "As tired as I've been, I'm likely to sleep through Dragon's Mass Eve anyway."

I forced a smile. "Okay. But you get yours tomorrow if you fall asleep."

He shrugged, then leaned over to dig around within the deep drawer in the nightstand. He pulled out a form—in triplicate—and handed it to me. "This," he said, "is for you."

I looked at it. I rubbed my eyes and looked at it again. "What's this?"

He cleared his voice. "It's . . . um . . . a requisition slip. I've been saving it for you. Your mother and I brought two with us when we rode west."

I read it, my eyes naturally drawn to the places where he'd taken the liberty of filling it out. As I realized what it was, I felt the anger burning hot in me and by instinct, I crumpled the requisition into as tight a ball as my white knuckled fist could make it. "I don't want a child," I said. "I don't *ever* want a child."

I tried to stand but his gnarled hand caught my arm and I turned on him. I nearly said something, nearly let the feelings that savaged me slip past my careful control. But I kept quiet. Still, he saw everything in my eyes and his own filled up with tears at the sight of my anger.

"I'm sorry," he said.

"Why?" I asked.

He blinked. "Why am I sorry?"

I shook my head. "No," I said. "Why do you think I should have a child?" Seeing his tears made my own fight harder to get out.

He patted my arm. "I thought when I met your mother that I knew what love was. But meeting you opened up a vast continent of love I never imagined could exist. How could I not want that for you?" His voice lowered and then my father said the last words that he would ever say to me. "Melody Constance Sheffleton-Farrelly, don't you know that you are the best gift anyone ever gave to me, Dragon's Mass Eve or not?"

I stood and bent to kiss his brow. Then, I left so he wouldn't see me crying. I tossed the ball of paper into my room and went outside into the yard to walk off the feelings that ambushed me. When I went back inside, I saw my father had gone to sleep amid the stories I'd written him over a lifetime of Dragon's Mass Eves together. And when I checked on him even later, I found he'd slipped away.

I gathered up the books, closed them, and stacked them neatly in his nightstand drawer. I carefully removed his spectacles and folded them up to lay them beside his bed.

Then I went to find something to wrap him in and wondered if the coming night would be cloudy or clear.

Motes swim. Light diffuses. Home rises.

We see it through a smoky glass. We watch it twitch and meep with each note of the framing song.

The Santaman laughs and beats his sword against his thigh: "Ho, ho, ho."

We few remaining weep and set our feet on emerald grass. We smell the reek of love upon the wind. We wipe our eyes. We wipe our eyes and look again.

Ahead a dragon.
Upon his back a world.

Our New Carved Home
The Santaman Cycle,
Authorized Standard Version
Verity Press, 2453 YD

You arrived in autumn amid the buzz of change.

But before that, while I waited for you, I started wrapping things up at our homestead on the edge of the world. I went through my father's papers and organized them, separating out his working notes from his personal notes. Most, I kept. But some I left for the mine's new owners.

I felt you kick for the first time while I was taking the civil service exam, and after I finished, the test proctor sought me out in the waiting room after everyone else had gone to let me know he'd not seen a score so high in well over twenty years.

I wasn't surprised at all when the offer came through, and once it did, I started negotiating the sale of the mine. I knew going in that whatever I sold it for would be vastly more than I could make in a lifetime on government salary, working in the cubicle maze of the Bureaucracy. But a clean start seemed somehow right to me, especially as your arrival drew closer and closer.

Still, I'm glad we had these three months together on the homestead where we both were born. Wandering the yard, it's been a strange, new mourning as I accept the reality that I'll likely not come back here again. You may when you're older. You might want to see where your grandmother and grandfather lay buried. You may want to see the house where you were born. And I'm sure folks around here will be curious to meet you, too.

There is a knock at the door on the morning of Dragon's Mass Eve and it startles you. I go to answer and find Parson Brown on the porch. He sees the truck the Bureaucracy has provided me, shoved full of everything we'll take with us when we leave. I've only left out enough to celebrate tonight and tomorrow, we start our weeks-long drive east and south.

"So," he says, "you really are going?"

I nod. "Tomorrow," I say. "Come in, Parson."

I brew him some tea while he plays with you and I can tell you're as uncomfortable with him as he is with you. When the tea is ready, I hold you while he drinks it, mindful of his shaking hands. I want to ask him about your father, but I don't. Last I heard, he'd ridden north with his sword and not long after, bits of gossip drifted back. I don't know who exactly wields it, but there are rumors of a young man in red with a terrible blade and he's earning quite a name for himself. I'm pretty sure it's him. But maybe it isn't. Maybe someone further north heard the cry of his heart. I doubt it, but it would be a fine story.

Drawler season didn't really subside this year—they pushed south all the way through summer—but the militias are holding them at Harrowfield and Lumner, and in a few weeks, I'll be working supply chain for the headquarters of a new standing army.

I don't ask about your father. And I don't tell Parson Brown your middle name is Simon, either. I know people are wondering and I'm okay with letting them wonder.

I look into your eyes and I find I could fall into them. They are brown like mine and like your grandfather's. The parson has to ask a second time before I realize he's speaking. "I'm sorry?"

"I was asking if you'd be joining us tonight," he says as he drains the last of his tea. "I've a new acolyte. Brother Timothy. He'll be giving the sermon." Parson Brown leans forward and tickles your chin. "I'm sure everyone is dying to meet little Drummond."

I smile. "Maybe," I tell him. "We'll see."

But I already know we won't be attending. Tonight, I'll make our hats and after I've nursed you, I'll eat rice stew and fruit salad. Then, we'll walk up the hill and I will hold you close as I recite words that don't need to be right or true to have their meaning for me. For us.

I think I understand my father's last Dragon's Mass Eve gift to me now when I see his face in yours. His attachment to his old, discarded religion makes sense to me now, too, though I had to meet you before I could fully comprehend the truest object of his faith.

Clear or cloudy, the only grace I'll ever need has already found me.

And the only home I'll ever want is you.

❄   ❄   ❄

Christmas is not full of joy and light for all, but in Charles de Lint's poignant story of friendship, he still offers the magic of hope. The presence of the dog, Fritzie, in the story brings to mind other stories of animals associated with Christmas. One of the editor's favorites is about the tabby cat that helped quiet Mary's newborn by cuddling up to the infant in the manger and purring him to sleep. In thanks, Mary blessed the cat. To this day, all true tabbies are still marked with an M on their brows as a sign of their service. (Right. The English letter M is an implausible anachronism, even for fantasy, but perhaps Mary knew a smattering of Greek—and Mariam in Greek is Μαριάμ.)

Pal o' Mine
❄
Charles de Lint

1

Gina always believed there was magic in the world. "But it doesn't work the way it does in fairy tales," she told me. "It doesn't save us. We have to save ourselves."

2

One of the things I keep coming back to when I think of Gina is walking down Yoors Street on a cold, snowy Christmas Eve during our last year of high school. We were out Christmas shopping. I'd been finished and had my presents all wrapped during the first week of December, but Gina had waited for the last minute as usual, which was why we were out braving the storm that afternoon.

I was wrapped in as many layers of clothes as I could fit under my overcoat and looked about twice my size, but Gina was just scuffling along beside me in her usual cowboy boots and jeans, a floppy felt hat pressing down her dark curls, and her hands thrust deep into the pockets of her pea jacket. She simply didn't pay any attention to the cold. Gina was good at that: ignoring inconveniences, or things she wasn't particularly interested in dealing with, much the way—I was eventually forced to admit that—I'd taught myself to ignore the dark current that was always present, running just under the surface of her exuberantly good moods.

"You know what I like best about the city?" she asked as we waited for the light to change where Yoors crosses Bunnett.

I shook my head.

"Looking up. There's a whole other world living up there."

I followed her gaze and at first I didn't know what she was on about. I looked through breaks in the gusts of snow that billowed around us, but couldn't detect anything out of the ordinary. I saw only rooftops and chimneys, multicolored Christmas decorations and the black strands of cable that ran in sagging geometric lines from the power poles to the buildings.

"What're you talking about?" I asked.

"The 'goyles," Gina said.

I gave her a blank look, no closer to understanding what she was talking about than I'd been before.

"The gargoyles, Sue," she repeated patiently. "Almost every building in this part of the city has got them, perched up there by the rooflines, looking down on us."

Once she'd pointed them out to me, I found it hard to believe that I'd never noticed them before. On that corner alone there were at least a half-dozen grotesque examples. I saw one in the archway keystone of the Annaheim Building directly across the street -a leering monstrous face, part lion, part bat, part man. Higher up, and all around, other nightmare faces peered down at us, from the corners of buildings, hidden in the frieze and cornice designs, cunningly nestled in corner brackets and the stone roof cresting. Every building had, them. *Every* building.

Their presence shocked me. It's not that I was unaware of their existence—after all, I was planning on architecture as a major in college. It's just that if someone had mentioned gargoyles to me before that day, I would have automatically thought of the cathedrals and castles of Europe not ordinary office buildings in Newford.

"I can't believe I never noticed them before," I fold her.

"There are people who live their whole lives here and never see them," Gina said.

"How's that possible?"

Gina smiled. "It's because of where they are looking down at us from just above our normal sightline. People in the city hardly ever look up."

"But still . . . "

"I know. It's something, isn't it? It really is a whole different world. Imagine being able to live your entire life in the middle of the city and never be noticed by anybody.

"Like a bag lady," I said.

Gina nodded. "Sort of. Except people wouldn't ignore you because you're some pathetic street person that they want to avoid. They'd ignore you because they simply couldn't *see* you."

That thought gave me a creepy feeling and I couldn't suppress a shiver, but I could tell that Gina was intrigued with the idea. She was staring at that one gargoyle, above the entrance to the Annaheim Building.

"You really like those things, don't you?" I said.

Gina turned to look at me, an expression I couldn't read sitting in the back of her eyes.

"I wish I lived in their world," she told me.

She held my gaze with that strange look in her eyes for a long heartbeat. Then the light changed and she laughed, breaking the mood. Slipping her arm in mine, she started us off across the street to finish her Christmas shopping.

When we stood on the pavement in front of the Annaheim Building, she stopped and looked up at the gargoyle. I craned my neck and tried to give it a good look myself, but it was hard to see because of all the blowing snow.

Gina laughed suddenly. "It knows we were talking about it."

"What do you mean?"

"It just winked at us."

I hadn't seen anything, but then I always seemed to be looking exactly the wrong way, or perhaps in the wrong way, whenever Gina tried to point out some magical thing to me. She was so serious about it.

"Did you see?" Gina asked.

"I'm not sure," I told her. "I think I saw something . . . "

Falling snow. The side of a building. And stone statuary that was pretty amazing in and of itself without the need to be animated as well. I looked up at the gargoyle again, trying to see what Gina had seen.

I wish I lived in their world.

It wasn't until years later that I finally understood what she'd meant by that.

3

Christmas wasn't the same for me as for most people, not even when I was a kid: my dad was born on Christmas day; Granny Ashworth, his mother, died on Christmas day when I was nine; and my own birthday was December 27th. It made for a strange brew come the holiday season, part celebration, part mourning, liberally mixed with all the paraphernalia that means Christmas: eggnog and glittering lights, caroling, ornaments, and, of course, presents.

Christmas wasn't centered around presents for me. Easy to say, I suppose, seeing how I grew up in the Beaches, wanting for nothing, but it's true. What enamored me the most about the season, once I got beyond the confusion of birthdays and mourning, was the idea of what it was supposed to be: peace and goodwill to all. The traditions. The idea of the miracle birth the way it was told in the Bible and more secular legends like the one about how for one hour after midnight on Christmas Eve, animals were given human voices so that they could praise the baby Jesus.

I remember staying up late the year I turned eleven, sitting up in bed with my cat on my lap and watching the clock, determined to hear Chelsea speak, except I fell asleep sometime after eleven and never did find out if she could or not. By the time Christmas came around the next year I was too old to believe in that sort of thing anymore.

Gina never got too old. I remember years later when she got her dog Fritzie, she told me, "You know what I like the best about him? The stories he tells me."

"Your dog tells you stories," I said slowly.

"Everything's got a voice," Gina told me. "You just have to learn how to hear it.

4

The best present I ever got was the Christmas that Gina decided to be my friend. I'd been going to a private school and hated it. Everything about it was so stiff and proper. Even though we were only children, it was still all about money and social standing and it drove me mad. I'd see the public school kids and they seemed so free compared to all the boundaries I perceived to be compartmentalizing my own life.

I pestered my mother for the entire summer I was nine until she finally relented and let me take the public transport into Ferryside where I attended Cairnmount Public School. By noon of my first day, I realized that I hated public school more.

There's nothing worse than being the new kid—especially when you were busing in from the Beaches. Nobody wanted anything to do with the slumming rich kid and her airs. I didn't have airs; I was just too scared. But first impressions are everything and I ended up feeling more left out and alone than I'd ever been at my old school. I couldn't even talk about it at home—my pride wouldn't let me. After the way I'd carried on about it all summer, I couldn't find the courage to admit that I'd been wrong.

So I did the best I could. At recess, I'd stand miserably on the sidelines, trying to look as though I was a part of the linked fence, or whatever I was standing beside at the time, because I soon learned it was better to be ignored than to be noticed and ridiculed. I stuck it out until just before Christmas break. I don't know if I would have been able to force myself to return after the holidays, but that day a bunch of boys were teasing me and my eyes were already welling with tears when Gina walked up out of nowhere and chased them off.

"Why don't you ever play with anybody?" she asked me.

"Nobody wants me to play with them," I said.

"Well, I do," she said and then she smiled at me, a smile so bright that it dried up all my tears.

After that, we were best friends forever.

5

Gina was the most outrageous, talented, wonderful person I had ever met. I was the sort of child who usually reacted to stimuli; Gina created them. She made up games, she made up stories, she made up songs. It was impossible to be bored in her company and we became inseparable, in school and out.

I don't think a day went by that we didn't spend some part of it together. We had sleepovers. We took art and music and dance classes together and if she won the prizes, I didn't mind, because she was my friend and I could only be proud of her. There was no limit to her imagination, but that was fine by me, too. I was happy to have been welcomed into her world and I was more than willing to take up whatever enterprise she might propose.

I remember one afternoon we sat up in her room and made little people out of found objects: acorn heads, seed eyes, twig bodies. We made clothes for them, and furniture, and concocted long extravagant family histories so that we ended up knowing more about them than we did our classmates.

"They're real now," I remember her telling me. "We've given them lives, so they'll always be real."

"What kind of real?" I asked, feeling a little confused because I was at that age when I was starting to understand the difference between what was make-believe and what was real.

"There's only one kind of real," Gina told me. "The trouble is, not everybody can see it and they make fun of those who can."

Though I couldn't know the world through the same perspective as Gina had, there was one thing I did know. "I would never make fun of you," I said.

"I know, Sue. That's why we're friends."

I still have the little twig people I made, wrapped up in tissue and stored away in a box of childhood treasures; I don't know what ever happened to Gina's.

We had five years together, but then her parents moved out of town— not impossibly far, but far enough to make our getting together a major effort—and we rarely saw each other more than a few times a year after that. It was mainly Gina's doing that we didn't entirely lose touch with each other. She wrote me two or three times a week, long chatty letters about what she'd been reading, films she'd seen, people she'd met, her hopes of becoming a professional musician after she finished high school. The letters were decorated with fanciful illustrations of their contents and sometimes included miniature envelopes in which I would find letters from her twig people to mine.

Although I tried to keep up my side, I wasn't much of a correspondent. Usually I'd phone her, but my calls grew further and further apart as the months went by. I never stopped considering her as a friend—the occasions when we did get together were among my best memories of being a teenager—but my own life had changed and I didn't have as much time for her anymore. It was hard to maintain a long-distance relationship when there was so much going on around me at home. I was no longer the new kid at school and I'd made other friends. I worked on the school paper and then I got a boyfriend.

Gina never wanted to talk about him. I suppose she thought of it as a kind of betrayal; she never again had a friend that she was as close to as she'd been with me.

I remember her mother calling me once, worried because Gina seemed to be sinking into a reclusive depression. I did my best to be there for her. I called her almost every night for a month and went out to visit her on the weekends, but somehow I just couldn't relate to her pain. Gina had always seemed so self-contained, so perfect, that it was hard to imagine her being as withdrawn and unhappy as her mother seemed to think she was. She put on such a good face to me that eventually the worries I'd had faded and the demands of my own life pulled me away again.

■ ■ ■

6

Gina never liked Christmas.

The year she introduced me to Newford's gargoyles we saw each other twice over the holidays: once so that she could do her Christmas shopping and then again between Christmas and New Year's when I came over to her place and stayed the night. She introduced me to her dog Fritzie, a gangly, wire-haired, long-legged mutt that she'd found abandoned on one of the country roads near her parents' place and played some of her new songs for me, accompanying herself on guitar.

The music had a dronal quality that seemed at odds with her clear high voice and the strange Middle Eastern decorations she used. The lyrics were strange and dark, leaving me with a sensation that was not so much unpleasant as uncomfortable, and I could understand why she'd been having so much trouble getting gigs. It wasn't just that she was so young and since most clubs served alcohol, their owners couldn't hire an underage performer; Gina's music simply wasn't what most people would think of as entertainment. Her songs went beyond introspection. They took the listener to that dark place that sits inside each and every one of us, that place we don't want to visit, that we don't even want to admit is there.

But the songs aside, there didn't seem to be any trace of the depression that had worried her mother so much the previous autumn. She appeared to be her old self, the Gina I remembered: opinionated and witty, full of life and laughter even while explaining to me what bothered her so much about the holiday season.

"I love the *idea* of Christmas," she said. "It's the hypocrisy of the season that I dislike. One time out of the year, people do what they can for the homeless, help stock the food banks, contribute to snowsuit funds and give toys to poor children. But where are they the rest of the year when their help is just as necessary? It makes me a little sick to think of all the money that gets spent on Christmas lights and parties and presents that people don't even really want in the first place. If we took all that money and gave it to the people who need it simply to survive, instead of throwing it away on ourselves, we could probably solve most of the problems of poverty and homelessness over one Christmas season."

"I suppose," I said. "But at least Christmas brings people closer together. I guess what we have to do is build on that."

Gina gave me a sad smile. "Who does it bring closer together?"

"Well . . . families, friends . . . "

"But what about those who don't have either? They look at all this closeness you're talking about and it just makes their own situation seem all the more desperate. It's hardly surprising that the holiday season has the highest suicide rate of any time of the year."

"But what can we do?" I said. "We can't just turn our backs and pretend there's no such thing as Christmas."

Gina shrugged, then gave me a sudden grin. "We could become Christmas commandos. You know," she added at my blank look. "We'd strike from within. First we'd convince our own families to give it up and then . . . "

With that she launched into a plan of action that would be as improbable in its execution as it was entertaining in its explanation. She never did get her family to give up Christmas, and I have to admit I didn't try very hard with mine, but the next year I did go visit the residents of places like St. Vincent's Home for the Aged and I worked in the Grasso Street soup kitchen with Gina on Christmas Day. I came away with a better experience of what Christmas was all about than I'd ever had at home.

But I just couldn't maintain that commitment all year round. I kept going to St. Vincent's when I could, but the sheer despair of the soup kitchens and food banks was more than I could bear.

7

Gina dropped out of college during her second year to concentrate on her music. She sent me a copy of the demo tape she was shopping around to the record companies in hopes of getting a contract. I didn't like it at first. Neither her guitar-playing nor her vocal style had changed much, and the inner landscape the songs revealed was too bleak, the shadows they painted upon the listener seemed too unrelentingly dark, but out of loyalty I played it a few times more and subsequent listenings changed that first impression.

Her songs were still bleak, but I realized that they helped create a healing process in the listener. If I let them take me into the heart of their darkness, they took me out again as well. It was the kind of music that while it appeared to wallow in despair, in actuality it left its audience stronger, more able to face the pain and heartache that awaited them beyond the music.

She was playing at a club near the campus one weekend and I went to see her. Sitting in front were a handful of hardcore fans, all pale-faced and dressed in black, but most of the audience didn't understand what she was offering them any more than I had the first time I sat through the demo tape. Obviously her music was an acquired taste—which didn't bode well for her career in a world where, more and more, most information was conveyed in thirty-second soundbites and audiences in the entertainment industry demanded instant gratification, rather than taking the time to explore the deeper resonances of a work.

She had Fritzie waiting for her in the claustrophobic dressing room behind the stage, so the three of us went walking in between her sets. That was the night she first told me about her bouts with depression.

"I don't know what it is that brings them on," she said. "I know I find it frustrating that I keep running into a wall with my music, but I also know that's not the cause of them either. As long as I can remember I've carried this feeling of alienation around with me; I wake up in the morning, in the middle of the night, and I'm paralyzed with all this emotional pain. The only people who have ever really helped to keep it at bay were first you, and now Fritzie."

It was such a shock to hear that her only lifelines were a friend who was hardly ever there for her and a dog. The guilt that lodged inside me then has never really gone away. I wanted to ask what had happened to that brashly confident girl who had turned my whole life around as much by the example of her own strength and resourcefulness as by her friendship, but then I realized that the answer lay in her music, in her songs that spoke of masks and what lay behind them, of puddles on muddy roads that sometimes hid deep, bottomless wells.

8

I was in the middle of studying for exams the following week, but I made a point of it to call Gina at least every day. I tried getting her to let me take her out for dinner on the weekend, but she and Fritzie were pretty much inseparable and she didn't want to leave him tied up outside the restaurant while we sat inside to eat. So I ended up having them over to the little apartment I was renting in Crowsea instead. She told me that night that she was going out west to try to shop her tape around to the big companies in L.A., and I didn't see her again for three months.

I'd been worried about her going off on her own, feeling as she was. I even offered to go with her, if she'd just wait until the semester was finished, but she assured me she'd be fine, and a series of cheerful cards and short letters—signed either by her or by just a big paw print—arrived in my letterbox to prove the point. When she finally did get back, she called me up and we got together for a picnic lunch in Fitzhenry Park.

Going out to the West Coast seemed to have done her good. She came back looking radiant and tanned, full of amusing stories concerning the ups and downs of her and Fritzie's adventures out there. She'd even got some fairly serious interest from an independent record label, but they were still making up their minds when her money ran out. Instead of trying to make do in a place where she felt even more like a stranger than she did in Newford, she decided to come home to wait for their response, driving back across the country in her old station wagon, Fritzie sitting up on the passenger seat beside her, her guitar in its battered case lying across the backseat.

"By the time we rolled into Newford," she said, "the car was just running on fumes. But we made it."

"If you need some money, or a place to stay . . . " I offered.

"I can just see the three of us squeezed into that tiny place of yours."

"We'd make do."

Gina smiled. "It's okay. My dad fronted me some money until the advance from the record company comes through. But thanks all the same. Fritzie and I appreciate the offer."

I was really happy for her. Her spirits were so high now that things had finally turned around and she could see that she was going somewhere with her music. She knew there was a lot of hard work still to come, but it was the sort of work she thrived on.

"I feel like I've lived my whole life on the edge of an abyss," she told me, "just waiting for the moment when it'd finally drag me down for good, but now everything's changed. It's like I finally figured out a way to live some place else away from the edge. *Far away.*"

I was going on to my third year at Butler U. in the fall, but we made plans to drive back to L.A. together in July, once she got the okay from the record company. We'd spend the summer together in La La Land, taking in the sights while Gina worked on her album. It's something I knew we were both looking forward to.

9

Gina was looking after the cottage of a friend of her parents when she fell back into the abyss. She never told me how she was feeling, probably because she knew I'd have gone to any length to stop her from hurting herself. All she'd told me before she went was that she needed the solitude to work on some new songs and I'd believed her. I had no reason to worry about her. In the two weeks she was living out there I must have gotten a half-dozen cheerful cards, telling me what to add to my packing list for our trip out west and what to leave off.

Her mother told me that she'd gotten a letter from the record company, turning down her demo. She said Gina had seemed to take the rejection well when she called to give her daughter the bad news. They'd ended their conversation with Gina already making plans to start the rounds of the records companies again with the new material she'd been working on. Then she'd burned her guitar and all of her music and poetry in a firepit down by the shore, and simply walked out into the lake. Her body was found after a neighbor was drawn to the lot by Fritzie's howling. The poor dog was shivering and wet, matted with mud from having tried to rescue her. They know it wasn't an accident because of the note she left behind in the cottage.

I never read the note. I couldn't.

I miss her terribly, but most of all I'm angry. Not at Gina, but at this society of ours that tries to make everybody fit into the same mold. Gina was unique, but she didn't want to be. All she wanted to do was fit in, but her spirit and her muse wouldn't let her. That dichotomy between who she was and who she thought she should be was what really killed her.

All that survives of her music is that demo tape. When I listen to it, I can't understand how she could create a healing process for others through that dark music, but she couldn't use it to heal herself.

10

Tomorrow is Christmas day and I'm going down to the soup kitchen to help serve the Christmas dinners. It'll be my first Christmas without Gina. My parents wanted me to come home, but I put them off until tomorrow night. I just want to sit here tonight with Fritzie and remember. He lives with me because Gina asked me to take care of him, but he's not the same dog he was when Gina was alive. He misses her too much.

I'm sitting by the window, watching the snow fall. On the table in front of me I've spread out the contents of a box of memories: The casing for Gina's demo tape. My twig people and the other things we made. All those letters and cards that Gina sent me over the years. I haven't been able to reread them yet, but I've looked at the drawings and I've held them in my hands, turning them over and over, one by one. The demo tape is playing softly on my stereo. It's the first time I've been able to listen to it since Gina died.

Through the snow I can see the gargoyle on the building across the street.

I know now what Gina meant about wanting to live in their world and be invisible. When you're invisible, no one can see that you're different.

Thinking about Gina hurts so much, but there's good things to remember, too. I don't know what would have become of me if she hadn't rescued me in that playground all those years ago and welcomed me into her life. It's so sad that the uniqueness about her that made me love her so much was what caused her so much pain.

The bells of St. Paul's Cathedral strike midnight. They remind me of the child I was, trying to stay up late enough to hear my cat talk. I guess that's what Gina meant to me. While everybody else grew up, Gina retained all the best things about childhood: goodness and innocence and an endless wonder. But she carried the downside of being a child inside her as well. She always lived in the present moment, the way we do when we're young, and that must be why her despair was so overwhelming for her.

"I tried to save her," a voice says in the room behind me as the last echo of St. Paul's bells fades away. "But she wouldn't let me. She was too strong for me."

I don't move. I don't dare move at all. On the demo tape, Gina's guitar starts to strum the intro to another song. Against the drone of the guitar's strings, the voice goes on.

"I know she'll always live on so long as we keep her memory alive," it says, "but sometimes that's just not enough. Sometimes I miss her so much I don't think *I* can go on."

I turn slowly then, but there's only me in the room. Me and Fritzie, and one small Christmas miracle to remind me that everything magic didn't die when Gina walked into the lake.

"Me, too," I tell Fritzie.

I get up from my chair and cross the room to where he's sitting up, looking at me with those sad eyes of his. I put my arms around his neck. I bury my face in his rough fur and we stay there like that for a long time, listening to Gina sing.

❄   ❄   ❄

In 1891, Pyotr Ilyich Tchaikovsky was commissioned to compose a ballet based on an adaptation of E. T. A. Hoffmann's story "The Nutcracker and the Mouse King." After completing the score, Tchaikovsky selected eight of the numbers from the ballet for a concert performance version: The Nutcracker Suite, Op. 71a. Premiering in March 1892, the suite was an immediate hit. The Nutcracker ballet, however, was not as well-received when it debuted in December of the same year. In the 1960s—after George Balanchine's 1954 staging for the New York City Ballet—it spread to dance companies across America and became a popular annual Christmas event. If the future predicted in this Hugo-winning novella is correct, Tchaikovsky's music will remain popular for a very long time.

The Nutcracker Coup
❋
Janet Kagan

Marianne Tedesco had *The Nutcracker Suite* turned up full blast for inspiration, and as she whittled she now and then raised her knife to conduct Tchaikovsky. That was what she was doing when one of the locals poked his delicate snout around the corner of the door to her office. She nudged the sound down to a whisper in the background and beckoned him in.

It was Tatep, of course. After almost a year on Rejoicing (that was the literal translation of the world's name), she still had a bit of trouble recognizing the Rejoicers by snout alone, but the three white quills in Tatep's ruff had made him the first real "individual" to her. Helluva thing for a junior diplomat not to be able to tell one local from another—but there it was. Marianne was desperately trying to learn the snout shapes that distinguished the Rejoicers to each other.

"Good morning, Tatep. What can I do for you?"

"Share?" said Tatep.

"Of course. Shall I turn the music off?" Marianne knew that *The Nutcracker Suite* was as alien to him as the rattling and scraping of his music was to her. She was beginning to like pieces here and there of the Rejoicer style, but she didn't know if Tatep felt the same way about Tchaikovsky.

"Please, leave it on," he said. "You've played it every day this week—am I right? And now I find you waving your knife to the beat. Will you share the reason?"

She *had* played it every day this week, she realized. "I'll try to explain. It's a little silly, really, and it shouldn't be taken as characteristic of human. Just as characteristic of Marianne."

"Understood." He climbed the stepstool she'd cobbled together her first month on Rejoicing and settled himself on his haunches comfortably to listen. At rest, the wicked quills adorning his ruff and tail seemed just that: adornments. By local standards, Tatep was a handsome male.

He was also a quadruped, and human chairs weren't the least bit of use to him. The stepstool let him lounge on its broad upper platform or sit upright on the step below that—in either case, it put a Rejoicer eye to eye with Marianne. This had been so successful an innovation in the embassy that they had hired a local artisan to make several for each office. Chornian's stepstools were a more elaborate affair, but Chornian himself had refused to make one to replace "the very first." A fine sense of tradition, these Rejoicers.

That was, of course, the best way to explain the Tchaikovsky. "Have you noticed, Tatep, that the farther away from home you go, the more important it becomes to keep traditions?"

"Yes," he said. He drew a small piece of sweetwood from his pouch and seemed to consider it thoughtfully. "Ah! I hadn't thought how very strongly you must need tradition! You're very far from home indeed. Some thirty light-years, is it not?" He bit into the wood, shaving a delicate curl from it with one corner or his razor-sharp front tooth. The curl he swallowed, then he said, "Please, go on."

The control he had always fascinated Marianne—she would have preferred to watch him carve, but she spoke instead. "My family tradition is to celebrate a holiday called Christmas."

He swallowed another shaving and repeated, "Christmas."

"For some humans Christmas is a religious holiday. For my family, it was more of . . . a turning of the seasons. Now, Esperanza and I couldn't agree on a date—her homeworld's calendar runs differently than mine— but we both agreed on a need to celebrate Christmas once a year. So, since it's a solstice festival, I asked Muhammad what was the shortest day of the year on Rejoicing. He says that's Tamemb Nap Ohd."

Tatep bristled his ruff forward, confirming Muhammad's date.

"So I have decided to celebrate Christmas Eve on Tarnemb Nap Ohd and to celebrate Christmas Day on Tememb Nap Chorr."

"Christmas is a revival, then? An awakening?"

"Yes, something like that. A renewal. A promise of spring to come."

"Yes, we have an Awakening on Tememb Nap Chorr as well."

Marianne nodded. "Many peoples do. Anyhow, I mentioned that I wanted to celebrate and a number of other people at the embassy decided it was a good idea. So, we're trying to put together something that resembles a Christmas celebration—mostly from local materials?"

She gestured toward the player. "That piece of music is generally associated with Christmas. I've been playing it because it gives me an anticipation of the Awakening to come."

Tatep was doing fine finishing work now, and Marianne had to stop to watch. The bit of sweetwood was turning into a pair of tommets—the Embassy staff had dubbed them "notrabbits" for their sexual proclivities—engaged in their mating dance. Tatep rattled his spines, amused, and passed the carving into her hands. He waited quietly while she turned it this way and that, admiring the exquisite workmanship.

"You don't get the joke," he said, at last.

"No, Tatep. I'm afraid I don't. Can you share it?"

"Look closely at their teeth."

Marianne, did, and got the joke. The creatures were tommets, yes, but the teeth they had were not tommet teeth. They were the same sort of teeth that Tatep had used to carve them. Apparently, "fucking like tommets" was a Rejoicer joke.

"It's a gift for Hapet and Achinto. They had *six* children! We're all pleased and amazed for them."

Four to a brood was the usual, but birthings were few and far between. A couple that had more than two birthings in a lifetime was considered unusually lucky

"Congratulate them for me, if you think it appropriate," Marianne said. "Would it be proper for the embassy to send a gift?"

"Proper and most welcome. Hapet and Achinto will need help feeding that many."

"Would you help me choose? Something to make children grow healthy and strong, and something as well to delight their senses."

"I'd be glad to. Shall we go to the market or the wood?"

"Let's go chop our own, Tatep. I've been sitting behind this desk too damn long. I could use the exercise."

As Marianne rose, Tatep put his finished carving into his pouch and climbed down. "You will share more about Christmas with me while we work? You can talk and chop at the same time."

Marianne grinned. "I'll do better than that. You can help me choose something that we can use for a Christmas tree, as well. If it's something that is also edible when it has seasoned for a few weeks' time, that would be all the more to the spirit of the festival."

The two of them took a leisurely stroll down the narrow cobbled streets. Marianne shared more of her Christmas customs with Tatep and found her anticipation growing apace as she did.

At Tatep's suggestion they paused at Killim the glassblower's, where Tatep helped Marianne describe and order a dozen ornamental balls for the tree. Unaccustomed to the idea of purely ornamental glass objects, Killim was fascinated. "She says," reported Tatep when Marianne missed a few crucial words of her reply, "she'll make a number of samples and you'll return on Debern Op Chorr to choose the most proper."

Marianne nodded. Before she could thank Killim, however, she heard the door behind her open, heard a muffled squeak of surprise, and turned. Halemtat had ordered yet another of his subjects clipped—Marianne saw that much before the local beat a hasty retreat from the door and vanished.

"Oh, god," she said aloud. "Another one." That, she admitted to herself for the first time, was why she was making such an effort to recognize the individual Rejoicers by facial shape alone. She'd seen no less than fifty clipped in the year she'd been on Rejoicing. There was no doubt in her mind that this was a new one—the blunted tips of its quills had been bright and crisp. "Who is it this time, Tatep?"

Tatep ducked his head in shame. "Chornian," he said.

For once, Marianne couldn't restrain herself. "Why?" she asked, and she heard the unprofessional belligerence in her own voice.

"For saying something I dare not repeat, not even in your language," Tatep said, "unless I wish to have *my* quills clipped."

Marianne took a deep breath. "I apologize for asking, Tatep. It was stupid of me." Best thing to do would be to get the hell out and let Chornian complete his errand without being shamed in front of the two of them. "Though," she said aloud, not caring if it was professional or not, "it's Halemtat who should be shamed, not Chornian."

Tatep's eyes widened, and Marianne knew she'd gone too far. She thanked the glassblower politely in Rejoicer and promised to return on Debem Op Chorr to examine the samples.

As they left Killim's, Marianne heard the scurry behind them—Chornian entering the shop as quickly and as unobtrusively as possible.

She set her mouth—her silence raging—and followed Tatep without a backward glance.

At last they reached the communal wood. Trying for some semblance of normalcy, Marianne asked Tatep for the particulars of an unfamiliar tree.

"*Huep*," he said. "Very good for carving, but not very good for eating." He paused a moment, thoughtfully. "I think I've put that wrong. The flavor is very good, but it's very low in food value. It grows prodigiously, though, so a lot of people eat too much of it when they shouldn't."

"Junk food," said Marianne, nodding. She explained the term to Tatep and he concurred. "Youngsters are particularly fond of it—but it wouldn't be a good gift for Hapet and Achinto."

"Then let's concentrate on good *healthy* food for Hapet and Achinto," said Marianne.

Deeper in the wood, they found a stand of the trees the embassy staff had dubbed *gnomewood* for its gnarly, stunted appearance. Tatep proclaimed this perfect, and Marianne set about to chop the proper branches. Gathering food was more a matter of pruning than chopping down, she'd learned, and she followed Tatep's careful instructions so she did not damage the tree's productive capabilities in the process.

"Now this one—just here," he said. "See, Marianne? Above the bole, for new growth will spring from the bole soon after your Awakening. If you damage the bole, however, there will be no new growth on this branch again."

Marianne chopped with care. The chopping took some of the edge off her anger. Then she inspected the gnomewood and found a second possibility. "Here," she said. "Would this be the proper place?"

"Yes," said Tatep, obviously pleased that she'd caught on so quickly. "That's right." He waited until she had lopped off the second branch and properly chosen a third, and then he said, "Chornian said Halemtat had the twining tricks of a *talemtat*. One of his children liked the rhyme and repeated it."

"*Talemtat* is the vine that strangles the tree it climbs, am I right?" She kept her voice very low.

Instead of answering aloud, Tatep nodded.

"Did Halemtat—did Halemtat order the child clipped as well?"

Tatep's eyelids shaded his pupils darkly. "The entire family. He ordered the entire family clipped."

So that was why Chornian was running the errands. He would risk his own shame to protect his family from the awful embarrassment—for a Rejoicer—of appearing in public with their quills clipped.

She took out her anger on yet another branch of the gnomewood. When the branch fell—on her foot, as luck would have it—she sat down in a heap, thinking to examine the bruise, then looked Tatep straight in the eye. "How long? How long does it take for the quills to grow out again?" After much of a year, she hadn't yet seen evidence that an adult's quills regenerated at all. "They do regrow?"

"After several Awakenings," he said. "The regrowth can be quickened by eating *welspeth*, but . . . "

But *welspeth* was a hothouse plant in this country. Too expensive for someone like Chornian.

"I see," she said. "Thank you, Tatep"

"Be careful where you repeat what I've told you. Best you not repeat it at all." He cocked his head at her and added with a rattle of quills, "I'm not sure where Halemtat would clip a human, or even if you'd feel shamed by a clipping, but I wouldn't like to be responsible for finding out."

Marianne couldn't help but grin. She ran a hand through her pale white hair. "I've had my head shaved—that was long ago and far away—and it was intended to shame me."

"Intended to?"

"I painted my naked scalp bright red and went about my business as usual. I set something of a new fashion and, in the end, it was the shaver who was—quite properly—shamed."

Tatep's eyelids once again shaded his eyes. "I must think about that," he said at last. "We have enough branches for a proper gift now, Marianne. Shall we consider the question of your Christmas tree?"

"Yes," she said. She rose to her feet and gathered up the branches. "And another thing as well . . . I'll need some more wood for carving. I'd like to carve some gifts for my friends, as well. That's another tradition of Christmas."

"Carving gifts? Marianne, you make Christmas sound as if it were a Rejoicing holiday!"

Marianne laughed. "It is, Tatep. I'll gladly share my Christmas with you."

Clarence Doggett was the Super Plenipotentiary Representing Terra to Rejoicing and today he was dressed to live up to his extravagant title in striped silver tights and a purple silk weskit. No less than four hoops of office jangled from his belt. Marianne had, since meeting him, conceived the theory that the more stylishly outré his dress the more likely he was to say yes to the request of a subordinate. Scratch that theory . . .

Clarence Doggett straightened his weskit with a tug and said, "We have no reason to write a letter of protest about Emperor Halemtat's treatment of Chornian. He's deprived us of a valuable worker, true, but . . . "

"Whatever happened to human rights?"

"They're not human, Marianne. They're aliens."

At least he hadn't called them "Pincushions" as he usually did, Marianne thought. Clarence Doggett was the unfortunate result of what the media had dubbed "the Grand Opening." One day humans had been alone in the galaxy, and the next they'd found themselves only a tiny fraction of the intelligent species. Setting up five hundred embassies in the space of a few years had strained the diplomatic service to the bursting point. Rejoicing, considered a backwater world, got the scrapings from the bottom of the barrel. Marianne was trying very hard not to be one of those scrapings, despite the example set by Clarence. She clamped her jaw shut very hard.

Clarence brushed at his fashionably large mustache and added, "It's not as if they'll *really* die of shame, after all."

"Sir," Marianne began.

He raised his hands. "The subject is closed. How are the plans coming for the Christmas bash?"

"Fine, sir," she said without enthusiasm. "Killim—she's the local glassblower—would like to arrange a trade for some dyes, by the way. Not just for the Christmas tree ornaments, I gather, but for some project of her own. I'm sending letters with Nick Minski to a number of glassblowers back home to find out what sort of dye is wanted."

"Good work. Any trade item that helps tie the Rejoicers into the galactic economy is a find. You're to be commended."

Marianne wasn't feeling very commended, but she said, "Thank you, sir."

"And keep up the good work—this Christmas idea of yours is turning out to be a big morale booster."

That was the dismissal. Marianne excused herself and, feet dragging, she headed back to her office. " 'They're not human,' " she muttered to herself. " 'They're aliens. It's not as if they'll *really* die of shame . . . ' " She slammed her door closed behind her and snarled aloud, "But Chornian can't keep up work and the kids can't play with their friends and his mate Chaylam can't go to the market. What if they starve?"

"They won't starve," said a firm voice.

Marianne jumped.

"It's just me," said Nick Minski. "I'm early." He leaned back in the chair and put his long legs up on her desk. "I've been watching how the neighbors behave. Friends—your friend Tatep included—take their leftovers to Chornian's family. They won't starve. At least, Chornian's family won't. I'm not sure what would happen to someone who is generally unpopular."

Nick was head of the ethnology team studying the Rejoicers. At least he had genuine observations to base his decision on.

He tipped the chair to a precarious angle. "I can't begin to guess whether or not helping Chornian will land Tatep in the same hot water, so I can't reassure you there. I take it from your muttering that Clarence won't make a formal protest?"

Marianne nodded . . .

He straightened the chair with a bang that made Marianne start. "Shit," he said. "Doggett's such a pissant."

Marianne grinned ruefully. "God, I'm going to miss you, Nick. Diplomats aren't permitted to speak in such matter-of-fact terms."

"I'll be back in a year. I'll bring you fireworks for your next Christmas." He grinned.

"We've been through that, Nick. Fireworks may be part of your family's Christmas tradition, but they're not part of mine. All that banging and flashing of light just wouldn't *feel* right to me, not on Christmas."

"Meanwhile," he went on, undeterred, "you think about my offer. You learned more about Tatep and his people than half the folks on my staff; academic credentials or no, I can swing putting you on the ethnology team. We're shorthanded as it is. I'd rather have skipped the rotation home this year, but . . . "

"You can't get everything you want, either."

He laughed. "I think they're afraid we'll all go native if we don't go home one year in five." He preened and grinned suddenly. "How d'you think I'd look in quills?"

"Sharp," she said and drew a second burst of laughter from him.

There was a knock at the door. Marianne stretched out a toe and tapped the latch. Tatep stood on the threshold, his quills still bristling from the cold. "Hi, Tatep—you're just in time. Come share."

His laughter subsiding to a chuckle, Nick took his feet from the desk and greeted Tatep in high-formal Rejoicer. Tatep returned the favor, then added by way of explanation, "Marianne is sharing her Christmas with me."

Nick cocked his head at Marianne. "But it's not for some time yet . . . "

"I know," said Marianne. She went to her desk and pulled out a wrapped package. "Tatep, Nick is my very good friend. Ordinarily, we exchange gifts on Christmas Day, but since Nick won't be here for Christmas, I'm going to give him his present now."

She held out the package. "Merry Christmas, Nick. A little too early, but—"

"You've hidden the gift in paper," said Tatep. "Is that also traditional?"

"Traditional but not necessary. Some of the pleasure is the surprise involved," Nick told the Rejoicer. With a sidelong glance and smile at Marianne, he held the package to his ear and shook it. "And some of the pleasure is in trying to guess what's in the package." He shook it and listened again.

"Nope, I haven't the faintest idea."

He laid the package in his lap.

Tatep flicked his tail in surprise. "Why don't you open it?"

"In my family, it's traditional to wait until Christmas Day to open your presents, even if they're wrapped and sitting under the Christmas tree in plain sight for three weeks or more."

Tatep clambered onto the stool to give him a stare of open astonishment from a more effective angle.

"Oh, no!" said Marianne. "Do you really mean it, Nick? You're *not* going to open it until Christmas Day?"

Nick laughed again. "I'm teasing." To Tatep, he said, "It's traditional in my family to wait—but it's also traditional to find some rationalization to open a gift the minute you lay hands on it. Marianne wants to see my expression; I think that takes precedence in this case."

His long fingers found a cranny in the paper wrapping and began to worry it ever so slightly. "Besides, our respective homeworlds can't agree on a date for Christmas . . . On some world today must be Christmas, right?"

"Good rationalizing," said Marianne, with a sigh and a smile of relief. "Right!"

"Right," said Tatep, catching on. He leaned precariously from his perch to watch as Nick ripped open the wrapping paper.

"Tchaikovsky made me think of it," Marianne said. "Although, to be honest, Tchaikovsky's nutcracker wasn't particularly traditional. This one is: take a close look."

He did. He held up the brightly painted figure, took in its green weskit, its striped silver tights, its flamboyant mustache. Four metal loops jangled at its carved belt, and Nick laughed aloud.

With a barely suppressed smile, Marianne handed him a "walnut" of the local variety.

Nick stopped laughing long enough to say, "You mean, this is a genuine, honest-to-god, *working* nutcracker?"

"Well, of course it is! My family's been making them for years." She made a motion with her hands to demonstrate. "Go ahead—crack that nut!"

Nick put the nut between the cracker's prominent jaws and, after a moment's hesitation, closed his eyes and went ahead.

The nut gave with an audible and very satisfying craaack! and Nick began to laugh all over again.

"Share the joke," said Tatep.

"Gladly," said Marianne. "The Christmas nutcracker, of which that is a prime example, is traditionally carved to resemble an authority figure—particularly one nobody much likes. It's a way of getting back at the fraudulent, the pompous. Through the years they've poked fun at everybody from princes to policemen to"—Marianne waved, a gracious hand at her own carved figure—"well, surely you recognize *him*."

"Oh, my," said Tatep, his eyes widening. "Clarence Doggett, is it not?" When Marianne nodded, Tatep said, "Are you about to get your head shaved again?"

Marianne laughed enormously. "If I do, Tatep, this time I'll paint my scalp red and green—traditional Christmas colors—and hang one of Killim's glass ornaments from my ear. Not likely, though," she added, to be fair. "Clarence doesn't go in for head shaving." To Nick, who had clearly taken in Tatep's "again," she said, "I'll tell you about it sometime."

Nick nodded and stuck another nut between Clarence's jaws. This time he watched as the nut gave way with an explosive bang. Still laughing, he handed the nutmeat to Tatep, who ate it and rattled his quills in laughter of his own. Marianne was doubly glad she'd invited Tatep to share the occasion—now she knew exactly what to make *him* for Christmas.

Christmas Eve found Marianne at a loss—something was missing from her holiday and she hadn't been able to put her finger on precisely what that something was.

It wasn't the color of the tree Tatep had helped her choose. The tree was the perfect Christmas-tree shape, and if its foliage was a red so deep it approached black, that didn't matter a bit. "Next year we'll have Killim make some green ornaments." Marianne said to Tatep, "for the proper contrast."

Tinsel—silver thread she'd bought from one of the Rejoicer weavers and cut to length—flew in all directions. All seven of the kids who'd come to Rejoicing with their ethnologist parents were showing the Rejoicers the "proper" way to hang tinsel, which meant more tinsel was making it onto the kids and the Rejoicers than onto the tree.

Just as well. She'd have to clean the tinsel off the tree before she passed it on to Hapet and Achinto—well-seasoned and just the thing for growing children.

Nick would really have enjoyed seeing this, Marianne thought. Esperanza was filming the whole party, but that just wasn't the same as being here.

Killim brought the glass ornaments herself. She'd made more than the commissioned dozen. The dozen glass balls she gave to Marianne. Each was a swirl of colors, each unique. Everyone ooohed and aaahed—but the best was yet to come. From her sidepack, Killim produced a second container. "Presents," she said. "A present for your Awakening Tree."

Inside the box was a menagerie of tiny, bright glass animals: notrabbits, fingerfish, wispwings. Each one had a loop of glass at the top to allow them to be hung from the tree. Scarcely trusting herself with such delicate objects of art, Marianne passed them on to George to string and hang.

Later, she took Killim aside and, with Tatep's help, thanked her profusely for the gifts. "Though I'm not sure she should have. Tell her I'll be glad to pay for them, Tatep. If she'd had them in her shop, I'd have snapped them upon the spot. I didn't know how badly our Christmas needed them until I saw her unwrap them."

Tatep spoke for a long time to Killim, who rattled all the while. Finally, Tatep rattled too. "Marianne, three humans have commissioned Killim to make animals for them to send home." Killim said something Marianne didn't catch. "Three humans in the last five minutes. She says, 'Think of this set as an advertisement.'"

"No, you may not pay me for them," Killim said, still rattling. "I have gained something to trade for my dyes."

"She says," Tatep began.

"It's okay, Tatep. That I understood."

Marianne hung the wooden ornaments she'd carved and painted in bright colors, then she unsnagged a handful of tinsel from Tatep's ruff, divided it in half, and they both flung it onto the tree. Tatep's handful just barely missed Matsimoto, who was hanging strings of beads he'd bought in the bazaar, but Marianne's got Juliet, who was hanging chains of paper cranes it must have taken her the better part of the month to fold. Juliet laughed and pulled the tinsel from her hair to drape it—length by length and *neatly*—over the deep red branches.

Then Kelleb brought out the star. Made of silver wire delicately filigreed, it shone just the way a Christmas-tree star should. He hoisted Juliet to his shoulders and she affixed it to the top of the tree and the entire company burst into cheers and applause.

Marianne sighed and wondered why that made her feel so down. "If Nick had been here," Tatep observed, "I believe he could have reached the top without an assistant."

"I think you're right," said Marianne. "I wish he were here. He'd enjoy this." Just for a moment, Marianne let herself realize that what was missing from this Christmas was Nick Minski.

"Next year," said Tatep.

"Next year," said Marianne. The prospect brightened her.

The tree glittered with its finery. For a moment they all stood back and admired it—then there was a scurry and a flurry, as folks went to various bags and hiding places and brought out the brightly wrapped presents. Marianne excused herself from Tatep and Killim and brought out hers to heap at the bottom of the tree with the rest.

Again there was a moment's pause of appreciation. Then Clarence Doggett—of all people—raised his glass and said, "A toast! A Christmas toast! Here's to Marianne, for bringing Christmas thirty light-years from old Earth!"

Marianne blushed as they raised their glasses to her. When they'd finished, she raised hers and found the right traditional response: "A Merry Christmas—and God bless us, every one!"

"Okay, Marianne. It's your call," said Esperanza. "Do we open the presents now or"—her voice turned to a mock whine—"do we *hafta* wait till tomorrow?"

Marianne glanced at Tatep. "What day is it now?" she asked. She knew enough about local time reckoning to know what answer he'd give.

"Why, today is Tememb Nap Chorr."

She grinned at the faces around her. "By Rejoicer reckoning, the day changes when the sun sets—it's been Christmas Day for an hour at least now. But stand back and let the kids find their presents first."

There was a great clamor and rustle of wrapping paper and whoops of delight as the kids dived into the pile of presents.

As Marianne watched with rising joy, Tatep touched her arm. "More guests," he said, and Marianne turned.

It was Chornian, his mate Chaylam, and their four children. Marianne's jaw dropped at the sight of them. She had invited the six with no hope of a response and here they were. "And all dressed up for Christmas!" she said aloud, though she knew Christmas was not the occasion. "You're as glittery as the Christmas tree itself," she told Chornian, her eyes gleaming with the reflection of it.

Ruff and tail, each and every one of Chornian's short-clipped quills was tipped by a brilliant red bead. "Glass?" she asked.

"Yes," said Chornian. "Killim made them for us."

"You look magnificent! Oh—how wonderful!" Chaylam's clipped quills had been dipped in gold; when she shifted shyly, her ruff and tail rippled with light. "You sparkle like sun on the water," Marianne told her. The children's ruffs and tails had been tipped in gold and candy pink and vivid yellow and—the last but certainly not the least—in beads every color of the rainbow.

"A kid after my own heart," said Marianne "I think that would have been my choice too." She gave a closer look. "No two alike, am I right? Come—join the party. I was afraid I'd have to drop your presents by your house tomorrow. Now I get to watch you open them, to see if I chose correctly."

She escorted the four children to the tree and, thanking her lucky stars she'd had Tatep write their names on their packages, she left them to hunt for their presents. Those for their parents she brought back with her.

"It was difficult," Chornian said to Marianne. "It was difficult to walk through the streets with pride but—we did. And the children walked the proudest. They give us courage."

Chaylam said, "If only on their behalf."

"Yes," agreed Chornian. "Tomorrow I shall walk in the sunlight. I shall go to the bazaar. My clipped quills will glitter, and I will not be ashamed that I have spoken the truth about Halemtat."

That was all the Christmas gift Marianne needed, she thought to herself, and handed the wrapped package to Chornian. Tatep gave him a running commentary on the habits and rituals of the human Awakening as he opened the package. Chornian's eyes shaded and Tatep's running commentary ceased abruptly as they peered together into the box.

"Did I get it right?" said Marianne, suddenly afraid she'd committed some awful faux pas. She'd scoured the bazaar for *welspeth* shoots and, finding none, she'd pulled enough strings with the ethnology team to get some imported.

Tatep was the one who spoke. "You got it right," he said. "Chorian thanks you." Chornian spoke rapid-fire Rejoicer for a long time; Marianne couldn't follow the half of it. When he'd finished, Tatep said simply, "He regrets that he has no present to give you."

"It's not necessary. Seeing those kids all in spangles brightened up the party—that's present enough for me!"

"Nevertheless," said Tatep, speaking slowly so she wouldn't miss a word. "Chornian and I make you this present."

Marianne knew the present Tatep drew from his pouch was from Tatep alone, but she was happy enough to play along with the fiction if it made him happy. She hadn't expected a present from Tatep and she could scarcely wait to see what it was he felt appropriate to the occasion.

Still, she gave it the proper treatment—shaking it, very gently, beside her ear. If there was anything to hear, it was drowned out by the robust singing of carols from the other side of the room. "I can't begin to guess, Tatep," she told him happily.

"Then open it."

She did. Inside the paper, she found a carving, the rich wine red of burgundy-wood, bitter to the taste and therefore rarely carved but treasured because none of the kids would gnaw on it as they tested their teeth. The style of carving was so utterly Rejoicer that it took her a long moment to recognize the subject, but once she did, she knew she'd treasure the gift for a lifetime.

It was unmistakably Nick—but Nick as seen from Tatep's point of view, hence the unfamiliar perspective. It was Looking Up At Nick.

"Oh, Tatep!" And then she remembered—just in time—and added, "Oh, Chornian! Thank you both so very much. I can't wait to show it to Nick when he gets back. Whatever made you think of doing Nick?"

Tatep said, "He's your best *human* friend. I know you miss him. You have no pictures; I thought you would feel better with a likeness."

She hugged the sculpture to her. "Oh, I do. Thank you, both of you." Then she motioned, eyes shining. "Wait. Wait right here, Tatep. Don't go away."

She darted to the tree and, pushing aside wads of rustling paper, she found the gift she'd made for Tatep. Back she darted to where the Rejoicers were waiting.

"I waited," Tatep said solemnly.

She handed him the package. "I hope this is worth the wait."

Tatep shook the package. "I can't begin to guess," he said.

"Then open it. *I* can't stand the wait!"

He ripped away the paper as flamboyantly as Nick had—to expose the brightly colored nutcracker and a woven bag full of nuts.

Marianne held her breath. The problem had been, of course, to adapt the nutcracker to a recognizable Rejoicer version. She'd made the Emperor Halemtat sit back on his haunches, which meant far less adaptation of the cracking mechanism. Overly plump, she'd made him, and spiky. In his right hand, he carried an oversized pair of scissors—of the sort his underlings used for clipping quills. In his left, he carried a sprig of *talemtat*, that unfortunate rhyme for his name.

Chornian's eyes widened. Again, he rattled off a spate of Rejoicer too fast for Marianne to follow . . . except that Chornian seemed anxious.

Only then did Marianne realize what she'd done. "Oh, my God, Tatep! He wouldn't clip your quills for having that, would he?"

Tatep's quills rattled and rattled. He put one of the nuts between Halemtat's jaws and cracked with a vengeance. The nutmeat he offered to Marianne, his quills still rattling. "If he does, Marianne, you'll come to Killim's to help me choose a good color for my glass beading."

He cracked another nut and handed the meat to Chornian. The next thing Marianne knew, the two of them were rattling at each other—Chornian's glass beads adding a splendid tinkling to the merriment.

Much relieved, Marianne laughed with them. A few minutes later, Esperanza dashed out to buy more nuts—so Chornian's children could each take a turn at the cracking.

Marianne looked down at the image of Nick cradled in her arm. "I'm sorry you missed this," she told it, "but I promise I'll write everything down for you before I go to bed tonight. I'll try to remember every last bit of it for you."

"Dear Nick," Marianne wrote in another letter some months later. "You're not going to approve of this. I find I haven't been ethnologically correct—much less diplomatic. I'd only meant to share my Christmas with Tatep and Chornian and, for that matter, whoever wanted to join in the festivities. To hear Clarence tell it, I've sent Rejoicing to hell in a handbasket.

"You see, it does Halemtat no good to clip quills these days. There are some seventy-five Rejoicers walking around town clipped and beaded—as gaudy and as shameless as you please. I even saw one newly male (teenager) with beads on the ends of his unclipped spines!

"Killim says thanks for the dyes, by the way. They're just what she had in mind. She's so busy, she's taken on two apprentices to help her. She makes 'Christmas ornaments' and half the art galleries in the known universe are after her for more and more. The apprentices make glass beads. One of them—one of Chornian's kids, by the way—hit upon the bright idea of making simple sets of beads that can be stuck on the ends of quills cold. Saves time and trouble over the hot glass method.

"What's more—

"Well, yesterday I stopped by to say 'hi' to Killim, when who should turn up but Koppen—you remember him? He's one of Halemtat's advisors? You'll never guess what he wanted: a set of quill-tipping beads.

"No, he hadn't had his quills clipped. Nor was he buying them for a friend. He was planning, he told Killim, to tell Halemtat a thing or two—I missed the details because he went too fast—and he expected he'd be clipped for it, so he was planning ahead. Very expensive *blue* beads for him, if you please, Killim!

"I find myself unprofessionally pleased. There's a thing or two Halemtat *ought* to be told . . .

"Meanwhile, Chornian has gone into the business of making nutcrackers. All right, so sue me, I showed him how to make the actual cracker work. It was that or risk his taking Tatep's present apart to find out for himself.

"I'm sending holos—including a holo of the one I made—because you've got to see the transformation Chornian's worked on mine. The difference between a human-carved nutcracker and a Rejoicer-carved nutcracker is as unmistakable as the difference between Looking Up At Nick and . . . well, *looking up at Nick.*

"I still miss you, even if you do think fireworks are appropriate at Christmas.

"See you soon—if Clarence doesn't boil me in my own pudding and bury me with a stake of holly through my heart."

Marianne sat with her light pen poised over the screen for a long moment; then she added, "Love, Marianne," and saved it to the next outgoing Dirt-bound mail.

Rejoicing
Midsummer's Eve
(Rejoicer reckoning)

Dear Nick—

This time it's not my fault. This time it's Esperanza's doing. Esperanza decided, for *her* contribution to our round of holidays, to celebrate

Martin Luther King Day. And she invited a handful of the Rejoicers to attend as well.

Now, the final part of the celebration is that each person in turn "has a dream." This is not like wishes, Nick. This is more on the order of setting yourself a goal, even one that looks to all intents and purposes to be unattainable, but one you will strive to attain. Even Clarence got so into the occasion that he had a dream that he would stop thinking of the Rejoicers as "Pincushions" so he could start thinking of them as Rejoicers. Esperanza said later Clarence didn't quite get, the point but for him she supposed that was a step in the right direction.

Well, after that, Tatep asked Esperanza, in his very polite fashion, if it would be proper for him to have a dream as well. There was some consultation over the proper phrasing—Esperanza says her report will tell you all about that—and then Tatep rose and said, "I have a dream—I have a dream that someday no one will get his quills clipped for speaking the truth."

(You'll see it on the recording. Everybody agreed that this was a good dream, indeed.)

After which, Esperanza had her, dream "for human rights for all."

Following which, of course, we all took turns trying to explain the concept of "human rights" to a half-dozen Rejoicers. Esperanza ended up translating five different constitutions for them—*and* an entire book of speeches by Martin Luther King . . .

Oh, god. I just realized . . . maybe it is my fault. I'd forgotten till just now. Oh. You judge, Nick.

About a week later Tatep and I were out gathering wood for some carving he plans to do—for Christmas, he says, but he wanted to get a good start on it—and he stopped gnawing long enough to ask me, "Marianne, what's 'human'?"

"How do you mean?"

"I think when Clarence says 'human,' he means something different than you do."

"That's entirely possible. Humans use words pretty loosely at the best of times—there, I just did it myself."

"What do you mean when you say 'human'?"

"Sometimes I mean the species *Homo sapiens*. When I say, *Humans use words pretty loosely*, I do. Rejoicers seem to be more particular about their speech, as a general rule."

"And when you say 'human rights,' what do you mean?"

"When I say 'human rights,' I mean *Homo sapiens* and *Rejoicing sapiens*. I mean any *sapiens*, in that context. I wouldn't guarantee that Clarence uses the word the same way in the same context."

"You think I'm human?"

"I *know* you're human. We're friends, aren't we? I couldn't be friends with—oh, a notrabbit—now, could I?"

He made that wonderful rattly sound he does when he's amused. "No, I can't imagine it. Then, if I'm human, I ought to have human rights."

"Yes," I said. "You bloody well ought to."

Maybe it *is* all my fault. Esperanza will tell you the rest—she's had Rejoicers all over her house for the past two weeks—they're watching every scrap of film she's got on Martin Luther King.

I don't know how this will all end up, but I wish to hell you were here to watch.

Love, Marianne

Marianne watched a Rejoicer child crack nuts with his Halemtat cracker and a cold, cold shiver went up her spine. That was the eleventh she'd seen this week. Chornian wasn't the only one making them, apparently; somebody else had gone into the nutcracker business as well. This was, however, the first time she'd seen a child cracking nuts with Halemtat's jaw.

"Hello," she said, stooping to meet the child's eyes. "What a pretty toy! Will you show me how it works?"

Rattling all the while, the child showed her, step by step. Then he (or she—it wasn't polite to ask before puberty) said, "Isn't it funny? It makes Mama laugh and laugh and laugh."

"And what's your mama's name?"

"Pilli," said the child. Then it added, "With the green and white beads on her quills."

Pilli—who'd been clipped for saying that Halemtat had been overcutting the imperial reserve so badly that the trees would never grow back properly.

And then she realized that, less than a year ago, no child would have admitted that its mama had been clipped. The very thought of it would have shamed both mother *and* child.

Come to think of it . . . she glanced around the bazaar and saw no less than four clipped Rejoicers shopping for dinner. Two of them she recognized as Chornian and one of his children, the other two were new to her. She tried to identify them by their snouts and failed utterly—she'd have to ask Chornian. She also noted, with utterly unprofessional satisfaction, that she *could* ask Chornian such a thing now. That too would have been unthinkable and shaming less than a year ago.

Less than a year ago. She was thinking in Dirt terms because of Nick. There wasn't any point dropping him a line; mail would cross in deep space at this late a date. He'd be here just in time for "Christmas." She wished like hell he was already here. He'd know what to make of all this, she was certain.

As Marianne thanked the child and got to her feet, three Rejoicers—all with the painted ruff of quills at their necks that identified them as Halemtat's guards—came waddling officiously up. "Here's one," said the largest. "Yes," said another. "Caught in the very act."

The largest squatted back on his haunches and said, "You will come with us, child. Halemtat decrees it."

Horror shot through Marianne's body.

The child cracked one last nut, rattled happily, and said, "I get my quills clipped?"

"Yes," said the largest Rejoicer. "You will have your quills clipped." Roughly, he separated child from nutcracker and began to tow the child away, each of them in that odd three-legged gait necessitated by the grip.

All Marianne could think to do was call after the child, "I'll tell Pilli what happened and where to find you!"

The child glanced over its shoulder, rattled again, and said, "Ask her could I have silver beads like Hortap!"

Marianne picked up the discarded nutcracker—lest some other child find it and meet the same fate—and ran full speed for Pilli's house.

At the corner, two children looked up from their own play and galloped along beside her until she skidded to a halt by Pilli's bakery. They followed her in, rattling happily to themselves over the race they'd run. Marianne's first thought was to shoo them off before she told Pilli what had happened, but Pilli greeted the two as if they were her own, and Marianne found herself blurting out the news.

Pilli gave a slow inclination of the head. "Yes," she said, pronouncing the words carefully so Marianne wouldn't miss them, "I expected that. Had it not been the nutcracker, it would have been words." She rattled. "That child is the most outspoken of my brood."

"But—" Marianne wanted to say, *Aren't you afraid?* but the question never surfaced.

Pilli gave a few coins to the other children and said, "Run to Killim's, my dears, and ask her to make a set of silver beads, if she doesn't already have one on hand. Then run tell your father what has happened." The children were off in the scurry of excitement. Pilli drew down the awning in front of her shop, then paused. "I think you are afraid for my child."

"Yes," said Marianne. Lying had never been her strong suit; maybe Nick was right—maybe diplomacy wasn't her field.

"You are kind," said Pilli. "But don't be afraid. Even Halemtat wouldn't dare to order a child *hashay*."

"I don't understand the term."

"*Hashay?*" Pilli flipped her tail around in front of her and held out a single quill. "Chippet will be clipped here," she said, drawing a finger across the quill about halfway up its length. "*Hashay* is to clip here." The finger slid inward, to a spot about a quarter of an inch from her skin. "Don't worry, Marianne. Even Halemtat wouldn't dare to *hashay* a child."

I'm supposed to be reassured, thought. Marianne. "Good," she said, aloud, "I'm relieved to hear that." In truth, she hadn't the slightest idea what Pilli was talking about—and she was considerably less than reassured by the ominous implications of the distinction. She'd never come across the term in any of the ethnologists' reports.

She was still holding the Halemtat nutcracker in her hands. Now she considered it carefully. Only in its broadest outlines did it resemble the one she'd made for Tatep. This nutcracker was purely Rejoicer in style and—she almost dropped it at the sudden realization—peculiarly *Tatep's* style of carving. Tatep was making them too?

If *she* could recognize Tatep's distinctive style, surely Halemtat could—what then?

Carefully, she tucked the nutcracker under the awning—let Pilli decide what to do with the object; Marianne couldn't make the decision for her—and set off at a quick pace for Tatep's house . . .

On the way, she passed yet another child with a Halemtat nutcracker. She paused, found the child's father, and passed the news to him that Halemtat's guards were clipping Pilli's child for the "offense." The father thanked her for the information and, with much politeness, took the nutcracker from the child.

This one, Marianne saw, was not carved in Tatep's style or in Chornian's. This one was the work of an unfamiliar set of teeth.

Having shooed his child indoors, the Rejoicer squatted back on his haunches. In plain view of the street, he took up the bowl of nuts his child had left uncracked and began to crack them, one by one, with such deliberation that Marianne's jaw dropped.

She'd never seen an insolent Rejoicer, but she would have bet money she was seeing one now. He even managed to make the crack of each nut resound like a gunshot. With the sound still ringing in her ears, Marianne quickened her steps toward Tatep's.

She found him at home, carving yet another nutcracker. He swallowed, then held out the nutcracker to her and said, "What do you think, Marianne? Do you approve of my portrayal?"

This one wasn't Halemtat, but his—for want of a better term—grand vizier, Corten. The grand vizier always looked to her as if he smirked. She knew the expression was due to a slightly malformed tooth but, to a human eye, the result was a smirk. Tatep's portrayal had the same smirk, only more so. Marianne couldn't help it . . . she giggled.

"Aha!" said Tatep, rattling up a rainstorm's worth of sound. "For once, you've shared the joke without the need of explanation!" He gave a long, grave look at the nutcracker. "The grand vizier has earned his keep this once!"

Marianne laughed, and Tatep rattled. This time the sound of the quills sobered Marianne. "I think your work will get you clipped, Tatep," she said, and she told him about Pilli's child.

He made no response. Instead, he dropped to his feet and went to the chest in the corner, where he kept any number of carvings and other precious objects. From the chest, he drew out a box. Three-legged, he walked back to her "Shake this! I'll bet you can guess what's inside."

Curious, she shook the box: it rattled. "A set of beads," she said.

"You see? I'm prepared. They rattle like a laugh, don't they? A laugh at Halemtat. I asked Killim to make the beads red because that was the color you painted your scalp when you were clipped."

"I'm honored . . . "

"But?"

"But I'm afraid for you. For *all* of you."

"Pilli's child wasn't afraid."

"No. No, Pilli's child wasn't afraid. Pilli said even Halemtat wouldn't dare *hashay* a child." Marianne took a deep breath and said, "But you're not a child." And I don't know what *hashay*ing does to a Rejoicer, she wanted to add.

"I've swallowed a taipseed," Tatep said, as if that said it all.

"I don't understand."

"Ah! I'll share, then. A taipseed can't grow unless it has been through the"—he patted himself—"stomach? digestive system?—of a Rejoicer. Sometimes they don't grow even then. To swallow a taipseed means to take a step toward the growth of something important. I swallowed a taipseed called 'human rights.'"

There was nothing Marianne could say to that but: "I understand."

Slowly, thoughtfully, Marianne made her way back to the embassy. Yes, she understood Tatep—hadn't she been screaming at Clarence for just the same reason? But she was terrified for Tatep—for them all.

Without consciously meaning, to, she bypassed the embassy for the little clutch of domes that housed the ethnologists. Esperanza—it was Esperanza she had to see. She was in luck. Esperanza was at home writing up one of her reports. She looked up and said, "Oh, good. It's time for a break!"

"Not a break, I'm afraid. A question that, I think, is right up your alley. Do you know much about the physiology of the Rejoicers?"

"I'm the expert," Esperanza said, leaning back in her chair. "As far as there is one in the group."

"What happens if you cut a Rejoicer's spine"—she held her fingers—"*this* close to the skin?"

"Like, a cat's claw, sort of. If you cut the tip, nothing happens. If you cut too far down, you hit the blood supply—and maybe the, nerve. The quill would bleed most certainly. Might never grow back properly. And it'd hurt like hell, I'm sure—like gouging the base of your thumbnail."

She sat forward suddenly. "Marianne, you're shaking. What is it?"

Marianne took a deep breath but couldn't stop shaking. "What would happen if somebody did that to all of Ta . . ."—she found she couldn't get the name out—"all of a Rejoicer's quills?"

"He'd bleed to death, Marianne." Esperanza took her hand and gave it a firm squeeze. "Now, I'm going to get you a good stiff drink and you are going to tell me all about it."

Fighting nausea, Marianne nodded. "Yes," she said with enormous effort. "Yes."

"Who the *hell* told the Pincushions about 'human rights'?" Clarence roared. Furious, he glowered down at Marianne and waited for her response.

Esperanza drew herself up to her full height and stepped between the two of them. "Martin Luther King told the Rejoicers about human rights.

You were there when he did it. Though you seem to have forgotten your dream, obviously the Rejoicers haven't forgotten theirs."

"There's a goddamned revolution going on out there!" Clarence waved a hand vaguely in the direction of the center of town.

"That is certainly what it looks like," Juliet said mildly. "So why are we here instead of out there observing?"

"You're here because I'm responsible for your safety."

"Bull," said Matsimoto. "Halemtat isn't interested in clipping us."

"Besides," said Esperanza. "The supply ship will be landing in about five minutes. Somebody's got to go pick up the supplies—and Nick. Otherwise, he's going to step right into the thick of it. The last mail went out two months ago. Nick's had no warning that the situation has"—she frowned slightly, then brightened as she found the proper phrase—"changed *radically*."

Clarence glared again at Marianne. "As a member of the embassy staff, you are assigned the job. You will pick up the supplies and Nick."

Marianne, who'd been about to volunteer to do just that, suppressed the urge to say, "Thank you!" and said instead, "Yes, sir."

Once out of Clarence's sight, Marianne let herself breathe a sigh of relief. The supply transport was built like a tank.

While Marianne wasn't any more afraid of Halemtat's wrath than the ethnologists were, she was well aware that innocent Dirt bystanders might easily find themselves stuck—all too literally—in a mob of Rejoicers. When the Rejoicers fought, as she understood it, they used teeth and quills. She had no desire to get too close to a lashing tailful. An unclipped quill was needle-sharp.

Belatedly, she caught the significance of the clipping Halemtat had instituted as punishment. Slapping a snout with a tail full of glass beads was not nearly as effective as slapping a snout with a morning star made of spines.

She radioed the supply ship to tell them they'd all have to wait for transport before they came out. Captain's gonna love that, I'm sure, she thought, until she got a response from Captain Tertain. By reputation he'd never set foot on a world other than Dirt and certainly didn't intend to do so now. So she simply told Nick to stay put until she came for him.

Nick's cheery voice over the radio said only, "It's going to be a very special Christmas this year."

"Nick," she said, "you don't know the half of it."

She took a slight detour along the way, passing the narrow street that led to Tatep's house. She didn't dare to stop, but she could see from the awning that he wasn't home. In fact, nobody seemed to be home . . . even the bazaar was deserted.

The supply truck rolled on, and Marianne took a second slight detour. What Esperanza had dubbed "the Grande Alle" led directly to Halemtat's imperial residence. The courtyard was filled with Rejoicers. Well-spaced Rejoicers, she saw, for they were—each and every one—bristled to their fullest extent. She wished she dared go for a closer look, but Clarence would be livid if she took much more time than normal reaching the supply ship. And he'd be checking—she knew his habits well enough to know that.

She floored the accelerator and made her way to the improvised landing field in record time. Nick waved to her from the port and stepped out. Just like Nick, she thought. She'd told him to wait in the ship until she arrived; he'd obeyed to the letter. It was all she could do to keep from hugging him as she hit the ground beside him. With a grateful sigh of relief, she said, "We've got to move fast on the transfer, Nick. I'll fill you in as we load."

By the time the two of them had transferred all the supplies from the ship, she'd done just that.

He climbed into the seat beside her, gave her a long thoughtful look, and said, "So Clarence has restricted all of the other ethnologists to the embassy grounds, has he?" He shook his head in mock sadness and clicked his tongue. "I see I haven't trained my team in the proper response to embassy edicts." He grinned at Marianne. "So the embassy advises that I stay off the streets, does it?"

"Yes," said Marianne. She hated being the one to tell him but he'd asked her. "The Super Plenipotentiary Et Cetera has issued a full and formal Advisory to all nongovernmental personnel . . . "

"Okay," said Nick. "You've done your job: I've been Advised. Now I want to go have a look at this revolution-in-progress." He folded his arms across his chest and waited.

He was right. All Clarence could do was issue an Advisory; he had no power whatsoever to keep the ethnologists off the streets. And Marianne wanted to see the revolution as badly as Nick did.

"All right," she said. "I *am* responsible for your safety, though, so best we go in the transport. I don't want you stuck." She set the supply transport into motion and headed back toward the Grande Allez.

Nick pressed his nose to the window and watched the streets as they went. He was humming cheerfully under his breath.

"Uh, Nick—if Clarence calls us . . . "

"We'll worry about that when it happens," he said.

Worry is right, thought Marianne, but she smiled. He'd been humming Christmas carols, like some excited child. Inappropriate as all hell, but she liked him all the more for it.

She pulled the supply transport to a stop at the entrance to the palace courtyard and turned to ask Nick if he had a good enough view. He was already out the door and making his way carefully into the crowd of Rejoicers. "Hey!" she shouted, and she hit the ground running to catch up with him. "Nick!"

He paused long enough for her to catch his arm, then said, "I need to see this, Marianne. It's my *job*."

"It's *my* job to see you don't get hurt."

He smiled. "Then you lead. I want to be over there where I can see and hear everything Halemtat and his advisors are up to."

Marianne harbored a brief fantasy about dragging him bodily back to the safety of the supply transport, but he was twice her weight and, from his expression, not about to cooperate. Best she lead, then. Her only consolation was that, when Clarence tried to radio them, there'd be nobody to pick up and receive his orders.

"Hey, Marianne!" said Chornian from the crowd. "Over here! Good view from here!"

And safer too. Grateful for the invitation, Marianne gingerly headed in Chornian's direction. Several quilled Rejoicers eased aside to let the two of them safely through. Better to be surrounded by beaded Rejoicers.

"Welcome back, Nick," said Chornian. He and Chaylam stepped apart to create a space of safety for the two humans. "You're just in time."

"So I see. What's going on?"

"Halemtat just had Pilli's Chippet clipped for playing with a Halemtat cracker. Halemtat doesn't *like* the Halemtat crackers."

Beside him, a fully quilled Rejoicer said, "Halemtat doesn't like much of anything. I think a proper prince ought to rattle his spines once or twice a year at least."

Marianne frowned up at Nick, who grinned and said, "Roughly translated: Hapter thinks a proper prince ought to have a sense of humor, however minimal."

"Rattle your spines, Halemtat!" shouted a voice from the crowd. "Let's see if you can do it."

"Yes," came another voice—and Marianne realized, it was Chornian's— "Rattle your spines, Great Prince of the Nutcrackers!"

All around them, like rain on a tin roof, came the sound of rattling spines. Marianne looked around—the laughter swept through the crowd, setting every Rejoicer in vibrant motion. Even the grand vizier rattled briefly, then caught himself, his ruff stiff with alarm.

Halemtat didn't rattle.

From his pouch, Chornian took a nutcracker and a nut. Placing the nut in the cracker's smirking mouth, Chornian made the bite cut through the rattling of the crowd like the sound of a shot. From somewhere to her right, a second crack resounded. Then a third . . . Then the rattling took up a renewed life

Marianne felt as if she were under water. All around her spines shifted and rattled. Chornian's beaded spines chattered as he cracked a second nut in the smirking face of the nutcracker.

Then one of Halemtat's guards ripped the nutcracker from Chornian's hands. The guard glared at Chornian, who rattled all the harder.

Looking over his shoulder to Halemtat, the guard called, "He's already clipped. What shall I do?"

"Bring me the nutcracker," said Halemtat. The guard glared again at Chornian, who had not stopped laughing, and loped back with the nutcracker in hand. Belatedly, Marianne recognized the smirk on the nutcracker's face.

The guard handed the nutcracker to the grand vizier—Marianne knew beyond a doubt that he recognized the smirk too.

"Whose teeth carved this?" demanded Halemtat.

An unclipped Rejoicer worked his way to the front of the crowd, sat proudly back on his haunches, and said, "Mine." To the grand vizier, he added, with a slight rasp of his quills that was a barely suppressed laugh, "What do you think of my work, Corten? Does it amuse you? You have a strong jaw."

Rattling swept the crowd again.

Halemtat sat up on his haunches. His bristles stood straight out. Marianne had never seen a Rejoicer bristle quite that way before. "Silence!" he bellowed.

Startled, either by the shout or by the electrified bristle of their ruler, the crowd spread itself thinner. The laughter had subsided only because each of the Rejoicers had gone as bristly as Halemtat. Chornian shifted slightly to keep Marianne and Nick near the protected cover of his beaded ruff.

"Marianne," said Nick softly, "that's Tatep."

"I know," she said. Without meaning to, she'd grabbed his arm for reassurance.

Tatep . . . He sat back on his haunches, as if fully at ease—the only sleeked Rejoicer in the courtyard. He might have been sitting in Marianne's office discussing different grades of wood, for all the excitement he displayed.

Halemtat, rage quivering, in every quill, turned to his guards and said, "Clip Tatep. *Hashay.*"

"No!" shouted Marianne, starting forward as she realized she'd spoken Dirtside and opened her mouth to shout it again in Rejoicer, Nick grabbed her and clapped a hand over her mouth.

"No!" shouted Chornian, seeming to translate for her, but speaking his own mind.

Marianne fought Nick's grip in vain. Furious, she bit the hand he'd clapped over her mouth. When he yelped and removed it—still not letting her free—she said, "It'll kill him!' He'll bleed to death! Let me go." On the last word, she kicked him hard, but he didn't let go.

A guard produced the ritual scissors and handed them to the official in charge of clipping. She held the instrument aloft and made the ritual display, clipping the air three times. With each snap of the scissors, the crowd chanted, "No. No. No."

Taken aback, the official paused. Halemtat clicked at her and she abruptly remembered the rest of the ritual. She turned to make the three ritual clips in the air before Halemtat.

This time the voice of the crowd was stronger. "No. No. No," came the shout with each snap.

Marianne struggled harder, as the official stepped toward Tatep . . .

Then the grand vizier scuttled to intercept. "No," he told the official. Turning to Halemtat, he said, "The image is mine. *I* can laugh at the caricature. Why is it, I wonder, that you can't, Halemtat? Has some disease softened your spines so that they no longer rattle?"

Marianne was so surprised she stopped struggling against Nick's hold— and felt the hold ease. He didn't let go, but held her against him in what was almost an embrace. Marianne held her breath, waiting for Halemtat's reply.

Halemtat snatched the ritual scissors from the official and threw them at Corten's feet. "You," he said. "You will *hashay* Tatep."

"No," said Corten. "I won't. My spines are still stiff enough to rattle."

Chornian chose that moment to shout once more, "Rattle your spines, Halemtat! Let us hear you rattle your spines!"

And without so much as a by-your-leave the entire crowd suddenly took up the chant: "Rattle your spines! Rattle your spines!"

Halemtat looked wildly around. He couldn't have rattled if he'd wanted to—his spines were too bristled to touch one to another. He turned his glare on the official, as if willing her to pick up the scissors and proceed.

Instead, she said, in perfect cadence with the crowd, "Rattle your spines!"

Halemtat made an imperious gesture to his guard—and the guard said, "Rattle your spines!"

Halemtat turned and galloped full tilt into his palace. Behind him the chant continued—"Rattle your spines! Rattle your spines!"

Then, quite without warning, Tatep rattled his spines. The next thing Marianne knew, the entire crowd was laughing and laughing and laughing at their vanished ruler.

Marianne went limp against Nick. He gave her a suggestion of a hug, then let her go. Against the rattle of the crowd, he said, "I thought you were going to get yourself killed, you idiot."

"I couldn't—I couldn't stand by and do *nothing*; they might have killed Tatep."

"I thought doing nothing was a diplomat's job."

"You're right; some diplomat I make. Well, after this little episode, I probably don't have a job anyhow."

"My offer's still open."

"Tell the truth, Nick. If I'd been a member of your team fifteen minutes ago, would you have let me go?"

He threw back his head and laughed. "Of course not," he said. "But at least I understand why you bit the hell out of my hand."

"Oh, god, Nick! I'm so sorry! Did I hurt you?"

"Yes," he said. "But I accept your apology—and next time, I won't give you that option!"

" 'Next time,' huh?"

Nick, still grinning, nodded.

Well, there was that to be said for Nick: he was realistic.

"Hi, Nick," said Tatep. "Welcome back."

"Hi, Tatep. Some show you folks laid on. What happens next?"

Tatep rattled the length of his body, "Your guess is as good as mine," he said. "I've never done anything like this before. Corten's still rattling. In fact, he asked me to make him a grand vizier nutcracker. I think I'll make him a present of it—for Christmas."

He turned to Marianne. "Share?" he said. "I was too busy to watch at the time. Were you and Nick mating? If you do it again, may I watch?"

Marianne turned a vivid shade of red, and Nick laughed entirely too much.

"You explain it to him," Marianne told Nick firmly. "Mating habits are not within my diplomatic jurisdiction. And I'm still in the diplomatic corps—at least, until we get back to the embassy."

Tatep sat back on his haunches, eagerly awaiting Nick's explanation. Marianne shivered with relief and said hastily, "No, it wasn't mating, Tatep. I was so scared for you I was going to charge in and—well, I don't know what I was going to do after that—but I couldn't just stand by and let Halemtat hurt you." She scowled at Nick and finished, "Nick was afraid I'd get hurt myself and wouldn't let me go."

Tatep's eyes widened in surprise. "Marianne, you would have fought for me?"

"Yes. You're my friend."

"Thank you," be said solemnly. Then to Nick, he said, "You were right to hold her back. Rattling is a better way than fighting." He turned again to Marianne. "You surprise me," he said. "You showed us how to rattle at Halemtat."

He shook from snout to tail-tip, with a sound like a hundred snare drums. "Halemtat turned tail and ran from our rattling!"

"And now?" Nick asked him.

"Now I'm going to go home. It's almost dinner time and I'm hungry enough to eat an entire tree all by myself." Still rattling, he added, "Too bad the hardwood I make the nutcrackers from is so bitter—though tonight I could almost make an exception and dine exclusively on bitter wood."

Tatep got down off his haunches and started for home. Most of the crowd had dispersed as well. It seemed oddly anticlimactic, until Marianne heard and saw the rattles of laughter ripple through the departing Rejoicers.

Beside the supply transport, Tatep paused. "Nick, at your convenience, I really *would* like you to share about human mating. For friendship's sake, I should know when Marianne is fighting and when she's mating. Then I'd know whether she needs help or—or what kind of help she needs. After all, some trees need help to mate . . ."

Marianne had turned scarlet again. Nick said, "I'll tell you all about it as soon as I get settled in again."

"Thank you." Tatep headed for home, for all the world as if nothing unusual had happened. In fact, the entire crowd, laughing as it was, might have been a crowd of picnickers off for home as the sun began to set.

A squawk from the radio brought Marianne back to business. No use putting it off. Time to bite the bullet and check in with Clarence—if nothing else, the rest of the staff would be worried about both of them.

Marianne climbed into the cab. Without prompting, Nick climbed in beside her. For a long moment, they listened to the diatribe that came over the radio, but Marianne made no move to reply. Instead, she watched the Rejoicers laughing their way home from the palace courtyard.

"Nick," she said. "Can you really laugh a dictator into submission?"

He cocked a thumb at the radio. "Give it a try," he said. "It's not worth cursing back at Clarence—you haven't his gift for bureaucratic invective."

Marianne also didn't have a job by the time she got back to the embassy. Clarence had tried to clap her onto the returning supply ship, but Nick stepped in to announce that Clarence had no business sending anybody from his ethnology staff home. In the end, Clarence's bureaucratic invective had failed him and the ethnologists simply disobeyed, as Nick had. All Clarence could do, after all, was issue a directive; if they chose to ignore it, the blame no longer fell on Clarence. Since that was all that worried Clarence, that was all right.

In the end, Marianne found that being an ethnologist was considerably more interesting than being a diplomat . . . especially during a revolution.

She and Nick, with Tatep, had taken time off from their mutual studies to choose this year's Christmas tree—from Halemtat's reserve. "Why," said Marianne, bemused at her own reaction, "do I feel like I'm cutting a Christmas tree with Thomas Jefferson?"

"Because you are," Nick said. "Even Thomas Jefferson did ordinary things once in a while. Chances are, he even hung out with his friends." He waved. "Hi, Tatep. How goes the revolution?"

For answer, Tatep rattled the length of his body.

"Good," said Nick.

"I may have good news to share with you at the Christmas party," added the Rejoicer.

"Then we look forward to the Christmas party even more than usual," said Marianne.

"And I brought a surprise for Marianne all the way from Dirt," Nick added. When Marianne lifted an eyebrow, he said, "No, no hints."

"Share?" said Tatep.

"Christmas Eve," Nick told him. "After you've shared your news, I think."

The tree-trimming party was in full swing. The newly formed Ad Hoc Christmas Chorus was singing Czech carols—a gift from Esperanza to everybody on both staffs. Clarence had gotten so mellow on the Christmas punch that he'd even offered Marianne her job back—if she was willing to be dropped a grade for insubordination. Marianne, equally mellow, said no, but said it politely.

Nick had arrived at last, along with Tatep and Chornian and Chaylam and their kids. Surprisingly, Nick stepped in between verses to wave the Ad Hoc Christmas Chorus to silence. "Attention, please," he shouted over the hubbub. "Attention, *please!* Tatep has an announcement to make." When he'd finally gotten silence, Nick turned to Tatep and said, "You have the floor."

Tatep looked down, then looked up again at Nick.

"I mean," Nick said, "go ahead and speak. Marianne's not the only one who'll want to know your news, believe me."

But it was Marianne Tatep chose to address.

"We've all been to see Halemtat," he said. "And Halemtat has agreed: No one will be clipped again unless five people from the same village agree that the offense warrants that severe a punishment. We will choose the five, not Halemtat. Furthermore, from this day forward, anyone may say anything without fear of being clipped. Speaking one's mind is no longer to be punished."

The crowd broke into applause. Beside Tatep, Nick beamed.

Tatep took a piece of parchment from his pouch. "You see, Marianne? Halemtat signed it and put his bite to it."

"How did you get him to agree?"

"We laughed at him—and we cracked our nutcrackers in the palace courtyard for three days and three nights straight, until he agreed," Chornian rattled. "He said he'd sign anything if we'd all just go away and let him sleep." He hefted the enormous package he'd brought with him and rattled again. "Look at all the shelled nuts we've brought for your Christmas party!"

Marianne almost found it in her heart to feel sorry for Halemtat. Grinning, she accepted the package and mounded the table with shelled nuts. "Those are almost too important to eat," she said, stepping back to admire their handiwork. "Are you sure they oughtn't to go into a museum?"

"The important thing," Tatep said, "is that I can say anything I want." He popped one of the nuts into his mouth and chewed it down. "Halemtat is a *talemtat*," he said, and rattled for the sheer joy of it.

"Corten looks like he's been eating too much briarwood," said Chornian, catching the spirit of the thing.

Not recognizing the expression, Marianne cast an eye at Nick, who said, "We'd say, 'Been eating a lemon.'"

One of Chonian's brood sat back on his/her haunches and said, "I'll show you Halemtat's guards—"

The child organized its siblings with much pomp and ceremony (except for the littlest, who couldn't stop rattling) and marched them back and forth. After the second repetition, Marianne caught the rough import of their chant: "We're Halemtat's guards/We send our regards/We wish you nothing but ill/Clip! We cut off your quill!"

After three passes, one child stepped on another's tail and the whole troop dissolved into squabbling among themselves and insulting each other. "You look like Corten!" said one, for full effect. The adults rattled away at them. The littlest one, delighted to find that insults could be funny, turned to Marianne and said, "Marianne! You're spineless!"

Marianne laughed even harder. When she'd caught her breath, she explained to the child what the phrase meant when it was translated literally into Standard. "If you want a good Dirt insult," she said, mischievously, "I give you 'birdbrain.'" All the sounds in that were easy for a Rejoicer mouth to utter—and when Marianne explained why it was an insult, the children all agreed that it was a very good insult indeed."

"Marianne is a birdbrain," said the littlest.

"No," said Tatep. "*Halemtat* is a birdbrain, not Marianne."

"Let the kid alone, Tatep," said Marianne. "The kid can say anything it wants!"

"True," said Tatep. "True!"

They shooed the children off to look for their presents under the tree, and Tatep turned to Nick. "Share, Nick—your surprise for Marianne."

Nick reached under the table. After a moment's searching he brought out a large bulky parcel and hoisted it onto the table beside the heap of Halemtat nuts. Marianne caught a double-handful before they spilled onto the floor.

Nick laid a protective hand atop the parcel. "Wait," he said. "I'd better explain. Tatep, every family has a slightly different Christmas tradition—the way you folks do for Awakening. This is part of my family's Christmas tradition. It's not part of Marianne's Christmas tradition—but, just this once, I'm betting she'll go along with me." He took his hand from the parcel and held it out to Marianne. "Now you can open it," he said.

Dropping the Halemtat nuts back onto the pile, Marianne reached for the parcel and ripped it open with enough verve to satisfy anybody's Christmas unwrapping tradition. Inside was a box, and inside the box a jumble of gaudy cardboard tubes—glittering in stars and stripes and polka dots and even an entire school of metallic green fish. "Fireworks!" said Marianne. "Oh, Nick . . . "

He put his finger to her lips. "Before you say another word—you chose today to celebrate Christmas because it was the right time of the Rejoicer year. You, furthermore, said that holidays on Dirt and the other human worlds don't converge—"

Marianne nodded.

Nick let that slow smile spread across his face. "But they do. This year, back on Dirt, today is the Fourth of July in the United States of America. The dates won't coincide again in our lifetimes but, just this once, they do. So, just this once—fireworks. You do traditionally celebrate Independence Day with fireworks, don't you?"

The pure impudence in his eyes made Marianne duck her head and look away but, in turning, she found herself looking right into Tatep's bright expectant gaze. In fact, all of the Rejoicers were waiting to see what Nick had chosen for her and if he'd chosen right.

"Yes," she said, speaking to Tatep but turning to smile at Nick. "After all, today's Independence Day right here on Rejoicing, too. Come on, let's go shoot off fireworks!"

For the next twenty minutes the night sky of Rejoicing was alive with Roman candles, shooting stars, and all the brightness of all the Christmases and all the Independence Days in Marianne's memory. In the streets, humans *oooh*ed and *aaah*ed and Rejoicers rattled. The pops and bangs even woke Halemtat, but all he could do was come out on his balcony and watch.

A day later Tatep reported the rumor that one of the palace guards even claimed to have heard Halemtat rattle. "I don't believe it for a minute," Nick added when he passed the tale on to Marianne.

"Me neither," she said, "but it's a good enough story that I'd like to believe it."

"A perfect Christmas tale, then. What would you like to bet that the story of 'The First Time Halemtat Rattled' gets told every Christmas from now on?"

"Sucker bet," said Marianne. Then the wonder struck her. "Nick? Do traditions start that easily—that quickly?"

He laughed. "What kind of fireworks would you like to have next year?"

"One of each," she said. "And about five of those with the gold fishlike things that swirl down and then go bam! at you when you least expect it."

For a moment, she thought he'd changed the subject, then she realized he'd answered her question. Wherever she went, for the rest of her life, her Christmas tradition would include fireworks—not just any fireworks, but Fourth of July fireworks. She smiled. "Next year, maybe, we should play Tchaikovsky's *1812 Overture* as well as *The Nutcracker Suite*."

He shook his head "No," he said, "*The Nutcracker Suite* has plenty enough fireworks all by itself—at least your version of it certainly did!"

❄   ❄   ❄

Although still kept to some extent in the U.K., the Christmas tradition of telling or reading ghost stories is one custom that either never caught on or is no longer enjoyed in the U.S. Washington Irving, in his The Sketch Book of Geoffrey Crayon, Gent. *(1819), wrote of a British parson "dealing forth strange accounts of popular superstitions and legends" on Christmas Day. Henry James framed his* The Turn of the Screw *(1898) as a tale told on Christmas Eve. M. R. James wrote in the preface to his* Ghost Stories of An Antiquary *(1904) that most of the stories "were read to patient friends, usually at the seasons of Christmas . . . " But the custom of telling scary tales on long, dark midwinter nights is probably an ancient one carried over into historic times. We can still enjoy it with this deliciously spooky and seasonally suitable story from Gene Wolfe.*

How the Bishop Sailed to Inniskeen
❄
Gene Wolfe

This is the story Hogan told us as we sat before our fire in the unroofed chapel, looking up at the niche above the door—the niche that had held the holy stone.

" 'Twas Saint Cian's pillow," said Hogan, "an' rough when he got it— rough as a pike's kiss. Smooth it was when he died, for his head had smoothed it sixty years. Couldn't a maid have done it nicer, an' where the stone had worn away was the Virgin. Her picture, belike, sir, in the markin's that'd been in the stone."

It sounded as if he meant to talk no more, so I said, "What would he want with a stone pillow, Pat?" This, though I knew the answer, simply because the night and the lonesome wind sweeping in off the Atlantic had made me hungry for a human voice.

"Not for his own sins, sure, for he'd none. But for yours, sir, an' mine. There was others, too, that come to live on this island."

"Other hermits, you mean?"

Hogan nodded. "An' when they was gone the fisherfolk come, me own folk with them. 'Twas they that built this chapel here, an' they set the holy stone above the door for he was dead an' didn't want it. When it was stormin' they'd make a broom, an' dip it in the water, an' sprinkle the holy stone, an' the storm would pass. But if it was stormin' bad, they'd carry the stone to the water an' dip it in."

I nodded, thinking how hard and how lonely life must have been for them on the Inniskeas, and of fishermen drowned. "What happened to it, Pat?"

"'Twas sunk in the bay in me grandfather's time." Hogan paused, but I could see that he was thinking—still talking in himself, as he himself would have said. "Some says it was the pirates an' some the Protestants. They told that to the woman that come from Dublin, an' she believed them."

I had been in Hogan's company for three days and was too sage a hound to go haring off after the woman from Dublin; in any event, I knew already that she was the one who had fenced the cromlech at the summit of the island. So I said, "But what do you think, Pat? What really happened to it?"

"The bishop took it. Me own grandfather saw him, him that was dead when I was born. Or me great-grandfather it might be, one or the other don't matter. But me father told me, an' the bishop took it Christmas Eve."

The wind was rising. Hogan's boat was snug enough down in the little harbor, but I could hear the breakers crash not two hundred yards from where we sat.

"There was never a priest here, only this an' a man to take care of it. O'Dea his name was."

Because I was already thinking of writing about some of the things he told me (though in the event I have waited so long), I said, "That was your grandfather, Pat, I feel certain."

"A relative, no doubt, sir," Hogan conceded, "for they were all relations on this island, more or less. But me grandfather was only a lad. O'Dea cared for the place when he wasn't out in his boat. 'Twas the women, you see, that wetted the holy stone, when the men were away."

I said, "It's a pity we haven't got it now, but if it's in the bay it ought to be wet enough."

"'Tis not, sir. 'Tis in Dublin, in their big museum there, an' dry as a bone. The woman from there fetched it this summer."

"I thought you said the bishop threw it into the bay."

"She had a mask for her face," Hogan continued, as though he had not heard me, "an' a rubber bathin' costume for the rest of her, an' air in a tin tied to her back, just like you see." (He meant, "as I have seen it on television.") "Three days she dove from Kilkelly's boat. Friday it was she brought it up in two pieces. Some say she broke it under the water to make the bringing up easier." Hogan paused to light his pipe.

I asked, "Did the bishop throw it into the bay?"

"In a manner of speakin', sir. It all began when he was just a young priest, do you see? The bishop that was before him had stuck close to the cathedral, as sometimes they will. In the old days it was not easy, journeyin'. Very bad, it was, in winter. If you'd seen the roads before they were made, you'd thank the Lord for General Wade."

Having had difficulties of my own in traveling around the west of Ireland in a newish Ford Fiesta, I nodded sympathetically.

"So this one, when he got the job, he made a speech. 'The devil take me,' he says, 'if ever I say Mass Christmas Eve twice in the same church.'"

"And the devil took him," I suggested.

"That he did not, sir, for the bishop was as good as his word. As the time wore on, there was many a one that begged him to stop, but there was no holdin' him. Come the tag end of Advent, off he'd go. An' if he heard that there was one place worse than another, it's where he went. One year a priest from Ballycroy went on the pilgrimage, an' he told the bishop a bit about Inniskeen, havin' been once or twice. 'Send word,' says the bishop, 'to this good man O'Dea. Tell him to have a boat waitin' for me at Erris.'

"They settled it by a fight, an' it was me grandfather's own father that was to bring him."

"Ah," I said,

"Me grandfather wanted to come along to help with the boat, sure, but his father wouldn't allow it, it was that rough, an' he had to wait in the chapel—right here, sir—with his mother. They was all here a long time before midnight, sure, talkin' the one to the other an' waitin' on the bishop, an' me grandfather—recollect he was but a little lad, sir—he fell asleep . . .

"Next thing he knew, his mother was shakin' him. 'Wake up, Sean, for he's come!' He wakes an' sits up, rubbin' his eyes, an' there's the bishop. But, Lord, sir, there wasn't half there that should've been! Late as the sun rises at Christmas, it was near the time.

"It didn't matter a hair to His Excellency. He shook all the men by the hand, an' smiled at all the women, an' patted me grandfather's head, an' blessed everybody. Then he begun the Mass. You never heard the like, sir. When they sang, there was angels singin' with them. Sure, they couldn't see them, but they knew that they were there an' they could hear them. An' when the bishop preached, they saw the Gates an' got the smell of Heaven. It was like cryin' for happiness, an' it was forever. Me father said the good man used to cry a bit himself when he talked of it—which he did, sir, every year about this time, until he left this world.

"When the Mass was over, the bishop blessed them all again, an' he give O'Dea a letter, an' O'Dea kissed his ring, which was an honor to him after. Me grandfather saw his father waiting to take the bishop back to Erris, an' knew he'd been in the back of them. Right back there, sir."

We were burning wreckage we had picked up on the beach earlier. Hogan paused to throw a broken timber on the fire.

"The stone, Pat," I said.

"The bishop took it, sir, sure. After he give the letter, he points at it, do you see." Hogan pointed to the empty niche. "An' he says, 'Sorry I am, O'Dea, but I must have that.'

"Then O'Dea gets up on a stool—'twas what they sat on here—an' gives it to him, an' off he goes with me grandfather's father.

"All natural, sir. But me grandfather lagged behind when the women went home, an' as soon as there wasn't one lookin', off he runs after the bishop, for he'd hopes his father'd allow him this time, it bein' not so rough as the night before. You know where the rock juts, sir? You took a picture from there."

"Of course," I said.

"Me grandfather run out onto that rock, sir, for there's a bit of a moon by then an' he's wantin' to see if they'd put out. They hadn't, sir. He sees his father there in the boat, holdin' it close in for the bishop. An' he sees the bishop holdin' the holy stone an' steppin' into it. Up comes the sun, an' devil a boat, or bishop, or father, or holy stone there is.

"Me grandfather's father's body washed up on Duvillaun, but never the bishop's. He'd wanted the holy stone, do you see, to weight him. Or some say to sleep on, there on the bottom. 'Tis the same thing, maybe."

I nodded. In that place, with the wind moaning around the ruined stone chapel, it did not seem impossible or even strange.

"They're all dead now, sir. There's not a man alive that was born on these islands, or a woman either. But they do say the ghosts of them that missed midnight Mass can be seen comin' over the bay Christmas Eve, for they was buried on the mainland, sir, most of 'em, or died at sea like the bishop. I never seen 'em, mind, an' don't want to."

Hogan was silent for a long time after that, and so was I.

At last I said, "You're suggesting that I come back here and have a look."

Hogan knocked out his pipe. "You've an interest in such things, sir, an' so I thought I ought to mention it. I could take you out by daylight an' leave you here with your food an' sleepin' bag, an' your camera. Christmas day, I'd come by for you again."

"I have to go to Bangor, Pat."

"I know you do, sir."

"Let me think about it. What was in the letter?"

" 'Twas after New Year's when they read it, sir, for O'Dea wouldn't let it out of his hands. Sure, there wasn't a soul on the island that could read, an' no school. It says the bishop had drowned on his way to Inniskeen to say the midnight Mass, an' asked the good people to make a novena for his soul. The priest at Erris wrote it, two days after Christmas."

Hogan lay down after that, but I could not. I went outside with a flashlight and roamed over the island for an hour or more, cold though it was.

I had come to Inniskeen, to the westernmost of Ireland's westernmost island group, in search of the remote past. For I am, among various other things, a writer of novels about that past, a chronicler of Xerxes and "King" Pausanias. And indeed the past was here in plenty. Sinking vessels from the Spanish Armada had been run aground here. Vikings had stridden the very beaches I paced, and earlier still, Neolithic people had lived here largely upon shellfish, or so their middens suggest . . .

And yet it seemed to me that night that I had not found the past, but the future; for they were all gone, as Hogan had said. The Neolithic people had fallen, presumably, before the modern Celtic Irish, becoming one of the chief strands of Irish fairy lore. The last of St. Cian's hermits had died in grace, leaving no disciple. The fishermen had lived here for two hundred years or more, generation after generation, harvesting the treacherous sea and tiny gardens of potatoes; and for a few years, there had actually been a whaling station on North Island.

No more.

The Norwegians sailed from their whaling station for the last time long ago. Long ago the Irish Land Commission removed the fisherfolk and resettled them; their thatched stone cottages are tumbling down, as the hermits' huts did earlier. Gray sea-geese nest upon Inniskeen again, and otters whistle above the whistling wind. A few shaggy black cattle are humanity's sole contribution; I cannot call them wild, because they do not know human beings well enough for fear. In the Inniskeas our race is already extinct. We stayed a hundred centuries and are gone.

I drove to Bangor the following day, December 22. There I sent two cables, made transatlantic calls, and learned only that my literary agent, who might perhaps have acted, had not the slightest intention of doing so before the holidays, and that my publishers, who might certainly have acted if they chose, would not.

Already all of Ireland, which delights in closing at every opportunity, was gleefully locking its doors. I would have to stay in Bangor over Christmas, or drive on to Dublin (praying the while for an open petrol station), or go back to Erris. I filled my rented Ford's tank until I could literally dabble my forefinger in gasoline and returned to Erris.

I will not regale you here with everything that went wrong on the twenty-fourth. Hogan had an errand that could neither be neglected nor postponed. His usually dependable motor would not start, so that eventually we were forced to beg the proprietor of the only store that carried such things to leave his dinner to sell us a spark plug. It was nearly dark before we pushed off, and the storm that had been brewing all day was ready to burst upon us.

"We're mad, you know," Hogan, told me. "Me as much as you." He was at the tiller, his pipe clenched between his teeth; I was huddled in the bow in a life jacket, my hat pulled over my ears. "How'll you make a fire, sir? Tell me that."

Through chattering teeth, I said that I would manage somehow.

"No, you won't, sir, for we'll never get there."

I said that if he was waiting for me to tell him to turn back, he would have to wait until we reached Inniskeen; and I added—bitterly—that if Hogan wanted to turn back I could not prevent him.

"I've taken your money an' given me word."

"We'll make it, Pat."

As though to give me the lie, lightning lit the bay.

"Did you see the island, then?"

"No," I said, and added that we were surely miles from it still.

"I must know if I'm steerin' right," Hogan said.

"Don't you have a compass?"

"It's no good for this, sir. We're shakin' too much." It was an ordinary pocket compass, as I should have remembered, and not a regular boat's compass in a binnacle.

After that I kept a sharp lookout forward. Low-lying North Island was invisible to my right, but from time to time I caught sight of higher, closer South Island. The land I glimpsed at times to our left might have been Duvillaun or Innisglora, or even Achill, or all three. Black Rock Light was visible only occasionally, which was somewhat reassuring. At last, when the final, sullen twilight had vanished, I caught sight of Inniskeen only slightly to our left. Pointing, I half rose in the bow as Hogan swung it around to meet a particularly dangerous comber. It lifted us so high that it seemed certain we were being flipped end for end; we raced down its back and plunged into the trough only to be lifted again at once.

"Hang on!" Hogan shouted. At that moment lightning cut the dark bowl of the sky from one horizon to the other.

I pointed, indeed, but I pointed back toward Erris. I would have spoken if I could, but I did not need to. In two hours or less we were sitting comfortably in Hogan's parlor, over whiskey toddies. The German tradition of the Christmas tree, which we Americans now count among American customs, has not taken much root in Ireland, but there was an Advent calendar with all its postage-stamp-sized windows wide, and gifts done up in brightly colored papers. And the little crèche (we would call it a crib set) with its as-yet empty manger, cracked, ethereal Mary, and devoted Joseph, had more to say about Christmas than any tree I have ever seen.

"Perhaps you'll come back next year," Hogan suggested after we had related our adventures, "an' then we'll have another go."

I shook my head.

His wife looked up from her knitting, and with that single glance understood everything I had been at pains to hide. "What was it you saw?" she asked.

I did not tell her, then or later. Nor am I certain that I can tell you. It was no ghost, or at least there was nothing of sheet or skull or ectoplasm, none of the conventional claptrap of movies and Halloween. In appearance, it was no more than the floating corpse of a rather small man with longish white hair. He was dressed in dark clothes, and his eyes—I saw them plainly as he rolled in the wave—were open. No doubt it was the motion of the water; but as I stared at him for half a second or so in the lightning's glare, it appeared to me that he raised his arm and gestured, invitingly and with the utmost good will, in the direction of Inniskeen.

I have never returned to Ireland, and never will. And yet I have no doubt at all that the time will soon come when I, too, shall attend his midnight Mass in the ruined chapel. What will follow that service, I cannot guess.

In Christ's name, I implore mercy for my soul.

❄   ❄   ❄

How can you go home for the holidays when home is no longer the magical place it used to be? And if you can't bear home without its lost magic, where do you go instead? Kenneth Grahame's classic fantasy The Wind in the Willows *is not usually associated with Christmas, but its fifth chapter,* Dulce Domum, *can stand alone as a charming seasonal tale. Ellen Kushner employs this brilliantly in a story that is, in some other aspects, more for adults than children.*

Dulce Domum
❆
Ellen Kushner

Come see my band, he'd say, and they pretty much always did.

—Europe, huh? she asked languidly. They were lying in her bed, which was where he liked to be after the show, after they'd seen the band. Good sex, and the comfort of warm skin, and just enough talking to make it real.

—R&B goes over big there. And they love Todd's chops: authentic African-American. They don't need to know he went to Buckley with us and played lacrosse.

—Buckley, huh? She named some friends she said had gone there, and he knew one or two, but not well. A lot of those kids had gone away to boarding school after ninth grade, while he stayed in Manhattan with his family.

—So do you like it there, in Europe?

He stretched. —It's OK.

—So do you, like, spend a lot of time in any one city?

She wanted to know if he had a girlfriend there. Already she was trying to figure out if he was serious material. Oops, time to go. He kissed her, and she tasted very sweet. —Just here, he said, and kissed her again. —New York is home.

New York was home, but in New York the band was no big deal. So they played in a few bars here, and they had dinner with their families, and escorted a friend's sister to a fundraiser for art or literacy or wildlife, depending, and maybe took a niece or a cousin's kid to see *Nutcracker*. Then the band went on the road again, the road across the sea, where playing the chords in tight jeans was enough, knowing home was always back here, waiting for him to take his place. His family was here, colorful and stable, in the stone castle with big windows on the park. A window would always be open for him to fly back through, no matter how big he got, or how long he was away.

He fell asleep as soon as he'd come, and she didn't wake him, which was nice of her. His eyes snapped open at first light. It was an old East Village apartment with leaky Venetian blinds. He was pulling on his jeans when he heard her say, Jet lag? and when he turned around she was spread out like a kid on the playground being an airplane, sleepily purring a sort of phlegmy *Vroom, vroom,* so he fell back onto her and improvised something about, *Be my jet plane, baby, ba-dum, ba-dum,* Gonna make your engine scream, so together they achieved one of those moments of intimacy that promise either a relationship's worth of in-jokes, or guaranteed embarrassment next time you meet.

He took her phone number, but he doubted he'd be back.

He called her late on Christmas Eve. She was home. She said, Come on up, which was good because he was standing at a payphone two blocks away, his cellphone deliberately run down, and it was raining.

She was wearing sweatpants and a fleece bathrobe with moons on it. The "I don't care if I'm attractive or not" gambit. He called her on it by falling to his knees before her, singing softly, "Oh, holy night, the stars are brightly shiiiiining . . . " So she took the cue and undid her sash.

In the castle where he grew up, two kings ruled. It was a brown stone fortress at the edge of Central Park; on rainy days their nanny would send his sister and him running up and down the back stairwell, to work off energy. That was their tower, the northeast corner of the big building. A famous musician lived on another floor, and sometimes in his tuxedo on his way to the Philharmonic he would use the back stairs, too, but they knew it was really their tower.

—You're not drunk, she said when she tasted his mouth. She seemed a little surprised. She must really like him.

He made an effort. —I'm sorry, he said. —I was just, you know, kind of wondering if, if you—

Her fingers were on his lips. —Shh. I know. I mean, I don't know, but I kind of do.

She let him fall on her, graceless and helpless. She was so warm, so alive.

■ ■ ■

He was allowed to think of them as kings. They were both golden, powerful men with strong wills and interesting work. When he was older, he'd made one joke about queens, and only one, and only once.

She wriggled around and took him in her mouth.

　　—Don't, he said. —Not now.

　　—Right. She came back up, and smooched his ear. —Full frontal?

　　He smiled in her hair. —Yeah.

And they were there right now, he thought, or tried not to think. There, in their castle, high above the Park, wondering when he was going to turn up to drink eggnog and light the fire and see the tree. If they were thinking of him at all. If they even had a tree this year.

He kept the last of his weight on his elbows, but he touched as much of her as he could, his front to hers, fitting her curves and pressing them down for the sense that there was something that could bear him, and she could.

　　They would ask his sister if she'd heard from him. They never pried, but when it came to something they both wanted, they didn't really care about privacy all that much. They didn't care that his phone was dead, or why.

　　"Kay doesn't let his battery run down."

　　"Not usually, no."

　　"Is he coming?"

　　He was. But not there.

—But we aren't *Oy Vey* Jews, she was explaining to him. He must have apologized for bothering her on Christmas Eve, and started her on her story: —My grandparents were, like, all Philharmonic subscription, Opera Guild, Metropolitan Museum members, and my mom went to Vassar . . . You know.

　　He knew. He hadn't cried, and that was good. He didn't, usually, but tonight he didn't trust himself. He smiled, and remembered to say, —So that's why you're home now? Waiting for stray lonely *goyim* to come in out of the rain?

　　She touched his hair. —It is my destiny. My spiritual practice, in return for killing your god. I feel I owe you something. Tomorrow I observe the ritual celebration of a movie and Chinese food, but for tonight . . . hot sex with a hunky blond. What about you? Your folks out of town?

He waited too long to say No, and she kept going: —Went to Aspen and forgot to book you a ticket? Gone to Vienna for the winter balls and left you to take care of the Shih Tzu?

—Nuh uh. He nuzzled her hair again. Her scalp smelt like herbs, and the ends of her hair a little like popcorn. He wasn't ready to leave, even though they were getting to the talky bit, and he should. Soon.

—It's okay, she went on; —I'm used to spending Christmas Eve with people who are depressed about their families. It's kind of a specialty. In college I had all these divorced friends —I mean, their parents were—and they were all upset, you know, spending Christmas Eve with one parent, and the Day with the other . . . so I'd make them come over and we'd do stupid kid stuff like painting on clown faces—you don't hate clowns, do you? Some people are really weirded out by them.

—My sister hates clowns. But I don't care. What else did you do?

—Well, we made French fries from scratch. She scrunched up her face.
—Boring, huh?

—Not really. Not if the point is to get someone to feel happy and normal. Food is good that way. My dad is, like, the king of comfort food. If you like whole steamed sea bass.

—Is your dad, um, Asian?

(And a second husband? Because he himself was blond? She was so obvious.)

—Naw, he's just a foodie. When he's jetlagged, he used to go to the Fulton Fish Market to get the first catch, back when it came in there at dawn. Makes his own duck confit. You know, like that. My other dad—

—Stepfather?

—No. Two dads, no mother.

—Oh, Peter! she chortled, and rather sharply he said, —*What?*

—Sorry. She ran a fingertip down his arm in apology. —Peter Pan. "Haven't got a mother."

—Lost boys, he said. —That's us, all right.

—Except for your sister.

She lay waiting to listen, but he could feel her quivering with another quote.

—Spit it out, he said, and she chortled, —"Girls are far too clever to fall out of their prams."

He pinned her deliciously down. —Better stop reminding me of my sister, or things could get weird.

—How weird? she purred.

He pulled back slightly and she gasped, —God, I'm an idiot. You're not there for a reason, and I—I'm sorry, I'm just an idiot. She bunched her fingers in his curls —Sorry— and kissed him.

He had kissed his sister exactly once. They were both fifteen, and both a little drunk, and she said, Okay, let's just get it over with, so they puckered up, but at the first sign of moist inner membrane they broke apart, going *Eew!* like six-year-olds, and Eloise said, Okay, so now can we stop worrying?

And he said something blindingly original like, Yeah, I guess.

He'd still been a little scared, then, that he'd like his sister the way her dad liked his dad. It was a huge relief, so huge they never spoke of it again. He was sure his sister was back home with them tonight. Eloise got along with both of them so well. Her own dad didn't scare her, even now.

This kiss was enthralling, deep and thoughtful. He always liked the kisses that happened after, building their way back to urgency, but not there yet, not urgent, just deep. He liked the way she assumed there would be an after, too. She wouldn't kick him out before he was ready to go.

—So it's just us, she murmured into his cheek. —Just you and me, and a city full of people full of their own crazy business out there, who don't know we're even here.

—With no idea what we're up to.

—Not a clue.

Was he talking too much? She seemed to want it, but did he?

Mouths licked and pinched and sucked between words. Words dropped in between their busy lips and teeth. She said, That's nice . . . and he occupied her mouth with his to keep words out, to keep words in.

—Not thinking of your sister now, huh? she asked him, and he moaned, —No— and so, of course, then he was.

His sister said he couldn't possibly remember the first time; they were too young. But that was her, not him. He was five whole months older. He remembered, really well.

They were in the living room high above the city, with all the glittering lights, the fire in the fireplace, the huge tree, the spread of cakes and fruit and decorated Christmas cookies—some the gifts of clients, the best ones baked by his dad—the spiced wine they each got a sip of . . . he could have been remembering any year, sure. The tree never seemed to get less huge, no matter how much he grew. Maybe their dads kept buying bigger ones. He wouldn't put it past them to think of that.

But he remembered seeing the book for the very first time that night. Eloise was on her own father's lap on the sofa, he was sitting on the floor next to them, and Linton reached one arm out around his little girl to show Kay the pictures. The book was little, with pale blue cloth and animals stamped on the front in gold, and the smell of the old paper rose up even through the pine and spices.

"He's going to get chocolate on it," his own dad said, but Linton just kept holding the book out to him.

"It's okay, Graham," Linton said. "They won't know it's not hundred-year-old chocolate by the time it goes to auction next."

"What about carbon dating?" muttered Eloise.

"That's just for dinosaurs and fossils," Kay said. "Gimme."

" 'Give it to me,' " Linton corrected.

"Please," added Graham.

He held the book carefully. There were line drawings of animals, almost on every page. They all wore clothes. You could tell the animals were still little, though, because of their being next to leaves and grass and things. There were colored pages, too, pretty and pale, of animals rowing boats. "Read," Kay said.

Linton opened the book, began reading something about spring-cleaning. Then he said, "No. Not tonight. I think it should be more . . . " He flipped through the pages, and began again:

Home! The call was clear, the summons was plain.

"Ratty!" Mole called, "hold on! It's my home, my old home! I've just come across the smell of it, and it's close by here, really quite close. And I must go to it, I must, I must!"

Kay had barely understood it, the first time, but it was the voice that mattered.

Home! Why, it must be quite close by him at that moment, his old home that he had hurriedly forsaken, that day when he first found the river.

The voice, warm and flexible and fluid like the river, taking him somewhere he'd never been before, introducing the two animals who were such good friends, and looked after each other when they were lost in the snow, and found the pathway to the Mole's little house in the ground, and Ratty made the fire and cooked some snacks, and then—and then—

—He's a musician, he said, —my other dad.

   —What kind?

   —Piano, mostly.

It was the harpsichord, really, but there was always one thing he changed or left out whenever he talked about them. He just did.

   —Jazz?

   —No. Classical. And new music. Downtown stuff.

   —Is that where you get it from, the music?

   —He's not my bio dad.

She pulled both his arms around her, flattening her breasts against him.
—Sorry.

   —He hates what I do, my band, anyway.

   —Music snob?

   —No. He thinks I've got no technique. And know what? He's right.

   —Ohhhh, you've got technique, all right. I love your technique.

Every year after that, Linton read from the book on Christmas Eve. The same chapter, *Dulce Domum*, where they're trudging through the snow on their way back to Rat's cozy River Bank digs, but Mole suddenly catches the scent of his old underground home, and they go and find it but then it's all cold and there's no food and then they build up a fire and then Rat finds some biscuits and sardines and then they light candles and then—and then they hear voices, and Mole says, "I think it must be the field-mice. They go round carol-singing this time of year," and then they open the door to the field-mice with lanterns and mittens and little red scarves and then—and then—

> *We others, who have long lost the more subtle of the physical senses, have not even proper terms to express an animal's intercommunications with his surroundings . . . and have only the word "smell," for instance, to include the whole range of delicate thrills which murmur in the nose of the animal night and day . . .*

   —Enjoying yourself?

He was giving her all he could, holding back carefully, holding back to observe her giving in to him, to observe how she enjoyed it, to admire his own skill and selfless self-restraint.

—Mrrrrrph . . .
—Is that a Yes? It is, isn't it? Cat got your tongue?
—You're evil.
—No I'm not. I'm good . . .

Linton tried reading Dickens once instead, and Eloise nearly had a meltdown. They were very young. Funny how, now that things were surreally bad, his sister was acting like nothing was wrong, and he was the one who couldn't stand it. Especially since it was her dad who was so messed up.

—Wait, she said. She pushed her tangled hair back from her eyes with the back of her wrist.
—What?
—My turn.
He tried to say No, but he shivered with delight as she did things, delicious things with him on Christmas Eve.
—Cat got your tongue? she purred.

He stopped dead in his tracks, his nose searching hither and thither . . .
A moment, and he had caught it again; and with it this time came recollection in fullest flood.

He lost it. She was giving him everything he wanted, and it was a terrible thing. All that physical pleasure, tricking him into feeling on top of the world, feeling powerful and invulnerable and joyous. And then—And then—
He heard the music.

Villagers all, this frosty tide,
Let your doors swing open wide

Linton at the harpsichord, the book in front of him so he could improvise right there as the little mice came to the door in the snow, and the lamps were held high, and they sang their carol:

Though wind may follow, and snow beside,
Yet draw us in by your fire to bide;
Joy shall be yours in the morning!

■ ■ ■

The very first year, Linton just spoke the words, fiddling around with underscoring as he read. The second year, though, he had composed a tune, secretly, to surprise them, and when he got to the field-mice he put the book down and went to his instrument, and rattled it off on the keyboard, singing with gusto.

They made him sing it again, in falsetto, to sound like mice. And after that they copied him, learned the tune, made harmonies. Every year since then, as Kay changed from treble to baritone, and Eloise's soprano grew from piping to rich, it was the song they sang on Christmas Eve.

Were they singing it now? He doubted it. He doubted it very much. If they were, he would be there. He would be there, singing, instead of right here, howling, as his pleasure refused to be staved off another measure.

"Oh, Ratty!" he cried dismally, "why ever did I do it? Why did I bring you to this poor, cold little place, on a night like this, when you might have been at River Bank by this time, toasting your toes before a blazing fire, with all your own nice things about you!"

Oh, and he knew he should be there now. He should be there with them. Even if they weren't singing. *Especially* if they weren't singing.

Omne animal triste post coitum.

All animals are sad after sex.

She nuzzled his neck. They were stuck together, the sheet wrapped around their legs, soaking up sweat and come. He started to shake.

He didn't know which he hated more, the idea that they weren't, despite what had happened, or the idea that they were: that somehow Linton was sitting gamely at the keyboard, pale and shaky—unless he was flushed, yeah, maybe he was flushed with a recent feeding from the bags in the fridge, for which Graham had called in every favor that years on the Board of the Sloan-Kettering could bring him—Linton sitting at the keyboard, eyes glittering with pleasure, young and strong and sure of himself for a few hours, until the daylight rolled around again and he had to go back in the—oh, no, it wasn't funny, but you had to laugh—the dark little place with the door where no light entered, where the bad kids were shut up in Victorian novels, the place where old coats were stored, fur coats that parted to reveal another kingdom, the dark place where hungry young men hid the truth until we all got enlightened and everything changed . . . and now his dad was back in there again because the light was so bad for him, he cried and he burned when it touched him—

—What is it? she said. —You're shaking. What's the matter?

—Nothing, he said. —I'm okay.

She rubbed some of the wet off him with an edge of the sheet, and reached down for a quilt, and pulled it over them both.

—I don't think you're feverish, she said. She felt his forehead with her wrist, and he couldn't help smiling, it was such a Wendy thing to do. —You're kind of cold, really.

—*Omne animal triste post coitum.* Only in my case, it's *chilly*, not *sad*.

—You're chilly *and* sad.

—It'll pass.

—OK.

She didn't say anything, just held him.

I want you to be here, his father had said. *I want to see you. We both do.*

I don't want to see him. He didn't say that. He'd never say that. He just wouldn't show up. It wasn't even that he didn't want to see him. He didn't want to hear the voice.

—Did you ever have a tree? he asked. —Or a Chanukah Bush or something?

She squeezed him in mild protest. —Tacky. If you want a tree, have a tree, I say. Don't try to whitewash it. Don't, like, frigging lie about it.

—So you wanted one.

—Well, yeah. Of course. A *tree* in your *house*? Come on.

—I like that you don't have one.

—Good. I'm glad. She stroked his hair. —But you know what? For you . . . for you, Kay, I might get one. If you wanted it.

—You would?

—And when my mother visited, I'd say that it was all your fault.

—You would?

—I would. You'd back me up, though, wouldn't you?

—I would. For you, I'd lie to a nice old lady who probably marched against the Pentagon and won't drink coffee that isn't Fair Trade certified.

—Hey, when did you meet my mom?

—So how is she?

—Fine. But I was just kidding.

—I know, he said. —But your family. Are they all right?

—Yeah. Sure. I just saw them last week. We always have this Chanukah party. Is there something—

—No. It's just . . . you never know. You never know when something's going to happen. I mean, one day you're all fine, and the next—the next —you just can't believe it. It's literally incredible. Like something you read in a book. Not something that could really happen. Not to anyone real. Not to anyone at all. Let alone someone you know. You see it, you know it, but you just cannot believe it. She told me, she even showed me, and I didn't believe her.

—Is she okay? Your sister, I mean.

—Eloise? She's fine.

—What about your dad?

—Graham's a busy man. A very busy man, these days. Calling in favors. Calling up doctors. Calling on one-eyed gypsies from Transylvania . . . No, they're fine. They're both fine. They don't know what happened, but they're sure it isn't catching.

She understood, at last, or thought she did. —Your other dad, she said. Is he . . . sick?

He made a little noise into her breast.

—Like, really, really sick? And you just can't face it?

He thought of the syringes on the table, the plastic bags in the fridge and in the microwave, heating to 98.6.

—You couldn't either, believe me.

—I know, she said. —I know. I hear about stuff, and I—I feel so lucky, sometimes.

—It's like—I can't go home. Home isn't even there anymore.

—I know. She tightened her hold. She waited, then said, —Is he all . . . different?

—Yeah. He used to be so—well, civilized. Disciplined. Controlled. And now —Now I wouldn't trust him with anything. Not the book, not anything. You can't turn your back on him. He's hungry all the time.

—He is?

—He'll eat anyone if he doesn't stop himself. He'd eat the fucking field-mice if he could!

—I thought it was supposed to make you not eat much, she said gently.

—He doesn't eat much. He doesn't eat anything. He used to like broccoli rabe and anchovies and crème caramel. He can't take real food at all, now.

She touched his wrist. —I'm really, really sorry.

—Yeah, well.

—I'm glad you're here.

—Yeah. Her warm fingers slipped around his wrist, soft against his pulse, like life holding onto life. She'd know if anything happened to him. She'd know . . . The radiator clanked, and, on the edge of sleep, he jumped.

"*Sii-lent night . . .*"

The sound drifted up from the radiator, no, from the window it was under, which rattled in a gust of wind, covering for a moment the words, the silly happy people out there singing in the street, and then it was, "*Allllll is calm . . . Allllll is bright . . .*"

"Yes, come along, field-mice," cried the Mole eagerly. "This is quite like old times! Shut the door after you. Pull up that settle to the fire."

She said, —I'll be your home, tonight.

—*Dulce Domum*, Kay said quietly.

—*Dulce*? Is that, like, ice cream?

—It's the chapter in the book, stupid. Latin for "Home, sweet home."

—I've got half a jar of *dulce de leche* from the corner bodega. When's the last time you ate?

—Breakfast, I guess.

—Get up, she said. —In my home, we make fried eggs and toast in the middle of the night when we're especially happy. It's a tradition.

And they braced themselves for the last long stretch, the home stretch, the stretch that we know is bound to end, sometime, in the rattle of the door-latch, the sudden firelight, and the sight of familiar things greeting us as long-absent travellers from far overseas.

❄   ❄   ❄

In this Hugo-nominated novella, there has been a worldwide collapse of technology. The Dominion—a portion of what was once the United States—is a place where science is scorned and a form of narrow-minded, bigoted Christianity rules. Christmas survives as one of four Universal Christian Holidays recognized by the Dominion; the others are Easter, Independence Day, and Thanksgiving. Which, despite the religious and patriotic trappings of this imagined future society, roughly parallel the other ancient pre-Christian seasonal festivals: spring (vernal) equinox, summer solstice, and autumnal equinox/harvest.

Julian: A Christmas Story
❄
Robert Charles Wilson

1

This is a story about Julian Comstock, better known as Julian the Agnostic or (after his uncle) Julian Conqueror. But it is not about his conquests, such as they were, or his betrayals, or about the War in Labrador, or Julian's quarrels with the Church of the Dominion. I witnessed many of those events—and will no doubt write about them, ultimately—but this narrative concerns Julian when he was young, and I was young, and neither of us was famous.

2

In late October of 2172—an election year—Julian and I, along with his mentor Sam Godwin, rode to the Tip east of the town of Williams Ford, where I came to possess a book, and Julian tutored me in one of his heresies.

It was a brisk, sunny day. There was a certain resolute promptness to the seasons in that part of Athabaska, in those days. Our summers were long, languid, and hot. Spring and fall were brief, mere custodial functions between the extremes of weather. Winters were short but biting. Snow set in around the end of December, and the River Pine generally thawed by late March.

Today might be the best we would get of autumn. It was a day we should have spent under Sam Godwin's tutelage, perhaps sparring, or target-shooting, or reading chapters from the Dominion History of the

Union. But Sam was not a heartless overseer, and the kindness of the weather had suggested the possibility of an Outing, and so we had gone to the stables, where my father worked, and drawn horses, and ridden out of the Estate with lunches of black bread and salt ham in our back-satchels.

We rode east, away from the hills and the town. Julian and I rode ahead; Sam rode behind, a watchful presence, his Pittsburgh rifle ready in the saddle holster at his side. There was no immediate threat of trouble, but Sam Godwin believed in perpetual preparedness; if he had a gospel, it was Be Prepared; also, Shoot First; and probably, Damn the Consequences. Sam, who was old (nearly fifty), wore a dense brown beard stippled with wiry white hairs, and was dressed in what remained presentable of his tan-and-green Army of the Californias uniform, and a cloak to keep the wind off. He was like a father to Julian, Julian's own true father having performed a gallows dance some years before. Lately he had been more vigilant than ever, for reasons he had not discussed, at least with me.

Julian was my age (seventeen), and we were approximately the same height, but there the resemblance ended. Julian had been born an aristo; my family was of the leasing class. His skin was clear and pale where mine was dark and lunar. (I was marked by the same Pox that took my sister Flaxie to her grave in '63.) His hair was long and almost femininely clean; mine was black and wiry, cut to stubble by my mother with her sewing scissors, and I washed it once a week or so—more often in summer, when the brook behind the cottage ran clean and cool. His clothes were linen and, in places, silk, brass-buttoned, cut to fit; my shirt and pants were course hempen cloth, sewn to a good approximation but obviously not the work of a New York tailor.

And yet we were friends, and had been friends for three years, since we met by chance in the forested hills west of the Duncan and Crowley Estate, where we had gone to hunt, Julian with his fine Porter & Earle cassette rifle and me with a simple muzzle-loader. We both loved books, especially the boys' books written in those days by an author named Charles Curtis Easton.[1] I had been carrying a copy of Easton's *Against the Brazilians*, illicitly borrowed from the Estate library; Julian had recognized the title, but refrained from ratting on me, since he loved the book as much as I did and longed to discuss it with a fellow enthusiast (of which there

---

[1]   Whom I would meet when he was sixty years old, and I was a newcomer to the book trade—but that's another story.

were precious few among his aristo relations)—in short, he did me an unbegged favor, and we became fast friends despite our differences.

In those early days I had not known how fond he was of blasphemy. But I had learned since, and it had not deterred me. Much.

We had not set out with the specific aim of visiting the Tip; but at the nearest crossroad Julian turned west, riding past cornfields and gourdfields already harvested and sun-whitened split-rail fences on which dense blackberry gnarls had grown up. The air was cool but the sun was fiercely bright. Julian and Sam wore broad-brimmed hats to protect their faces; I wore a plain linen pakool hat, sweat-stained, rolled about my ears. Before long we passed the last rude shacks of the indentured laborers, whose near-naked children gawked at us from the roadside, and it became obvious we were going to the Tip, because where else on this road was there to go?—unless we continued east for many hours, all the way to the ruins of the old towns, from the days of the False Tribulation.

The Tip was located far from Williams Ford to prevent poaching and disorder. There was a strict pecking order to the Tip. This is how it worked: professional scavengers hired by the Estate brought their pickings from the ruined places to the Tip, which was a pine-fenced enclosure (a sort of stockade) in a patch of grassland and prairie flowers. There the newly-arrived goods were roughly sorted, and riders were dispatched to the Estate to make the highborn aware of the latest acquisitions, and various aristos (or their trusted servants) would ride out to claim the prime gleanings. The next day, the leasing class would be allowed to sort through what was left; after that, if anything remained, indentured laborers could rummage among it, if they calculated it worthwhile to make the journey.

Every prosperous town had a Tip; though in the east it was sometimes called a Till, a Dump, or an Eebay.

Today we were fortunate: several wagonloads of scrounge had lately arrived, and riders had not yet been sent to notify the Estate. The gate was manned by a Home Guard, who looked at us suspiciously until Sam announced the name of Julian Comstock; then the guard briskly stepped aside, and we went inside the enclosure.

Many of the wagons were still unloading, and a chubby Tipman, eager to show off his bounty, hurried toward us as we dismounted and moored our horses. "Happy coincidence!" he cried. "Gentlemen!" Addressing mostly Sam by this remark, with a cautious smile for Julian and a disdainful sidelong glance at me. "Anything in *particular* you're looking for?"

"Books," Julian said promptly, before Sam or I could answer.

"Books! Ordinarily, I set aside books for the Dominion Conservator . . . "

"The boy is a Comstock," Sam said. "I don't suppose you mean to balk him."

The Tipman reddened. "No, not at all . . . in fact we came across something in our digging . . . *a sort of library in miniature* . . . I'll show you, if you like."

This was intriguing, especially to Julian, who beamed as if he had been invited to a Christmas party. We followed the stout Tipman to a freshly-arrived canvasback wagon, from which a laborer was tossing bundled piles into a stack beside a tent.

These twine-wrapped bales were books . . . old, tattered, and wholly free of the Dominion Stamp of Approval. They must have been more than a century old; for although they were faded they had obviously once been colorful and expensively printed, not made of stiff brown paper like the Charles Curtis Easton books of modern times. They had not even rotted much. Their smell, under the cleansing Athabaska sunlight, was inoffensive.

"Sam!" Julian whispered. He had already drawn his knife and was slicing through the twine.

"Calm down," suggested Sam, who was not an enthusiast like Julian.

"Oh, but—Sam! We should have brought a cart!"

"We can't carry away armloads, Julian, nor would we ever have been allowed to. The Dominion scholars will have all this. Though perhaps you can get away with a volume or two."

The Tipman said, "These are from Lundsford." Lundsford was the name of a ruined town thirty or so miles to the southeast. The Tipman leaned toward Sam Godwin, who was his own age, and said: "We thought Lundsford had been mined out a decade ago. But even a dry well may freshen. One of my workers spotted a low place off the main excavations—a sort of *sink-hole*: the recent rain had cut it through. Once a basement or warehouse of some kind. Oh, sir, we found good china there, and glasswork, and many more books than this . . . most were mildewed, but some had been protected under a kind of stiff oilcoth, and were lodged beneath a partially-collapsed ceiling . . . there had been a fire, but they survived it . . . "

"Good work, Tipman," Sam Godwin said.

"Thank you, sir! Perhaps you could remember me to the great men of the Estate?" And he gave his name (which I have forgotten).

Julian had fallen to his knees amidst the compacted clay and rubble of the Tip, lifting up each book in turn and examining it with wide eyes. I joined him in his exploration.

I had never much liked the Tip. It had always seemed to me a haunted place. And of course it was haunted: that was its purpose, to house the revenants of the past, ghosts of the False Tribulation startled out of their century-long slumber. Here was evidence of the best and worst of the people who had inhabited the Years of Vice and Profligacy. Their fine things were very fine, their glassware especially, and it was a straitened aristo indeed who did not possess antique table-settings rescued from some ruin or other. Sometimes one might find silver utensils in boxes, or useful tools, or coins. The coins were too plentiful to be worth much, individually, but they could be worked into buttons or other adornments. One of the high-born back at the Estate owned a saddle studded with copper pennies all from the year 2032. (I had occasionally been enlisted to polish it.)

But here also was the trash and inexplicable detritus: "plastic," gone brittle with sunlight or soft with the juices of the earth; bits of metal blooming with rust; electronic devices blackened by time and imbued with the sad inutility of a tensionless spring; engine parts, corroded; copper wire rotten with verdigris; aluminum cans and steel barrels eaten through by the poisonous fluids they had once contained—and so on, almost ad infinitum.

Here, too, were the in-between things, the curiosities, the ugly or pretty baubles, as intriguing and as useless as seashells. ("Put down that rusty trumpet, Adam, you'll cut your lip and poison your blood!"—my mother, when we had gone to the Tip many years before I met Julian. There had been no music in the trumpet anyway; its bell was bent and corroded through.)

More than that, though, there was the uneasy knowledge that these things, fine or corrupt, had survived their makers—had proved more imperishable than flesh or spirit (for the souls of the secular ancients were almost certainly not first in line for the Resurrection).

And yet, these books . . . they tempted; they proclaimed their seductions boldly. Some were decorated with impossibly beautiful women in various degrees of undress. I had already sacrificed my personal claim to virtue with certain young women at the Estate, whom I had recklessly kissed; at the age of seventeen I considered myself a jade, or something like one; but these images were so frank and impudent they made me blush and look away.

Julian simply ignored them, as he had always been invulnerable to the charms of women. He preferred the larger and more densely written material—he had already set aside a textbook of Biology, spotted and discolored but largely intact. He found another volume almost as large, and handed it to me, saying, "Here, Adam, try this—you might find it enlightening."

I inspected it skeptically. The book was called *The History of Mankind In Space.*

"The moon again," I said.

"Read it for yourself."

"Tissue of lies, I'm sure."

"With photographs."

"Photographs prove nothing. Those people could do anything with photographs."

"Well, read it anyway," Julian said.

In truth the idea excited me. We had had this argument many times, Julian and I, especially on autumn nights when the moon hung low and ponderous on the horizon. People have walked there, he would say. The first time he made this claim I laughed; the second time I said, "Yes, certainly: I once climbed there myself, on a greased rainbow—" But he had been serious.

Oh, I had heard these stories before. Who hadn't? Men on the moon. What surprised me was that someone as well-educated as Julian would believe them.

"Just take the book," he insisted.

"What: to keep?"

"Certainly to keep."

"Believe I will," I muttered, and I stuck the object in my back-satchel and felt both proud and guilty. What would my father say, if he knew I was reading literature without a Dominion stamp? What would my mother make of it? (Of course I would not tell them.)

At this point I backed off, and found a grassy patch a little away from the rubble, where I could sit and eat some of the lunch I had packed, and watch Julian, who continued to sort through the detritus with a kind of scholarly intensity. Sam Godwin came and joined me, brushing a spot on an old timber so he could recline without soiling his uniform, such as it was.

"He sure loves those old books," I said, making conversation.

Sam was often taciturn—the very picture of an old veteran—but he nodded and spoke familiarly: "He's learned to love them. I helped teach him. I wonder if that was wise. Maybe he loves them too much. It might be they'll kill him, one of these days."

"How, Sam? By the apostasy of them?"

"Julian's too smart for his own good. He debates with the Dominion clergy. Just last week I found him arguing with Ben Kreel[2] about God, history, and such abstractions. Which is precisely what he must *not* do, if he wants to survive the next few years."

"Why, what threatens him?"

"The jealousy of the powerful," Sam said, but he would say no more on the subject, only sat and stroked his graying beard, and glanced occasionally, and uneasily, to the east.

The day went on, and eventually Julian had to drag himself from his nest of books with only a pair of prizes: the *Introduction To Biology* and another volume called *Geography of North America*. Time to go, Sam insisted; better to be back at the Estate by supper; in any case, riders had been sent ahead, and the official pickers and Dominion curators would soon be here to cull what we had left.

But I have said that Julian tutored me in one of his apostasies. Here is how it happened. We stopped, at the drowsy end of the afternoon, at the height of a ridge overlooking the town of Williams Ford, the grand Estate upstream of it, and the River Pine as it cut through the valley on its way from the mountains of the West. From this vantage we could see the steeple of the Dominion Hall, and the revolving wheels of the grist mill and the lumber mill, and so on, blue in the long light and hazy with woodsmoke, colored here and there with what remained of the autumn foliage. Far to the south a railway bridge crossed the gorge of the Pine like a suspended thread. *Go inside*, the weather seemed to proclaim; *it's fair but it won't be fair for long; bolt the window, stoke the fire, boil the apples; winter's due.* We rested our horses on the windy hilltop, and Julian found a blackberry bramble where the berries were still plump and dark, and we plucked some of these and ate them.

This was the world I had been born into. It was an autumn like every autumn I could remember. But I could not help thinking of the Tip and its ghosts. Maybe those people, the people who had lived through the Efflorescence of Oil and the False Tribulation, had felt about their homes and neighborhoods as I felt about Williams Ford. They were ghosts to me, but they must have seemed real enough to themselves—must have *been* real; had not realized they were ghosts; and did that I mean I was also a ghost, a revenant to haunt some future generation?

---

[2]   Our local representative of the Council of the Dominion; in effect, the Mayor of the town.

Julian saw my expression and asked me what was the matter. I told him my thoughts.

"Now you're thinking like a philosopher," he said, grinning.

"No wonder they're such a miserable brigade, then."

"Unfair, Adam—you've never seen a philosopher in your life." Julian believed in Philosophers and claimed to have met one or two.

"Well, I *imagine* they're miserable, if they go around thinking of themselves as ghosts and such."

"It's the condition of all things," Julian said. "This blackberry, for example." He plucked one and held it in the pale palm of his hand. "Has it always looked like this?"

"Obviously not," I said, impatiently.

"Once it was a tiny green bud of a thing, and before that it was part of the substance of the bramble, which before that was a seed inside a blackberry—"

"And round and round for all eternity."

"But no, Adam, that's the point. The bramble, and that tree over there, and the gourds in the field, and the crow circling over them—they're all descended from ancestors that didn't quite resemble them. A blackberry or a crow is a *form*, and forms change over time, the way clouds change shape as they travel across the sky."

"Forms of what?"

"Of DNA," Julian said earnestly. (The *Biology* he had picked out of the Tip was not the first *Biology* he had read.)

"Julian," Sam warned, "I once promised this boy's parents you wouldn't corrupt him."

I said, "I've heard of DNA. It's the life force of the secular ancients. And it's a myth."

"Like men walking on the moon?"

"Exactly."

"And who's your authority on this? Ben Kreel? The *Dominion History of the Union*?"

"Nothing is changeless except DNA? That's a peculiar argument even from you, Julian."

"It would be, if I were making it. But DNA *isn't* changeless. It struggles to remember itself, but it never remembers itself perfectly. Remembering a fish, it imagines a lizard. Remembering a horse, it imagines a hippopotamus. Remembering an ape, it imagines a man."

"Julian!" Sam was insistent now. "That's quite enough."

"You sound like a Darwinist," I said.

"Yes," Julian admitted, smiling in spite of his unorthodoxy, the autumn sun turning his face the color of penny copper. "I suppose I do."

That night, I lay in bed until I was reasonably certain both my parents were asleep. Then I rose, lit a lamp, and took the new (or rather, very old) *The History of Mankind In Space* from where I had hidden it behind my oaken dresser.

I leafed through the brittle pages. I didn't read the book. I *would* read it, but tonight I was too weary to pay close attention, and in any case I wanted to savor the words (lies and fictions though they might be), not rush through them. Tonight I wanted only to sample the book; in other words, to look at the pictures.

There were dozens of photographs, and each one captured my attention with fresh marvels and implausibilities. One of them showed— or purported to show—men standing on the surface of the moon, just as Julian had described.

The men in the picture were evidently Americans. They wore flags stitched to the shoulders of their moon clothing, an archaic version of our own flag, with something less than the customary sixty stars. Their clothing was white and ridiculously bulky, like the winter clothes of the Inuit, and they wore helmets with golden visors that disguised their faces. I supposed it must be very cold on the moon, if explorers required such cumbersome protection. They must have arrived in winter. However, there was no ice or snow in the neighborhood. The moon seemed to be little more than a desert, dry as a stick and dusty as a Tipman's wardrobe.

I cannot say how long I stared at this picture, puzzling over it. It might have been an hour or more. Nor can I accurately describe how it made me feel . . . larger than myself, but lonely, as if I had grown as tall as the stars and lost sight of everything familiar. By the time I closed the book the moon had risen outside my window—the *real* moon, I mean; a harvest moon, fat and orange, half-hidden behind drifting, evolving clouds.

I found myself wondering whether it was truly possible that men had visited that celestial body. Whether, as the pictures implied, they had ridden there on rockets, rockets a thousand times larger than the familiar Independence Day fireworks. But if men had visited the moon, why hadn't they stayed there? Was it so inhospitable a place that no one wished to remain?

Or perhaps they had stayed, and were living there still. If the moon was such a cold place, I reasoned, people residing on its surface would be forced to build fires to keep warm.

There seemed to be no wood on the moon, judging by the photographs, so they must have resorted to coal or peat. I went to the window and examined the moon minutely for any sign of campfires, pit mining, or other lunar industry. But I could see none. It was only the moon, mottled and changeless. I blushed at my own gullibility, replaced the book in its hiding place, chased these heresies from my mind with a prayer (or a hasty facsimile of one), and eventually fell asleep.

3

It falls to me to explain something of Williams Ford, and my family's place in it—and Julian's—before I describe the threat Sam Godwin feared, which materialized in our village not long before Christmas.[3]

Situated at the head of the valley was the font of our prosperity, the Duncan and Crowley Estate. It was a country estate (obviously, since we were in Athabaska, far from the eastern seats of power), owned by two influential New York mercantile families, who maintained their villa not only as a source of income but as a kind of resort, safely distant (several days' journey by train) from the intrigues and pestilences of city life. It was inhabited—ruled, I might say—not only by the Duncan and Crowley patriarchs but by a whole legion of cousins, nephews, relations by marriage, high-born friends, and distinguished guests in search of clean air and rural views. Our corner of Athabaska was blessed with a benign climate and pleasant scenery, according to the season, and these things attract idle aristos the way strong butter attracts flies.

It remains unrecorded whether the town existed before the Estate or vice versa; but certainly the town depended on the Estate for its prosperity. In Williams Ford there were essentially three classes: the Owners, or aristos; below them the leasing class, who worked as smiths, carpenters, coopers, overseers, gardeners, beekeepers, etc., and whose leases were repaid in service; and finally the indentured laborers, who worked as field hands, inhabited rude shacks along the west bank of the Pine, and received no compensation beyond bad food and worse lodging.

My family occupied an ambivalent place in this hierarchy. My mother was a seamstress. She worked at the Estate as had her parents before her.

---

[3]   I beg the reader's patience if I detail matters that seem well-known. I indulge the possibility of a foreign audience, or a posterity to whom our present arrangements are not self-evident.

My father, however, had arrived in Williams Ford as a transient, and his marriage to my mother had been controversial. He had "married a lease," as the saying has it, and had been taken on as a stable hand at the Estate in lieu of a dowry. The law allowed such unions, but popular opinion frowned on it. We had few friends of our own class, my mother's blood relations had since died (perhaps of embarrassment), and as a child I was often mocked and derided for my father's low origins.

On top of that was the issue of our religion. We were—because my father was—Church of Signs. In those days, every Christian church in America was required to have the formal approval of the Board of Registrars of the Dominion of Jesus Christ on Earth. (In popular parlance, "The Church of the Dominion," but this was a misnomer, since every church is a Dominion Church if it is recognized by the Board. Dominion Episcopal, Dominion Presbyterian, Dominion Baptist—even the Catholic Church of America since it renounced its fealty to the Roman Pope in 2117—all are included under the Dominionist umbrella, since the purpose of the Dominion is not to be a church but to certify churches. In America we are entitled by the Constitution to worship at any church we please, as long as it is a genuine Christian congregation and not some fraudulent or satanistic sect. The Board exists to make that distinction. Also to collect fees and tithes to further its important work.)

We were, as I said, Church of Signs, which was a marginal denomination, shunned by the leasing class, recognized but not fully endorsed by the Dominion, and popular mostly with illiterate indentured workers, among whom my father had been raised. Our faith took for its master text that passage in Mark which proclaims, "In my Name they will cast out devils, and speak in new tongues; they will handle serpents, and if they drink poison they will not be sickened by it." We were snake-handlers, in other words, and famous beyond our modest numbers for it. Our congregation consisted of a dozen farmhands, mostly transients lately arrived from the southern states. My father was its deacon (though we did not use that name), and we kept snakes, for ritual purposes, in wire cages on our back acre, next to the outbuilding. This practice contributed very little to our social standing.

That had been the situation of our family when Julian Comstock arrived as a guest of the Duncan and Crowley families, along with his mentor Sam Godwin, and when Julian and I met by coincidence while hunting.

At that time I had been apprenticed to my father, who had risen to the rank of an overseer at the Estate's lavish and extensive stables. My father loved animals, especially horses.

Unfortunately I was not made in the same mold, and my relations with the stable's equine inhabitants rarely extended beyond a brisk mutual tolerance. I did not love my job—which consisted largely of sweeping straw, shoveling ordure, and doing in general those chores the older stablehands felt to be beneath their dignity—so I was pleased when it became customary for a household amanuensis (or even Sam Godwin in person) to arrive and summon me away from my work at Julian's request. (Since the request emanated from a Comstock it couldn't be overruled, no matter how fiercely the grooms and saddlers gnashed their teeth to see me escape their autocracy.)

At first we met to read and discuss books, or hunt together; later, Sam Godwin invited me to audit Julian's lessons, for he had been charged with Julian's education as well as his general welfare. (I had been taught the rudiments of reading and writing at the Dominion school, and refined these skills under the tutelage of my mother, who believed in the power of literacy as an improving force. My father could neither read nor write.) And it was not more than a year after our first acquaintance that Sam presented himself one evening at my parents' cottage with an extraordinary proposal.

"Mr. and Mrs. Hazzard," Sam had said, putting his hand up to touch his cap (which he had removed when he entered the cottage, so that the gesture looked like a salute), "you know of course about the friendship between your son and Julian Comstock."

"Yes," my mother said. "And worry over it often enough—matters at the Estate being what they are."

My mother was a small woman, plump, but forceful, with ideas of her own. My father, who spoke seldom, on this occasion spoke not at all, only sat in his chair holding a laurel-root pipe, which he did not light.

"Matters at the Estate are exactly the crux of the issue," Sam Godwin said. "I'm not sure how much Adam has told you about our situation there. Julian's father, General Bryce Comstock, who was my friend as well as my commanding officer, shortly before his death charged me with Julian's care and well-being—"

"Before his death," my mother pointed out, "at the gallows, for treason."

Sam winced. "True, Mrs. Hazzard, I can't deny it, but I assert my belief that the trial was rigged and the verdict indefensible. Defensible or not, however, it doesn't alter my obligation as far as the son is concerned. I promised to care for the boy, Mrs. Hazzard, and I mean to keep my promise."

"A Christian sentiment." Her skepticism was not entirely disguised.

"As for your implication about the Estate, and the practices of the young heirs and heiresses there, I couldn't agree more. Which is why I approved and encouraged Julian's friendship with your son. Apart from Adam, Julian has no true friends. The Estate is such a den of venomous snakes—no offense," he added, remembering our religious affiliation, and making the common but mistaken assumption that congregants of the Church of Signs necessarily like snakes, or feel some kinship with them—"no offense, but I would sooner allow Julian to associate with, uh, scorpions," striking for a more palatable simile, "than abandon him to the sneers, machinations, ruses, and ruinous habits of his peers. That makes me not only his teacher but his constant companion. But I'm almost three times his age, Mrs. Hazzard, and he needs a reliable friend more nearly of his own growth."

"What do you propose, exactly, Mr. Godwin?"

"What I propose is that I take on Adam as a second student, full-time, and to the ultimate benefit of both boys."

Sam was usually a man of few words—even as a teacher—and he seemed as exhausted by this oration as if he had lifted some great weight.

"As a student, but a student of *what*, Mr. Godwin?"

"Mechanics. History. Grammar and composition. Martial skills—"

"Adam already knows how to fire a rifle."

"Pistolwork, sabrework, fist-fighting—but that's only a fraction of it," Sam added hastily. "Julian's father asked me to cultivate the boy's mind as well as his reflexes."

My mother had more to say on the subject, chiefly about how my work at the stables helped offset the family's leases, and how difficult it would be to do without those extra vouchers at the Estate store. But Sam had anticipated the point. He had been entrusted by Julian's mother—that is to say, the sister-in-law of the President—with a discretionary fund for Julian's education, which could be tapped to compensate for my absence from the stables. And at a handsome rate. He quoted a number, and the objections from my parents grew considerably less strenuous, and were finally whittled away to nothing. (I observed all this from a room away, through a gap in the door.)

Which is not to say no misgivings remained. Before I set off for the Estate the next day, this time to visit one of the Great Houses rather than the stables, my mother warned me not to tangle myself too tightly with the affairs of the high-born. I promised her I would cling to my Christian virtues. (A hasty promise, less easily kept than I imagined.[4])

"It may not be your morals that are at risk," she said. "The high-born conduct themselves by different standards than we use, Adam. The games they play have mortal stakes. You do know that Julian's father was hung?"

Julian never spoke of it, but it was a matter of public record. I repeated Sam's assertion that Bryce Comstock had been innocent.

"He may well have been. That's the point. There has been a Comstock in the Presidency for the past thirty years, and the current Comstock is said to be jealous of his power. The only real threat to the reign of Julian's uncle was the ascendancy of his brother, who made himself dangerously popular in the war with the Brazilians. I suspect Mr. Godwin is correct, that Bryce Comstock was hanged not because he was a bad General but because he was a successful one."

No doubt such scandals were possible—I had heard stories about life in New York City, where the President resided, that would curl a Cynic's hair. But what could these things possibly have to do with me? Or even Julian? We were only boys.

Such was my naiveté.

4

The days had grown short, and Thanksgiving had come and gone, and so had November, and snow was in the air—the tang of it, anyway—when fifty cavalrymen of the Athabaska Reserve rode into Williams Ford, escorting an equal number of Campaigners and Poll-Takers.

Many people despised the Athabaskan winter. I was not one of them. I didn't mind the cold and the darkness, not so long as there was a hard-coal heater, a spirit lamp to read by on long nights, and the chance of wheat cakes or headcheese for breakfast. And Christmas was coming up fast—one of the four Universal Christian Holidays recognized by the

---

[4]   Julian's somewhat feminine nature had won him a reputation among the other young aristos as a sodomite. That they could believe this of him without evidence is testimony to the tenor of their thoughts, as a class. But it had occasionally redounded to my benefit. On more than one occasion, his female acquaintances—sophisticated girls of my own age, or older—made the assumption that I was Julian's intimate companion, in a physical sense. Whereupon they undertook to cure me of my deviant habits, in the most direct fashion. I was happy to cooperate with these "cures," and they were successful, every time.

Dominion (the others being Easter, Independence Day, and Thanksgiving). My favorite of these had always been Christmas. It was not so much the gifts, which were generally meager—though last year I had received from my parents the lease of a muzzle-loading rifle of which I was exceptionally proud—nor was it entirely the spiritual substance of the holiday, which I am ashamed to say seldom entered my mind except when it was thrust upon me at religious services. What I loved was the combined effect of brisk air, frost-whitened mornings, pine and holly wreaths pinned to doorways, cranberry-red banners draped above the main street to flap cheerfully in the cold wind, carols and hymns chanted or sung—the whole breathless confrontation with Winter, half defiance and half submission. I liked the clockwork regularity of these rituals, as if a particular cog on the wheel of time had engaged with neat precision. It soothed; it spoke of eternity.

But this was an ill-omened season.

The Reserve troops rode into town on the fifteenth of December. Ostensibly, they were here to conduct the Presidential Election. National elections were a formality in Williams Ford. By the time our citizens were polled, the outcome was usually a foregone conclusion, already decided in the populous Eastern states—that is, when there was more than one candidate, which was seldom. For the last six electoral years no individual or party had contested the election, and we had been ruled by one Comstock or another for three decades. Election had become indistinguishable from acclamation.

But that was all right, because an election was still a momentous event, almost a kind of circus, involving the arrival of Poll-Takers and Campaigners, who always had a fine show to put on.

And this year—the rumor emanated from high chambers of the Estate, and had been whispered everywhere—there was to be a movie shown in the Dominion Hall.

I had never seen any movies, though Julian had described them to me. He had seen them often in New York when he was younger, and whenever he grew nostalgic—life in Williams Ford was sometimes a little sedate for Julian's taste—it was the movies he was provoked to mention. And so, when the showing of a movie was announced as part of the electoral process, both of us were excited, and we agreed to meet behind the Dominion Hall at the appointed hour.

Neither of us had any legitimate reason to be there. I was too young to vote, and Julian would have been conspicuous and perhaps unwelcome as the only aristo at a gathering of the leasing class. (The high-born had been polled independently at the Estate, and had already voted proxies for their indentured labor.) So I let my parents leave for the Hall early in the evening, and I followed surreptitiously, and arrived just before the event was scheduled to begin. I waited behind the meeting hall, where a dozen horses were tethered, until Julian arrived on an animal borrowed from the Estate stables. He was dressed in his best approximation of a leaser's clothing: hempen shirt and trousers of a dark color, and a black felt hat with its brim pulled low to disguise his face.

He dismounted, looking troubled, and I asked him what was wrong. Julian shook his head. "Nothing, Adam—or nothing yet—but Sam says there's trouble brewing." And here he regarded me with an expression verging on pity. "War," he said.

"There's always war."

"A new offensive."

"Well, what of it? Labrador's a million miles away."

"Obviously your sense of geography hasn't been much improved by Sam's classes. And we might be *physically* a long distance from the front, but we're *operationally* far too close for comfort."

I didn't know what that meant, and so I dismissed it. "We can worry about that after the movie, Julian."

He forced a grin and said, "Yes, I suppose so. As well after as before."

So we entered the Dominion Hall just as the lamps were being dimmed, and slouched into the last row of crowded pews, and waited for the show to start.

There was a broad stage at the front of the Hall, from which all religious appurtenances had been removed, and a square white screen had been erected in place of the usual pulpit or dais. On each side of the screen was a kind of tent in which the two players sat, with their scripts and dramatic gear: speaking-horns, bells, blocks, a drum, a pennywhistle, *et alia*. This was, Julian said, a stripped-down edition of what one might find in a fashionable New York movie theater. In the city, the screen (and thus the images projected on it) would be larger; the players would be more professional, since script-reading and noise-making were considered fashionable arts, and the city players competed with one another for roles; and there might be a third player stationed behind the screen for dramatic narration or additional "sound effects." There might even be an orchestra, with thematic music written for each individual production.

Movies were devised in such a way that two main characters, male and female, could be voiced by the players, with the male actor photographed so that he appeared on the left during dialogue scenes, and the female actor on the right. The players would observe the movie by a system of mirrors, and could follow scripts illuminated by a kind of binnacle lamp (so as not to cast a distracting light), and they spoke their lines as the photographed actors spoke, so that their voices seemed to emanate from the screen. Likewise, their drumming and bell-ringing and such corresponded to events within the movie.[5]

"Of course, they did it better in the secular era," Julian whispered, and I prayed no one had overheard this indelicate comment. By all reports, movies had indeed been spectacular during the Efflorescence of Oil—with recorded sound, natural color rather than black-and-gray, etc. But they were also (by the same reports) hideously impious, blasphemous to the extreme, and routinely pornographic. Fortunately (or *unfortunately*, from Julian's point of view) no examples have survived; the media on which they were recorded was ephemeral; the film stock has long since rotted, and "digital" copies are degraded and wholly undecodable. These movies belonged to the twentieth and early twenty-first centuries—that period of great, unsustainable, and hedonistic prosperity, driven by the burning of Earth's reserves of perishable oil, which culminated in the False Tribulation, and the wars, and the plagues, and the painful dwindling of inflated populations to more reasonable numbers.

Our truest and best American antiquity, as the *Dominion History of the Union* insisted, was the nineteenth century, whose household virtues and modest industries we have been forced by circumstance to imperfectly restore, whose skills were practical, and whose literature was often useful and improving.

But I have to confess that some of Julian's apostasy had infected me. I was troubled by unhappy thoughts even as the torchieres were extinguished and Ben Kreel (our Dominion representative, standing in front of the movie screen) delivered a brief lecture on Nation, Piety, and Duty. *War*, Julian had said, implying not just the everlasting War in Labrador but a new phase of it, one that might reach its skeletal hand right into Williams Ford—and then what of me, and what of my family?

---

[5]   The illusion was quite striking when the players were professional, but their lapses could be equally astonishing. Julian once recounted to me a New York movie production of Wm. Shakespeare's *Hamlet,* in which a player had come to the theater inebriated, causing the unhappy Denmark to seem to exclaim "Sea of troubles—(an unprintable oath)—I have troubles of my own," with more obscenities, and much inappropriate bell-ringing and vulgar whistling, until an understudy could be hurried out to replace him.

"We are here to cast our ballots," Ben Kreel said in summation, "a sacred duty at once to our country and our faith, a country so successfully and benevolently stewarded by its leader, President Deklan Comstock, whose Campaigners, I see by the motions of their hands, are anxious to get on with the events of the night; and so, without further ado, et cetera, please direct your attention to the presentation of their moving picture, *First Under Heaven*, which they have prepared for our enjoyment—"

The necessary gear had been hauled into Williams Ford under a canvas-top wagon: a projection apparatus and a portable Swiss dynamo (probably captured from the Dutch forces in Labrador), powered by distilled spirits, installed in a sort of trench or redoubt freshly dug behind the church to muffle its sound, which nevertheless penetrated through the plank floors like the growl of a huge dog. This vibration only added to the sense of moment, as the last illuminating flame was extinguished and the electric bulb within the huge black mechanical projector flared up.

The movie began. As it was the first I had ever seen, my astonishment was complete. I was so entranced by the illusion of photographs "come to life" that the substance of the scenes almost escaped me . . . but I remember an ornate title, and scenes of the Second Battle of Quebec, recreated by actors but utterly real to me, accompanied by drum-banging and shrill pennywhistling to represent the reports of shot and shell. Those at the front of the auditorium flinched instinctively; several of the village's prominent women came near to fainting, and clasped the hands or arms of their male companions, who might be as bruised, come morning, as if they had participated in the battle itself.

Soon enough, however, the Dutchmen under their cross-and-laurel flag began to retreat from the American forces, and an actor representing the young Deklan Comstock came to the fore, reciting his Vows of Inauguration (a bit prematurely, but history was here truncated for the purposes of art)—that's the one in which he mentions both the Continental Imperative and the Debt to the Past. He was voiced, of course, by one of the players, a *basso profundo* whose tones emerged from his speaking-bell with ponderous gravity. (Which was also a slight revision of the truth, for the genuine Deklan Comstock possessed a high-pitched voice, and was prone to petulance.)

The movie then proceeded to more decorous episodes and scenic views representing the glories of the reign of Deklan Conqueror, as he was known to the Army of the Laurentians, which had marched him to his ascendancy in New York City. Here was the reconstruction of Washington,

DC (a project never completed, always in progress, hindered by a swampy climate and insect-borne diseases); here was the Illumination of Manhattan, whereby electric streetlights were powered by a hydroelectric dynamo, four hours every day between six and ten p.m.; here was the military shipyard at Boston Harbor, the coal mines and foundries and weapons factories of Pennsylvania, the newest and shiniest steam engines to pull the newest and shiniest trains, etc., etc.

I had to wonder at Julian's reaction to all this. This entire show, after all, was concocted to extoll the virtues of the man who had contrived the death by hanging of his father. I could not forget—and Julian must be constantly aware—that the current President was a fratricidal tyrant. But Julian's eyes were riveted on the screen. This reflected (I later learned) not his opinion of contemporary politics but his fascination with what he preferred to call "cinema." This making of illusions in two dimensions was never far from his mind—it was, perhaps, his "true calling," and would culminate in the creation of Julian's suppressed cinematic masterwork, *The Life and Adventures of the Great Naturalist Charles Darwin* . . . but that tale remains for another telling.

The present movie went on to mention the successful forays against the Brazilians at Panama during Deklan Conqueror's reign, which may have struck closer to home, for I saw Julian wince once or twice.

As for me . . . I tried to lose myself in the moment, but my attention was woefully truant.

Perhaps it was the strangeness of the campaign event, so close to Christmas. Perhaps it was the *The History of Mankind In Space* which I had been reading in bed, a page or two at a time, almost every night since our journey to the Tip. Whatever the cause, I was beset by a sudden anxiety and sense of melancholy. Here I was in the midst of everything that seemed familiar and ought to be comforting—the crowd of the leasing class, the enclosing benevolence of the Dominion Hall, the banners and tokens of the Christmas season—and it all felt suddenly *ephemeral*, as if the world were a bucket from which the bottom had dropped out.

Perhaps this was what Julian had called "the philosopher's perspective." If so, I wondered how the philosophers endured it. I had learned a little from Sam Godwin—and more from Julian, who read books of which even Sam disapproved—about the discredited ideas of the Secular Era. I thought of Einstein, and his insistence that no particular point of view was more privileged than any other: in other words his "general relativity," and its claim that the answer to the question "What is real?" begins with the question "Where are you standing?" Was that all I was, here in the cocoon of Williams Ford—a Point of View? Or was I an incarnation of a molecule of DNA, "imperfectly remembering," as Julian had said, an ape, a fish, and an amoeba?

Maybe even the Nation that Ben Kreel had praised so extravagantly was only an example of this trend in nature—an imperfect memory of another century, which had itself been an imperfect memory of all the centuries before it, and so back to the dawn of Man (in Eden, or Africa, as Julian believed).

Perhaps this was just my growing disenchantment with the town where I had been raised—or a presentiment that it was about to be stolen away from me.

The movie ended with a stirring scene of an American flag, its thirteen stripes and sixty stars rippling in sunlight—betokening, the narrator insisted, another four years of the prosperity and benevolence engendered by the rule of Deklan Conqueror, for whom the audience's votes were solicited, not that there was any competing candidate known or rumored. The film flapped against its reel; the electric bulb was extinguished. Then the deacons of the Dominion began to reignite the wall lights. Several of the men in the audience had lit pipes during the cinematic display, and their smoke mingled with the smudge of the torchieres, a blue-gray thundercloud hovering under the high arches of the ceiling.

Julian seemed distracted, and slumped in his pew with his hat pulled low. "Adam," he whispered, "we have to find a way out of here."

"I believe I see one," I said; "it's called the door—but what's the hurry?"

"Look at the door more closely. Two men of the Reserve have been posted there."

I looked, and what he had said was true. "But isn't that just to protect the balloting?" For Ben Kreel had retaken the stage and was preparing to ask for a formal show of hands.

"Tom Shearney, the barber with a bladder complaint, just tried to leave to use the jakes. He was turned back."

Indeed, Tom Shearney was seated less than a yard away from us, squirming unhappily and casting resentful glances at the Reserve men.

"But after the balloting—"

"This isn't about balloting. This is about conscription."

"Conscription!"

"Hush!" Julian said hastily, shaking his hair out of his pale face. "You'll start a stampede. I didn't think it would begin so soon . . . but we've had certain telegrams from New York about setbacks in Labrador, and the call-up of new divisions. Once the balloting is finished the Campaigners will probably announce a recruitment drive, and take the names of everyone present and survey them for the names and ages of their children."

"We're too young to be drafted," I said, for we were both just seventeen.

"Not according to what I've heard. The rules have been changed. Oh, you can probably find a way to hide out when the culling begins—and get away with it, considering how far we are from anywhere else. But my presence here is well-known. I don't have a mob or family to melt away into. In fact it's probably not a coincidence that so many Reserves have been sent to such a little village as Williams Ford."

"What do you mean, not a coincidence?"

"My uncle has never been happy about my existence. He has no children of his own. No heirs. He sees me as a possible competitor for the Executive."

"But that's absurd. You don't *want* to be President—do you?"

"I would sooner shoot myself. But Uncle Deklan has a jealous bent, and he distrusts the motives of my mother in protecting me."

"How does a draft help him?"

"The entire draft is not aimed at me, but I'm sure he finds it a useful tool. If I'm drafted, no one can complain that he's excepting his own family from the general conscription. And when he has me in the infantry he can be sure I find myself on the front lines in Labrador— performing some noble but suicidal trench attack."

"But—Julian! Can't Sam protect you?"

"Sam is a retired soldier; he has no power except what arises from the patronage of my mother. Which isn't worth much in the coin of the present realm. Adam, is there another way out of this building?"

"Only the door, unless you mean to break a pane of that colored glass that fills the windows."

"Somewhere to hide, then?"

I thought about it. "Maybe," I said. "There's a room behind the stage where the religious equipment is stored. You can enter it from the wings. We could hide there, but it has no door of its own."

"It'll have to do. If we can get there without attracting attention."

But that was not too difficult, for the torchieres had not all been re-lit, much of the hall was still in shadow, and the audience was milling about a bit, and stretching, while the Campaigners prepared to record the vote that was to follow—they were meticulous accountants even though the final tally was a foregone conclusion and the ballrooms were already booked for Deklan Conqueror's latest inauguration. Julian and I shuffled from one shadow to another, giving no appearance of haste, until we were close to the foot of the stage; there we paused at an entrance to the storage room, until a goonish Reserve man who had been eyeing us was called away by a superior officer to help dismantle the projecting equipment. We ducked through the curtained door into near-absolute darkness. Julian stumbled over some obstruction (a piece of the church's tack piano, which had been disassembled for cleaning in 2165 by a traveling piano-mechanic, who had died of a stroke before finishing the job), the result being a woody "clang!" that seemed loud enough to alert the whole occupancy of the church, but evidently didn't.

What little light there was came through a high glazed window that was hinged so that it could be opened in summer for purposes of ventilation. It was a weak sort of illumination, for the night was cloudy, and only the torches along the main street were shining. But it registered as our eyes adjusted to the dimness. "Perhaps we can get out that way," Julian said.

"Not without a ladder. Although—"

"What? Speak up, Adam, if you have an idea."

"This is where they store the risers—the long wooden blocks the choir stands on when they're racked up for a performance. Perhaps those—"

But he was already examining the shadowy contents of the storage room, as intently as he had surveyed the Tip for ancient books. We found the likely suspects, and managed to stack them to a useful height without causing too much noise. (In the church hall, the Campaigners had already registered a unanimous vote for Deklan Comstock and had begun to break the news about the conscription drive. Some few voices were raised in futile objection; Ben Kreel was calling loudly for calm—no one heard us rearranging the unused furniture.)

The window was at least ten feet high, and almost too narrow to crawl through, and when we emerged on the other side we had to hang by our fingertips before dropping to the ground. I bent my right ankle awkwardly as I landed, though no lasting harm was done.

The night, already cold, had turned colder. We were near the hitching posts, and the horses whinnied at our surprising arrival and blew steam from their gaping nostrils. A fine, gritty snow had begun to fall. There was not much wind, however, and Christmas banners hung limply in the frigid air.

Julian made straight for his horse and loosed its reins from the post. "What are we going to do?" I asked.

"You, Adam, will do nothing but protect your own existence as best you know how; while I—"

But he balked at pronouncing his plans, and a shadow of anxiety passed over his face. Events were moving rapidly in the realm of the aristos, events I could barely comprehend.

"We can wait them out," I said, a little desperately. "The Reserves can't stay in Williams Ford forever."

"No. Unfortunately neither can I, for Deklan Conqueror knows where to find me, and has made up his mind to remove me from the game of politics like a captured chesspiece."

"But where will you go? And what—"

He put a finger to his mouth. There was a noise from the front of the Dominion Church Hall, as of the doors being thrown open, and voices of congregants arguing or wailing over the news of the conscription drive. "Ride with me," Julian said. "Quick, now!"

We did not follow the main street, but caught a path that turned behind the blacksmith's barn and through the wooded border of the River Pine, north in the general direction of the Estate. The night was dark, and the horses stepped slowly, but they knew the path almost by instinct, and some light from the town still filtered through the thinly falling snow, which touched my face like a hundred small cold fingers.

"It was never possible that I could stay at Williams Ford forever," Julian said. "You ought to have known that, Adam."

Truly, I should have. It was Julian's constant theme, after all: the impermanence of things. I had always put this down to the circumstances of his childhood, the death of his father, the separation from his mother, the kind but aloof tutelage of Sam Godwin.

But I could not help thinking once more of *The History of Mankind In Space* and the photographs in it—not of the First Men on the Moon, who were Americans, but of the Last Visitors to that celestial sphere, who had been Chinamen, and whose "space suits" had been firecracker-red. Like the Americans, they had planted their flag in expectation of more visitations to come; but the End of Oil and the False Tribulation had put paid to those plans.

And I thought of the even lonelier Plains of Mars, photographed by machines (or so the book alleged) but never touched by human feet. The universe, it seemed, was full to brimming with lonesome places. Somehow I had stumbled into one. The snow squall ended; the uninhabited moon came through the clouds; and the winter fields of Williams Ford glowed with an unearthly luminescence.

"If you must leave," I said, "let me come with you."

"No," Julian said promptly. He had pulled his hat down around his ears, to protect himself from the cold, and I couldn't see much of his face, but his eyes shone when he glanced in my direction. "Thank you, Adam. I wish it were possible. But it isn't. You must stay here, and dodge the draft, if possible, and polish your literary skills, and one day write books, like Mr. Charles Curtis Easton."

That was my ambition, which had grown over the last year, nourished by our mutual love of books and by Sam Godwin's exercises in English Composition, for which I had discovered an unexpected talent.[6] At the moment it seemed a petty dream. Evanescent. Like all dreams. Like life itself. "None of that matters," I said.

"That's where you're wrong," Julian said. "You must not make the mistake of thinking that because nothing lasts, nothing matters."

"Isn't that the philosopher's point of view?"

"Not if the philosopher knows what he's talking about." Julian reined up his horse and turned to face me, something of the imperiousness of his famous family entering into his mien. "Listen, Adam, there is something important you can do for me—at some personal risk. Are you willing?"

"Yes," I said immediately.

"Then listen closely. Before long the Reserves will be watching the roads out of Williams Ford, if they aren't already. I have to leave, and I have to leave tonight. I won't be missed until morning, and then, at least at first, only by Sam. What I want you to do is this: go home—your parents will be worried about the conscription, and you can try to calm them down—but don't allude to any of what happened tonight—and first

---

[6]   Not a talent that was born fully-formed, I should add. Only two years previously I had presented to Sam Godwin my first finished story, which I had called "A Western Boy: His Adventures in Enemy Europe." Sam had praised its style and ambition, but called attention to a number of flaws: elephants, for instance, were not native to Brussels, and were generally too massive to be wrestled to the ground by American lads; a journey from London to Rome could not be accomplished in a matter of hours, even on "a very fast horse"—and Sam might have continued in this vein, had I not fled the room in a condition of acute auctorial embarrassment.

thing in the morning, make your way as inconspicuously as possible into the Estate and find Sam. Tell him what happened at the Church Hall, and tell him to ride out of town as soon as he can do so without being caught. Tell him he can find me at Lundsford. That's the message."

"Lundsford? There's nothing at Lundsford."

"Precisely: nothing important enough that the Reserves would think to look for us there. You remember what the Tipman said in the fall, about the place he found those books? A low place near the main excavations. Sam can look for me there."

"I'll tell him," I promised, blinking against the cold wind, which irritated my eyes.

"Thank you, Adam," he said gravely. "For everything." Then he forced a smile, and for a moment was just Julian, the friend with whom I had hunted squirrels and spun tales: "Merry Christmas," he said. "Happy New Year!"

And wheeled his horse about, and rode away.

5

There is a Dominion cemetery in Williams Ford, and I passed it on the ride back home—carved stones sepulchral in the moonlight—but my sister Flaxie was not buried there.

As I have said, the Church of Signs was tolerated but not endorsed by the Dominion. We were not entitled to plots in the Dominion yard. Flaxie had a place in the acreage behind our cottage, marked by a modest wooden cross, but the cemetery put me in mind of Flaxie nonetheless, and after I returned the horse to the barn I stopped by Flaxie's grave (despite the shivery cold) and tipped my hat to her, the way I had always tipped my hat to her in life.

Flaxie had been a bright, impudent, mischievous small thing—as golden-haired as her nickname implied. (Her given name was Dolores, but she was always Flaxie to me.) The Pox had taken her quite suddenly and, as these things go, mercifully. I didn't remember her death; I had been down with the same Pox, though I had survived it. What I remembered was waking up from my fever into a house gone strangely quiet. No one had wanted to tell me about Flaxie, but I had seen my mother's tormented eyes, and I knew the truth without having to be told. Death had played lottery with us, and Flaxie had drawn the short straw.

(It is, I think, for the likes of Flaxie that we maintain a belief in Heaven. I have met very few adults, outside the enthusiasts of the established Church, who genuinely believe in Heaven, and Heaven was scant consolation for my grieving mother. But Flaxie, who was five, had believed in it fervently—imagined it was something like a meadow, with wildflowers blooming, and a perpetual summer picnic underway—and if that childish belief soothed her in her extremity, then it served a purpose more noble than truth.)

Tonight the cottage was almost as quiet as it had been during the mourning that followed Flaxie's death. I came through the door to find my mother dabbing her eyes with a handkerchief, and my father frowning over his pipe, which, uncharacteristically, he had filled and lit. "The draft," he said.

"Yes," I said. "I heard about it."

My mother was too distraught to speak. My father said, "We'll do what we can to protect you, Adam. But—"

"I'm not afraid to serve my country," I said.

"That's a praiseworthy attitude," my father said glumly, and my mother wept even harder. "But we don't yet know what might be necessary. Maybe the situation in Labrador isn't as bad as it seems."

Scant of words though my father was, I had often enough relied on him for advice, which he had freely given. He was fully aware, for instance, of my distaste for snakes—for which reason, abetted by my mother, I had been allowed to avoid the sacraments of our faith, and the venomous swellings and occasional amputations occasionally inflicted upon other parishioners—and, while this disappointed him, he had nevertheless taught me the practical aspects of snake-handling, including how to grasp a serpent in such a way as to avoid its bite, and how to kill one, should the necessity arise.[7] He was a practical man despite his unusual beliefs.

But he had no advice to offer me tonight. He looked like a hunted man who has come to the end of a cul-de-sac, and can neither go forward nor turn back.

I went to my bedroom, although I doubted I would be able to sleep. Instead—without any real plan in mind—I bundled a few of my possessions for easy carrying. My squirrel-gun, chiefly, and some notes and writing, and *The History of Mankind In Space*; and I thought I should add some salted pork, or something of that nature, but I resolved to wait until later, so my mother wouldn't see me packing.

---

[7]   "Grasp it where its neck ought to be, behind the head; ignore the tail, however it may thrash; and crack its skull, hard and often enough to subdue it." I had recounted these instructions to Julian, whose horror of serpents far exceeded my own: "Oh, I could never do such a thing!" he had exclaimed. This surfeit of timidity may surprise readers who have followed his later career.

■ ■ ■

Before dawn, I put on several layers of clothing and a heavy pakool hat, rolled down so the wool covered my ears. I opened the window of my room and clambered over the sill and closed the glass behind me, after I had retrieved my rifle and gear. Then I crept across the open yard to the barn, and saddled up a horse (the gelding named Rapture, who was the fastest, though this would leave my father's rig an animal shy), and rode out under a sky that had just begun to show first light.

Last night's brief snowfall still covered the ground. I was not the first up this winter morning, and the cold air already smelled of Christmas. The bakery in Williams Ford was busy making nativity cakes and cinnamon buns. The sweet, yeasty smell filled the northwest end of town like an intoxicating fog, for there was no wind to carry it away. The day was dawning blue and still.

Signs of Christmas were everywhere—as they ought to be, for today was the Eve of that universal holiday—but so was evidence of the conscription drive. The Reservists were already awake, passing like shadows in their scruffy uniforms, and a crowd of them had gathered by the hardware store. They had hung out a faded flag and posted a sign, which I could not read, because I was determined to keep a distance between myself and the soldiers; but I knew a recruiting-post when I saw one. I did not doubt that the main ways in and out of town had been put under close observation.

I took a back way to the Estate, the same riverside road Julian and I had traveled the night before. Because of the lack of wind, our tracks were undisturbed. We were the only ones who had recently passed this way. Rapture was revisiting his own hoof-prints.

Close to the Estate, but still within a concealing grove of pines, I lashed the horse to a sapling and proceeded on foot.

The Duncan-Crowley Estate was not fenced, for there was no real demarcation of its boundaries; under the Leasing System, everything in Williams Ford was owned (in the legal sense) by the two great families. I approached from the western side, which was half-wooded and used by the aristos for casual riding and hunting. This morning the copse was not inhabited, and I saw no one until I had passed the snow-mounded hedges which marked the beginning of the formal gardens. Here, in summer, apple and cherry trees blossomed and produced fruit; flowerbeds gave forth symphonies of color and scent; bees nursed in languid ecstasies. But now it was barren, the paths quilted with snow, and there was no one visible but the senior groundskeeper, sweeping the wooden portico of the nearest of the Estate's several Great Houses.

The Houses were dressed for Christmas. Christmas was a grander event at the Estate than in the town proper, as might be expected. The winter population of the Duncan-Crowley Estate was not as large as its summer population, but there was still a number of both families, plus whatever cousins and hangers-on had elected to hibernate over the cold season. Sam Godwin, as Julian's tutor, was not permitted to sleep in either of the two most luxurious buildings, but bunked among the elite staff in a white-pillared house that would have passed for a mansion anywhere but here. This was where he had conducted classes for Julian and me, and I knew the building intimately. It, too, was dressed for Christmas; a holly wreath hung on the door; pine boughs were suspended over the lintels; a Banner of the Cross dangled from the eaves. The door was not locked, and I let myself in quietly.

It was still early in the morning, at least as the aristos and their elite helpers calculated time. The tiled entranceway was empty and still. I went straight for the rooms where Sam Godwin slept and conducted his classes, down an oaken corridor lit only by the dawn filtering through a window at the long end. The floor was carpeted and gave no sound, though my shoes left damp footprints behind me.

At Sam's particular door, I was confronted with a dilemma. I could not knock, for fear of alerting others. My mission as I saw it was to deliver Julian's message as discreetly as possible. But neither could I walk in on a sleeping man—could I?

I tried the handle of the door. It moved freely. I opened the door a fraction of an inch, meaning to whisper, "Sam?"—and give him some warning.

But I could hear Sam's voice, low and muttering, as if he were talking to himself. I listened more closely. The words seemed strange. He was speaking in a guttural language, not English. Perhaps he wasn't alone. It was too late to back away, however, so I decided to brazen it out. I opened the door entirely and stepped inside, saying, "Sam! It's me, Adam. I have a message from Julian—"

I stopped short, alarmed by what I saw. Sam Godwin—the same gruff but familiar Sam who had taught me the rudiments of history and geography—was practicing *black magic*, or some other form of witchcraft: *on Christmas Eve!* He wore a striped cowl about his shoulders, and leather lacings on his arm, and a boxlike implement strapped to his forehead; and his hands were upraised over an arrangement of nine candles mounted in a brass holder that appeared to have been scavenged from some ancient

Tip. The invocation he had been murmuring seemed to echo through the room: Bah-*rook*-a-*tah*-atten-*eye*-hello-hey-noo . . .

My jaw dropped.

"Adam!" Sam said, almost as startled as I was, and he quickly pulled the shawl from his back and began to unlace his various unholy riggings.

This was so irregular I could barely comprehend it.

Then I was afraid I *did* comprehend it. Often enough in Dominion school I had heard Ben Kreel speak about the vices and wickedness of the Secular Era, some of which still lingered, he said, in the cities of the East—irreverence, irreligiosity, skepticism, occultism, depravity. And I thought of the ideas I had so casually imbibed from Julian and (indirectly) from Sam, some of which I had even begun to believe: Einsteinism, Darwinism, space travel . . . had I been seduced by the outrunners of some New Yorkish paganism? Had I been duped by Philosophy?

"A message," Sam said, concealing his heathenish gear, "what message? Where is Julian?"

But I could not stay. I fled the room.

Sam barreled out of the house after me. I was fast, but he was long-legged and conditioned by his military career, strong for all his forty-odd years, and he caught me in the winter gardens—tackled me from behind. I kicked and tried to pull away, but he pinned my shoulders.

"Adam, for God's sake, settle down!" cried he. That was impudent, I thought, invoking God, him—but then he said, "Don't you understand what you saw? I am a Jew!"

A Jew!

Of course, I had heard of Jews. They lived in the Bible, and in New York City. Their equivocal relationship with Our Savior had won them opprobrium down the ages, and they were not approved of by the Dominion. But I had never seen a living Jew in the flesh—to my knowledge—and I was astonished by the idea that Sam had been one all along: *invisibly*, so to speak.

"You deceived everyone, then!" I said.

"I never claimed to be a Christian! I never spoke of it at all. But what does it matter? You said you had a message from Julian—give it to me, damn you! Where is he?"

I wondered what I should say, or who I might betray if I said it. The world had turned upside-down. All Ben Kreel's lectures on patriotism and fidelity came back to me in one great flood of guilt and shame. Had I been a party to treason as well as atheism?

But I felt I owed this last favor to Julian, who would surely have wanted me to deliver his intelligence whether Sam was a Jew or a Mohammedan: "There are soldiers on all the roads out of town," I said sullenly. "Julian went for Lundsford last night. He says he'll meet you there. Now *get off of me!*"

Sam did so, sitting back on his heels, deep anxiety inscribed upon his face. "Has it begun so soon? I thought they would wait for the New Year."

"I don't know what has begun. I don't think I know anything at all!" And, so saying, I leapt to my feet and ran out of the lifeless garden, back to Rapture, who was still tied to the tree where I had left him, nosing unproductively in the undisturbed snow.

I had ridden perhaps an eighth of a mile back toward Williams Ford when another rider came up on my right flank from behind. It was Ben Kreel himself, and he touched his cap and smiled and said, "Do you mind if I ride along with you a ways, Adam Hazzard?"

I could hardly say no.

Ben Kreel was not a pastor—we had plenty of those in Williams Ford, each catering to his own denomination—but he was the head of the local Council of the Dominion of Jesus Christ on Earth, almost as powerful in his way as the men who owned the Estate. And if he was not a pastor, he was at least a sort of shepherd to the townspeople. He had been born right here in Williams Ford, son of a saddler; had been educated, at the Estate's expense, at one of the Dominion Colleges in Colorado Springs; and for the last twenty years he had taught elementary school five days a week and General Christianity on Sundays. I had marked my first letters on a slate board under Ben Kreel's tutelage. Every Independence Day he addressed the townsfolk and reminded them of the symbolism and significance of the Thirteen Stripes and the Sixty Stars; every Christmas, he led the Ecumenical Services at the Dominion Hall.

He was stout and graying at the temples, clean-shaven. He wore a woolen jacket, tall deer hide boots, and a pakool hat not much grander than my own. But he carried himself with an immense dignity, as much in the saddle as on foot. The expression on his face was kindly. It was always kindly. "You're out early, Adam Hazzard," he said. "What are you doing abroad at this hour?"

"Nothing," I said, and blushed. Is there any other word that so spectacularly represents everything it wants to deny? Under the circumstances, "nothing" amounted to a confession of bad intent. "Couldn't sleep," I added hastily. "Thought I might shoot a squirrel or so." That would explain the rifle strapped to my saddle, and it was at least remotely plausible; the squirrels were still active, doing the last of their scrounging before settling in for the cold months.

"On Christmas Eve?" Ben Kreel asked. "And in the copse on the grounds of the Estate? I hope the Duncans and Crowleys don't hear about it. They're jealous of their trees. And I'm sure gunfire would disturb them at this hour. Wealthy men and Easterners prefer to sleep past dawn, as a rule."

"I didn't fire," I muttered. "I thought better of it."

"Well, good. Wisdom prevails. You're headed back to town, I gather?"

"Yes, sir."

"Let me keep you company, then."

"Please do." I could hardly say otherwise, no matter how I longed to be alone with my thoughts.

Our horses moved slowly—the snow made for awkward footing—and Ben Kreel was silent for a long while. Then he said, "You needn't conceal your fears, Adam. I know what's troubling you."

For a moment I had the terrible idea that Ben Kreel had been behind me in the hallway at the Estate, and that he had seen Sam Godwin wrapped in his Old Testament paraphernalia. Wouldn't that create a scandal! (And then I thought that it was exactly such a scandal Sam must have feared all his life: it was worse even than being Church of Signs, for in some states a Jew can be fined or even imprisoned for practicing his faith. I didn't know where Athabaska stood on the issue, but I feared the worst.) But Ben Kreel was talking about conscription, not about Sam.

"I've already discussed this with some of the boys in town," he said. "You're not alone, Adam, if you're wondering what it all means, this military movement, and what might happen as a result of it. And I admit, you're something of a special case. I've been keeping an eye on you. From a distance, as it were. Here, stop a moment."

We had come to a rise in the road, on a bluff above the River Pine, looking south toward Williams Ford from a little height.

"Gaze at that," Ben Kreel said contemplatively. He stretched his arm out in an arc, as if to include not just the cluster of buildings that was the town but the empty fields as well, and the murky flow of the river, and the wheels of the mills, and even the shacks of the indentured laborers down in the low country. The valley seemed at once a living thing, inhaling the crisp atmosphere of the season and breathing out its steams, and a portrait, static in the still blue winter air. As deeply rooted as an oak, as fragile as a ball of Nativity glass.

"Gaze at that," Ben Kreel repeated. "Look at Williams Ford, laid out pretty there. What is it, Adam? More than a place, I think. It's a way of life. It's the sum of all our labors. It's what our fathers have given us and it's what we give our sons. It's where we bury our mothers and where our daughters will be buried."

Here was more Philosophy, then, and after the turmoil of the morning I wasn't sure I wanted any. But Ben Kreel's voice ran on like the soothing syrup my mother used to administer whenever Flaxie or I came down with a cough.

"Every boy in Williams Ford—every boy old enough to submit himself for national service—is just now discovering how reluctant he is to leave the place he knows best. Even you, I suspect."

"I'm no more or less willing than anyone else."

"I'm not questioning your courage or your loyalty. It's just that I know you've had a little taste of what life might be like elsewhere—given how closely you associated yourself with Julian Comstock. Now, I'm sure Julian's a fine young man and an excellent Christian. He could hardly be otherwise, could he, as the nephew of the man who holds this nation in his palm. But his experience has been very different from yours. He's accustomed to cities—to movies like the one we saw at the Hall last night (and I glimpsed you there, didn't I? Sitting in the back pews?)—to books and ideas that might strike a youth of your background as exciting and, well, *different*. Am I wrong?"

"I could hardly say you are, sir."

"And much of what Julian may have described to you is no doubt true. I've traveled some myself, you know. I've seen Colorado Springs, Pittsburgh, even New York City. Our eastern cities are great, proud metropolises—some of the biggest and most productive in the world— and they're worth defending, which is one reason we're trying so hard to drive the Dutch out of Labrador."

"Surely you're right."

"I'm glad you agree. Because there is a trap certain young people fall into. I've seen it before. Sometimes a boy decides that one of those great cities might be a place he can *run away* to—a place where he can escape all the duties, obligations, and moral lessons he learned at his mother's knee. Simple things like faith and patriotism can begin to seem to a young man like burdens, which might be shrugged off when they become too weighty."

"I'm not like that, sir."

"Of course not. But there is yet another element in the calculation. You may have to leave Williams Ford because of the conscription. And the thought that runs through many boys' minds is, if I must leave, then perhaps I ought to leave on my own hook, and find my destiny on a city's streets rather than in a battalion of the Athabaska Brigade . . . and you're good to deny it, Adam, but you wouldn't be human if such ideas didn't cross your mind."

"No, sir," I muttered, and I must admit I felt a dawning guilt, for I had in fact been a little seduced by Julian's tales of city life, and Sam's dubious lessons, and *The History of Mankind In Space*—perhaps I *had* forgotten something of my obligations to the village that lay so still and so inviting in the blue near distance.

"I know," Ben Kreel said, "that things haven't always been easy for your family. Your father's faith, in particular, has been a trial, and we haven't always been good neighbors—speaking on behalf of the village as a whole. Perhaps you've been left out of some activities other boys enjoy as a matter of course: church activities, picnics, common friendships . . . well, even Williams Ford isn't perfect. But I promise you, Adam: if you find yourself in the Brigades, especially if you find yourself tested in time of war, you'll discover that the same boys who shunned you in the dusty streets of your home town become your best friends and bravest defenders, and you theirs. For our common heritage ties us together in ways that may seem obscure, but become obvious under the harsh light of combat."

I had spent so much time smarting under the remarks of other boys (that my father "raised vipers the way other folks raise chickens," for example) that I could hardly credit Ben Kreel's assertion. But I knew little of modern warfare, except what I had read in the novels of Mr. Charles Curtis Easton, so it might be true. And the prospect (as was intended) made me feel even more shame-faced.

"There," Ben Kreel said: "Do you hear that, Adam?"

I did. I could hardly avoid it. The bell was ringing in the Dominion church, calling together one of the early ecumenical services. It was a silvery sound on the winter air, at once lonesome and consoling, and I wanted almost to run toward it—to shelter in it, as if I were a child again.

"They'll want me soon," Ben Kreel said. "Will you excuse me if I ride ahead?"

"No, sir. Please don't mind about me."

"As long as we understand each other, Adam. Don't look so downcast! The future may be brighter than you expect."

"Thank you for saying so, sir."

I stayed a while longer on the low bluff, watching as Ben Kreel's horse carried him toward town. Even in the sunlight it was cold, and I shivered some, perhaps more because of the conflict in my mind than because of the weather. The Dominion man had made me ashamed of myself, and had put into perspective my loose ways of the last few years, and pointed up how many of my native beliefs I had abandoned before the seductive Philosophy of an agnostic young aristo and an aging Jew.

Then I sighed and urged Rapture back along the path toward Williams Ford, meaning to explain to my parents where I had been and reassure them that I would not suffer too much in the coming conscription, to which I would willingly submit.

I was so disheartened by the morning's events that my eyes drifted toward the ground even as Rapture retraced his steps. As I have said, the snows of the night before lay largely undisturbed on this back trail between the town and the Estate. I could see where I had passed this morning, where Rapture's hoofprints were as clearly written as figures in a book. (Ben Kreel must have spent the night at the Estate, and when he left me on the bluff he would have taken the more direct route toward town; only Rapture had passed this way.) Then I reached the place where Julian and I had parted the night before. There were more hoofprints here, in fact a crowd of them—

And I saw something else written (in effect) on the snowy ground— something which alarmed me.

I reined up at once.

I looked south, toward Williams Ford. I looked east, the way Julian had gone the previous night.

Then I took a bracing inhalation of icy air, and followed the trail that seemed to me most urgent.

6

The east-west road through Williams Ford is not heavily traveled, especially in winter.

The southern road—also called the "Wire Road," because the telegraph line runs alongside it—connects Williams Ford to the railhead at Connaught, and thus sustains a great deal of traffic. But the east-west road goes essentially nowhere: it is a remnant of a road of the secular ancients, traversed mainly by Tipmen and freelance antiquarians, and then only in the warmer months. I suppose, if you followed the old road as far as it would take you, you might reach the Great Lakes, or somewhere farther east, in that direction; and, the opposite way, you could get yourself lost among washouts and landfalls in the Rocky Mountains. But the railroad—and a parallel turnpike farther south—had obviated the need for all that trouble.

Nevertheless, the east-west road was closely watched where it left the outskirts of Williams Ford. The Reserves had posted a man on a hill overlooking it, the same hill where Julian and Sam and I had paused for blackberries on our way from the Tip last October. But it is a fact that the Reserve troops were held in Reserve, and not sent to the front lines, mainly because of some disabling flaw of body or mind; some were wounded veterans, missing a hand or an arm; some were too simple or sullen to function in a disciplined body of soldiers. I cannot say anything for certain about the man posted as lookout on the hill, but if he was not a fool he was at least utterly unconcerned about concealment, for his silhouette (and that of his rifle) stood etched against the bright eastern sky for all to see. But maybe that was the intent: to let prospective fugitives know their way was barred.

Not *every* way was barred, however, not for someone who had grown up in Williams Ford and hunted everywhere on its perimeter. Instead of following Julian directly I rode north a distance, and then through the crowded lanes of an encampment of indentured laborers (whose ragged children gaped at me from the glassless windows of their shanties, and whose soft-coal fires made a smoky gauze of the motionless air). This route connected with lanes cut through the wheat fields for the transportation of harvests and field-hands—lanes that had been deepened by years of use, so that I rode behind a berm of earth and snake rail fences, hidden from the distant sentinel. When I was safely east, I came down a cattle-trail that reconnected me with the east-west road.

On which I was able to read the same signs that had alerted me back at Williams Ford, thanks to the fine layer of snow still undisturbed by any wind.

Julian had come this way. He had done as he had intended, and ridden toward Lundsford before midnight. The snow had stopped soon thereafter, leaving his horse's hoof-prints clearly visible, though softened and half-covered.

But his were not the only tracks: there was a second set, more crisply defined and hence more recent, probably set down during the night; and this was what I had seen at the crossroads in Williams Ford: evidence of pursuit. Someone had followed Julian, without Julian's knowledge. This had dire implications, the only redeeming circumstance being the fact of a single pursuer rather than a company of men. If the powerful people of the Estate had known that it was Julian Comstock who had fled, they would surely have sent an entire brigade to bring him back. I supposed Julian had been mistaken for a simple miscreant, a labor refugee, or a youngster fleeing the conscription, and that he had been followed by some ambitious Reservist. Otherwise that whole imagined battalion might be right behind me . . . or perhaps soon *would* be, since Julian's absence must have been noted by now.

I rode east, adding my own track to these two.

Before long it was past noon, and I began to have second thoughts as the sun began to angle toward an early rendezvous with the southwestern horizon. What exactly did I hope to accomplish? To warn Julian? If so, I was a little late off the mark . . . though I hoped that at some point Julian had covered his tracks, or otherwise misled his pursuer, who did not have the advantage I had, of knowing where Julian meant to stay until Sam Godwin could arrive. Failing that, I half-imagined *rescuing* Julian from capture, even though I had but a squirrel rifle and a few rounds of ammunition (plus a knife and my own wits, both feeble enough weapons) against whatever a Reservist might carry. In any case these were more wishes and anxieties than calculations or plans; I had no fully formed plan beyond riding to Julian's aid and telling him that I had delivered my message to Sam, who would follow along as soon as he could discreetly leave the Estate.

And then what? It was a question I dared not ask myself—not out on this lonely road, well past the Tip now, farther than I had ever been from Williams Ford; not out here where the flatlands stretched on each side of the path like the frosty plains of Mars, and the wind, which had been absent all morning, began to pluck at the fringes of my coat, and my shadow elongated in front of me like a scarecrow gone riding. It was cold and getting colder, and soon the winter moon would be aloft, and me with only a few ounces of salt pork in my saddlebag and a few matches to make a fire if I was able to secure any kindling by nightfall. I began to wonder if I had gone quite insane. At several points I thought: I could go back; perhaps I hadn't yet been missed; perhaps it wasn't too late to sit down to a Christmas Eve dinner with my parents, raise a glass of cider to Flaxie and to Christmases past, and wake in time to hear the ringing-in of the Holiday and smell the goodness of baked bread and Nativity apples drenched in cinnamon and brown sugar. I mused on it repeatedly, sometimes with tears in my eyes; but I let Rapture continue carrying me toward the darkest part of the horizon.

Then, after what seemed endless hours of dusk, with only a brief pause when both Rapture and I drank from a creek which had a skin of ice on it, I began to come among the ruins of the secular ancients.

Not that there was anything spectacular about them. Fanciful drawings often portray the ruins of the last century as tall buildings, ragged and hollow as broken teeth, forming vine-encrusted canyons and shadowy cul-de-sacs.[8] No doubt such places exist—most of them in the uninhabitable Southwest, however, where "famine sits enthroned, and waves his scepter over a dominion expressly made for him," which would rule out vines and such tropical items†[9]—but most ruins were like the ones I now passed, mere irregularities (or more precisely, *regularities*) in the landscape, which indicated the former presence of foundations. These terrains were treacherous, often concealing deep basements that could open like hungry mouths on an unwary traveler, and only Tipmen loved them. I was careful to keep to the path, though I began to wonder whether Julian would be as easy to find as I had imagined—"Lundsford" was a big locality, and the wind had already begun to scour away the hoofprints I had relied on for navigation.

I was haunted, too, by thoughts of the False Tribulation of the last century. It was not unusual to come across desiccated human remains in localities like this. Millions had died in the worst dislocations of the End of Oil: of disease, of internecine strife, but mostly of starvation. The Age of Oil had allowed a fierce intensity of fertilization and irrigation of the land, which had fed more people than a humbler agriculture could support. I had seen photographs of Americans from that blighted age, thin as sticks, their children with distended bellies, crowded into "relief camps" that would soon enough be transformed into communal graves when the imagined "relief" failed to materialize. No wonder, then, that our ancestors had mistaken those decades for the Tribulation of prophecy. What was astonishing was how many of our current institutions—the Church, the Army, the Federal Government—had survived more or less intact. There was a passage in the Dominion Bible that Ben Kreel had read whenever the subject of the False Tribulation arose in school, and which

---

8   Or "culs-de-sac"? My French is rudimentary.

9   Though Old Miami or Orlando might begin to fit the bill.

I had committed to memory: The field is wasted, the land mourns; for the corn is shriveled, the wine has dried, the oil languishes. Be ashamed, farmers; howl, vinekeepers; howl for the wheat and the barley, for the harvest of the field has perished . . .

It had made me shiver then, and it made me shiver now, in these barrens which had been stripped of all their utility by a century of scavenging. Where in this rubble was Julian, and where was his pursuer?

It was by his fire I found him. But I was not the first to arrive.

The sun was altogether down, and a hint of the aurora borealis played about the northern sky, dimmed by moonlight, when I came to the most recently excavated section of Lundsford. The temporary dwellings of the Tipmen—rude huts of scavenged timber—had been abandoned here for the season, and corduroy ramps led down into the empty digs.

Here the remnants of last night's snow had been blown into windrows and small dunes, and all evidence of hoofprints had been erased. But I rode slowly, knowing I was close to my destination. I was buoyed by the observation that Julian's pursuer, whoever he was, had not returned this way from his mission: had not, that is, taken Julian captive, or at least had not gone back to Williams Ford with his prisoner in tow. Perhaps the pursuit had been suspended for the night.

It was not long—though it seemed an eternity, as Rapture short-stepped down the frozen road, avoiding snow-hidden pitfalls—before I heard the whickering of another horse, and saw a plume of smoke rising into the moon-bright sky.

Quickly I turned Rapture off the road and tied his reins to the low remnants of a concrete pillar, from which rust-savaged iron rods protruded like skeletal fingers. I took my squirrel rifle from the saddle holster and moved toward the source of the smoke on foot, until I was able to discern that the fumes emerged from a deep declivity in the landscape, perhaps the very dig from which the Tipmen had extracted *The History of Mankind In Space*. Surely this was where Julian had gone to wait for Sam's arrival. And indeed, here was Julian's horse, one of the finer riding horses from the Estate (worth more, I'm sure, in the eyes of its owner, than a hundred Julian Comstocks), moored to an outcrop . . . and, alarmingly, here was another horse as well, not far away. This second horse was a stranger to me; it was slat-ribbed and elderly-looking; but it wore a military bridle and the sort of cloth bib—blue, with a red star in the middle of it—that marked a mount belonging to the Reserves.

I studied the situation from behind the moon-shadow of a broken abutment.

The smoke suggested that Julian had gone beneath ground, down into the hollow of the Tipmen's dig, to shelter from the cold and bank his fire for the night. The presence of the second horse suggested that he had been discovered, and that his pursuer must already have confronted him.

More than that I could not divine. It remained only to approach the contested grounds as secretively as possible, and see what more I could learn.

I crept closer. The dig was revealed by moonlight as a deep but narrow excavation, covered in part with boards, with a sloping entrance at one end. The glow of the fire within was just visible, as was the chimney-hole that had been cut through the planking some yards farther down. There was, as far as I could discern, only one way in or out. I determined to proceed as far as I could without being seen, and to that end I lowered myself down the slope, inching forward on the seat of my pants over ground that was as cold, it seemed to me, as the wastelands of the Arctic north.

I was slow, I was cautious, and I was quiet. But I was not slow, cautious, or quiet *enough*; for I had just progressed far enough to glimpse an excavated chamber, in which the firelight cast a kaleidoscopic flux of shadows, when I felt a pressure behind my ear—the barrel of a gun—and a voice said, "Keep moving, mister, and join your friend below."

I kept silent until I could comprehend more of the situation I had fallen into.

My captor marched me down into the low part of the dig. The air, if damp, was noticeably warmer here, and we were screened from the increasing wind, though not from the accumulated odors of the fire and the stagnant must of what had once been a basement or cellar in some commercial establishment of the secular ancients.

The Tipmen had not left much behind: only a rubble of broken bits of things, indistinguishable under layers of dust and dirt. The far wall was of concrete, and the fire had been banked against it, under a chimney-hole that must have been cut by the scavengers during their labors. A circle of stones hedged the fire, and the damp planks and splinters in it crackled with a deceptive cheerfulness. Deeper parts part of the excavation, with ceilings lower than a man standing erect, opened in several directions.

Julian sat near the fire, his back to the wall and his knees drawn up under his chin. His clothes had been made filthy by the grime of the place. He was frowning, and when he saw me his frown deepened into a scowl.

"Go over there and get beside him," my captor said, "but give me that little bird rifle first."

I surrendered my weapon, modest as it was, and joined Julian. Thus I was able to get my first clear look at the man who had captured me. He appeared not much older than myself, but he was dressed in the blue and yellow uniform of the Reserves. His Reserve cap was pulled low over his eyes, which twitched left and right as though he were in constant fear of an ambush. In short he seemed both inexperienced and nervous—and maybe a little dim, for his jaw was slack, and he was evidently unaware of the dribble of mucous that escaped his nostrils as a result of the cold weather. (But as I have said before, this was not untypical of the members of the Reserve, who were kept out of active duty for a reason.)

His weapon, however, was very much in earnest, and not to be trifled with. It was a Pittsburgh rifle manufactured by the Porter & Earl works, which loaded at the breech from a sort of cassette and could fire five rounds in succession without any more attention from its owner than a twitch of the index finger. Julian had carried a similar weapon but had been disarmed of it; it rested against a stack of small staved barrels, well out of reach, and the Reservist put my squirrel rifle beside it.

I began to feel sorry for myself, and to think what a poor way of spending Christmas Eve I had chosen. I did not resent the action of the Reservist nearly as much as I resented my own stupidity and lapse of judgment.

"I don't know who you are," the Reservist said, "and I don't care—one draft-dodger is as good as the next, in my opinion—but I was given the job of collecting runaways, and my bag is getting full. I hope you'll both keep till morning, when I can ride you back into Williams Ford. Anyhow, none of us shall sleep tonight. I won't, in any case, so you might as well resign yourself to your captivity. If you're hungry, there's a little meat."

I was never less hungry in my life, and I began to say so, but Julian interrupted: "It's true, Adam," he said, "we're fairly caught. I wish you hadn't come after me."

"I'm beginning to feel the same way," I said.

He gave me a meaningful look, and said in a lower voice, "Is Sam—?"

"No whispering there," our captor said at once.

But I divined the intent of the question, and nodded to indicate that I had delivered Julian's message, though that was by no means a guarantee of our deliverance. Not only were the exits from Williams Ford under close watch, but Sam could not slip away as inconspicuously as I had, and if Julian's absence had been noted there would have been a redoubling of the guard, and perhaps an expedition sent out to hunt us. The man who had captured Julian was evidently an outrider, assigned to patrol the roads for runaways, and he had been diligent in his work.

He was somewhat less diligent now that he had us in his control, however, for he took a wooden pipe from his pocket, and proceeded to fill it, as he made himself as comfortable as possible on a wooden crate. His gestures were still nervous, and I supposed the pipe was meant to relax him; for it was not tobacco he put into it.

The Reservist might have been a Kentuckian, for I understand the less respectable people of that State often form the habit of smoking the silk of the female hemp plant, which is cultivated prodigiously there. Kentucky hemp is grown for cordage and cloth and paper, and as a drug is less intoxicating than the Indian hemp of lore; but its mild smoke is said to be pleasant for those who indulge in it, though too much can result in sleepiness and great thirst.

Julian evidently thought these symptoms would be welcome distractions in our captor, and he gestured to me to remain silent, so as not to interrupt the Reservist in his vice. The Reservist packed the pipe's bowl with dried vegetable matter from an oilcloth envelope he carried in his pocket, and soon the substance was alight, and a slightly more fragrant smoke joined the effluvia of the camp-fire as it swirled toward the rent in the ceiling.

Clearly the night would be a long one, and I tried to be patient in my captivity, and not think too much of Christmas matters, or the yellow light of my parents' cottage on dark winter mornings, or the soft bed where I might have been sleeping if I had not been rash in my deliberations.

7

I began by saying this was a story about Julian Comstock, and I fear I lied, for it has turned out mainly to be a story about myself.

But there is a reason for this, beyond the obvious temptations of vanity and self-regard. I did not at the time know Julian nearly as well as I thought I did.

Our friendship was essentially a boys' friendship. I could not help reviewing, as we sat in silent captivity in the ruins of Lundsford, the things we had done together: reading books, hunting in the wooded foothills west of Williams Ford, arguing amiably over everything from Philosophy and Moon-Visiting to the best way to bait a hook or cinch a bridle. It had been too easy, during our time together, to forget that Julian was an aristo with close connections to men of power, or that his father had been famous both as a hero and as a traitor, or that his uncle Deklan Comstock, the President, might not have Julian's best interests at heart.

All that seemed far away, and distant from the nature of Julian's true spirit, which was gentle and inquisitive—a naturalist's disposition, not a politician's or a general's. When I pictured Julian as an adult, I imagined him contentedly pursuing some scholarly or artistic adventure: digging the bones of pre-Noachian monsters out of the Athabaska shale, perhaps, or making an improved kind of movie. He was not a warlike person, and the thoughts of the great men of the day seemed almost exclusively concerned with war.

So I had let myself forget that he was *also* everything he had been before he came to Williams Ford. He was the heir of a brave, determined, and ultimately betrayed father, who had conquered an army of Brazilians but had been crushed by the millstone of political intrigue. He was the son of a powerful woman, born to a powerful family of her own—not powerful enough to save Bryce Comstock from the gallows, but powerful enough to protect Julian, at least temporarily, from the mad calculations of his uncle. He was both a pawn and a player in the great games of the aristos. And while I had forgotten all this, Julian had not—these were the people who had made him, and if he chose not to speak of them, they nevertheless must have haunted his thoughts.

He was, it is true, often frightened of small things—I still remember his disquiet when I described the rituals of the Church of Signs to him, and he would sometimes shriek at the distress of animals when our hunting failed to result in a clean kill. But tonight, here in the ruins, I was the one who half-dozed in a morose funk, fighting tears; while it was Julian who sat intently still, gazing with resolve from beneath the strands of dusty hair that straggled over his brows, as coolly calculating as a bank clerk.

When we hunted, he often gave me the rifle to fire the last lethal shot, distrusting his own resolve.

Tonight—had the opportunity presented itself—I would have given the rifle to him.

I half-dozed, as I said, and from time to time woke to see the Reservist still sitting in guard. His eyelids were at half-mast, but I put that down to the effect of the hemp flowers he had smoked. Periodically he would start, as if at a sound inaudible to others, then settle back into place.

He had boiled a copious amount of coffee in a tin pan, and he warmed it whenever he renewed the fire, and drank sufficiently to keep him from falling asleep. Of necessity, this meant he must once in a while retreat to a distant part of the dig and attend to physical necessities in relative privacy. This did not give us any advantage, however, since he carried his Pittsburgh rifle with him, but it allowed a moment or two in which Julian could whisper without being overheard.

"This man is no mental giant," Julian said. "We may yet get out of here with our freedom."

"It's not his *brains* so much as his *artillery* that's stopping us," said I.

"Perhaps we can separate the one from the other. Look there, Adam. Beyond the fire— back in the rubble."

I looked.

There was motion in the shadows, which I began to recognize.

"The distraction may suit our purposes," Julian said, "unless it becomes fatal." And I saw the sweat that had begun to stand out on his forehead, the terror barely hidden in his eyes. "But I need your help."

I have said that I did not partake of the particular rites of my father's church, and that snakes were not my favorite creatures. This is true. As much as I have heard about surrendering one's volition to God—and I had seen my father with a Massassauga Rattler in each hand, trembling with devotion, speaking in a tongue not only foreign but utterly unknown (though it favored long vowels and stuttered consonants, much like the sounds he made when he burned his fingers on the coal stove)—I could never entirely assure myself that I would be protected by divine will from the serpent's bite. Some in the congregation obviously had not been: there was Sarah Prestley, for instance, whose right arm had swollen up black with venom and had to be amputated by Williams Ford's physician . . . but I will not dwell on that. The point is, that while I *disliked* snakes, I was not especially *afraid* of them, as Julian was. And I could not help admiring his restraint: for what was writhing in the shadows nearby was a nest of snakes that had been aroused by the heat of the fire.

I should add that it was not uncommon for these collapsed ruins to be infested with snakes, mice, spiders, and poisonous insects. Death by bite or sting was one of the hazards routinely faced by Tipmen, including concussion, blood poisoning, and accidental burial. The snakes, after the Tipmen ceased work for the winter, must have crept into this chasm anticipating an undisturbed hibernation, of which we and the Reservist had unfortunately deprived them.

The Reservist—who came back a little unsteadily from his necessaries—had not yet noticed these prior tenants. He seated himself on his crate, scowled at us, and studiously refilled his pipe.

"If he discharges all five shots from his rifle," Julian whispered, "then we have a chance of overcoming him, or of recovering our own weapons. But, Adam—"

"No talking there," the Reservist mumbled.

"—you must remember your father's advice," Julian finished.

"I said keep quiet!"

Julian cleared his throat and addressed the Reservist directly, since the time for action had obviously arrived: "Sir, I have to draw your attention to something."

"What would that be, my little draft dodger?"

"I'm afraid we're not alone in this terrible place."

"Not alone!" the Reservist said, casting his eyes about him nervously. Then he recovered and squinted at Julian. "I don't see any other persons."

"I don't mean persons, but vipers," said Julian.

"Vipers!"

"In other words—snakes."

At this the Reservist started again, his mind perhaps still slightly confused by the effects of the hemp smoke; then he sneered and said, "Go on, you can't pull that one on me."

"I'm sorry if you think I'm joking, for there are at least a dozen snakes advancing from the shadows, and one of them[10] is about to achieve intimacy with your right boot."

"Hah," the Reservist said, but he could not help glancing in the indicated direction, where one of the serpents—a fat and lengthy example—had indeed lifted its head and was sampling the air above his bootlace.

The effect was immediate, and left no more time for planning. The Reservist leapt from his seat on the wooden crate, uttering oaths, and danced backward, at the same time attempting to bring his rifle to his shoulder and confront the threat. He discovered to his dismay that it was not a question of *one* snake but of *dozens*, and he compressed the trigger of the weapon reflexively. The resulting shot went wild. The bullet impacted near the main nest of the creatures, causing them to scatter with astonishing speed, like a box of loaded springs—unfortunately for the hapless Reservist, who was directly in their path. He cursed vigorously

---

10   Julian's sense of timing was exquisite, perhaps as a result of his theatrical inclinations.

and fired four more times. Some of the shots careened harmlessly; at least one obliterated the midsection of the lead serpent, which knotted around its own wound like a bloody rope.

"Now, Adam!" Julian shouted, and I stood up, thinking: My father's advice?

My father was a taciturn man, and most of his advice had involved the practical matter of running the Estate's stables. I hesitated a moment in confusion, while Julian advanced toward the captive rifles, dancing among the surviving snakes like a dervish. The Reservist, recovering somewhat, raced in the same direction; and then I recalled the only advice of my father's that I had ever shared with Julian:

Grasp it where its neck ought to be, behind the head; ignore the tail, however it may thrash; and crack its skull, hard and often enough to subdue it.

And so I did just that—until the threat was neutralized.

Julian, meanwhile, recovered the weapons, and came away from the infested area of the dig.

He looked with some astonishment at the Reservist, who was slumped at my feet, bleeding from his scalp, which I had "cracked, hard and often."

"Adam," he said. "When I spoke of your father's advice—I meant the *snakes.*"

"The snakes?" Several of them still twined about the dig. But I reminded myself that Julian knew very little about the nature and variety of reptiles. "They're only corn snakes," I explained.[11] "They're big, but not venomous."

Julian, his eyes gone large, absorbed this information.

Then he looked at the crumpled form of the Reservist again.

"Have you killed him?"

"Well, I hope not," I said.

8

We made a new camp, in a less populated part of the ruins, and kept a watch on the road, and at dawn we saw a single horse and rider approaching from the west. It was Sam Godwin.

Julian hailed him, waving his arms. Sam came closer, and looked with some relief at Julian, and then speculatively at me. I blushed, thinking of how I had interrupted him at his prayers (however unorthodox those prayers might have been, from a purely Christian perspective), and how

---

[11]   Once confined to the southeast, corn snakes have spread north with the warming climate. I have read that certain of the secular ancients used to keep them as pets—yet another instance of our ancestors' willful perversity.

poorly I had reacted to my discovery of his true religion. But I said nothing, and Sam said nothing, and relations between us seemed to have been regularized, since I had demonstrated my loyalty (or foolishness) by riding to Julian's aid.

It was Christmas morning. I supposed that did not mean anything in particular to Julian or Sam, but I was poignantly aware of the date. The sky was blue again, but a squall had passed during the dark hours of the morning, and the snow "lay round about, deep and crisp and even." Even the ruins of Lundsford were transformed into something soft-edged and oddly beautiful. I was amazed at how simple it was for nature to cloak corruption in the garb of purity and make it peaceful.

But it would not be peaceful for long, and Sam said so. "There are troops behind me as we speak. Word came by wire from New York not to let Julian escape. We can't linger here more than a moment."

"Where will we go?" Julian asked.

"It's impossible to ride much farther east. There's no forage for the animals and precious little water. Sooner or later we'll have to turn south and make a connection with the railroad or the turnpike. It's going to be short rations and hard riding for a while, I'm afraid, and if we do make good our escape we'll have to assume new identities. We'll be little better than draft dodgers or labor refugees, and I expect we'll have to pass some time among that hard crew, at least until we reach New York City. We can find friends in New York."

It was a plan, but it was a large and lonesome one, and my heart sank at the prospect.

"We have a prisoner," Julian told his mentor, and he took Sam back into the excavated ruins to explain how we had spent the night.

The Reservist was there, hands tied behind his back, a little groggy from the punishment I had inflicted on him but well enough to open his eyes and scowl. Julian and Sam spent a little time debating how to deal with this encumbrance. We could not, of course, take him with us; the question was how to return him to his superiors without endangering ourselves unnecessarily.

It was a debate to which I could contribute nothing, so I took a little slip of paper from my back-satchel, and a pencil, and wrote a letter.

It was addressed to my mother, since my father was without the art of literacy.

You will no doubt have noticed my absence, I wrote. It saddens me to be away from home, especially at this time (I write on Christmas Day).

But I hope you will be consoled with the knowledge that I am all right, and not in any immediate danger.

(This was a lie, depending on how you define "immediate," but a kindly one, I reasoned.)

In any case I would not have been able to remain in Williams Ford, since I could not have escaped the draft for long even if I postponed my military service for some few more months. The conscription drive is in earnest; the War in Labrador must be going badly. It was inevitable that we should be separated, as much as I mourn for my home and all its comforts.

(And it was all I could do not to decorate the page with a vagrant tear.)

Please accept my best wishes and my gratitude for everything you and Father have done for me. I will write again as soon as it is practicable, which may not be immediately. Trust in the knowledge that I will pursue my destiny faithfully and with every Christian virtue you have taught me. God bless you in the coming and every year.

That was not enough to say, but there wasn't time for more. Julian and Sam were calling for me. I signed my name, and added, as a postscript:

Please tell Father that I value his advice, and that it has already served me usefully. Yrs. etc. once again, Adam.

"You've written a letter," Sam observed as he came to rush me to my horse. "But have you given any thought to how you might mail it?"

I confessed that I had not.

"The Reservist can carry it," said Julian, who had already mounted his horse.

The Reservist was also mounted, but with his hands tied behind him, as it was Sam's final conclusion that we should set him loose with the horse headed west, where he would encounter more troops before very long. He was awake but, as I have said, sullen; and he barked, "I'm nobody's damned mailman!"

I addressed the message, and Julian took it and tucked it into the Reservist's saddlebag. Despite his youth, and despite the slightly dilapidated condition of his hair and clothing, Julian sat tall in the saddle. I had never thought of him as high-born until that moment, when an aspect of command seemed to enter his body and his voice. He said to the Reservist, "We treated you kindly—"

The Reservist uttered an oath.

"Be quiet. You were injured in the conflict, but we took you prisoner, and we've treated you in a more gentlemanly fashion than we were when the conditions were reversed. I am a Comstock—at least for the moment—

and I won't be spoken to crudely by an infantryman, at any price. You'll deliver this boy's message, and you'll do it gratefully."

The Reservist was clearly awed by the assertion that Julian was a Comstock—he had been laboring under the assumption that we were mere village runaways—but he screwed up his courage and said, "Why should I?"

"Because it's the Christian thing to do," Julian said, "and if this argument with my uncle is ever settled, the power to remove your head from your shoulders may well reside in my hands. Does that make sense to you, soldier?"

The Reservist allowed that it did.

And so we rode out that Christmas morning from the ruins in which the Tipmen had discovered *The History of Mankind In Space*, which still resided in my back-satchel, vagrant memory of a half-forgotten past.

My mind was a confusion of ideas and anxieties, but I found myself recalling what Julian had said, long ago it now seemed, about DNA, and how it aspired to perfect replication but progressed by remembering itself imperfectly. It might be true, I thought, because our lives were like that—*time itself* was like that, every moment dying and pregnant with its own distorted reflection. Today was Christmas: which Julian claimed had once been a pagan holiday, dedicated to Sol Invictus or some other Roman god; but which had evolved into the familiar celebration of the present, and was no less dear because of it.

(I imagined I could hear the Christmas bells ringing from the Dominion Hall at Wiliams Ford, though that was impossible, for we were miles away, and not even the sound of a cannon shot could carry so far across the prairie. It was only memory speaking.)

And maybe this logic was true of people, too; maybe I was already becoming an inexact echo of what I had been just days before. Maybe the same was true of Julian. Already something hard and uncompromising had begun to emerge from his gentle features—the first manifestation of a new Julian, a freshly *evolved* Julian, called forth by his violent departure from Williams Ford, or slouching toward New York to be born.

But that was all Philosophy, and not much use, and I kept quiet about it as we spurred our horses in the direction of the railroad, toward the rude and squalling infant Future.

❄ ❄ ❄

Amelia, thanks to time-travel tech, makes herself into something of a ghost from the future and one who, when seen, looks quite normal. But Charles Dicken's Ghost of Chrisimas Yet to Come in A Christmas Carol *had a frightening and vague mien—perhaps indicative of the uncertainty of the future—and never spoke: "It was shrouded in a deep black garment, which concealed its head, its face, its form, and left nothing of it visible save one outstretched hand. But for this it would have been difficult to detach its figure from the night, and separate it from the darkness by which it was surrounded . . . [Scrooge] felt that it was tall and stately when it came beside him, and that its mysterious presence filled him with a solemn dread. He knew no more, for the Spirit neither spoke nor moved."*

Loop

❄

Kristine Kathryn Rusch

Amelia could not believe she was actually sitting there. The log was cold and damp beneath her jeans. The trees above dripped water. Out in the mist, an owl called, followed by the faint echo of a dog barking. Laughter from the porch made her cringe.

Above the ground fog, the sky was clear. Stars twinkled and a tiny satellite made its consistent way around the heavens. Her cheeks tingled with chill.

She could still feel the controls, clutched in her left palm. The sharp plastic edges bit into her skin.

Somehow she hadn't imagined it would be like this. Somehow she had thought the device would send her into the middle of an extended memory: she would be sitting on the porch, Tyler's hand warm on her knee, Jeanne and Paul beside them, the smell of eggnog in the air. She had wanted to relive it all, not observe it from the side.

"More eggnog anyone?" Tyler's voice had a deep richness. It warmed her. She longed to crawl onto the porch, knock her old self out of the way, and sit beside him again.

She had tried that when she first arrived. Her hands went through them all—and they hadn't noticed. She felt like Emily in *Our Town*: trapped in the best memory of her life, and no one saw her.

"Me," her own voice replied. It sounded higher, more confident than it did from the inside.

"Yeah, and a little more rum," Paul said.

"None for me." Jeannie's southern accent had an air of falseness. Amelia didn't remember her well. Paul had broken up with Jeanne after dating her for only a year.

A long time ago.

It had all been a long time ago.

Amelia got up off the log, brushed the water off her jeans (—how could she feel that and not her friends on the porch?—), and let herself in the back door. The kitchen was as she remembered it: done in browns and tans, filled with too many dishes, too many books, and too many papers. The room smelled like turkey and pumpkin pies cooled on the counter. A calico cat—Nerdboy! She hadn't thought of Nerdboy in years—slept on an overstuffed kitchen chair.

Tyler stood over a large punchbowl filled with eggnog batter. With his right hand, he poured a steaming bowl of hot rum into the mixture. His dark hair curled over his collar, and his broad shoulders strained at his denim workshirt.

She had forgotten how slim he was, how graceful his movements. As she walked toward him, Nerdboy looked up. His tail thumped against the chair, and his ears went back. He growled.

Tyler half-turned. "What is it, Nerdie?"

She froze there, waiting for him to see her. Nerdboy growled again.

"There's nothing there, kiddo," Tyler said, and returned to the eggnog. In the living room, the opening strains of the Elvis Presley version of "Blue Christmas" blared before someone turned the stereo down.

"Hey, you hiding in there or what?" Paul yelled.

"Coming!" Tyler ladled eggnog into three glass cups, looped his fingers through the handles, and carried them into the living room. Amelia followed. A fifteen-foot Douglas fir dwarfed the room, decorated only in colored lights and clear glass balls. Elvis crooned in the background, and brightly wrapped packages huddled under the tree. Her younger self patted the couch for Tyler. He handed Paul a cup before sitting down.

Her younger self looked up and the smile froze on her face. She grabbed Tyler's wrist, nearly spilling some eggnog on his shirt. "Tyler, look. There she is again. That woman."

Tyler set his cup on the coffee table before looking up. Amelia didn't move. She wanted them to see her. She wanted him to see her. "Hon, it's shadows."

"No," Paul said. "I see someone too." He stepped out of the living room. Amelia walked toward him. If Paul believed, then Tyler would too. Then she could touch him again—

She squeezed the controls tightly, holding her breath as Paul walked into the darkened hallway. The machine squealed, and light shattered around her.

She could see nothing for what felt like an eternity. Then the white light faded into red and green spots. The air was warm, warmer than it had been in the house. She didn't move, uncertain of where she was.

The spots cleared and she found herself in the lab. The lab was as empty as it had been when she got there hours—a day?—ago. The forlorn Christmas tree left a pile of needles on the tiled floor. The Happy Holidays banner had come loose from its nails and the middle sagged. Dirty cups sat on the worktables and gift-wrap overflowed from the wastebaskets.

It took a moment before she focused on the figure sitting in the middle of the mess. It was another version of herself—the version she had seen in the mirror that morning—fifty-six, slightly overweight, with deep, sad lines forming around her mouth, and silver hairs overpowering the black ones in her short haircut.

Something was wrong. She shouldn't be able to see herself. Not here. Not in the now. She should be in herself, experiencing the moment from the inside.

Perhaps that was a moment from her past. Perhaps that was what she had looked like before she had gone to the memory. Perhaps she hadn't come all the way back.

She looked down at the controls, but they were still hidden by that incredibly bright light. She couldn't feel her left hand.

Tyler would have known what to do. Tyler always test-ran the equipment, while she stayed back and monitored the progress from the Now-station. Only no one was monitoring for her. No one could see if the small red malfunction light was blinking.

It would be so easy, she had said to herself after having too much rum and eggnog alone in that big empty house. Just a little trip back, set for only ten minutes: routine. No one would argue with routine.

No one would even notice. No one was scheduled to return to the lab until the day after New Year's, and that was Mark and Christy, the junior team, who would test all the equipment to see if everything was running properly for the week's experiments. Mark and Christy were grad students who had only been on the Project since Tyler died. Even if they saw the malfunction button blinking, they wouldn't know what to do about it.

Not that it mattered. No one had survived in the time stream this long. Tyler had thought it impossible to last more than a day. The government forensic experts who had autopsied him had thought some temporal distortion had killed him. They had warned her to pick the next traveler carefully—someone young with a lot of stamina and no family history of severe medical problems. Having anyone else travel would jeopardize the government funding and the Defense Department approval.

Amelia didn't know how long she had been in the stream. Tyler had never mentioned a white light.

She closed her eyes and reached for her left hand. Her fingers encountered fabric. She followed it until she felt her left wrist bone—with her right hand, as if it were someone else's wrist—then slid her fingers around to the controls. The plastic was cold. She couldn't feel any of the indented keys. She fumbled, reached, and heard an explosion loud as a clap of thunder.

The sun warmed her face. Her back was wet. An odd tingling ran up her left side. Her left arm had gone to sleep. She opened her eyes and found herself staring at a sky so blue it looked like it had been painted by a child who loved bright colors.

Water lapped around her, pushing at her clothes, raising her off the ground and then retreating. A hesitant lover, uncertain of his touch. She smiled and reached for Tyler as she had every morning since she was twenty-five.

He was gone.

She sat up, memory returning. Her left arm dragged in the sand, the control fused to her hand as if she too were made of some sort of synthetic. The sand was white, the air humid. The branches on the palm trees swayed with the gentle breeze. To her left the ocean stretched as far as she could see. To her right, the beach ended in a rise that led to a modified Spanish adobe.

Amelia had never been here before.

She stood. Her arm swung heavy and useless beside her. Water dripped off her hair, and down her clothes. Her tennis shoes were soaked. That sensation bothered her most of all. She slipped off one shoe, then the other, picked them up and walked barefoot across the hot sand.

Halfway to the adobe, her feet encountered stone. The stone path led through a hedge of oversized ferns. She walked through it and stood on a rise overlooking a shaded verandah. Small groups of white wicker furniture surrounded a small swimming pool. Two large glass doors were propped open. Thin white curtains blew inside the house, revealing more white furniture and a white carpet. A serving tray bearing a glass filled with brown liquid floated by itself through the double doors. It stopped near one of the furniture groupings.

" . . . can't." A woman's voice floated up toward Amelia. Amelia walked down the rise beside the pool, looking for the source of the voice.

A young woman sat in one of the wicker lounge chairs, slim legs crossed at the ankles. She wore a sheer white wrap with bikini bottoms underneath. Her feet were bare. Her right hand rested on a glass table, the beverage beside her. The serving unit floated back toward the house.

"I know this isn't the most festive place to spend Christmas. But—" her voice broke "—Grandmama's funeral is tomorrow, and all the relatives will already be here."

Amelia couldn't see the phone at all, but she knew it had to be there. The young woman was speaking into the air. Amelia wondered how the young woman heard the voice on the other end. She walked closer, remaining half-hidden, uncertain if the young woman could see her.

Then she stopped. The young woman had long black hair, a narrow face, and wide dark eyes.

She looked like Tyler.

She looked exactly like Tyler.

Amelia sat on one of the wicker chairs near the pool. Her left hand bumped the edge of the chair, sending a dull ache to her shoulder. The unit squealed and light eased out of its sides. The fingers on her right hand tingled.

A lump rose in her throat. She and Tyler had never had children. On purpose. So what had brought her here, to this woman, near Christmas? It was somewhere beyond Now, somewhere in the future, judging by the devices. Had Tyler had a child he hadn't told her about? He had had so many relationships before they met.

"No, look. I'm sorry," the young woman said. "I can't talk any more." She moved her right hand slightly and sighed. The connection had been severed somehow. Then she sat forward and squinted in Amelia's direction.

"Grandmama?"

The young woman reached for Amelia.

"Grandmama?" she repeated.

The light grew brighter. Amelia reached back. Their fingers met, but did not touch. Instead, the light engulfed her, and she could no longer see.

The gifts were open. Brightly colored wrapping paper lay in shreds on the floor. Paul and Tyler sat cross-legged on the hardwood floor, playing with Matchbox trucks. Jeanne and Amelia's younger self leaned on the back of the couch, arms crossed, and made snide comments about boys always being boys.

Amelia stood next to Paul. His red truck skid across the floor and went through her feet. Her entire left side tingled, and the tingle had grown in her right fingers. She wanted to kneel next to Tyler and ask him what was happening. She wanted him to reassure her that everything was all right.

But everything was not all right. She was wasting away. Tyler had had the same symptoms, spread over a longer period.

She crouched, her left hand scraping the smooth wood floor. Paul started, then slid back, grabbing Tyler's arm as he moved. "There she is," Paul said.

"Where?" Amelia's younger self stepped forward. Jeanne followed.

Tyler looked up. "I don't see anything."

"Jesus," Paul said. "It looks like your mother, Amelia."

"Mother was never in this house," Amelia's younger self said.

Amelia remained still. She met Paul's gaze steadily.

"Where?" Tyler asked.

"Right next to me," Paul said.

Suddenly Tyler saw her. She recognized the light in his eyes. "My God," he said. He got up and walked around her. She stifled the urge to move with him. Then he tried to put his hand on her shoulder. She leaned into the touch, but his hand went right through her.

"My God," he repeated. "This isn't your mother, Amelia. This is you."

Amelia nodded. Tyler jumped back.

"This isn't possible," Amelia's younger self said. "I'm right here. I'm alive."

"And so is she." Tyler crouched in front of Amelia. His cheeks were flushed. "You can hear me, can't you?"

"Yes," she said.

"Yes," he whispered. "But I can't hear you." He tried to touch her again, and frowned as his hand went through her. "It's some kind of distortion field. You're not a ghost at all."

"I'm alive," Amelia said. She had to repeat it twice before Tyler understood.

"It is a distortion field. Time experiments?"

The older Tyler would have yelled at her for giving his younger self that much information, but she didn't know what it would hurt now. He had already seen her.

She nodded.

"My God," he said. "They work."

She shook her head and touched her arm. "Help me," she said. "Please. Help me."

"She's asking for help," Paul said. "Tyler—"

But Paul's voice was fading. The light had returned: brighter this time. It burned into her left hand, along her side. She cried out in pain—and then the light engulfed her.

Colors flashed behind her closed eyelids. She was on a cold, hard floor. Her head ached. She sat up and rubbed her forehead with her good hand before opening her eyes.

The lab again. Her Now-self still huddled over the controls like they were her last link to sanity. She stared at her Now-self for a moment. Had she really looked that lost before stepping into the time stream? She used to pity women who looked like that after they had lost their man. Tyler had been dead six months. She still had the experiments, their house, their friends.

But they all felt so empty without him. An ache grew in her chest.

It's a dream, Tyler had said. We're living a dream.

She made herself get up. She swayed a bit, unused to moving without the help of her left arm. She walked around the benches to her Now-Self. Her Now-self was fiddling with the controls. Amelia remembered that moment: she only had time to return to one memory. She had to make it a good one.

Odd that she hadn't picked one with her and Tyler alone.

But she had been thinking Christmas, since it was the loneliness of the holidays that had driven her to the lab in the first place. And the best Christmas had been that first one in the country house, with Paul and Jeanne. She and Paul and Tyler had always compared the others to that one, thinking that nothing could measure up.

But it didn't really seem that special now. Perhaps it had been special because it had been the first.

Her Now-self looked up and gasped. Amelia sat on the bench across from her. Her Now-self reached out just as the air exploded around them.

■ ■ ■

She couldn't get air. Her mouth was filled with water. Her right arm flailed. She opened her eyes to a blue distorted world. Under water. She was under water. She had to reach the surface or she would drown.

She kicked up, three good strong kicks that pushed her to the air. She spit the water out of her mouth and took deep, thankful breaths. Water rippled around her. Her presence had disturbed it. She was in a pool. The pool she had seen near the adobe house. She kicked her way to the ladder on the pool's deep end, and grabbed onto the metal railing with her right hand. The tingling had progressed into her wrist. She could barely move the hand at all.

She was running out of time.

She climbed out and sat on the side, breathing heavily. The young woman was asleep in her lounge chair, left arm covering her beautiful face. Amelia knew better than to try and touch her. The people were not real but the places were, as if they were a revolving set for a cosmic play.

Amelia grabbed a towel off the stack and wiped the water from her face. The humid air almost felt cool. She wrapped the towel around her neck, and wandered inside the house.

The main room was white with white furniture: obviously for entertaining. The back rooms had beds in them with clothes scattered about. The young woman did not live alone. A cat slept in the middle of one of the beds, and gave Amelia the evil eye as she passed.

She stopped in the only bedroom that looked as if it hadn't been used recently. The bed was an oversized four-poster like the one she and Tyler had had, with pale pink sheets under a pink and brown patterned spread. But that wasn't what drew her. What drew her were the pictures on the walls.

Some looked familiar: an early date with Tyler at a seafood place; a prize-winning photo of their first lab. But others were dream photos: her in a white wedding gown, Tyler in a black tux smiling down at her; both of them smiling in professional photography fashion at the tiny baby she held in her arms. Then baby pictures and school pictures of a young girl surrounded by family groupings with Tyler aging as he had and the temporal distortion wasting him away. He wore another tux for the young girl's wedding, looking proud and fatherly, and after that, he appeared in no more pictures even though they continued to chronicle the girl, and then her daughter—the young woman Amelia had seen outside.

She sighed and leaned on the bed. Her body was shaking. A life that she hadn't lived, complete with photographs. This had probably been her room until she died.

The shaking turned into a shudder. A life she hadn't lived. A life she could never live, even if she had married Tyler and had a child. She would die in this time stream—in this loop—and no one would know. They would just think she had disappeared.

She stared at the photos, and watched as they vanished in a blur of light.

She awoke to the sound of voices. Tyler was hunched over her, a frown on his too-young face. "She's back," he said.

Amelia couldn't move either arm. She wanted to sit up, but knew she didn't dare, not in front of this young Tyler, not with the chance of losing her balance.

"What's happening to you?" he asked.

She wished he could hear her. She would tell him and maybe he would find a solution. Still, it wouldn't hurt to try. "I'm trapped," she said. "I'm stuck in a loop."

He understood the part about being trapped. She had to repeat herself three times before he said: "Loop? Like in the movies?"

Not exactly, because she did move forward in each time period. She just kept visiting the same three settings. But she nodded anyway.

"Loop," he said reflectively. The tree lights winked behind him.

"I still think she's a ghost," Paul said, from somewhere behind them. "I don't care about the scar on the chin. She looks like Amelia's mother."

Tyler shook his head just a little. He smiled at her with the love she had missed. He knew her, just as she would have known him. It didn't matter that she had a younger self watching somewhere in the background.

The light was back, eating Tyler, making him disappear. The loops were shorter now. "Tyler," she said, wishing she could reach for him. She didn't want to lose him again—

—but when she came to herself she was back in the lab, propped against the large black lab table near the front of the room. The numbness had started in her feet. She looked at her arms. They seemed to be hers, except for her left hand, with the control fused to her skin.

She had jumped back too far. She had known there would be that risk. Tyler had said that when he went on trips longer than ten years he always felt depleted. But she had thought she could deal with depleted.

Her Now-self left the bench and walked over to Amelia. Her Now-self wore a ring on the third finger of her left hand. Had Amelia altered something by appearing? Or had she slipped into another life, another time? Had that trapped her?

Her Now-self's hands were shaking. They passed over Amelia's useless left hand, and her Now-self swallowed, hard. "Your control is broken," her Now-self said.

"I know," Amelia said.

But her Now-self was looking down and didn't seem to hear. Even in this place, she couldn't speak to herself.

Her Now-self set the control down. "Here," she said. "If I don't touch it, you can. Take mine."

Amelia shook her head. She couldn't move her arms. She smiled a little sadly. She would die here.

"You're the woman we saw all those years ago, aren't you?" Her Now-self asked.

Amelia nodded. She was getting too tired to speak.

"You went to see him, didn't you?" Her Now-self asked. "Just like I was going to."

Amelia smiled a little. She had seen him, one last time. And he had smiled at her. He loved her, no matter who or when she was.

"And it was wrong. It trapped you." Her Now-self stood. "When he—when he was alive, he made me promise to never come here by myself. He knew, didn't he?"

"He guessed," Amelia said, even though her Now-self couldn't hear.

"And all the precautions," her Now-self said quietly. "He was trying to protect me. He said, before he died, that he would always love me. And I didn't believe him. I had to see—"

Amelia nodded. The tingle filled her entire body. The light was returning, and the sound was fading. She had done this. She had made the changes, by appearing in her own past. As a ghost.

She wanted to tell her Now-self not to go, but she couldn't. She couldn't move at all.

The light faded one final time. Amelia knew something supported her, but she couldn't feel it beneath the tingle in her body. As the red and green dots dissipated, she found herself on the four-poster bed in the adobe house, staring at the pictures on the wall.

They hadn't changed: she and Tyler gazing happily at each other, the baby between them; Tyler, giving away the bride. It took a moment before she understood what the photographs meant. They meant that her Now-self had heard, had understood. Her alternate self, the one who had married Tyler, born a child, and worked on the project, had set the controls aside, faced the dark and lonely house, and conquered it.

A breeze moved the curtains. The air had a fresh, salty smell here that she could have grown to love. A movement caught the corner of her eye. She tried to turn her head, but couldn't. The floorboards creaked, and the young woman in the white shift appeared at the edge of Amelia's vision.

"Grandmama," the woman said, kneeling beside the bed, "Grandmama, I miss you so."

Amelia smiled her last smile at the woman she and Tyler had helped make in a world she would never remember. "I missed you too, honey," she said as the light took her. "I missed you too."

❄   ❄   ❄

La Befana, mentioned near the end of this haunting tale, is an Italian Christmas tradition. The ragged old lady rides a broomstick—or carries it over her shoulder supporting a bag—and delivers gifts to children on Epiphany Eve. (Epiphany marks the Twelfth Day of Christmas and the day the Magi made their visit to the infant Jesus.) M. Rickert relates one version of the Befana legend. Another variation casts her as a mother who had lost her own child. Insane with grief, not accepting the death, she bundles the infant's belongings up and goes in search of him. She finds the Christ child instead, and gives the bundle to him. The woman—who has suffered so much she appears to be an old crone—is granted the gift of being the mother of all children for one night each year: mostly rewarding her offspring, but occasionally letting some know they must improve their ways.

The Christmas Witch
❄
M. Rickert

The children of stone collect bones, following cats through twisted narrow streets, chasing them away from tiny birds, dead gray mice (with sweet round ears, pink inside like seashells), and fish washed on rocky shore. The children show each other their bone collections, tiny white femurs, infinitesimal wings, jawbones with small teeth intact. Occasionally, parents find these things; they scold the little hoarder, or encourage the practice by setting up a science table. It's a stage children go through, they assume, this fascination with structure, this cold approach to death. The parents do not discuss it with each other, except in passing. ("Oh yes, the skeleton stage.") The parents do not know, they do not guess that once the found bones are tossed out or put on display, the children begin to collect again. They collect in earnest.

Rachel Boyle has begun collecting bones, though her father doesn't know about it, of course. Her mother, being dead, might know. Rachel can't figure that part out. Her mother is not a ghost, the Grandma told her, but a spirit. The Grandma lives far away, in Milwaukee. Rachel didn't even remember her when she came for the funeral. "You remember me, honey, don't you?" she asked and Rachel's father said, "Of course she remembers you." Rachel went in the backyard where she tore flowers while her father and the Grandma sat at the kitchen table and cried. After the Grandma left, Rachel and her father moved to Stone.

Rachel doesn't get off the school bus at her house, because her father is still at work. She gets off at Peter Williamson's house. The first time she found Peter with his bone collection spread out before him on the bedroom floor she thought it was gross. But the second time she sat across from him and asked him what they were for.

Peter shrugged. "You know," he said.

Rachel shook her head.

"Didn't they teach you anything in Boston? They're for Wilmot Redd, the witch. You know. A long time ago. An old lady. She lived right here in Stone. They hung her. There's a sign about her on Old Burial Hill but she's not buried there. No one knows where she ended up."

That's when Rachel began collecting bones. She stored them in her sock drawer, she stored them under her bed, she had several in her jewelry box, and two chicken legs buried in the flowerpot from her mother's funeral. The flowers were dead, but it didn't matter, she wouldn't let her father throw them out.

For Halloween, Rachel wants to be dead but her father says she can't be. "How about a witch?" he says, "Or a princess?"

"Peter's going to be dead," she says. "He'll have a knife going right through the top of his head, and blood dripping down his face."

"How about a cat? You can have a long tail and whiskers."

"Mariel is going to be a pilgrim."

"You can be a pilgrim."

"Pilgrims are dead! Jeez, Dad, didn't they teach you anything in Boston?"

"Don't talk to me like that."

Rachel sighs, "Okay, I'll be a witch."

"Fine, we'll paint your face green and you can wear a wig."

"Not that kind of witch."

Her father turns out the light and kisses her on the forehead before he leaves her alone in the dark. All of a sudden Rachel is scared. She thinks of calling her father. Instead, she counts to fifty before she pulls back the covers and sneaks around in the dark of her room, gathering the bones, which she pieces together into a sort of puzzle shape of a funny little creature, right on top of her bed. She uses a skull, and a long bone that might be from a fish, the small shape of a mouse paw, and a couple of chicken legs. She sucks her thumb while she waits for it to do the silly dance again.

On Tuesday, Mrs. Williamson has a doctor's appointment. Rachel still gets off the bus with Peter. They still go to his house. There, the baby-sitter waits for them. Her name is Melinda. She has long blonde hair, a pierced navel, pierced tongue, ears pierced all the way around the edge, and rings on every finger. She wraps her arms around Peter and wrestles him to the floor. He screams but he is smiling. After a while she lets go and turns to Rachel.

Rachel wishes Melinda would wrap her arms around her, but she doesn't. "My name's Melinda," she says. Rachel nods. Her father already told her. He wouldn't let her be watched by a stranger. "Who wants popcorn?" Melinda says and races Peter into the kitchen. Rachel follows even though she doesn't really like popcorn.

Peter tells Melinda about his plans for Halloween. He tells her about the knife through his head while the oil heats up in the pan. Melinda tosses in a kernel. Peter runs out of the room.

"What are you going to be?" Melinda asks but before Rachel can answer, Peter is back in the kitchen, the knife in his head, blood dripping around the eyes. Melinda says, "Oh gross, that's so great, it looks really gross." The kernel pops. Melinda pours more kernels into the pan and then slaps the lid on. "Hey, dead man," she says, "How about getting the butter?"

Peter gets a stick of butter out of the refrigerator. He places it on the cutting board. He takes a sharp knife out of the silverware drawer. Popcorn steam fills the kitchen. Rachel feels sleepy, sitting at the island. She leans her head into her hand; her eyes droop. Peter makes a weird sound and drops the knife on the counter. Blood trickles from his finger and over the butter. Melinda sets the pan on a cold burner, turns off the stove, and wraps Peter's finger in paper towel. Rachel isn't positive but she thinks Peter is crying beneath his mask.

"It's okay," Melinda says. "It's just a little cut." She steers Peter through the kitchen toward the bathroom. Rachel looks at the blood on the butter; one long red drop drips down the side. She stares at the kitchen window, foggy with steam. For a second she thinks someone is standing out there, watching, but no one is. Peter and Melinda come back into the kitchen. Peter no longer has the knife through his head. His hair is stuck up funny, his face, pink, and he has a band-aid on his finger. He sits at the island beside Rachel but doesn't look at her. Melinda slices the bloody end of butter and tosses it into the trash. She cuts a chunk off, places it in a glass bowl and sticks it in the microwave. "So, what are you going to be for Halloween?"

"Wilmot Redd," Rachel says.

"You can't," says Melinda.

"Don't you know anything?" Peter asks.

"Be nice, Peter." Melinda pours the popcorn into a big purple bowl and drips melted butter over it. "You can't be Wilmot Redd."

"Why not?"

Melinda puts ice in three glasses and fills them with Dr. Pepper. She sits down at the island, across from Peter and Rachel. "If I tell you, you can't tell your dad."

Rachel has heard about secrets like this. When a grownup tells you not to tell your parents something, it is a bad secret. Rachel is thrilled to be told one. "I won't," she says.

"Okay, I know you think witches wear pointy black hats and act like the bad witch in *The Wizard of Oz* but they don't. Witches are just regular people and they look and dress like everyone else. Stone is full of witches. I can't tell you who all is a witch, but you would be surprised. Who knows? Maybe you'll grow up to be a witch yourself. All that stuff about witches is a lie. People have been lying about witches for a very long time. And that's what happened to Wilmot Redd. Maybe she wasn't even a witch at all, but one thing for sure she wasn't an evil witch. That's the part that's made up about witches and that's what they made up about her, and that's how come she wound up dead. You can't dress up as Wilmot Redd. We just don't make fun of her in Stone. Even though it happened a long time ago, most people here still feel really bad about it. Most people think she was just an old woman who was into herbs and shit, don't tell your dad I said 'shit' either, all right? Making fun of Wilmot Redd is like saying you think witches should be hung. You don't think that do you? All right then, so don't dress up as Wilmot Redd. You can go as a made-up witch, but leave poor Wilmot Redd out of it. No one even knows what happened to her, I mean after she died. That's how much she didn't matter. They threw her body off a cliff somewhere. No one even knows where her bones ended up. They could be anywhere."

"Do you collect bones?" Rachel asks and Peter kicks her.

"Why would I do that?" Melinda says. "You have some weird ideas, kid."

Witches everywhere. Teacher witches, mommy and daddy witches, policeman witches too, boy witches and girl witches, smiling witches, laughing witches, bus driver witches. Who is not a witch in Stone? Rachel isn't, she knows that for sure. Rachel makes special requests for chicken "with the bones," she says, and she eats too much, giving herself a stomachache. "How many bones do you need?" her father asks, because Rachel has told him she needs them for a

school project. "I don't know," she says. "Jack just keeps saying I need more."
"Jack sounds kind of bossy," her father says.

Rachel nods. "Yeah, but he's funny too."

Finally, Halloween arrives. Rachel goes to school dressed as a made-up witch. She notices that there are several of them on the bus and the playground. They start the morning with doughnuts and apple cider and then they do math with questions like two pumpkins plus one pumpkin equals how many pumpkins.

Rachel raises her hand and the lady at the front of the room who says she is Miss Engstrom, their teacher, but who doesn't look anything like her, says, "Yes, Rachel?"

"How many bones does it take to make a body?"

"That's a very good question," the lady says. She's wearing a long purple robe and she has black hair that keeps sliding around funny on her head. "I'll look that up for you, Rachel, but in the meantime, can you answer my question? You have two pumpkins and then your mother goes to the store and comes home with one more pumpkin, how many pumpkins do you have?"

"Her mother is dead," a skeleton in the back of the room says.

"I don't care," says Rachel.

"I mean your father," the lady says. "I meant to say your father goes to the store."

But Rachel just sits there and the lady calls on someone else.

They get an extra long recess. Cindi Becker tears her princess dress on the swing and cries way louder than Peter cried when he cut his finger. Somebody dressed all in black, with a black hood, won't speak to anyone but walks slowly through the playground, stopping occasionally to point a black-gloved finger at one of the children. When one of the kindergartners gets pointed at, he runs, screaming, back to his teacher, who is dressed up as a pirate.

Rachel finds Peter with the knife in his head and says, "Don't tell, but I'm still going to be Wilmot Redd tonight." The boy turns to her, but doesn't say anything at all, just walks away. After a while, Rachel realizes that there are three boys on the playground with knives in their heads, and she isn't sure if the one she spoke to was Peter.

They don't have the party until late in the afternoon. The lady who says she is Miss Engstrom turns off the lights and closes the drapes.

Rachel raises her hand. The lady nods at her.

"When my mom went to the store a bad man shot her—"

The lady waves her arms, as if trying to put out a fire, the purple sleeves dangling from her wrists. "Rachel, Rachel," she says. "I'm so sorry about your mother. I should have said your father went to the store. I'm really sorry. Maybe I should tell a story about witches."

"My mother is not a witch," Rachel says.

"No, no of course she's not a witch. Let's play charades!"

Rachel sits at her desk. She is a good girl for the most part. But she has learned that even without her face painted, she can pretend to be listening when she isn't. Nobody notices that she isn't playing their stupid game. Later, when she is going to the bus, the figure all dressed in black points at her. She feels the way the kindergartner must have felt. She feels like crying. But she doesn't cry.

She gets off the bus at Peter Williamson's house with Peter who acts crazy, screaming for no reason, letting the door slam right in her face. I hate you, Peter, she thinks, and is surprised to discover that nothing bad happens to her for having this thought. But when she opens the door, Melinda is standing there, next to Peter who still has the knife in his head. "Don't you understand? You can't dress up as Wilmot Redd."

"Where's Mrs. Williamson?" Rachel asks.

"She had to go to the doctor's. Did you hear me?"

"I'm not," Rachel says, walking past Melinda. "Can't you see I'm just a made-up witch?"

"Is that what you're wearing tonight?"

Rachel nods.

"Who wants popcorn?" Melinda says. Rachel sticks her tongue out at Peter. He just stands there, with the knife in his head.

"Hey, aren't you guys hungry?" Melinda calls from the kitchen.

Peter runs, screaming, past Rachel. She walks in the other direction, to Peter's room. She knows where he keeps his collection, in his bottom drawer. Peter hasn't said anything about it, maybe he hasn't noticed, but Rachel has been stealing bones from him for some time now. Today she takes a handful. She doesn't have any pockets so she drops the bones into her Halloween treat bag from school. She is careful not to set the bag down. She is still carrying it when her father comes to get her.

They walk home together, through the crooked streets of Stone. The sky is turning gray. Ghosts and witches dangle from porches and crooked trees behind picket fences. Pumpkins grin blackly at her.

Rachel's father says that after dinner Melinda is coming over.

"She just wants to see what kind of witch I am," Rachel says.

Her father smiles, "Yes, I'm sure you're right. Also, I asked her if she could stay and pass out treats while I go with you. That way no one will play a trick on us."

"Melinda might," Rachel says, but her father just laughs, as if she were being funny.

When they get home, Rachel goes into her bedroom while her father makes dinner. He's making macaroni and cheese, her favorite, though tonight, the thought of it makes her strangely queasy. Rachel begins to gather the bones from all the various hiding places, the box under her bed, the sock drawer. She puts them in a pillowcase. When her father calls her for dinner, she shoves the pillowcase under her bed.

In the kitchen, a man stands next to the stove with a knife in his head. Rachel screams, and her father tears off the mask. He tells her he's sorry. "See," he lifts the mask up by the knife. "It's just something I bought at the drugstore. I thought it would be funny."

Rachel tries to eat but she doesn't have much of an appetite. She picks at the yellow noodles until the doorbell rings. Her father answers it and comes back with Melinda who smiles and says, "How's the little witch?"

"Not dead," Rachel answers.

Rachel's father looks at her as if she has a knife in her head.

They go from house to house begging for candy. The witches of Stone drop M&M's, peanut butter cups, and popcorn balls into Rachel's plastic pumpkin. Once, a ghost answers the door, and once, when she reaches into a bowl for a small Hershey's bar, a green hand pops up through the candy and tries to grab her. Little monsters, giant spiders, made-up witches, and bats weave gaily around Rachel and her father. The pumpkins, lit from within, grin at her. Rachel thinks of Wilmot Redd standing on Old Burial Hill watching all of them, waiting for her to bring the bones.

But when Rachel gets home, the bones are gone. The pillowcase, filled with most of her collection and shoved under her bed, is missing. Rachel runs into the living room, just in time to see Melinda leaving with a white bundle under her arm. Rachel stands there, in her fake witch costume and thinks, *I wish you were dead.* She has a lot of trouble getting to sleep that night. She cries and cries and her father asks her over and over again if it's because of her mother. Rachel doesn't tell him about the bones. She doesn't know why. She just doesn't.

Two days later, Melinda is killed in a car accident. Rachel's father wipes tears from his eyes when he tells her. Mrs. Williamson cries when she thinks Peter and Rachel aren't watching. But Peter and Rachel don't cry.

"She stole my bones," Rachel says.

"Mine too," says Peter. "She stole a bunch of them."

Melinda's school picture is on the front page of the newspaper, beside a photograph of the fiery wreck.

"That's what she gets," Rachel says, "for stealing."

Peter frowns at Rachel.

"Wanna trade?" she asks.

He nods. Rachel trades a marshmallow pumpkin for a small bone shaped like a toe.

That night, after her father kisses her on the forehead and turns off the light, she takes her small collection of bones and tries to make them dance, but the shape is all wrong. It just lies there and doesn't do anything at all.

The day of Melinda's funeral, Rachel's father doesn't go to work. He's a lawyer in Boston and it isn't easy, the way it is for some parents, to stay home on a workday, but he does. He picks Rachel up at school just after lunch.

The funeral is in a church in the new section of Stone, far from the harbor and Old Burial Hill. On the way there, they pass a group of people carrying signs.

"Close your eyes," her father says.

Rachel closes her eyes. "What are they doing?"

"They're protesting. They're against abortion."

"What's abortion?"

"Okay, you can open them. Abortion is when a woman is pregnant and decides she doesn't want to be pregnant."

"You mean like magic?"

"No, it's not magic. She has a procedure. The procedure is called having an abortion. When that's over, she's not pregnant anymore."

Rachel looks out the car window at the pumpkins with collapsed faces, the falling ghosts, a giant spiderweb dangling in a tree. "Dad?"

"Mmhm?"

"Can we move back to Boston?"

Her father glances down at her. "Don't you feel safer here? And you already have so many friends. Mrs. Williamson says you and Peter get along great. And there's your friend, Jack. Maybe we can have him over some Saturday."

"Melinda said there are a lot of witches in Stone."

Her father whistles, one long low sound. "Well, she was probably just trying to be funny. Here we are." They are parked next to a church. "This is where Melinda's funeral is."

"Okay," says Rachel but neither of them move to get out of the car.

"Let's say a prayer for Melinda," her father says.

"Here?"

He closes his eyes and bows his head while Rachel watches a group of teenage girls in cheerleading uniforms hugging on the church steps.

"Now, do you wanna get ice cream?"

Rachel can't believe she's heard right. She knows about funerals and they don't have anything to do with ice cream, but she nods, and he turns the car around, right in the middle of the street, just as the church bells ring. Rachel's father drives all the way back to the old section of Stone, where they stop for ice cream. Rachel has peppermint stick and her father has vanilla. They walk on the sidewalk next to the water and watch the seagulls. Rachel tries not to think about Wilmot Redd who stands on Old Burial Hill, waiting.

Her father looks at his watch. "We have to get going," he says. "It's almost time for Peter to get off the bus."

"Peter?"

"His mother has to go to the doctor's. I told her he could come to our house."

Rachel's father goes out to meet Peter when he gets off the bus and they walk in together, talking about the Red Sox. They walk right past Rachel. "Dad?" she says but he doesn't answer. She follows them into the kitchen. Her father is spreading cream cheese on a bagel for Peter. Later, when she is playing in her bedroom with him, Rachel says, "I wish your mom had an abortion," which makes Peter cry. When her father comes into the room he makes her tell him what she did and she tells him she didn't do anything but Peter tells on her and her father says she is grounded.

Miss Engstrom tells them that they are very lucky to live in Stone, so near to Danvers and Salem and the history of witches. Rachel says that she knows there are a lot of witches in Stone and Miss Engstrom laughs and then all the children laugh too. Later, on the playground, Stella Miner and Leanne Green hold hands and stick out their tongues at Rachel, and Minnity Dover throws pebbles at her. Miss Engstrom catches Minnity and makes her sit on the bench for the rest of recess. Rachel swings so high that she can imagine she is flying. When the bell rings, she comes back to Earth where Bret and Steve Keeter, the twins, and Peter Williamson wait for her. "We wish your mom had an abortion," Peter says. The twins nod their golden heads.

"You don't even know what that means," says Rachel and runs past them, toward Miss Engstrom who stands beside the open door, frowning.

"Rachel," she says, "You're late." But she doesn't say anything to the boys, who come in behind Rachel, whispering.

"Shut up!" Rachel shouts.

Miss Engstrom sends Rachel to the office. The principal says he is going to call her father. Rachel sits in the office until it's almost time to go home, and then she goes back to the classroom for her books and lunchbox.

"Wanna know what we did while you were gone?" Clara Vanmeer whispers when they line up for the bus.

Rachel ignores her. She knows what they did. They are witches, all of them, and they put some kind of spell on her. *I wish you were all dead*, Rachel thinks, and she really means it. It worked with Melinda, didn't it? But not her mom. She never wished her mom would die. Never never never. Who did? Who wished that for her mother who used to call her Rae-Rae and made chocolate chip pancakes and was beautiful? Rachel hugs her backpack and stares out the window at the witches of Stone, picking their kids up from school. The bus drives past rotten pumpkins and fallen graveyards. Rachel's head hurts. She hopes Mrs. Williamson will let her take a nap but when they get there, the house is locked. Peter rings the doorbell five hundred times, and pulls on the door but Rachel just sits on the step. Nobody is home, why can't he just get that through his head? Finally, Peter starts to cry. "Shut up," Rachel says. She has to say it twice before he does.

"Where's my mother?" Peter asks, wiping his nose with the sleeve of his jacket.

"How should I know?" Rachel watches a small black cat with a tiny silver bell around its neck emerge from the bush at the neighbor's house. Unfortunately, it is not carrying a dead bird or mouse.

Peter starts crying again. Loudly. Rachel's head hurts. "Shut up!" she says, but he just keeps crying. She stands up and readjusts her backpack.

Rachel is already walking down the tiny sidewalk when Peter calls for her to wait. They walk to Rachel's house, but of course that is locked as well. Peter starts crying again. Rachel takes off the backpack and sets it on the step. The afternoon sun is low, the sky gray and fuzzy like a sweater. Her head hurts and she's hungry. Also, Peter is really annoying her. "I want my mother," he says.

"Well, I want my mother too," Rachel says. "But that doesn't help. She's dead, okay? She's dead."

"My mom's dead?" Peter screams, so loud that Rachel has to cover her ears with her hands. That's when Mrs. Williamson comes running up the sidewalk. Peter doesn't even see her at first because he's so hysterical. Mrs. Williamson runs to Peter. She sits down beside him, says his name, and touches him on the shoulder. He looks up and shouts, "Mom!" He wraps his arms around her, saying over and over again, "You're not dead." Rachel resists the temptation to look down the sidewalk to see if her own mother is coming. She knows she is not.

They walk back to the Williamsons' house together. Rachel, trying not to drag her backpack, follows. "I'm sorry," she hears Mrs. Williamson say. "I had a doctor's appointment and I got caught in traffic. I tried to call the school, but I was too late, and then I tried to find someone to come to the house, but no one was home."

Peter says something to Mrs. Williamson. She can't hear him and she leans over so he can whisper in her ear. Rachel stands behind them, watching. Mrs. Williamson turns and stares at Rachel. "Did you tell him I was dead?" she asks.

Rachel shakes her head no, but she can tell Mrs. Williamson doesn't believe her.

"When the Pilgrims came to America they wanted to live in a place where they could practice their religion. They were trying to be good people. So when they saw someone doing something they thought was bad, they wanted to stop it. Bad meant the devil to them. They didn't want to be around the devil. They wanted to be around God." Miss Engstrom stands at the front of the room dressed as a Puritan. She puts the Puritan dress on every day for Social Studies. Her cheeks are pink and her hair is sticking to her face. She is trying to help them understand what happened, she says, but Cindi Becker has said, more than once, that her mom doesn't want Miss Engstrom teaching them religion. "It's not religion," Miss Engstrom says, "it's History."

Every day Miss Engstrom puts on the Pilgrim dress and pretends she's a Puritan. The children are supposed to pretend they are witches. "Act natural," she tells them. "Just be yourselves." But when they do, they get in trouble; they have to stand in the stockade or go to the jail in the back of the room. The stockade is made out of cardboard, and the jail is just chairs in a circle. Rachel hates to be put in either place. By the fourth lesson, she has figured out how to sit at her desk with her hands neatly folded. When Miss Engstrom asks Rachel what she is doing, she says, "Praying" and Miss Engstrom tells her what a good Puritan she is. By the sixth lesson the class is filled with good Puritans, sitting with neatly folded hands. Only Charlie Dexter is stuck in the stockade and Cindi Becker is in the jail in the back of the room. Miss Engstrom says that they are probably witches. Rachel decides that Social Studies is her favorite subject. She looks forward to the next lesson. What will happen to the witches when they go on trial? But the next day they have a substitute and the day after that, another. They have so many substitutes Rachel can't remember their names. One day, one of the substitutes tells the class that she is their new teacher.

"What happened to Miss Engstrom?" Rachel asks.

"My mother had her fired," says Cindi Becker.

"She's not coming back," the teacher says. "Now, let's talk about Thanksgiving."

Rachel is so excited about Thanksgiving she can't stand it. A whole turkey! Think of the bones! Each night Rachel rearranges her bone collection. It is a difficult time of year for it. Cats still wander the crooked streets of Stone but they are either eating everything they kill, or killing less, because there are few bones to be found. Rachel arranges and rearranges, trying to form the shape that will dance for her. Damn that Melinda, Rachel thinks. What would happen if Rachel had bones like that in her collection? Human bones?

Rachel has a fit when her father tells her they are going to the Williamsons' house for Thanksgiving. "This will be better," he says. "You can play with Peter and his cousins. Don't you think it would be lonely with just you and me at our house?"

"The bones!" Rachel cries. "I want the bones!"

"What are you talking about?" her father asks.

Rachel sniffs. "I want the turkey bones."

Rachel's father stares at her. He is cutting an apple and he stands, holding the knife, staring at her.

"You know, for my project."

"Are you still doing that, now that Miss Engstrom is gone?"

Rachel nods. Her father says, "Well, we can make a turkey. But not on Thursday. On Thursday we're going to the Williamsons'."

The night before Thanksgiving though, her father gets a phone call. He says, "Oh, I am so sorry." And, "No, no please don't even worry about us." He nods his head a lot. "Please know you are in our prayers. Let us know if we can do anything." After he hangs up the phone he sits in his chair and stares at the TV screen. Finally, he says, "It looks like you got your wish."

He looks at his watch, and then, all in a hurry, they drive to the grocery store, where he buys a turkey, bags of stuffing, and pumpkin pie. He throws the food into the cart. Rachel can tell that he is angry but she doesn't ask him what's wrong. She'd rather not know. Besides, she has other stuff to worry about. Like is there a bad man in this store? Will he shoot them the way he shot her mother?

When they get home her father says, "Mrs. Williamson lost the baby."

"What baby?" Rachel asks.

"She was pregnant. But she lost it."

Rachel remembers, once, when Mrs. Williamson got angry at Peter when he came home from school without his sweater. "You can't be so careless all the time," Rachel remembers her saying.

"Well, she shouldn't be so careless," Rachel says.

"Rachel, you have to start learning to think about other people's feelings once in a while."

Rachel thinks about the lost baby, out in the dark somewhere. "Mrs. Williamson is stupid," she says.

Rachel's father, holding a can of cranberry sauce with one hand, points toward her room with the other. "You go to your room," he says. "And think about what you're saying."

Rachel runs to her room. She slams the door shut. She throws herself on her bed and cries herself to sleep. When she wakes up there is no light shining under the door. She doesn't know what time it is, but she thinks it is very late. She gets up and begins collecting bones from all the hiding places; bones in her socks, bones in her underwear drawer, bones in a box under the bed, bones in her jewelry box, and bones in her stuffed animals, cut open with the scissors she's not supposed to use. She hums as she assembles and reassembles the bones until at last they quiver and shake. She thinks they are going to dance for her but instead, they stab her with their sharp little points.

"Stop it," Rachel says. She takes them apart again, stores them in separate places and goes to sleep, crying for her mother.

The next morning, Rachel watches the parade on TV while her father makes stuffing and cleans the turkey. When the phone rings, he brings it to Rachel, and turns the TV sound off. The Grandma asks her how school is going and how she likes living in Stone, and finally, how is she? Rachel answers each question, "Fine," while watching a silent band march across the TV. The Grandma asks to speak to her father again and Rachel goes to the kitchen. Her father reaches for the phone and says, "My God, Rachel, what happened to your arms?" Rachel looks down at her arms. There are small red spots and tiny bruises all over them.

"She has bruises all over her arms," her father says.

Rachel grabs a stick of celery and walks toward the living room. Her father follows, still holding the phone. "Rachel, what happened to your arms?"

Rachel turns and smiles at him. Ever since her mom died, her dad has been trying hard. Rachel knows this, and she knows that he doesn't know she knows this. But there are certain things he isn't very good at. Rachel is positive that if her mom were still alive, she wouldn't even have to ask what had happened, she'd know. Rachel feels sorry for her dad but she doesn't want to tell him about the bones. Look what happened when she barely even mentioned them to Melinda. So Rachel makes something up instead. "Miss Engstrom," she says.

"What are you talking about? Miss Engstrom? She isn't even your teacher anymore."

Rachel only smiles, sweetly, at her father. He repeats what she told him, into the phone. Rachel walks into the living room. She wraps herself in the red throw and sits in front of the TV, watching the balloon man fill up the screen as she munches on celery. How many bones does it take, anyway? Miss Engstrom never did answer her question.

Later, when the doorbell rings, her father shouts, "I'll get it," which is sort of strange because she is never allowed to answer the door. She hears voices and then her father comes into the room with a policeman and a policewoman. Rachel thinks they've come to arrest her. She's a liar, a thief, and a murderer, so it had to happen. Still, she feels like crying now that it has.

Her father has been talking to her, she realizes, but she has no idea what he's said. He turns the sound off the TV and he and the policeman walk out of the room together. The policewoman stays with Rachel. She sits right next to Rachel on the couch. For a while they watch the silent parade, until the policewoman says, "Can you tell me what happened to your arms, Rachel?"

"I already told my dad," Rachel says.

The policewoman nods. "The thing is, I just want to make sure he didn't leave anything out."

"I don't want to get in trouble."

"You're not in trouble. We are here to help. Okay, honey? Can I see your arms?"

Rachel shakes her head, no.

The policewoman nods. "Who hurt you, Rachel?"

Rachel turns to look at her. She has blond hair and brown eyes with yellow flecks in them. She looks at Rachel very closely. As if she knows the truth about her.

"You can tell me," she says.

"The bones," Rachel whispers.

"What about the bones?"

"But you can't tell anyone."

"I might have to tell someone," the policewoman says.

So Rachel refuses to speak further. She shows the lady her arms, but only because she figures it will make her go away, and it does. After she looks at Rachel's arms the policewoman goes out in the kitchen with her dad and the policeman. Rachel turns up the volume. Jessica Simpson, dressed in white fur, like a kitten without the whiskers, is singing. Her voice fills up the room, but Rachel can still hear the murmuring sound of the grownups talking in the kitchen. Then the door opens and closes and she hears her father saying good-bye. Rachel's father comes and stands in the room, watching her. He doesn't say anything and Rachel doesn't either but later, when they are eating turkey together he says, "You might still be just a little girl but you can get grownups in a lot of trouble by telling lies."

Rachel nods. She knows this. Miss Engstrom taught them all about the history of witches. Rachel chews the turkey leg clean. It was huge and she is quite full, but now she has a turkey leg, almost as big as a human bone, to add to her collection. She sets it on her napkin next to her plate. As if he can read her mind her father says, "Rachel, no more bones."

"What?"

"Your bone collection. It's done. Over. Find something else to collect. Seashells. Buttons. Barbie dolls. No more bones."

Rachel knows better than to argue. Instead, she asks to be excused. Her father doesn't even look at her; he just nods. Rachel goes to her bedroom and searches through the mess of clothes in the wicker chair until she finds her Halloween costume. When her father comes to tell her it's time for bed, he says, "You can wear that one last time but then we're putting it away until next year."

"Can I sleep in it?" Rachel asks.

Her father shrugs. "Sure, why not?" He smiles, but it is a pretend smile. Rachel smiles a pretend smile back. She crawls into bed, dressed like a pretend witch. Her father kisses her on the forehead and turns out the light. Rachel lies there until she counts to a hundred and then she sits up. She gathers the bones, whispering in the dark.

A few days later, the witch costume has been packed away, the first dusting of snow has sprinkled the crooked streets and picket fences of Stone, and Rachel has forgotten all about how angry she was at her father. Since Mrs. Williamson lost the baby, she no longer watches Rachel. Rachel thinks this is a good idea because she doesn't feel safe with Mrs. Williamson, but she hates being in school all day. All the other children have been picked up from the after school program and it's just Rachel and Miss Carrie who keep looking out the school window, saying, "Boy, your dad sure is late."

Rachel sits at the play table, making a design with the purple, blue, green, and yellow plastic shapes. She is good at putting things together and Miss Carrie compliments her work. Rachel remembers putting the spell on her father and she regrets it. She pretends the shapes are bones, she puts them together and then she takes them apart, she whispers, trying to say the words backward, but it is hard to do and Miss Carrie, who isn't a real grownup at all, but a high school girl like Melinda, says, "Uh, you're starting to creep me out."

Miss Carrie calls her mother, using the purple cell phone she carries in the special cell phone pocket of her jeans. "I don't know what to do," she says. "Rachel is still here. Her dad is really late. Hey, Rache, what's your last name again?" Rachel tells Carrie and Carrie tells her mom. Just then, Mrs. Williamson arrives. She is wearing a raincoat, even though it isn't raining, and her hair is a mess. She tells Carrie that she is taking Rachel home. Rachel doesn't want to go with Mrs. Williamson, the baby loser, but Carrie says, "Oh, great," to Mrs. Williamson and then says into the phone, "Never mind, someone finally came to pick her up." She is still talking to her mother when Rachel leaves with Mrs. Williamson who doesn't say anything until they are in the car.

"Peter told me what you said, Rachel, about how I should have had an abortion, and I want you to know, that sort of talk is not allowed in our house. I really don't even want you playing with Peter anymore. Not one word about abortion or dead mothers or anything else you have up your sleeve, do you understand?"

Rachel nods. She is looking out the window at a house decorated with tiny white icicle lights hanging over the windows. "Where's my dad?" she asks.

Mrs. Williamson sighs, "He's been delayed."

Rachel is afraid to ask what that means. When they get to the Williamsons' house, Mrs. Williamson pretends to be nice. She asks Rachel if her book bag is too heavy and offers to carry it. Rachel shakes her head. She is afraid to say anything for fear that it will be the wrong thing. There is a big wreath on the back door of the Williamsons' house and it has a bell on it that rings when they go inside. Mr. Williamson and Peter are eating at the kitchen table. The house is deliciously warm but it smells strange.

Mrs. Williamson takes off her raincoat and hangs it from a peg in the wall. Rachel drops her book bag below the coats, and stands there until Mrs. Williamson tells her to hang up her coat and sit at the table.

When Rachel sits down Mr. Williamson points a chicken leg at her and says, "Now listen here, young lady—" but Mrs. Williamson interrupts him.

"I already talked to her," she says.

Rachel is mashing her peas into her potatoes when her father arrives. He thanks Mr. and Mrs. Williamson and he says, "How you doing?" to Peter though Peter doesn't answer. Mrs. Williamson invites him to stay for dinner but he says thank you, he can't. Rachel leaves her plate on the table and no one tells her to clear it. She puts on her coat. Her father picks up her backpack. He thanks the Williamsons again and then taps Rachel's shoulder. Hard.

"Thank you," Rachel says.

They walk out to the car together, their shoes squeaking on the snow. The Williamsons' house is decorated with white lights; the neighbors have colored lights and two big plastic snowmen with frozen grins and strange eyes on their front porch.

"What did you say to that policewoman?" Rachel's father asks.

He isn't looking at Rachel. He is staring out the window, the way he does when he is driving in Boston.

"Miss Engstrom didn't do it," she says.

"They seem to think I hurt you, do you understand—" He doesn't finish what he is saying. He pulls into their driveway, but instead of getting out of the car to open the garage door, he sits there. "Just tell the truth, Rachel, okay? Just tell the truth. You know what that is, don't you?"

"I did," Rachel says. She feels like crying and also, she thinks she might throw up.

"Who did that to you, then? Who did that to your arms?"

"The bones."

"The bones?"

Rachel nods.

"What bones?"

"You know."

Her father makes a strange noise. He is bent over, and his eyes are shut. Praying, Rachel thinks. The car is still running. Rachel looks out the window. She cranes her neck so she can see the Sheekles' yard. They have it decorated with six reindeer made out of white lights. The car door slams. Rachel watches her father open the garage door. She watches him walk back to the car, lit by the headlights, his neck bent as if he is looking for something very important that he has lost.

"Dad?" Rachel says when he gets back in the car. "Are you mad?"

He shakes his head. He eases the car into the garage, turns off the ignition. They walk to the house together. When they get inside, he says, "Okay, I want all of them."

"All of what?" Rachel says, though she thinks she knows.

"That bone collection of yours. I want it."

"No, Dad."

He shakes his head. He stands there in his best winter coat, his gloves still on, shaking his head. "Rachel, why would you want to keep them, if they are hurting you?"

It's a good question. Rachel has to think for a moment before she answers. "Not all the time," she says. "Mostly they don't. They used to be my friend."

"The bones?"

Rachel nods.

"The bones used to be your friend?"

"Jack," she says.

He doesn't look at her. He is angry! He lied when he said he wasn't.

"Rachel," he says, softly, "honey? Let's get the bones. Okay? Let's put them away . . . where they can't . . . bones aren't . . . Jesus Christ." He slams his fist on the kitchen table. Rachel jumps. He covers his face with his hands. "Jesus Christ, Marla," he says.

Marla is Rachel's mother's name.

Rachel isn't sure what to do. She takes off her hat and coat. Then she walks into her bedroom and begins gathering the bones. After a while she realizes her father is standing in the doorway, watching.

Rachel hands her father all the bones. "Be careful," she says, "They killed Melinda." He doesn't say anything. That night he forgets to tell Rachel when to go to sleep. She changes into her pajamas, crawls into bed, and waits but he forgets to kiss her. He sits in the living room, making phone calls. The words drift into Rachel's room, "bones, mother murdered, lies, problems in school." Rachel thinks about Christmas. What will she get this year? Will she get a new Barbie? Will she get anything? Or has she been a bad girl? Will someone kill her father? Will Mrs. Williamson come to take care of her, and then lose her the way she lost the baby? Will Santa Claus save her? Will God? Will anyone? Will they get white lights for their tree or colored? Every year they switch but Rachel can't remember what they had last year. Rachel hopes it's a colored light year, because she likes the colored lights best. The last thing she hears before she falls asleep is her father's distant voice. "Bones," he says. "Yes that's right, bones."

The next morning, Rachel's father tells her she isn't going to school. She's going with him to Boston. "I made an appointment for you, okay, honey? I think you need a woman to talk to. So I made an appointment with Dr. Trentwerth."

Rachel is happy not to go to school with the nasty children of Stone. She is happy not to have to sit in the classroom and listen to Mrs. Fizzure who never dresses like a Puritan and doesn't put anyone in the stockade or jail. Rachel is happy to go to Boston. They listen to Christmas music the whole way there. Rachel's appointment isn't until ten o'clock, so she has to sit in her dad's office and be very quiet while he does his work. He gives her paper and pens and she draws pictures of Christmas trees and ghosts while she waits. When it's time to go to her appointment, her father looks at her pictures and says, "These are very nice, Rachel." Rachel actually thinks they are sort of scary though she didn't draw the ghosts the way a kindergartner would, all squiggly lines and black spot eyes. She made them the way they really are, a lady smiling next to a Christmas tree, a baby asleep on a floor, a cat grinning.

Dr. Trentwerth has a long gray braid that snakes down the side of her neck. She's wearing an orange sweater and black pants. Her earrings are triangles of tiny gold bells. She says hello to Rachel's father but she doesn't shake his hand. She shakes Rachel's hand, as if she might be someone important. They leave her father sitting on the couch looking at a magazine.

Rachel is disappointed by the doctor's office. There are little kid toys everywhere. A stuffed giraffe, a dollhouse, blocks, trucks, and baby dolls with pink baby bottles. Rachel doesn't know what she's supposed to do. "Be polite," she remembers her father telling her.

"You have a nice room," Rachel says. "Would you like some tea?" the doctor asks. "Or hot cocoa?" Rachel walks past all the baby toys and sits in the chair by the window. "Cocoa please," she says. Dr. Trentwerth turns the electric teakettle on. "Your father tells me you've been having some trouble with your bone collection," she says. "He doesn't believe me." "He said the bones hurt you." Rachel nods. Shrugs. "But not all the time. Like I said. Just once." The doctor tears open a packet of hot cocoa, which she empties into a plain white mug. She pours the water into it. "Let's just let that sit for a while," she says. "It's very hot. Whose bones hurt you, Rachel?"

Rachel sighs. "Cat bones, mice bones, chicken bones, you know."

Dr. Trentwerth nods. "Your father says you moved to Stone after your mother died. What was that like?"

"We were both really sad, me and Dad. Everyone was. We got a lot of flowers." Dr. Trentwerth hands the mug to Rachel. "Careful, it's still hot." Dr. Trentwerth is right. It is hot. Rachel brings it toward her mouth but it is too hot. She sets it, carefully, on the table next to the chair. "Tell me about where you live," the doctor says as she sits down across from Rachel.

"Well, everyone is a witch," Rachel says. "Okay, not everyone, but almost everyone and one time, a long time ago, there was a woman there named Wilmot Redd and some people came and took her away 'cause they said all witches had to die. They hung her and no one did anything about it. Miss Engstrom, she was my teacher, got taken away too, and Melinda, my baby-sitter, died, but that's because she stole the bones and now my father has them and I don't want him to die but he probably will. Mrs. Williamson is this lady who sometimes takes care of me and she looks real nice but she loses babies and she lost one and no one even is looking for it. If my mom was still alive she would rescue me."

"And the bones?"

"They used to keep me company at night."

"Where would you be when the bones kept you company, Rachel?"

"In my room."

"In your bedroom?"

"Mmhhm."

"I see."

"But then they stopped being nice and started hurting me."

"Whose bones, Rachel?"

"My dad has them now."

"Where did your dad's bones hurt you?"

"They were still mine then."

"Where did the bones hurt you, Rachel?"

"On my body."

"Where on your body?"

Suddenly, Rachel has a bad feeling. How does she know Dr. Trentwerth isn't one of them too? Rachel reaches for her mug and sips the hot cocoa. Dr. Trentwerth sits there, watching.

The moon is not a bone. Rachel knows this, but when the moon stares down at her, like an eye socket, Rachel wonders if she is just a small insect rattling around inside a giant skull. She knows this isn't true. She's not a baby, after all. She knows this isn't how reality works, but she can't help herself. Sometimes she imagines flying up to the moon, and climbing right through that hole to find everyone she's ever lost on the other side. She doesn't care about Melinda but she cares a lot about her mom and dad.

Rachel no longer lives in Stone and she no longer lives with her father. A lady and two policemen came to school one day and took Rachel away. She was cutting paper snowflakes at the time, and little bits of paper fluttered from her clothes as they walked to the car. Now Rachel lives with the Freemans. Big plastic candy canes line the walk up to the Freemans' front porch, which is decorated with blinking colored lights. A wreath with tiny gift-wrapped packages glued to it hangs on the front door. (But there are no gifts inside, Rachel checked.) The house smells sweet with the scent of holiday candles. Mrs. Freeman tells Rachel to be careful around the candles and not to bother Mr. Freeman when he is watching TV, which is most of the time.

Rachel's bedroom is in the back of the house. It has green itchy carpet and two twin beds and a dresser that is mostly blue, with some patches of yellow and lime green, as though someone started to paint it and then gave up on the project. The curtains on Rachel's window are faded tiny blue flowers with yellow centers and they are Rachel's favorite things in the room. Lying in her bed, Rachel can look out the window at the moon and imagine crawling right out of her world into a better one.

On the first night, Mrs. Freeman came into the bedroom and held Rachel while she cried and told her things would get better. In the morning, Mr. Freeman drove Rachel to school. He walked with a limp and he burped a lot, but before he left her in the school office he told her she was a brave girl and everything was going to be better soon.

"The Freemans are nice," the lady who took Rachel away from Stone told her. "Mrs. Freeman was once in the same situation you are in. She understands just what you're going through. And Mr. Freeman is a retired police officer. He got shot a few years ago. You're lucky to go there."

But Rachel didn't feel like a lucky girl, even when the Freemans took her to the Christmas tree lot and let her choose their tree, or when Mrs. Freeman put lotion on Rachel's chapped hands, or when they took her to an attorney's office, a very important woman who acted as if everything Rachel said mattered.

Rachel doesn't feel lucky until the day Mr. Freeman says, "Rachel, the lawyers think you should go back and live with your father." Mrs. Freeman cries and says, "Tomorrow's Christmas Eve, how can they do this?"

But Rachel is so happy she almost pees in her pants. When the lady comes to pick Rachel up, Mrs. Freeman says, "I have half a mind not to let you take her."

But Mr. Freeman says, "Rachel, get your suitcase." Mrs. Freeman hugs Rachel so tightly that for a second she is afraid she really isn't going to let her go, but then she does.

The lady who waits for Rachel says, "This isn't my fault. This is hard for all of us."

"It's hardest for her," Mrs. Freeman says and after that, Rachel doesn't hear the rest.

Down the street the Mauley kids are building a snowman. "I hate you, George Mauley," Rachel screams at the top of her lungs.

"What did you do that for?" the lady asks. "Get in the car."

But Rachel has no idea why she did it. As they drive past the Mauley children, Rachel turns her face toward the window, so her back is to the lady. She sticks her tongue out at George Mauley but he is busy putting stones in the snowman's eyes and doesn't notice.

"I want you to know, you are not alone," the woman says. "Maybe things didn't work out this time, but we are watching. You just keep telling the truth, Rachel, and I promise you things will get better."

It starts snowing. Not a lot, just tiny flakes fluttering down the white sky. Rachel remembers the snowflake she had been cutting when the lady took her away from Stone. What happened to her snowflake?

"Here we are then," the lady says. "Don't forget your suitcase." They walk into a big restaurant with orange booths along the wall and tiny Christmas trees on the tables. The waitresses wear brown dresses with white aprons and little half-circle hats that look like miniature spaceships crashed into all their heads. A woman is standing in one of the booths, waving and calling Rachel's name. The lady walks toward her. Rachel follows.

The woman wraps her arms around Rachel. She smells like soap. When she lets go of Rachel, she doesn't stand up but stays at Rachel's level, staring at her. Pink lipstick is smeared above her lips so she looks a little bit like she has three lips. Her eyebrows are drawn high on her forehead, beneath curls that are a strange shade of pink and orange, and she wears poinsettia earrings. "You remember me, don't you, honey?" she says. Then she looks up at the lady and frowns. "You can go now." She pulls Rachel close; together they pivot away from the lady. "Here, let me take that." She leans over and takes Rachel's suitcase. Rachel looks over her shoulder at the lady who is already walking away. "You don't remember me, do you? It's me. Grandma."

"Where's Dad?"

The Grandma sighs. "Are you hungry?" She guides Rachel into the booth and then slides in across from her. "This has all been expensive, you know. The lawyers and everything. He's at work. But he'll be home by the time we get there. Do you want a hamburger? A chocolate shake? What did you say to those people? Okay, I promised I wouldn't talk about it. Don't touch the little tree, Rachel, can't you just sit still for five minutes? It's just for looking."

Rachel's stomach feels funny. "Can I have an egg?"

"An egg? What kind of egg? Don't you want a hamburger?"

Rachel shakes her head. She starts to cry.

"Don't cry," the Grandma says. "It's over, all right? If you want an egg, you can have an egg. Were the people mean to you, Rachel? Did anyone hurt you?"

"Fried, please," Rachel says. "And can I have toast?"

"You can tell me, you know," the Grandma says. "Did anything happen to you while you were gone? Did anyone touch you in a bad way?"

Rachel is tired of the questions about bad touch. She is tired of grownups. Also she is cold. She just looks at the Grandma and after a while the Grandma says, "We decorated the tree last night. Your father hadn't even bought one yet. But don't worry; I set him straight about that. After everything you've been through! Well, he just wasn't thinking clearly. He's been through a lot too. Blue Spruce. It looks real nice."

The waitress comes and the Grandma orders a fried egg and toast for Rachel and the fish platter for herself. The waitress says, "Rachel?"

Miss Engstrom! Dressed as a waitress!

"Do you know each other?" the Grandma says.

"I used to be Rachel's teacher," Miss Engstrom says.

"In Boston?" asks the Grandma.

Miss Engstrom shakes her head, "No, in Stone. How are you, Rachel? Are you having a good holiday? Do you like your new teacher?"

"Wait, I know who you are. I know all about you."

"I wish you would come back," Rachel says.

"I forbid you to speak to my granddaughter, do you hear me? Where's the manager?"

Miss Engstrom's face does something strange, it sort of collapses, like an old Jack o' Lantern, but she shakes her head and everything goes back to normal. She smiles a fake smile at Rachel and walks away. The Grandma says, "She's the one who hurt you, isn't she? Where's that social worker when you need her? Why didn't you tell them about her, Rachel? Could you just tell me that?"

"Miss Engstrom never hurt me," Rachel says. "She was nice."

"Nice? She left bruises on your arms, Rachel."

Rachel sighs. She is sooo tired of stupid grownups and their stupid questions. "I told everyone," she says, "it wasn't her. It wasn't my dad, okay? It was the bones that did it."

"What bones? What are you talking about?"

But Rachel doesn't answer. She's learned a thing or two about answering adults' questions. Instead, she picks up the saltshaker and salts the table. The Grandmother grabs the shaker. "Just sit and wait for your egg," she says. "Maybe you could use this time to think about what you've done."

Rachel folds her hands neatly in front of her, just as she learned to do in Miss Engstrom's class. She is still sitting like that when Miss Engstrom returns with their order.

"You can eat now, Rachel," the Grandmother says. Rachel unfolds her hands and cuts her egg. The yellow yolk breaks open and smears across her plate. She can feel both Miss Engstrom and the Grandmother watching, but she pretends not to notice. The music is "Frosty the Snowman." Rachel eats her egg and hums along.

"Stop humming," says the Grandma, then, to Miss Engstrom, "You can go. We don't want anything else."

Miss Engstrom touches Rachel's head, softly. Rachel looks up at Miss

Engstrom and sees that she is crying. Miss Engstrom nods at Rachel, one quick nod, as if they have agreed on something, then she sets the bill down on the table and walks away.

"Your father will be happy to see you," the Grandmother says. "Eat your egg. We've still got a long drive ahead of us."

Rachel's father does act happy to see her. He says, "I am so happy you are home," but he hugs her as if she is covered in mud and he doesn't want to get his clothes dirty.

The Christmas tree is already decorated. Rachel stares at it and the Grandma says, "Do you like it? We did it last night to surprise you." It is lit with tiny white lights, and oddly decorated with gold and white balls.

"Where are our ornaments?" Rachel asks.

"We decided to do something different this year," the Grandma says. "Don't you just love white and gold?"

Rachel doesn't know what to say. Clearly she is not expected to tell the truth.

"Why don't you go unpack," the Grandma says, nodding at the suitcase. "Make yourself at home," she laughs.

Rachel is surprised, when she enters her bedroom, to discover that her bed is gone, replaced by two twin beds, just like at the Freemans'. One bed is covered with Rachel's old stuffed animals; they stare at her with their black eyes. She assumes this is her bed. Rachel inspects the animals and discovers that the ones she had cut open and stuffed with bones have been sewn shut, all except her white bear and he is missing. The other bed is covered with a pink lacy spread and several fat pillows. Next to it is a small table with a lamp, a glass of water, a few wadded tissues, and a stack of books.

"Surprise!" the Grandma says. "We're roomies now. Isn't this fun?"

Rachel nods. Apparently this is the right thing to do. The Grandma lifts the suitcase onto Rachel's bed. "Now, let's unpack your things and we can just forget about your little adventure and get on with our lives." The Grandma begins unpacking Rachel's suitcase, refolding the clothes before she puts them in the dresser. "Didn't anyone there help you with your clothes?" she says, frowning.

Rachel shrugs.

The Grandma closes the suitcase, clasps it shut, and puts it in the closet, right next to a set of plaid luggage. "Do you want a cookie? How about a gingerbread man? I've been baking up a storm, let me tell you."

Rachel follows the Grandma into the kitchen. Baking up a storm? she thinks. Maybe the Grandma is a witch; that would explain a lot. Her father is in the kitchen, talking on the phone, but when he sees her, he stops. He smiles at her, with the new smile of his and then he says, "She just walked into the kitchen. Can I call you back?" The Grandma is talking at the same time, something about chocolate chip eyes. Rachel's father says, "I love you too," softly, into the phone but Rachel stares at him in shock. Is he talking to her mother? Rachel knows that doesn't make sense. She's not a baby, after all, but who is he talking to?

"Here," the Grandma says, "choose."

Rachel looks down into the cookie tin the Grandma has thrust before her. Gingerbread men lie there with chocolate chip eyes and wrinkled red mouths. ("Dried cranberry," the Grandma says.) Rachel chooses the one at the top and immediately begins eating his face. Her father sits across from her and shakes his head when the Grandma thrusts the tin toward him. "I missed you," he says.

The gingerbread man is spicy but the eyes and nose are sweet. Rachel doesn't care for the mouth but that part is gone fast enough.

"Your grandmother has been nice enough to come here to live with us."

The Grandmother sets a glass of milk down in front of Rachel. "Oh, I was ready for a change. Who needs Milwaukee?"

Rachel doesn't know what to say about any of it. She chews her gingerbread man and drinks her milk. Her father and the Grandma seem to have run out of ideas as well. They simply watch her eat. When she's finished, she yawns and the Grandmother says, "Time for bed."

Rachel looks at her father, expecting him to do something. Just because she yawned doesn't mean she's ready for bed! But her father isn't any help.

"Say good night," the Grandma says.

"Good night," says Rachel. She gets up, pushes the chair in, and rinses her glass. The Grandma follows her into the bedroom. She stays there the whole time Rachel is getting undressed. Rachel feels embarrassed but she doesn't know what else to do, so she pretends she doesn't mind the Grandma sitting on her bed talking about how much fun it's going to be to share the room. "Every night just like a slumber party," she says. After Rachel goes to the bathroom, brushes her teeth, and washes her face and hands, the Grandma tells her to kneel by her bed. The Grandma, complaining the whole time about how difficult it is, kneels down beside her.

"Lord," she says. "Please help Rachel understand right from wrong, reality from imagination, truth from lies and all that. Thank you for sending her home. Do you have anything to add? Rachel?"

Rachel can't think of anything to say. She shakes her head. The Grandma makes a lot of noise as she stands up again.

Rachel crawls into bed and the Grandma tucks the covers tight. So tight that Rachel feels like she can't breathe, then the Grandma kisses Rachel's forehead and turns out the light. Rachel waits, for a long time, for her father to come in to kiss her good night but he never does.

It is very dark when Rachel wakes up. The room is dark and there is no light shining under the door. It takes a moment for Rachel to realize why she's woken up. A soft rustling sound is coming from the closet.

"Grandma?" Rachel whispers, and then, louder, "Grandma?"

The Grandma wakes up, sputtering, "Marla? Is that you?"

"No. It's me, Rachel. Do you hear that noise?"

They listen for a while. It seems, to Rachel, a very long time and she is just starting to worry that the Grandma will think she is lying when the rustling starts again.

"We've got a mouse," the Grandma says. "Don't worry, I have a feeling Santa Claus might bring you a cat this year."

Very soon the Grandma is snoring in her bed. The rustling sound stops and then, just as Rachel is falling asleep, starts again. Rachel stares into the dark with burning eyes. It doesn't matter what the grownups do, she realizes, she's not safe anywhere.

Carefully, Rachel feels around in the dark for her bunny slippers. She picks up a shoe by mistake, and is startled by how large it is until she realizes it must belong to the Grandmother. She sets it down and picks up first one slipper, and then the other.

Her bunny slippers on, Rachel tiptoes out of the bedroom into the hallway, which is softly lit by the white glow of the Sheekles' Christmas-light reindeer. Rachel isn't sleepwalking, she is completely awake, but she feels strange, as though somehow she is both entirely awake and asleep at the same time. Rachel feels like she hears a voice calling from a great distance. But she isn't hearing it with her ears; it's more like a feeling inside, a feeling inside and outside of herself too. This doesn't make sense, Rachel knows, but this is what is happening. Maybe the grownups aren't right about anything, about what is real, or what is possible.

When she walks outside, the bitter cold hits Rachel hard. But she does not go back to her warm bed, instead she walks in the deadly dark of

Stone, lit by occasional Christmas lights, and the few cars from which she hides, all the way to Old Burial Hill where the graves stand in the oddly blue snow, marking the dead who once lived there.

Rachel isn't afraid. She lies down. It is cold. Well, of course it is. She shivers, staring up at the stars, which, come to think of it, look like chips of bones. Maybe the skull she's been trapped in has been smashed open by some giant child who is, even now, searching through the pieces, hoping to find her. She closes her eyes.

"No, no. Not your bones. You've misunderstood everything."

Rachel opens her eyes. Standing before her is the old woman.

"Get up. Stamp your feet."

Rachel just lies there so the woman pulls her up.

"Are you a witch?" Rachel asks.

"Clap your hands and stamp your feet."

"Are you real?"

But the old woman is gone and Rachel's father is running toward her. "What are you doing here?" he says. "Rachel, what is happening to you?"

He wraps her tight in his arms and picks her up. One of her bunny slippers falls from her foot and lands softly on the snow-covered grave but he doesn't notice. He is running down the hill. Rachel, bouncing in his arms, watches the bunny slipper get smaller and smaller. She holds her father tight.

The Grandma is waiting for them in the kitchen where she is heating milk on the stove. She has on a flowered robe; her pinky-red hair, sparkling in the light, circles her face like a clown.

"She was in the graveyard," Rachel's father says.

The Grandma touches Rachel's bare arm with her own icy fingers. "Get a blanket. She's chilled to the bone."

Rachel's father sets her on the kitchen chair. He gently pries her fingers from around his neck. "I'll be right back," he says. "You have to let me go."

Rachel watches the doorway until he returns, carrying the white comforter from his bed. He wraps Rachel in it ("like a sausage," he used to say in happier times) then sits down with her on his lap.

Rachel's father kisses her head. She starts to feel warm. "Rachel," her father says, "never do that again. We'll visit your mother's grave in Boston more often, if that's what you want, but don't just leave in the middle of the night. Don't scare us like that."

Rachel nods. The Grandmother hands her a Santa Claus-face mug of hot chocolate, and sets another on the table in front of Rachel's father.

Rachel sips her hot chocolate, gives the Grandma a close look.

"Good, isn't it?" the Grandma says.

Rachel nods.

"Milk. That's the secret ingredient. None of that watery stuff."

The Grandmother sets the tin of gingerbread men on the table and Rachel reaches for one, teetering on her father's lap. He hands her a gingerbread man and takes one for himself.

"Well, it's a good thing you didn't fall asleep out there," the Grandma says.

Rachel swallows the gingerbread foot. "I started to but someone woke me up. I think it was that witch, Wilmot Redd. She found me and she made me stand up. She told me she didn't want my bones."

Rachel's father and the Grandmother look at each other. Rachel stops chewing and stares straight ahead, waiting to see if her father will make her get off his lap or if the Grandma will call the lady to come and take her away again.

"Rachel, Wilmot Redd was just some old lady. A fisherman's wife," Rachel's father says, gently.

The Grandma sits down at the kitchen table. She looks at Rachel so hard that Rachel finally has to look back at her. The Grandma's face is extraordinarily white and Rachel thinks it looks just a little bit like a paper snowflake.

"I think I know who it might have been," she says, "Have you ever heard of La Befana? She's an old woman. Much older than me. And scary looking. Ugly. She carries around a big old sack filled with gifts that she gives to children. A long time ago the three wise men stopped by her house to get directions to Bethlehem, to see the Christ Child, you know. And after she gave them directions they invited her along but she didn't go with them 'cause she had too much housework to do. Of course she immediately regretted being so stupid and she's been trying to catch up ever since, so she goes around giving gifts to all the children just in case one of them is the Savior she neglected to visit, all those years ago, just 'cause she had dirty laundry to take care of. I bet that's who helped you tonight. Old La Befana herself." The Grandmother turns to look at Rachel's father. "It's about time this family had some luck, right? And what could be luckier than to be part of a real live Christmas miracle?"

Rachel's father hugs her and says, "Well, this little miracle better go to bed. Tomorrow is Christmas Eve, you don't want to sleep through it, do you?"

The Grandmother takes the mug of hot chocolate and the half-eaten gingerbread man from Rachel. Her father carries her to bed, tucks her in, and kisses her forehead. Rachel is falling asleep, listening to the faint murmuring voices of her father and the Grandmother, when she hears the noise. She goes to the closet, opens it, and sees right away, the Halloween treat bag in the corner, rustling as though the mouse is trapped inside. She is just about to shut the door when the small hand reaches out of the bag, grasps the paper edge, and another hand appears, and then, a tiny, bone head.

"Is that you?" Rachel whispers.

The bones don't answer. They just come walking toward her, their sharp points squeaking.

Rachel slams the closet door shut. She runs out of her room. The Grandma and her father are sitting next to the tree. When they turn to her, their faces are flicked with yellow, blue and green, they grin the wide skeletal grin of skulls. "Honey, is something the matter?" her father asks. Rachel shakes her head. "Are you sure? You look like you've seen—"

The Grandma interrupts, "Is it the mouse? Did you see the mouse?"

Rachel nods.

"Don't worry about it," the Grandma says, "Maybe Santa Claus will bring you a kitty this year."

Rachel refuses to go back to bed until her father and the Grandmother walk with her. They tuck her in, and again her father kisses her forehead, and the Grandma does the same, and then they leave her alone in the dark. After a while she hears the bones squeaking across the floor. Rachel feels around in the dark until she finds the Grandmother's big shoe. Rachel waits until she hears the squeaking start once more. When it does, she pounds where the sound comes from, and the first two times, she hits only the floor but the next five or six, she hears the breaking of bones, the small cries and curses. Her father and Grandmother run into the room and turn on the light. "Well, you killed it," the Grandma says, looking at her, strangely. "I'll go get the broom and dustpan."

Rachel's father doesn't say anything. They just stand there, looking at the mess on the floor, and then at the mess on the bottom of the Grandmother's shoe.

Later, after it's all cleaned up, Rachel crawls back into bed. She pulls the blankets to her chin, and rolls to her side. Her father and the Grandmother stand there for a while before they walk out of the room. For a long time Rachel listens in the dark but all she hears is her own breathing, and she falls asleep to the comforting sound.

When she wakes again it is Christmas Eve and snowing outside, glistening white flakes that tumble down the sky from the snow queen's garden, the Grandma says.

Because it is a special day the Grandma lets Rachel have gingerbread cookies and hot chocolate for breakfast on the couch while her father sleeps late. "He's worn out after everything you've been through," the Grandma says. Occasionally Rachel thinks she hears mewing from her father's room but the Grandma says, "Anyone can sound like a cat. It's probably just a sound he makes in his sleep. You, for instance, last night you were singing in your sleep."

"I was?" Rachel asks.

"Didn't anyone ever tell you that before? You sing in your sleep."

"I do?"

The Grandma nods. "You're a very strange little girl, you know," she says.

Rachel chews the gingerbread face and sighs.

"Now what do you suppose this is all about?"

The Grandma stands next to the Christmas tree, looking out the window. Rachel gets off the couch and squeezes between the Grandma and the tree. A gray cat meanders down the crooked sidewalk in front of the house. In its mouth it holds a limp mouse. Walking behind the cat is a straggling line of children in half-buttoned winter coats and loosely tied scarves, tiptoeing in boots and wet sneakers, not talking to each other or catching snowflakes on their tongues, only intently watching the cat with their bright eyes.

"Like the Pied Piper," the Grandma says.

Rachel shrugs and goes back to the couch. "It's just a bunch of the little kids," she says. "Who's the Pied Piper?"

The Grandma sighs. "Don't they teach you anything important these days?"

Rachel shakes her head.

"Well, it looks like I'll have to," the Grandma says.

And she does.

❄   ❄   ❄

Translated literally from the original Greek, the Gospel of Matthew relates how magi *(the plural of a word most commonly translated as* magician, *although the meaning would have also included practitioners of astrology, alchemy, and those with other forms of esoteric knowledge) from the rising [of the sun]—showed up in Jerusalem seeking a child who had been born King of the Jews. In Orson Scott Card's story we find—among other things—they may have come from* very *far away, indeed, and why they choose to make gifts of gold, frankincense, and myrrh.*

Wise Men

❄

Orson Scott Card

I got control of Lytrotis, a half-Greek adviser to King Herod of Judea, in the year 734 of the Roman Republic. It was the 27th year of the Peace of Augustus. It was the last year of Herod's life.

My control over Lytrotis was complete. He had thought I was a god, and that I would make him great—never guessing that the only power I had was the power to take control of his body, shunting him aside.

He discovered how I had lied to him within moments of my taking possession, but it was too late for him then. I was too strong for him, too experienced. He screamed with all his might, he wrestled with me day and night, and to me his screams were the bleating of a lamb, and his writhing was the fluttering of a moth.

Eloi, my enemy, had given poor Lytrotis what he had denied to me: a featherless biped body to dwell in, with all its pleasures and pains, with those clever little hands, with eyes that saw so clearly and yet saw nothing at all, and with a mouth to speak . . . so that lies could be told.

Lies! Ah, how sweet to tell lies again. During my time between bodies I felt like a prisoner, able to communicate only as we evyonim do in our bodiless state, showing memories to each other, utter truth, so that we stand exposed before each other, all our memories and motives known.

As I stood exposed before Eloi on that terrible day six thousand years before, when he cast us down into the Earth. The featherless bipeds had already spread themselves throughout the world, had already acquired the rudiments of language and the making of tools. They were ripe to be possessed by us, the evyonim, the massless wanderers through the darkness of spacetime, but Eloi had a plan to make these bipeds immortal, the bonds between beast and evyon permanent.

"They are not to be exploited," he said, "they are to be elevated. Your bodiless aeons are over. It is time for you to become like me, if you can—tied to the physical world again, yet masters of all things. If you can."

His plan was a foolish one. Full of chances for failure. The bodies were too delicious. Once we had tasted them, we would not want to let them go. Yet most of us would lose them. I had seen it before, hadn't I? On the world of the cherubim, the world of the seraphim, the world of the nagidim, the world of the yaminim—only a tiny fraction of the evyonim were able to keep the beast they rode, and all the rest were given a stunted, crippled, broken version . . . because that's all that Eloi thought that they deserved.

"This time," I said, "we will do it my way. I will not discard them the way you do. I will save them all."

How they rejoiced! But Eloi only looked at his beloved, his darling of darlings, his chosen one, his Beyn, he whose real name I am incapable of saying and whose face I am forbidden to see.

"I will live and die for them," he said. "I will save all who master the beasts and then live to serve the good of all."

"The weak, you mean," I said. "The ones who cower. When *I* have mastered my beast, I will not cower." I was so brave, and all who saw my courage were rapt with admiration.

In that moment the evyonim chose, and because we cannot lie, Eloi could sort us all at once. One-third of them were mine, two-thirds his. But even if nine-tenths had chosen me, he would have done the same, for the evyonim are nothing to him unless they grovel to him. He cast me down, and my one-third with him, and kept the rest as his darlings, and then he gave them beasts to ride, one by one as they were born.

But they were weak and I was strong. I took whatever beast I wanted. I could not expel the darlings whose beast I usurped—they remained there, watching me with terror and admiration as I rode the beast the way it was meant to be ridden. And when I was done with it, I discarded it—they could have the ruins of it for whatever days or weeks or years it might have left. They had seen what greatness could do with a featherless biped; their own life was pitiful by comparison.

Yet every beast I used, I knew I could not keep. The day would come when all his darlings had their beasts, and then he would bind them, the ones he chose: evyon to biped, inseparable, immortal, filled with irresistible power, and yet still the pitiful, cowering, subservient, rule-bound darling without a spark of self-will in it.

And I would have nothing.

One chance I had, and it was now. For I saw the preparations—they could not be hidden from me. The bodiless darlings who sang to the shepherds, unable to hide their joy. The baby that plunged into the world. I knew who it was inside the little beast. He was here to do what he had promised—live and die for them, and then rise with the power to make the beasts immortal and bind it to the evyon, so it was no more hungry, but filled now; not evyon but immortal and inseparable ish, beynim like the Beyn.

The despicable darlings.

But if he failed, then all of them were broken, all of them were lost.

When he cast me down everyone thought that I was finished. But he hasn't the power to destroy us. He can *deprive* us, cut us off, leave us hungering forever, but he cannot make us cease to exist, just as he can't create a single one of us. We can only be found and named, located and led, linked to beasts and thus empowered. We don't *belong* to him! We are not his *property!*

I was cast out, but I knew that when they all saw the failure of his plan—not just the evyonim, but all the ones he had made immortal, who carried out his orders—they would see that he was *wrong*.

It is the thing they will not bear, you see. They will not follow him then, if his plan fails. It all falls apart. Chaos is reborn out of his miserable, pinched-off order when they cease to trust in him.

And so I watched and waited all those centuries, until the time came at last. I watched the starships dart between the worlds, the convergence of the beynim. I saw how it all led to now, to here, to Judea, to the people he had fooled into thinking they were chosen but had really enslaved to his niggling laws and then abandoned.

I stood afar off, unable to look directly at the entry of the Beyn into this world. But I knew the nature of the beast.

A baby. Weak. Killable.

Now that Eloi was committed, there was no second chance. *This* was the only body that his beloved Beyn could ever bind with. If I killed it early, before it came into its power, then his darlings could never be bound. Their beasts would stay in their graves. None would rise. They would be lost forever.

Like me.

Eloi knew the danger, of course. And so he hid his Beyn from me. Somewhere in Judea. Somewhere in the lands ruled by Herod. That's all I knew.

So I came to Lytrotis and studied him, all his desires and dreams. Then I began to reach inside him and kindle little fires, wakening and strengthening the hopes and wishes that were useful to me. He felt my presence and thought that all those fires were promises. Did he want a little power? I showed him his own dreams of taking life and giving death. Did he want honor? I showed him his own face wearing the majesty of kings. He wanted all of it. I never lied to him. I showed him his own darkest desires and he lied to himself, convincing himself that if he let me in, I would give it all to him. I never *said*.

Fool, Lytrotis! Let me in, and your *beast* will have it all, but I will be the rider. Are there pleasures? Yes, you'll feel a pale echo of what I, the master of this body, feel. But the choices are all mine, until I tire of this beast and let you have it back.

Until that day, Lytrotis had been a hanger-on, one that Herod tolerated because he was a flatterer and because he was young and attractive. But now, with me inside and in control, with a tongue, with *language*, I began to be able to lie in earnest. Not flattery, but good advice, based on my thousands of years of learning how the darlings can be controlled.

Herod had long felt his kingdom slipping away. The Romans loomed and circled like vultures: Die, Herod, they seemed to say, and your kingdom will drop into our hands, no matter how you buttress it.

Herod built the Jews a temple, and they still despised him. He built cities and filled them with Greeks, and they looked down on him. He killed his wife and three of his sons when they conspired against him and still he was not safe. As his body aged and sickened, he had nothing left.

Then I took over the body of this sycophant and suddenly Herod began to hear wisdom.

The good news I promised him came true. My warnings saved him several times. All I said to Herod was the purest truth. The only lie was this: that he could trust me.

"In my old age, to have such an adviser as you," he said once. "If I had known you earlier . . . "

But if I had known earlier that *this* was the time and place, the kingdom would have been mine, and Herod a discarded corpse somewhere.

As for taking *him* over—what good would that have done me? He was nearly a corpse already. Sick, in constant pain. His beast would die too soon. I had to use Herod's power to kill the Beyn, and Lytrotis gave me the means to do it. Herod listened to me. Herod trusted me. Herod did what I told him to do.

I set his agents to searching Judea from end to end—as well as other places heavily infested with Jews, like Galilee and Syria and Egypt. I learned when the baby had been born, but no names, and the parents could have taken it somewhere else by now, for all I knew. Then Eloi tipped his hand.

Three travelers came into Judea, and my agents brought me word before Herod knew of them.

"They're strange men," said Jerubbel. "I thought that they were kings, but they claim not to be. Merely educated men. Sages."

"But strange—what do you mean by that?"

"Foreign, but not from any place we know of. None of the kingdoms of Parthia—they speak Persian and Aramaic, but they aren't from any place in Parthia. Names of farther places have been spoken to them, but they claim not to be from any of them. Not India or China, not Samarkand or the Isles of the Sea. 'From the East,' is all they say."

"What do they look like?"

Jerubbel shook his head. "I stare at them intently, but at once my gaze shifts away and I can't remember what I saw. When I don't focus my eyes on them, I can see that there are three—two tall, one short. They ride on dromedaries, with six more camels behind them, laden with supplies. They have servants who *can* be looked at—ordinary men. *Those* I can tell you about; I talked to them. Two Assyrians, a Babylonian, an Elamite, an Armenian. But they all say the same: I don't know what they look like, or where they're from, or what the language is that they speak among themselves."

"Aren't the servants afraid to be with such strange men?" I asked.

"They are," said Jerubbel. "But the pay is good, and these 'wise men' are mild-tempered and never beat them. So the servants stay, and talk of these marvels to men like me."

"Take this report to Herod as soon as you can," I said, "but don't speak to him of how you can't actually look at them. That will frighten him, and he'll either want to kill them or refuse to see them. Speak to him when I am at his side."

Jerubbel did what I asked, and when Herod heard of these wise men from unknown lands, he sat in thought.

"What a great opportunity," I said.

"Why?" he asked.

"They come from lands that Rome has never heard of," I said. "And yet they came to you."

"But they *haven't* come to me."

"They entered Judea," I said. "You are king here. Send for them. They will come."

"I don't want to see them," he said. For sometimes Herod had more wisdom than was useful to me. "They don't belong here."

"They *don't* belong here," I agreed, "which is why you must meet them, so you can learn their business. How can a king be safe with strangers in the land?"

So Herod's men went out and within two days the Wise Men walked into his court and I laid eyes on them for the first time.

I almost laughed aloud.

Of course they could not be looked upon by these beasts. They were not of this species of featherless biped, not even of this planet, and did not want to be known for what they were. A seraph, a yamin, a nagid. The seraph's wings were hidden under a cloak, but I could see them moving as he walked; the yamin's nearly spineless movements made him seem to seep across the floor like something liquid; the nagid hobbled, trying not to move in the great two-footed hops that are native to his race.

All of them chosen as beasts for evyonim to bind with because they were like enough to Eloi: A large brain, language, hands that made tools. All of life on every planet bent itself to creating beasts that Eloi could employ as mounts for those who served him, as Eloi himself once mounted such a beast on yet another world, and bound to it, and made the thing immortal.

It stops here, I thought, as seraph, yamin, and nagid approached. I was not *bound* to Lytrotis's beast, so I was not blinded as Eloi's darlings were, seeing only the beast-face and never the evyon within. I could not be deceived by their fendings and shadowings. I was not yet trapped within the brain.

The seraph was the one called Asdruel. The yamin was not known to me, but that is because they are not comfortable at such low gravity and rarely come to the world where I have been imprisoned. The nagid was a little pest named Lemuel who liked to write sentimental poetry and have it translated into every language he could find. Such vanity—supposedly against the rules, but apparently his poems pleased Eloi and so the poems continued to slither their way into every culture.

And because of who they were, and what they were, I knew why they were here. The Beyn would not have power to raise his body from the dead unless they began the transformation now, the deep binding that no other of Eloi's darlings was pure enough to undergo without destroying the body in the process. It had to happen before the baby came into its language, preferably before he began to walk upright. They would have the chemicals, the bioforms, or as these bipeds would say, the potions and the spells.

They would also have the little baby's home address.

No, I could not follow them. They would know me then. But here in Herod's court, I could hide inside Lytrotis and not be recognized.

I could see that Herod was in a mood to be surly and abrupt, but oil was what we needed now, not vinegar. "Be kind and helpful to them, my king," I whispered in his ear, "and they will tell us all we need to know."

By now Herod took my counsel almost before I gave it.

"Why do such esteemed ambassadors come to my poor kingdom?" asked Herod, his voice soft and meek.

Ah yes, thought I, this is the Herod who somehow got *both* Octavian and Antony to back him, so he could keep his kingdom no matter which of them might triumph in their civil war.

"We come in search of him who is born king of the Jews," said Asdruel, for his mouth was best suited to framing the speech of these bipeds. Herod understood him easily, as did all the court; only I could hear how strained his voice was to make such difficult sounds.

"You may speak to me in Greek," said Herod. "Or Aramaic."

"It is Hebrew in which the prophecies were written," said Asdruel. "We saw the star of the newborn king blaze brightly in the east, and we have come to add our poor selves to his worthship."

"Judea we knew," added Lemuel, his voice squeaking. No one seemed to notice, or if they did, they did not care. Always these "wise men" deflected from themselves whatever they did not want the bipeds to notice. But I was not deflected. I could not be fooled. "Judea, but not where in the land. It is larger than we thought."

I leaned to Herod's ear. "Your own wise men will search out the answer."

"Small compared to Rome," said Herod. "Towns and villages, where Rome is nations and cities. Yet we also have the Law and the Prophets, and men skilled in the searching of them. Perhaps we have a book you have not read, a prophecy you do not know. Stay here and dine, and wash yourselves from your journey. Before your meal and bath are over, we will have whatever answer can be found."

I was amused at the thought of a yamin washing in plain water—it would osmote every vital mineral right out of his body. So defenseless, the yaminim. Not that he could die—these three were already dead and then restored, made immortal on their own worlds. But the water would boil away from him and it might be hard to conceal completely from the bipeds.

"We will eat, and bathe," said Asdruel. "And eagerly we await your counsel."

Within a few minutes, Herod had all the Hasmoneans and Sadducees that always lingered in the court, hoping to be the next one named high priest. "Find me where this 'king of the Jews' is supposed to be born," said Herod to them, not oily *now*, but full of vinegar. "And when you find it, tell me why *I* was never told of such a portentous birth."

"O King," said one of them, "if we told you of every rumored Anointed One, it would take you hours every day to hear of them. They're country bumpkins, most of them, with delusions. Their neighbors and families hush them up or hide them away. They do no harm. They are possessed."

It was true. I let many of my followers amuse themselves by taking over the bodies of mental weaklings and then pretending to be the Beyn. Why not? It amused me and confused his darlings.

Apparently it wasn't hard to find. Several of these priests and scholars had suggestions within the hour, but they were too farfetched. Yet in scarcely more time than the idiotic ones, the right prophecy turned up.

And so Herod had the young scholar who found it read the words aloud. " 'And thou Bethlehem, in the land of Judea, art not the least among the princes, for out of thee shall come a Governor that shall rule my people.' Who can the governor be, except the Anointed?"

The Wise Men seemed content with that, nodding and smiling. "Yes," said Asdruel, "that is right."

"We feel the rightness of it when it's . . . right," screeched Lemuel.

Oh yes, that one was a poet.

"Then I, who am Idumean," said Herod, "who serve as king only until this long-awaited one is born—my life's work is complete and I can die content."

Asdruel and Lemuel and the yamin bowed—though the yamin was already so near the floor as to make no difference. "Your faithfulness as steward of the newborn king will not be forgotten."

I was sure of that.

"I beg you to tell me now," said Herod, "what day the star you saw appeared, so that we can learn his age and help you find him."

The three of them looked from one to another. I almost made Lytrotis laugh aloud, for of course they couldn't say—they had been on other planets, where other time-systems were employed."

"We have been so long upon the road," said Asdruel, "and started from three different kingdoms. We expect the child must be nearly one year old by now."

I could see Herod's skin begin to flush. Because he was a suspicious old fool, he thought he was being lied to. "It is often so," I whispered, "in people of their country. They do not have the calendar of Julius, you see."

"Ah," said Herod softly, nodding, the color fading from his cheek. "Of course it is hard to know the day, when you do not have that excellent calendar."

"We will find him," said Asdruel. "Easily, now that we know the name of the town. We beg your permission now, O King, to leave your presence and greet the baby who has been born among the Jews."

"Go, yes," said Herod—for he needed no prompting from me, when the course was obvious. "Go and seek out the little boy. Only do me this kindness, I beg of you, noble visitors. I am old, and travel little from this home that has become the prison of my declining years. But for this glorious event I will—I must—set out from here so I may prostrate myself before the One for whom I have kept such long vigil."

Oh, yes, Herod, that is well-played, I said, without letting the words slip out. I do not have to teach treachery to *you*.

"Of course we will return to you," said Asdruel.

The ability to lie, I thought, of course it rose with you, Asdruel, when you claimed your new immortal body from the stone where your old dead one had lain. A liar like me, that's what you are, only I'm condemned and hated for it, and you're one of his loftiest Messengers, entrusted with an errand such as *this*.

The Wise Men rose up and went away, the whole procession of them.

Since I knew they were not coming back, I sent three men to follow them, so they could note what house they entered.

But that was just to satisfy old Herod, who thought he knew my plan.

I did not *follow* them. I ran ahead—myself, using the legs of Lytrotis's beast, which had not run in years. But he was young, and if these years of luxury had sapped his strength, I had the power to drive the beast as Lytrotis had never bothered to drive it. I was there when they arrived. I saw them pass through the streets. I felt the little dagger in my sleeve. I had practiced with it. I knew that it would drop into my hand when I needed it.

They deflected the eyes of others—all knew of their passing, but had no memory of their faces, their misshapen bodies, the strangeness of it all. Only I could see. And so I followed, always keeping a building between us, so they did not see me, could not have guessed that I was there.

It was a little house—the kind that is rented to a young family starting out. A tall and quiet man who worked with his hands, of a social class that Lytrotis barely knew existed. But I knew him—one of Eloi's favorite darlings. And the mother! She came out and tucked herself under her husband's arm, and I knew her well. These were strong, and faithful to Eloi—they would never have let me in the way Lytrotis did. Nor could I have stayed inside them if they had—there was no place in them where disharmony left space for me to tear them open from the inside. Maddening, that the only evyonim I could work with were the vain and stupid ones, the easily deceived, the greedy ones who dreamed of things that would destroy them if they ever got them. Lytrotis.

He felt me despising him and seethed in the corner of his old self where I still tolerated his presence.

There was no room for these Wise Men in the house, still less for their servants. But they could go into the garden of the larger house next door, and so the young mother ran to the neighbor and asked consent. Apparently it was given, and the mother returned.

Through the garden gate the Wise Men went, and their servants followed, carrying the gifts that they had brought with them to honor the newborn king.

Only I knew what they were. A small chest of the kind commonly used to transport frankincense; a largish covered phial in which the waxy form of myrrh was often carried. And a dozen small bags, tight-knotted and carried in a larger bag; by the weight, it could only be metal, and I knew that it was gold.

The gold was useless—it was only there to deceive.

As for the frankincense and myrrh, they were anything but that. Philter and bioform, that was what they held. The tools to transform the baby into the kind of being who could only die if he permitted it, and never lost the connection with his body even if he did.

The gifts—the tools of the operation—were laid out upon a low stone table in the garden.

Meanwhile, the father and mother had gone back into their house, and now they came out again, a toddler in their arms. I could not be sure of his age, for I could not look at him. I could sense his heft, his size in their arms, but I am forbidden to look upon the Beyn, either through the eyes of a beast or with my own perceptions. I am blind to him. But not to his presence.

If you drive a dagger deep, and slash with it, the body of a baby is so small you are bound to hit something vital, and inflict a fatal wound.

So as the parents carried him from house to house, I drifted among the neighbors, sliding ever closer.

At the gate, when they stopped to pass through single file, I was close enough.

I reached out my hand as if to caress the babe, as several of the neighbors had already done. There was no knife in my hand; I would not let the blade appear until my fingers were already close. None would see the blade, not even as I made the first deep slashes. My hand would cover it from sight. The connection of Beyn to bipedal corpse would be severed in that moment, never to be restored, the body never to be taken up again. All in ruins, all his plans. Vindication. Vengeance. Breaking up and tearing down. What I had lived for all these centuries.

The blade was dropping into place; I felt it against my palm; and then there was something cool against my forehead. Cool, and yet it burned. I would have recoiled from it but I could not, for it did not hurt the skin of the body that I occupied; it was me it hurt. The hidden me, that no one here had seen.

It was the hand of Asdruel against my brow.

And then the hand of the creeping yamin cupping my knee, and the hand of Lemuel the nagid poet on my chest over my heart.

But not *my* brow, not *my* knee, not *my* chest, not *my* heart. Lytrotis's. Miserable puny weakling fool that he was, he was the darling that Eloi had bound this body to; he was soothed and calmed by their touch, while I was set aflame and felt torture and tearing beyond anything that I had known before.

"Lytrotis," said Asdruel softly. "I am Asdruel."

"Lemuel," screeched the nagid.

And the voice of the yamin rasped his name: "Hhasah."

"In the name of the Beyn," said Asdruel, "we command this spirit to come out of him."

The knife was in my hand. I am the strongest of my kind. The Beyn was trapped in a baby's body, and seeing only what the babe could see and knowing only what the babe could know. He could not bring his power to bear against me. And they did not know my name.

I gripped the knife. Though I burned white-hot at every point where my immaterial evryon self connected with the beast, I pushed the blade forward.

The baby gurgled and laughed. The baby said a word.

"Or," he said. It once had been my name. Yet it might just as easily have been a random sound, no word at all.

"Or," whispered Asdruel. "Once you were of the mighty, a son of the morning. But here you have no power. This body is not yours. In the name of the Beyn, and by his power, which he put in us, we command you to come out."

But I could not obey them. For as they spoke, I was already gone.

Not gone—I was still *there*. My boundaries, as far as they could be detected at all, were entirely contained within the body of the beast called Lytrotis. But I did not connect with the beast at any point. It belonged to Lytrotis entirely.

I could sense how he flowed again into every corner of the beast and made it his again. A homecoming it was for him. And in his joy, relief, and gratitude, he wept and sank to his knees.

"Rise up," rasped Hhasah. "Come in and see what we do here."

But Lytrotis did not rise.

"Why are you afraid?" screeched Lemuel. "You are free now."

"I fear it will come back," said Lytrotis, "and take me again."

"It will not," said Asdruel. "We have forbidden it."

And it was true. I could not even hold the thought of taking Lytrotis's beast again. It fled my mind each time I tried to think of it; finally I gave it up so I could think at all.

Lytrotis rose to his feet and let himself be drawn inside the garden. As he went, Hhasah reached up into his sleeve and took the knife and then pushed it hiltfirst into his own body—such malleable flesh, these yaminim, with nonce pockets wherever they needed them, for as long as they were needed.

I could not ride in Lytrotis now. I was outside the gate. I could not pass through it. The barrier was impenetrable. And I was blind to it. Whatever went on inside, I could not sense it. For where the Beyn was, I could not, an unprotected evyon, go.

But I did not have to see. I knew. The bioforms were introduced to him as he was anointed; the philter was used to lave his body, and it entered him at pores and mouth, and he inhaled the fumes.

Inside the beast, the links to the evyon of the Beyn were made firm and eternal. Mortal, yes, the body still was that—it could be killed. But only if the Beyn was willing to let it happen.

I should not have done it myself. I should have trained someone, told him to avert his gaze when it was time to kill.

But these were the darlings, after all. Even the greedy fools like Lytrotis were Eloi's darlings, or had been, once. When they came close enough they would withhold the blow. It would not even take the hands of the Wise Men to stop them. Only when he allowed it would they touch him violently, and pierce him, and slay him.

The shock of it faded. The grief. The disappointment. All that was left to me was rage.

But rage could not exist for long so close to him. He didn't like it, and now I had no beast to hold me in one place upon the surface of Earth. I felt myself pushed away as if by the blow of a giant's fist, and then I was on a mountain top, far from Bethlehem, far from Judea, far from Rome. A mountain covered with ice.

Too late now to stop him when it would have been the easiest. But I would find a way.

Meanwhile, I had foreseen the possibility. I am not so vain as to deny the possibility of being beaten, and so I had my plans already laid. Herod's order was already given. The soldiers were already marching. There were eighteen babies under two years of age within the village, and another six in nearby homes. They would die at the first light of dawn.

And one of them would be the Beyn. Bound up now so that he could rise again, but deprived of all his opportunity to teach them how to prepare for death so they, too, could rise. This or that piece of Eloi's plan might be carried out, but not all. They would see it, all the evyonim, all the beynim, all the seraphim and cherubim, yaminim and nagidim, they would see.

I know. The story is already familiar to you.

How the Wise Men left in darkness and went home another way, where Herod's men could never find them—for they boarded their starship and flew off in a starlike blaze into the night.

And the parents and the baby, they were also warned, and while they had no starship to carry them away, they had the dromedaries and the servants of the Wise Men, and gold enough to pay them.

Gold enough to live in exile for ten years in Alexandria, among the Jews and Greeks of that city, with all the learning of the world to draw upon in his education.

And I was left with the bitter knowledge that every step of mine had been foreseen before I took it. Gold! I had not guessed its purpose. It was his armor; it was gold that supported the Beyn and his parents in Egypt until the atrocities of Herod were forgotten, and no one looked any longer for the babe that had been visited by the strange, unseeable Wise Men from the east.

What was left to me? To act out my part in the plan. And what was my part?

To tempt him and fail to introduce impurity into him.

To use the teachers and scholars to trip him up and confuse him and expose the fact that Eloi cared nothing for these people; but always he had an answer, and the common folk continued to follow him and listen to his words.

And finally, when it was time, when he allowed it, to have him killed.

Useless. Worse than useless—essential to the plan I hated with all my heart.

Yet as he died, I was there, inside a Roman soldier, and they heard me cry out in his voice: "Yes, take that, you Beyn of Eloi!"

But even those exultant words of mine, as I rejoiced in his suffering, were written down another way, as if I were testifying of him; as if I were afraid.

Worst of all, when he put himself together again, eternal evyon with domesticated beast, he changed you all, all the darlings. We could not possess your bodies any more, not as we used to; you could fight us now and keep us out. Even when the evyonim succumbed to us, we could not feel the passion and the pain of the beast, not as we used to. Otherwise you would have known the bitterness of captivity within a beast controlled by someone else, by me. The Beyn has protected you all your life, and you never knew it, and didn't care.

All this you see so clearly now, because you are separated from your beast, and now I cannot lie to you. But you recognize me, don't you? You know how often I have whispered to you, I or one of those who serve me. You know how I played upon your worst desires—or your best, when that served my purpose.

I could not stop the Beyn, I never could, I know that now. He was too strong for me, and Eloi watched over him.

But you I *can* stop. I *have* stopped you. See how unclean you are? I taught you how to be this thing of filth, and you learned my lessons well, and went beyond them to become a master of self-indulgence and destruction.

Now you see me naked and you know the truth about us both. Do you think that he'll accept you now?

This is not my story and it never was. It is *our* story.

You belong to me.

❄   ❄   ❄

Despite our standard legends, the Fangborn—vampires and werewolves—are really the good guys who protect and serve humanity. Like Christmas, they are all about hope. In her Agatha- and Macavity Award-winning holiday story, Dana Cameron tells of a Fangborn brother-and-sister detective team who discover evil in a form they think is impossible. (It is much easier to accept such fantasy fiction than some of the odd superstitions associated with Christmas. In some Eastern European countries, for example, it is thought babies born or conceived on Christmas Eve are more likely to become a werewolves than others. Stranger still, ethnologist Tatomir Vukanović wrote that some Serbian villagers believed pumpkins kept after Christmas turned into vampires.)

The Night Things Changed
❄
Dana Cameron

I pounded up the stairs to the roof and slammed open the door; the wintry air lashed my face. My sister the vampire was stretched out on her stomach, nearly naked, under the pale December sun.

She wasn't moving. I knew from her phone call the news was bad, but . . .

"Claudia?" I swallowed; my mouth was dry. "Claud?"

She stirred and opened her eyes blearily. Her face was drawn, she moved stiffly. Claudia relaxed when she saw it was me, fastened the bikini top behind her neck, then sat up.

I turned away, blushing. "Aw, jeez, Claud. Do you have to?"

"What? I'm covered. Gerry, take a pill. No one can see me up here. We picked the place for that very reason."

She was right; evergreen shrubs and dead, leafy vines—a forest of green in the summer—sheltered her place from every side, leaving the roof open to the sky. Despite the crust of snow on the ground, she wasn't even shivering.

It was such a small bikini, though. I kept quiet: she'd think I was being a prude.

"I don't even need to wear a bathing suit when I'm alone," she said, reading my face.

"Yeah, you do, as long as I'm your brother." I *am* a prude; sue me. No guy likes to think about his sister being ogled, especially not when she looked good enough to model that bikini. And I wished she'd cut her long dark hair. It was just too dangerous in a fight.

I changed the topic. "I got your message. I was worried."

She nodded; her shoulders sagging. "A bad one, this morning. It means work for us."

Things had been so quiet lately, it had to happen. "Tell me."

"It was in the emergency room." Claudia "happens" to go through the emergency room a lot, trolling for trouble. "This guy was in for sutures, a cut on his arm he said he got slipping on ice. He was giving Eileen a hard time, and I got a whiff of him. I asked her to send him to me for 'post-trauma assessment.'"

Claudia glanced at me; there were dark smudges under her eyes. She looked beat. "He barged into my office, got angry when I told him he had to wait his turn. Very aggressive, all id, defensive as Hell. Maybe there's a hurt little kid somewhere under all that armor, but he's being led by a really thuggish protector-self."

I hate when she talks like a shrink, but it's how she gets things straight in her own head. "Was he big?"

She nodded. "And he uses it. He doesn't mind threatening people, liked the idea he was scaring me. And then . . . when I stood up to him, he took a swing at me."

I nodded, bristling. She was obviously okay, but I hated hearing this kind of stuff. It was part of our job, and I knew Claudia could take care of herself, but it still chafed. Call me overprotective. "And?"

"He missed. That made him crazy. He tried again." She shrugged. "And then I bit him."

I nodded again; it didn't make me feel much better. If biting had cured the guy, she wouldn't have called me, just saved it for the next time we got together for dinner. "Anyone see you?"

"The door was shut. He knocked me down, then ran out of the office." She paused. "He's a really bad one—"

"We'll get him. We always get the bad guys," I said, confident.

She shook her head. "There was something weirdly, profoundly, wrong about him."

"You're just tired. We always—"

"No, Gerry!" Her sharp tone startled me. "This is different. His reaction . . . I can't get the taste out of my mouth. It's like . . . I could work on him for a year, and still not get anywhere."

Her eyes filled up, and I knew that she'd been thrown for a loop. Professionally and personally, Claudia is a proud person.

"Scootch over," I said. I didn't say any more, just sat down on the lounge and put my arm around her. I resisted the urge to take off my jacket and put it over her shoulders, because the sun was the best thing for a vampire in need of healing, even the weak sun of a Massachusetts midwinter. And besides, I needed my coat myself. I always seem to feel the cold.

Prudish. Overprotective. Chilly. In a lot of ways, we werewolves are just big pussies.

After getting Claudia's promise that she'd take it easy, I took the copy of the file she had and visited the address of "J. Smith."

J. Smith? Proof once again that evil is not creative.

I didn't need to get out of the pickup, but I did. As I figured, the place—a double-decker—was abandoned, my footprints the first breaking the new fall of snow surrounding it. As I nosed around, I picked up lots of strong residual scents, most of them unhappy: drugs and sex, pain and fear. There was something in the background, an ugly smell that made my skin crawl; I didn't know if our guy had been there, but the recognizable odor of evil called me to Change . . .

Not here, not now. Save it for tonight, when you might be able to do something about it . . .

I reluctantly followed my tracks back to my truck and decided to pick up the trail at the hospital. Construction and early holiday mall shoppers had turned Route 128 into a slushy parking lot, but the F150 handled well with her new snow tires. I tuned the radio to the Leftover Lunch on WFNX and crept toward Union Hospital in Lynn.

I like being a werewolf for the same reasons I liked being a cop. Sure, it's a lonely job and I see life's tragedies, but then I fix them. I help people, I make the world a better place, and I'm good at it. I *like* being one of the good guys. I get a sense of satisfaction I bet your average CPA never gets. Or maybe they do; what do I know? I'm just Gerry Steuben, regular guy, North Shore born and bred, with a CJ degree from Salem State, recently early-retired from the Salem PD. My tax forms say I'm a PI now, but I don't do domestics, insurance fraud, or repo. I'll go to the end of the earth to find lost kids, though, and never charge a cent. But I mostly stick to the family business, which is eradicating evil from the world.

Sounds like I'm full of myself, doesn't it? Not if you know the truth about my type. Our type. The Fangborn, Pandora's Orphans, the ones the ancients called "Hope," supposedly trapped at the bottom of the box. But according to *our* legends, the First Fangborn got out, and it's a good thing they did, too, for when evil was released into the world, so was the means of destroying it. Vampires and werewolves, the first to clean the blood and ease the pain, the second to remove irredeemable evil when we find it. Our instincts are infallible, our senses attuned to evil. True evil—not the idiot who cuts you off in traffic or steals your newspaper—exists, and we're here to fight it. We're the ones evil can't touch, the superheroes you never see, if we do our jobs right. I believe that to the core of my soul, and it's the best feeling in the world.

Imagine the world today if we didn't put the brakes on evil. Funny, since the Fangborn have always been depicted as the most depraved killers in every mythology. My kind aren't the most fertile in the world—there are less than one thousand of us in the United States—and when you normals turned from hunting to agriculture, you started popping out kids like it was going out of style. But we're the children of Hope, so we do what we can, and every bit helps.

As for those myths: It's not the turn of the moon but the call of evil that makes us Change, though I can manage it if I'm pissed off enough. I don't have hair on the palms of my hands, though for a while when I turned thirteen, I was afraid of that happening for other reasons. Claudia says I obsess about anyone touching my stuff, but can you name one guy who isn't territorial? When we order pizza, Claudia always asks for roasted garlic. She relies on the mirror by her front door to remind her to dress like other people when it's cold. She also *claims* she's allergic to silver, but that's because she thinks it looks tacky against her skin.

In reality, we're big on family and secrecy. Me and Claud live in Salem because eastern Massachusetts was where our family was needed, back in the day. Grandpa had a sense of humor about it: "Ven ve move from de old country, I tink, 'Here, dey like tings dat go bump in de night, so ve vill giff dem bumps in de night!'" he'd cackle. I miss the old guy like crazy, but our presence has nothing to do with the witchcraft trials; it was just easier to hide a bunch of Germans with funny habits among the Polish and Russian immigrants in nineteenth-century Salem. Protective coloring is all-important. Around here, not only do you have tales of witchcraft, but there are rumors of a sea monster (a nineteenth-century gimmick concocted by ferry owners and innkeepers), pirate treasures, and haunted houses. What's the occasional sighting of a big dog by moonlight against all that?

The traffic finally nudged its way to my exit and I pulled into the hospital parking lot. Many Fangborn are nurses, doctors, shrinks, cops, even clergy. Any job that gets us close to the public, the people who need protection, is a good job for us.

I didn't even have to roll down the window. The stench hit me from outside the cab of the truck. It was all I could do to keep my hands from turning to claws on the wheel and my human brain focused on parking. I killed the engine as soon as I could, clutching the Saint Christopher medal that's been on my neck since my first Communion. I don't care whether he's a saint; I'm not that religious. My mother gave it to me, and it helps to have something to focus on when resisting the Change. Claudia was right: this guy was a bad one. Smith had escaped her—which was saying something—and then left a trail that a normal could follow, if he'd understood why he was suddenly feeling queasy and irritable. There wasn't a sound of bird or beast anywhere nearby, not even a seagull.

True evil has the smell of rotting meat, sewer filth, sickrooms. Add the feeling you get when you realize something life-alteringly bad is happening, something you can't do anything about, and you'll get close to what I felt. But my senses are a hundred times sharper than yours.

The good thing is that smell brings on the Change and that brings power.

I opened the door cautiously. The wind shifted and I found I could manage without going furry, so I visited the ER. The nurses told me the doc who'd treated "J. Smith" was gone.

I thanked them, then tried Claudia's office. The scent was stronger here, possibly because of his attack on Claudia, but there was something else I couldn't place: it set my teeth on edge. The assistant Claudia shared with the other shrinks told me I'd just missed my sister, that she'd been really shook up by a patient. I feigned surprise—Claudia could get into a lot of trouble for talking about the case with me, much less giving me the file—and said I'd check on her.

I tracked the scent back to the parking lot, where the guys at the valet stand said that a guy had caught a cab dropping someone off, a local company.

Just then Eileen came out, a tart little nurse who'd always had a cup of coffee and a kind word for me when I'd been on the force. Claudia'd said she was the nurse handling Smith's case. We exchanged hellos.

"You heard about Claudia?"

"Yeah." I exhaled, whistling.

"She's okay. Guy was a bruiser. Came in to get stitched up, said it was a slip, but I know a bottle slash when I see one. Street fight, probably."

I nodded.

"Claudia gave me the high sign, so I sent him along to her. A post-trauma chat, I told him. Oh!" Eileen said, remembering. "It gets better. Weems brought him in. Said he found him in the middle of the street, and hauled him in to get him patched up. Too bad you missed him, you guys could have caught up on old times."

She grinned a mean grin; everyone knew Weems and I hated each other.

"My bad luck," I said. I stuck my hands in my pockets. "Apart from this guy, you been busy?"

She shook her head. "Not the past two days. Not even a bumsicle." She glanced at the steely sky. "That'll change. Snow tonight."

I nodded; I could smell that, too. We both knew that between the cold, the holidays, and the law of averages, soon enough there'd be accidents, drunk drivers, domestic disputes, and the homeless who'd freeze to death. The usual.

"Well, the kids will like it." She zipped herself up. "They're out of school after today. Jumping out of their little skins already, the little monsters."

"Oh, come on," I said. "Kids should be excited about Christmas." I like Christmas. I like the effort people make. I like presents. I like the hope. Like I said, we Fangborn are all about Hope.

"Yeah, I guess." Eileen looked uneasy, though. "I've got this feeling, Gerry. Everyone's on edge. Maybe it's the low pressure or the full moon, but there's something up. Watch yourself out there."

The ER was always hopping during the full moon. My people aren't the only ones who feel its power.

"I will, thanks. And you take care. Keep up with the patch."

Eileen was startled. "How did you—?"

I grinned. "You've been out here for five minutes and didn't light up." I didn't tell her I could smell the difference in her clothing, see the slight weight gain, feel her nerves humming with the strain of not reaching for that crumpled box of relief . . .

We wished each other Merry Christmas and I left. The trail from the taxi was blasted by the mall traffic and the nearby landfill, so I headed to Ziggy's Donuts in Salem, where the cabbies hung out. It didn't hurt that Annie worked there, a girl I'd been kinda hung up on for a while.

I ordered a jelly-filled because Annie was on the counter. I had been trying to get up my nerve to ask her out on a date. It was one of my New Year's resolutions—from this year. But we chatted while she got my donut, and I didn't say anything dumb, so I counted it a success. Maybe even a sign. I found a seat before I did something impetuous and stupid.

I'd have to soon: time was almost running out on my resolution, and I keep my promises.

It's hard, when you're a guy, to ask out a cute girl. I'm okay, I'm not hideous, though personally I think I look better as a wolf. I built my own house when our folks died, I have a decent income and a boat that's paid for, and my place is spotless because I don't like surprises.

But it's even harder, when you're Fangborn, to ask a normal out. The two species can mate, though most of us Fangborn prefer to keep to our own kind. A mixed mating has a lower chance of producing a were or vamp than two Fangborn, but that's pretty low odds, too; how my parents lucked out and got *two*, one of each, I don't know. As far as I understand, it's all about recessive genes, but it doesn't make the initial discussion any easier. "Hey, sweetie? When I said my family was strange, I didn't mean regular, dysfunctional-strange . . . "

My cabbie came in then, sweating profusely, probably thinking he was coming down with the flu; I could smell Smith on him, even though they'd probably only brushed fingers when Smith paid. I waited until the cabbie ordered his coffee—even Annie's smile didn't help him—and then I approached him. He wasn't supposed to tell me where he took his fare, but I slid a twenty across the table and got the address of a no-tell motel on the edge of town. Then I asked to check his cab, to see whether Smith had dropped anything, I said.

"Help yourself," he said, shivering around his coffee cup. "It's open."

I was feeling pleased with myself when Weems pulled up alongside me in the parking lot. As he locked up the cruiser, he didn't speak, but gave me a nod along with the hairy eyeball. I nodded back, and kept moving.

We had never liked each other, and now he harbors the deep suspicion most cops have for PIs. He's always made my hackles rise. I couldn't put my finger on the reason, so I did the best I could to avoid him.

Annie knew him, too. Well enough to know that she could look forward to a full six-percent tip.

I waited until Weems was tearing into his bear claw, then opened the door to the cab—

. . . the screech of brakes before a crash . . . a phone ringing at 3:30 in the morning . . . the gush of blood from a wound that is deeper than you thought . . .

I could barely keep myself standing. I slammed the door, and stumbled back to my truck, not even waiting to calm myself before I fled into the traffic and away from that cab.

■ ■ ■

"What's next?" Claudia said, when I returned to her condo two hours later. She looked a little better and was now dressed in shorts and a T-shirt that said I ♥ SPIKE. She was barefoot, making us coffee. I still felt sick and I was freezing just looking at her. Her place is all white wood and glass and bare surfaces, which she calls "clean lines." The Christmas tree and lights looked out of place there, but I was glad of them.

I tried to get myself together. "After I left Ziggy's, I checked the motel. He paid cash, left no forwarding address. No luck at the other fleabags, either. I cast around for a while, but he wasn't doing any walking and I couldn't get anything from car tracks." I didn't tell her I'd driven halfway to New Hampshire before I'd gotten hold of myself, and used my work to keep from spinning into another panic. I wrapped my arms around myself, trying to feel less hollow, trying not to puke watching the cream swirl around the top of the coffee.

She saw me hesitate. "Gerry, what's wrong? You look like seven kinds of Hell."

I pushed the coffee away from me. "Every time I've caught a noseful of Smith, it's almost knocked me off my feet. You were right, he's bad."

"Yeah, bad. But why did I take so long to bounce back after I saw him? And you, you're always psyched up, all bloodlusty and rarin' to go, when you find a bad guy. What's different about Smith?"

"I dunno." I shrunk down into myself, not wanting to talk.

"That's not helpful." She went into psychiatrist mode. "Okay, you can't say what's wrong with *Smith*. What do *you* feel?"

"Claudia—"

"Humor me."

I shivered. She was right, but I really didn't want to discuss it. "Every time I think about Smith, I get sick, I feel confused. It's like the world's upside down, like I'm chasing my own tail—"

I shoved the chair back and bolted for the sink. I made it, just before the donut made a repeat appearance, and turned on the tap while I retched. Much as I wanted it to, the sound of running water didn't block out Claudia's exclamation.

"Oh, my God, Gerry. He's one of *us*."

"He can't be." I wiped off my mouth and turned to her.

"That's got to be it. It explains so much—our reactions, his, the way he went berserk in the office—"

"He's just a psycho," I said. But I knew she was right.

"No, Gerry." She took a deep breath. "He's evil. And he's one of *us*!"

"There's no such thing as an evil Fangborn, Claudia," I said. "Not in all our history." "Maybe not in our history, but what about our future? I've got to check in with the family, let them know what's going on. Maybe the oracles will have something for us. This is *amazing*—"

A sudden, childish urge hit me. "Claud, don't."

"Don't tell the family?"

I nodded. I just didn't want any of this to be true.

"Gotta do it, Gerry. We can't let Smith get away, and if he's what we think he is, they all need to know. This is *big*."

I shrugged miserably.

She put her hand on my shoulder. "It's scary, yes, the idea of evil appearing in our form, with our powers. It's also a tremendous revelation. Gerry, it can tell us a lot about who we are, maybe more than the geneticists or the oracles can, and it can tell us about the nature of evil. It may even foretell the final battle against evil, Gerry. The one where we win. Who wouldn't want to be present for that?"

Her eyes were alight and her fangs peeked out with her excitement.

I hated her for being excited, but at least that helped shake off the overwhelming emptiness I felt. Time to man up, Gerry. We're still the good guys—

It's just that the bad guys had never looked like us before.

I nodded. "Okay, you contact the family, and I'll hit the Internet. Smith's out there, and until we get a clue or a scent, we're just gonna have to wait."

We exchanged a look. Sensing the presence of evil is one thing. Being able to find it before it acts is quite another. And the idea of evil in the form of a Fangborn was just plain terrifying.

I went home, and no sooner opened the door than I was attacked by a mass of muscle and fur.

"Beemer, get off!" I peeled the big, brown-striped tom off my shoulder and dumped him on the couch. As a kitten, Beemer jumping from the staircase railing onto me was impressive and cute as Hell. Now that he was in the fifteen-pound class, it was less amusing. To me, anyway. Beemer still thought it was a riot. But even he couldn't cheer me up tonight.

As I heated a shepherd's pie I got over at Henry's Market, I listened to the police scanner, but didn't hear anything that would help. As Beemer washed himself on the leather couch next to me, I drank too much and flipped around the TV—a beaut, 40-inch plasma, with controls to put the *Enterprise* to shame—but there was nothing to keep my attention. Ditto the Internet and the new issue of *Maxim*. If you wanted proof that my kind are born, not made, just do the math: if we could turn normals, not a single lingerie model would be left unbitten. Trust me.

Frustrated in every sense of the word, I didn't drift off until just before the alarm rang.

Groaning, I got up, dumped kibble into Beemer's bowl, and hit the bricks, not because I had a lead, but because I had a headache worse than any hangover. The memory of evil left unchecked is one of the downsides of the job, and I didn't even want to think about what Smith meant.

I walked by Ziggy's, but Annie wasn't working. The day outside matched my insides: granite gray, cold, depressing. Even the telephone poles were decorated to suit my mood: the neighborhood was papered with missing pet flyers. I knew how I'd feel if Beemer ever went missing: it'd be a crappy Christmas for the kids worrying about Kitty-Cakes or Bongo or Maxie . . .

Focus on the job, Gerry. Keep it together.

Down by the Willows, I caught a faint scent. The Salem Willows is an amusement park, very small and dated. It's mostly Whack-a-Mole and fried dough stands and rackety rides during the summer. In the winter, it's a wasteland, boarded up and abandoned.

It wasn't abandoned now: Salem PD, state police, and the ME vans were there. My vision and hearing sharpened, and my olfactory nerves went crazy. Smith had been here, not long ago.

Weems was also there. This time, he came right over to me.

"Steuben. Been seeing a lot of you lately." He only reaches my chin, and he's kinda pudgy, so short-man syndrome never helped things between us.

That's why werewolves and vamps have such crappy reputations. The local authorities always notice us sniffing around crime scenes and figure we're the bad guys.

I sipped my coffee. "Been seeing a lot of you, too, Weems. Funny, huh?"

"I ain't laughing." He crossed his arms. "What're you doing here?"

"I'm looking for the guy at the hospital who knocked my sister around."

His face softened, just a little. "Your sister, she's okay."

Suggesting I was not. "C'mon, Weems. I'm trying to catch an asshole here."

"And what're *we* doing?" For an instant, I thought he'd either hit me or have a heart attack. He balled up his fists and turned a shade of red that would have made Santa's tailors envious.

"You know what I mean." I tried to look desperate, no stretch, under the circumstances. "Man, come on. It's *Claudia*."

The stories would have you believe that vampires are incredibly alluring. It's true, they produce a pheromone that seems to make people around them comfortable, which helps vamps in their healing work. Add a good dose of empathy, and yes, vampires hold a definite attraction for normals, who think of it as sexual.

Something about Claudia had long ago hit Weems hard, right between the eyes. She'd hate me throwing her under the bus like that, but if it got me past his defensiveness . . .

I could see that Weems was torn, but he wasn't going to pass up anything that made him look good in front of Claudia. "We got one vic, and it's a wet one. Or it was, a couple of days ago: it's pretty dried up now." Weems looked greenish; he never could stand the sight of blood. "Chest sliced open . . . and the heart removed."

"Jesus." I swallowed. "Got an ID?"

"Homeless guy. My guess, he was either flopping in the shed over there, or he was lured in."

"You said *sliced* open?"

"You're a ghoul, Steuben." He sighed. "ME says a big knife, it looks like. They need more tests."

I nodded. If there was one thing we could agree on, it was the reluctance of the ME to spill details.

He hesitated. "The chest was opened up like . . . ah, jeez. It reminded me of one of those Advent calendars. The skin pulled back square, and the ribs broken to get the heart out."

Maybe he didn't like me seeing him queasy, maybe he just regretted telling me as much as he did, but Weems's face hardened. "Get lost, Steuben. I find you nosing around, you'll be sorry."

"Merry Christmas to you, too, Weems." I left.

"They found a body," I said, after I let myself into Claudia's condo.

Claudia was excited. "Yeah, I know, I just heard it on the news." It was her day off and while Claud was waiting to hear something solid back from the family—who were going crazy over the news—she was trying to work out a profile for Smith. Maybe she was doing rote work for the same reason I was: to keep from thinking about our world being turned inside out. I still felt like I had the pins knocked out from under me and I hated that uncertainty.

"Down the Willows?" I said, surprised. That was quick.

"No, pulled from the harbor." She frowned. "The woman had been in there about a week. They said 'mutilated,' which usually means something worse."

"So was mine." I told her what I'd just learned from Weems. "They know who she was?"

"A local prostitute, was all they said."

"There's a chance it's not the same guy, not our guy—" I said.

"I'm not willing to bet on that."

"Me, neither."

"He's selecting people on the periphery of society," she said. "Going for those who live under the radar."

I considered where the trail had led me: the abandoned drug den, the dry spell in the emergency room, and—oh, Hell. Three missing cats in one neighborhood was just too much coincidence. I told Claudia. "I guess he's been doing this for a while."

She nodded. "And is escalating. He's refining his ritual, getting bolder, going for less vulnerable, more public targets. It's typical that he started with animals." The look on her face didn't bode well for Smith when we caught him. "Gerry, it's only going to get worse from here. I'm guessing that he's attributing some special significance to the date—the full moon, Christmas . . . "

Suddenly, I knew. "It *is* Christmas," I said. I told her Weems's description of the corpse, what he'd said about Advent calendars. "Doesn't that sound like what you're talking about? Little, uh, treats leading up to the big day?"

She nodded. "Right. Christmas. Good eyes on Weems."

I snorted. "He's my hero." But Christmas was just two days away. "My question is, Why did Smith have to call a cab?"

"He didn't have a car," she answered promptly. "Weems brought him in, right?"

I made a face at her. "But if Smith is responsible for the murders, he must have a car."

"He can't afford to let it go out in public. Too many people could see . . . what?"

"Bloodstains? Cracked window?"

"Too recognizable," she said. "A truck with a business logo on it, contractors, deliveries—"

"Right, it's got to blend in, but not the sort of thing you'd drive for private stuff." I thought a minute, then an idea hit me. "Like a police car. Maybe it isn't Smith! Maybe it's Weems!"

"Gerry. Get real. Weems is your bête noir, and he's a dickhead, but he's not our guy."

"He was at the hospital." I ticked off my reasons on my fingers, *loving* that Smith might just be a garden-variety psycho, his trail confused by Weems. "He was at the donut shop. He's been dogging my tracks all day, and every time I saw him, I felt the call to Change."

"All places you'd expect to see a cop investigating the same case as we are. Have you ever wanted to Change because of Weems before now?" She put her hand on mine; it was warm as toast. "I know you don't like him, but you're getting distracted by this. You've always been so damned sure about everything—"

That was the problem: I couldn't be sure about anything anymore if Smith was Fangborn.

I pulled away. "I don't think so. I think you were picking up on his vibes, the same time you were dealing with some ordinary, run-of-the-mill loony, and that's why you thought it was Smith."

"You're wrong," she said. "Weems has nothing to do with this. I think you want it to be Weems so you don't have to consider that there might be an evil out there we haven't seen before. I get it, Ger: you want things to be cut-and-dried. But now we know . . . it can't be like that."

"Whatever." I turned away.

"Don't dismiss me, Gerry."

You know about that traditional conflict between werewolves and vampires? It's really just a sibling thing.

"Claudia, just because—"

"Sssh!" Claudia was pointing to the TV.

The news was on. A school bus, its driver, and six kids were missing from their daycare center.

"Okay," I said, "we've got the fake address at the Point, a murder at the Willows, a body in the harbor. Throw in the missing pets, and we have someone with a familiarity with the waterfront. That's a couple of big neighborhoods to cover."

"He needs space, and he needs a place where people won't hear . . .

screams." Claudia was looking at the map spread out in front of us. "He's sticking with what's familiar to him, which is good for us, but he's also an organized psychopath, which is bad."

"The houses are too close together, here and here," I said, pointing out two neighborhoods. "That leaves the warehouses in the industrial park down at the Point and the coal plant down here." I pointed to a neighborhood that was near, by water, but on the other side of town, by land.

"A school bus is going to stick out in either place," Claudia said. "Is he going to take them out to sea?"

"If he is, we're pretty well screwed," I said. "Protective coloring— where can you take six crying kids and a school bus where no one will notice?"

We looked at each other, then simultaneously at one of the neighborhoods we had just rejected. A short distance from my own house, separated by large parking lots and a playing field, was the middle school, now empty for the holidays.

It's not that we need the moon to shift, though that helps. It's easier to run around as a wolf when there aren't many people around. It's easier to pick up a faint trail with the dust settled from the day. It's not that we need the moon, but somehow, it makes it easier for me, the same way the sun takes the poison out of vamps like Claudia. You'd have to talk to our scientists who are working out exactly how we Fangborn work, but if you think of it like a vulture's bare head helping to kill the bacteria they pick up, or photosynthesis, taking nutrients from the sunlight, that's probably close. All I know is that Claudia couldn't taste the blood and clean it, cauterize the wound, and numb the memory without sunlight to charge her up. And in the same way—don't ask me how, I'm not one of the geeks—I get recharged by the moon.

Plus, lots of bad guys also wait for night to work. Makes it easier on us all.

The moon was full and low on the horizon as we parked down the street from the school. We ran down the plan again: check the school and then call the cops if we find anything.

Simple, if we were right. If we weren't already too late.

"Got the gear?" I asked Claudia.

She nodded, held up the leash—her excuse for being out with a very large dog—and a charged cell phone. As for me, while I hate what people inflict on their pets—birthday parties, pedicures, Halloween costumes—I will always be grateful for the dog-clothing craze. And grateful to the guy who invented stretch fabrics: my Lycra doggie track suit makes it a heck of a lot easier if I have to Change back to human and don't want to be buck-naked.

Claudia doubled the knots on her bootlaces, tied her hair back, and we went into the schoolyard.

The bus was there, all right, on the side, cold and silent as an empty grave. Sure, school was out and it was night, but who notices a school bus outside a school? The schoolyard had been badly plowed, so there were no clear tracks, but it only took me a minute to find the basement door they'd used, the lock broken.

The reek hit me as soon as we got the door open. This time, I didn't resist the Change.

The rush of adrenaline and endorphins and other hormones blotted out whatever pain shrieking bones forced through evolutionary growth in an instant might bring. Nature wouldn't be so cruel as to put this burden on us without compensation. The bloodlust didn't hurt, either, and it was only Claud's warning hand on my back that reminded me not to howl with the delight of it.

Smith's spoor was worse than any I'd ever smelled, overwhelming the traces of new linoleum, old wax, and textbooks. It was nearly unbearable to my lupine nose, but one thought, a bloodthirsty, simple joy, cleared of all human doubt and fear, overwhelmed even that:

It was time to track and to tear.

I stepped out of my boots and glanced up at Claud, who was down on one knee; the reek was hitting her just as badly. It was always harder for her; vamps don't have the same chemical buffer that protects wolves. Her skin took on a violet cast visible even in the shadows, and her eyes were wide and bright. Her facial features broadened, her nose receded, and her fingers lengthened.

She stood up, shook herself, and nodded. As she packed my boots into her backpack, I saw the gleam of her viperish fangs extending, the glint of a streetlight on the fine pattern of snakescale, an armor of supple, thickened skin. Snakes have always been associated with healing and transformation—there's a reason they're on the staff of Asclepius—but they've got a rep for danger, too.

I whined and stared at her neck. Her hand went up, and she found the pearls she'd forgotten to take off.

"Thankths," she said, with a slight hiss. Still largely humanoid, fangs and a forked tongue make speech awkward, but not impossible. She stowed the necklace in her bag, and nodded.

I led the way, as stealthy as a shadow. I cast around, stopped, panted, and tried again, but with no luck. There was no one single track to pick up. Smith'd been here long enough for the basement to be so saturated with his stench that I could barely breathe.

I couldn't detect the children. I hoped we weren't too late.

Claudia nodded. She pointed at the first door, and we both listened. Nothing.

She tried it; locked solid.

The next was an unlocked closet. The stink was there, too, but less. The bus driver was stashed in there. There was a pulse, faint and fading.

Claudia fanged down, called 911. We continued.

The next door opened silently; I could smell WD-40 recently applied to the hinges. No way to tell Claud, but she pointed to the duct tape across the lock, and I nodded. We went in.

The children were there. Even under Smith's foulness, I could tell they were alive. I felt a surge of delight.

They were drugged, only half-awake; a light on the playground offered just enough illumination for a normal to see forms without detail. My nose told me of full diapers, fear, and baby shampoo.

Smith was nowhere around. We went quietly, just in case.

"Hang on," Claudia said. She Changed back about halfway, just enough to keep her powers on deck, but not so far that the first thing the kids saw was a pale purple lady with no nose and very big teeth.

She went over to them quickly. "Hey, you guys? Let's get you fixed up and we'll get you home, okay? My dog Chewie is going to do some tricks for you. He's really big, but he's really, really friendly. Chewie, come!"

That was my cue. I knew to play it dumb and sweet over in the faint light so the kids would focus on me. That way, they'd be less afraid and they wouldn't notice Claudia practicing her leech-craft. I spend my time fighting evil, not practicing party tricks, but whenever I fell over, the kids laughed, so it was okay. And as soon as Claudia got one kid untied, her razor nails dancing scalpels over the duct tape, I was there, his new best friend, and they were so busy patting me they forgot to be afraid. Under the guise of inspecting their wounded hands, she got to work, biting their wrists, narcotizing the pain, neutralizing their terror, sucking out Smith's drugs, dimming their memories. I could sense her body reacting to the blood and emotion she was taking in, her muscles rippling, nearly all trace of humanity lost from her features even as she healed the little ones.

She'd just finished the last one when *he* was on her. Even as I picked up

on the fresh scent—snow mixed with spoiled milk and rotting fish heads—
Smith rocketed from the shadows, moving faster than anything human.

If I knew he was there, it meant Claudia knew, too. She shoved the kid
toward me as Smith landed on her. She rolled with him as far away from
us as she could.

In spite of Claudia's ministrations, the kids whimpered. I grabbed the
last one by the hood of her jacket and gently pulled her the rest of the
way to the group. I stood between them and the brawl, nudging the kids
to stand behind me, thankful Disney had removed their fear of large wild
animals.

It took everything I had to keep from jumping in and ripping Smith
apart, but I had to keep the children safe. And there's not much that can
stop my sister when she's pissed and Changed; for all her tweedy skirts and
bookishness, she's as much a warrior as I am.

Smith was putting up a pretty good fight and the sonofabitch knew
how to use a knife: Claudia would need a week on the roof to recover
from this. I was glad of the dark, that the children's eyes weren't as sharp
as mine, that they couldn't see the amount of blood that Claudia was
letting.

She was winning. Maybe Smith wasn't Fangborn, maybe just some
kind of freak human genetic anomaly—

You could practically feel the energy she expended fill the room,
almost blotting out the horror of Smith. Righteous violence in the cause
of justice—

I let out a low growl; there was *too* much energy, the air was sizzling as
if every Fangborn in New England was Changing next to me.

Claudia screamed.

Smith had Changed. An unholy transformation, something never before
seen in the world as I knew it: evil taking on the shape of a werewolf.

If I'd had time for rational, human thought, I would have been slowed
by what *shouldn't* have been happening, by what was impossible, but the
pull to attack was so strong I almost burst out of my skin. I bunched up
and launched myself at Smith.

Claudia threw herself out of the way as I bowled the other wolf out of
the room. We skidded into the hallway, unable to get a purchase on the
cold, polished cement floor. With a scrabble of claws, I was up, but he was
just a second faster and knocked me down again, snapping at my eyes. I
slashed at his gut and jerked my head out of the way, feeling his hot breath
and drool on my ears. I whipped around and grabbed at his muzzle; I was

bigger than he was and he almost pulled away before I closed my teeth. I caught him, barely, by the tender tip of his nose and the soft skin under his jaw. Teeth slid through flesh and I held on; he tried to push me away with his front paws, but was more effective with his rear claws, raking across my belly.

I smelled my own blood, but held on for dear life. He couldn't pull out of my grasp without tearing himself and I couldn't let him go.

The door opened and cold air washed over us. I heard a shout and recognized Weems.

He shouted again. I could smell Weems's fear. Weems drew his pistol. He was going to shoot. Well, I couldn't let him shoot *me*. I let go and Smith hurled himself at the doorway and Weems.

Thoughts flashed through my head: If Smith landed on Weems, I could grab him before he did much damage. If he knocked Weems out of the way, or took a bullet or six, so much the better for me.

Damn. He bolted right past Weems. He couldn't afford to get caught as a werewolf any more than I could. The prospect of decades of lab experiments made a life sentence at Cedar Junction look like a week at Sandals.

Sweat-soaked polyester, terror, boiled coffee, and roast beef: Weems had had dinner at Big Freddy's. If I planted a dirty, doggy paw in his face as I chased after Smith, I'm sure it was an accident.

Smith was nowhere to be seen as I raced down the street away from the school, but it didn't matter: he was leaving a trail of blood that any Cub Scout could have followed, and his scent was so strong there might as well have been a spotlight on him.

I cut through snowy backyards and vaulted a chain-link fence: Christmas lights lit the snow and the smell of cooking meats and seafood wasn't even a momentary distraction. Another burst of speed brought me down to the historic district on the waterfront, the eighteenth-century houses decorated with candles and garlands.

The tear in my belly was bad; I could feel the shock of the cold air through fur even as my muscle reknit itself. There was a sharp pain whenever I moved my left hind leg. The icy snow, dirty with sand and road salt, packed itself in between the pads of my paws, slowing me down and throwing off my gait. Blood—mine and Smith's—was matted in my fur, and my jaw ached.

The trail of blood was getting heavier, though: Smith was also slowing down. In spite of my wounds, I sped up, eager to end this.

But part of me hoped Smith would never stop. If he stopped, I'd kill him, and my job would be finished. Then I'd have to think about what was happening. I wasn't sure if my frail human brain could deal with it.

I leapt onto a back porch, tensed, then sailed over the back of the deck onto the sidewalk of Derby Street. I skidded on the icy bricks of the crosswalk, and barely missed getting hit by an Escalade. I yelped, feeling the breeze as the SUV swerved past.

The waterfront opened up in front of me. The heavy clouds parted for an instant and the full moon shone down on the blood that led straight down Derby Wharf, which stretched out a quarter of a mile into the harbor.

Unless Smith wanted to swim in life-sucking cold water toward the winking lights of Marblehead, he had nowhere to go except back to me. I grinned, as only a wolf drunk on power can.

There was no one out, and I was glad; it was usually a place for evening strolls, the marks of lesser canines blazoned against the snowbanks. I padded down the wide gravel path, catching my breath, preparing myself for the last fight.

Smith was smarter than I gave him credit for. He timed his attack for the instant the lighthouse lamp whirled toward me, washing the shadows together and reducing my field of vision.

Keeping my eyes lowered and narrowed, my ears back, I made myself wait until the last moment. Then I sprang at him, just as hard as I could. I caught Smith with his head still up, and seized him by the throat, biting down with every bit of strength I had.

His momentum carried him over me, and as he fell, his own weight tore his flesh off in my mouth. Hot blood poured and he dropped dead at my feet.

He might have been a predator with a hero's weapons, but I was a hero with true purpose.

I spat out the fur and gore as the moonlight flooded the wharf and harbor. Steam rose from the wounds of the dead wolf, blood black on the snow. Power from the kill, from having slain one of my own kind, almost knocked me off my feet, and it was possible I was the first one ever in history to have experienced it.

Evil just doesn't exist in the Fangborn. At least, it hadn't before now.

I threw my head back and howled, my inhuman blood singing, the completeness and rightness of my triumph dizzying.

But somewhere in the back of my brain, the part that stays human, I knew it was the last time I'd feel that way.

· · ·

On Christmas Eve, Claudia found me down in the basement of my house. It's finished with mats on the floors and walls so we can train in private.

"That's some sweat you're working up there," she yelled. She was wearing her T-shirt with the bull's-eye printed over her heart, the one that says GO AHEAD AND TRY IT, BUFFY.

I was flaked out on the floor in three layers of sweats, my headphones on, music turned to eleven. I considered her statement, then showed her a finger.

She came over to the stereo, cranked it up to fourteen or twenty so I had to pull the headphones off, then she switched off the CD. She glanced at the player.

"*Disintegration.* Nice. And have you been down here since yesterday, moping out to The Cure? I'm going to take my old CDs away from you if you're going to behave like an adolescent."

"I am an adolescent." And I am, by my people's standards. Just a pup.

"I get that. Gerry, you *peed* on Weems's car!"

I shrugged. It seemed like the thing to do at the time.

After I'd returned, still wolfself, to the school, Claudia had sold most of the story to a suspicious Weems. She was out walking her dog when she saw the school bus. Not wanting to feel like a fool if it wasn't the missing children, she'd explored, then found the kids. The kids, still under her chemical thrall, had confirmed it: the scary man's dog had attacked the nice lady's doggie, who chased both the bad guys away. Weems later found Smith's body at the wharf, dead, without a mark on him save for his stitched-up arm.

She knelt beside me. "Gerry, Smith is a shock; I buy that. I was rattled, too. It's scary as Hell. The family computer lists have been lighting up with the discussion, and none of the historians have anything like this. *Ever.*"

"I'm not scared, Claud," I said. "And I get that this is major. It's just that . . ."

I took a breath; it was even harder to say out loud than it was to admit to myself. "I liked knowing that we Fangborn were the righteous ones, and that whatever we hunted was *always* wrong. No doubts, never. I always thought it was the payoff for the work we do." It also meant, no matter what my opinion, that Weems was at least nominally on our side.

She cocked her head. "You mean, in addition to the super strength, healing, and longevity?"

"Yeah."

"And the rush that comes after the Change?"

"Well . . . yeah."

She frowned. "You're young and you're being greedy and you're forgetting the First Lesson."

I scowled. "'The work is the reward.' You sound like Grandpa."

"There's a good reason for that. He was right." She hunkered down against the wall next to me. "Look, everyone reaches a crisis of faith at some point in his life. For me, it was trying to figure out if we had the right to live outside human law, learning the difference between *law* and *justice*. It's part of the life. It makes us understand what it is to be human, why that's precious and to be protected. Normals never get half of what we have, and go through life in doubt."

"We're not human, Claud. Never will be. And now we get the doubt, too."

She shook her head. "We're closer to them than anything else. Biologically and spiritually. We need that connection. And you know that killing Smith was right, even if he was one of us."

But no Fangborn had ever killed Fangborn before. No Fangborn had ever manifested pure evil before . . . I couldn't turn off the voice in my head.

Claudia talked for a long time about the community of the Fangborn, duty, honor, and all that crap. I listened. A lot of it made sense.

I nodded. "You're right. I need time, that's all. Thanks."

"No problem. I'm just glad I got here before you got into the Nine Inch Nails." Relief flooded her features, which told me exactly how rocky she thought I looked. "So. You packed?"

"No. It won't take me long." This year, our Christmas present to each other was tickets to Aruba. Expensive, but we both needed the sunshine right now.

She nodded, then eyed me sternly. "But you're gonna go to midnight Mass, right?"

"Probably. I gotta go for a walk, first. Clear my head." I hauled myself up, muscles stiff not from the fight, but from lying around. Any harm I take while wolfself heals rapidly, as long as I remain wolfy, but any hurt I get while in human form reappears when I revert back to human form.

"Good. I'll see you there. And Gerry?"

"Yeah, Claud?"

She wrinkled her nose. "Take a shower, would you?"

I flipped her the bird again, and got my jacket. She smiled as she left, and I knew I had her convinced. That's the good thing about having a shrink for a sister: you learn what they look for and you can give it to them.

Yes, her words made sense. They just did nothing to take away my pain.

I pulled on my duck boots, hat, scarf, and gloves. I probably didn't need so much—it was over thirty degrees—but ever since the fight, I just couldn't get warm.

I walked a long time and found myself at the foot of Derby Wharf. I went out far enough to let the holiday lights of the street fall behind me, until I was alone in the frigid dark. Bloodstains blurred the snow, which had been trampled by the locals looking for the serial killer's savage dog. A fierce hellhound roaming Salem, one more myth in the making.

I watched the lighthouse beam skim the surface of the dark water. Listened to the soft slap of waves against the stone wharf. Anyone with a lick of insight could feel the remnants of the power that had been expended here.

In our family's annals, there was nothing like this, but now I had to wonder: Who else had we missed? Or if this was a really new development, what did it mean? The only thing I knew was that my certainty about my place in the world—my armor and my sword—was shattered.

I felt the silence all around me, city noises muffled by the snow, and tried to find the bottom of the sea of pain I felt. The uncertainty was crushing, the loss of faith like the loss of a limb. I felt broken and made a fool of, mocked by the universe for my belief.

I took a deep breath, the kind you take at the crossroads when the dark man shows up and offers you the world in exchange for your grubby soul. As I watched the obsidian water, I took another breath and realized that if I couldn't manage the leap of faith that Claudia described, then I had to make a leap of another kind.

Down the street from Derby Wharf is a little bar called In a Pig's Eye. It's a local joint; there's no television and they pull the best pints in town.

Annie works there nights.

It was about half full, the folks who were getting one more drink in before Mass and the ones whose family were the other strangers on bar stools.

"Jeez, Gerry, you been sick or something? You look kinda peaky." She set down a coaster in front of me. "Winter Warmer?"

"Thanks. Just . . . out of it, I guess." I suddenly remembered my rank-smelling sweats and two days' growth of beard, and kept my jacket zipped. Hell.

"I bet. I read about Claudia in the paper. You must have *freaked*."

One of the things I've learned to live with is the fact that I'll never get credit for being on the scene, for doing the job. "I worry about her, but she's good at taking care of herself." Then I couldn't resist, sweats or no. "And besides. Chewie wouldn't let anything happen to her."

She put the dark beer down in front of me, a perfect half inch of froth at the top. "No. He's a sweetie."

I felt myself flush, remembering the perfume of Annie's ankles, her hand on the back of my neck as she talked to Claudia one summer night. We'd been coming home from work and I'd still been intoxicated by the kill when we ran into Annie. It's one of my fondest memories. "You like dogs?"

She shrugged. "Depends. Like people, really. You gotta take them one at a time, you know?"

Ask her out, I told myself, ask her out right now, coffee, a drink, anything, or so help me, I'll— "How do you feel about Aruba?" I felt myself go red again: that was not what I meant to say. It was too much, too soon, too pimp, oh shit—

Annie stopped wiping down the bar.

Suddenly, the bottomless water seemed a better choice.

"I'd prefer to start with a drink, maybe dinner," she said slowly. "That is, if you're really, actually, *finally* getting the guts to ask me out?"

"Uh . . . yeah." I swallowed. "That okay?"

"Yeah. But it took you long enough." She glanced at me. "You tough guys, you're all just pussycats. You aren't always a big pussycat, are you, Gerry?"

Mostly I'm a big wolf, I thought giddily. "Never again," I vowed. "How's tomorrow night?"

"Can't." She looked at me funny. "It's Christmas tomorrow, remember? I'm going snowshoeing at Bradley Palmer State Park in the morning."

I wrinkled my brow. An odd tradition, but nice, I s'pose . . .

She blew out her cheeks. "You know I'm Wiccan, right? I like Christmas, but I observe the Solstice."

She looked a little defensive, but I could barely contain myself. I forced myself to take a deep breath. "Trust me when I say that mixed relationships are not a problem for me."

She relaxed, then gave me a look that warmed me instantly, straight through. "If you invite me over for breakfast, I'll ditch the snowshoeing. But I have to leave by noon, because I promised Kelly I'd take her shift at the shelter so she can be with her family."

"Breakfast is at nine o'clock!" I could barely get the words out fast enough.

"Claudia won't mind?"

"Nah. I'll call her when I get home." Claudia had been pushing me to ask Annie out from the first time I'd mentioned her. "She's good people, not an evil bone in her body," Claudia'd said. And Claudia knows bones, good and evil.

"I'll be there." Annie smiled, so sexy I felt my knees go to jelly. "I made a batch of my famous chocolate-chip muffins; I'll bring them."

Into nature, civic-minded, and a cook? I realized I was grinning like an idiot, so I drank the rest of my beer, to keep from proposing to her right then and there, my head ringing with every Christmas carol ever written.

❄   ❄   ❄

Nina Kiriki Hoffman's novella, a World Fantasy Award finalist, focuses on two strangers who connect on Christmas Eve, and—although these are not the only gifts they exchange—find items in a drugstore to wrap and give one another. The tradition is connected with the gifts of the Magi and the secret generosity of Saint Nicholas, a fourth-century Bishop of Myra. Saturnalia, the Roman winter festival, involved some gift-giving, as did the new year celebration of Kalends. As for wrapping gifts, the Victorians used plain brown paper and later tissue paper; printed wrapping paper came along after the turn of the century.

Home for Christmas
❉
Nina Kiriki Hoffman

Matt spread the contents of the wallet on the orange shag rug in front of her, looking at each item. Three oil company charge cards; an auto club card, an auto insurance card; a driver's license which identified the wallet's owner as James Plainfield, thirty-eight, with an address bearing an apartment number in one of the buildings downtown; a gold MasterCard with a hologram of the world on it; a gold Amex card; six hundred and twenty-three dollars, mostly in fifties; a phone credit card, a laminated library card; five tan business cards with "James Plainfield, Architect" and a phone number embossed on them in brown ink; receipts from a deli, a bookstore, an art supply store; a ticket stub from a horror movie; and two scuffed color photographs, one of a smiling woman and the other of a sullen teenage girl.

The wallet, a soft camel-brown calfskin, was feeling distress. —He's lost without me,— it cried, —he needs me; he could be dead by now. Without me in his back pocket he's only half himself.—

Matt patted it and yawned. She had been planning to walk the frozen streets later that night while people were falling asleep, getting her fill of Christmas Eve dreams for another year, feeding the hunger in her that only quieted when she was so exhausted she fell asleep herself. But her feet were wet and she was tired enough to sleep now. She was going to try an experiment: this year, hole up, drink cocoa, and remember all her favorite dreams from Christmas Eves past. If that worked, maybe she could change her life style, stay someplace long enough to . . . to . . . she wasn't sure. She hadn't stayed in any one place for more than a month in years.

"We'll go find him tomorrow morning," she said to the wallet. Although tomorrow was Christmas. Maybe he would have things to do, and be hard to find.

—Now!— cried the wallet.

Matt sighed and leaned against the water heater. Her present home was the basement of somebody's house; the people were gone for the Christmas holidays and the house, lonely, had invited her in when she was looking through its garbage cans a day after its inhabitants had driven off in an overloaded station wagon.

—He'll starve,— moaned the wallet, —he'll run out of gas and be stranded. The police will stop him and arrest him because he doesn't have identification. We have to rescue him *now*.—

Matt had cruised town all day, listening to canned Christmas music piped to the freezing outdoors by stores, watching street-corner Santas ringing bells, cars fighting for parking spaces, shoppers whisking in and out of stores, their faces tense; occasionally she saw bright dreams, a parent imagining a child's joy at the unwrapping of the asked-for toy, a man thinking about what his wife's face would look like when she saw the diamond he had bought for her, a girl finding the perfect book for her best friend. There were the dreams of despair, too: grief because five dollars would not stretch far enough, grief because the one request was impossible to fill, grief because weariness made it too hard to go on.

She had wandered, wrapped in her big olive-drab army coat, never standing still long enough for anyone to wonder or object, occasionally ducking into stores and soaking up warmth before heading out into the cold again, sometimes stalling at store windows to stare at things she had never imagined needing until she saw them, then laughing that feeling away. She didn't need anything she didn't have.

She had stumbled over the wallet on her way home. She wouldn't have found it—it had slipped down a grate—except that it was broadcasting distress. The grate gapped its bars and let her reach down to get the wallet; the grate was tired of listening to the wallet's whining.

—Now,— the wallet said again.

She loaded all the things back into the wallet, getting the gas cards in the wrong place at first, until the wallet scolded her and told her where they belonged. "So," Matt said, slipping the wallet into her army jacket pocket, "if he's lost, stranded, and starving, how are we going to find him?"

—He's probably at the Time-Out. The bartender lets him run a tab sometimes. He might not have noticed I'm gone yet.—

She knew the Time-Out, a neighborhood bar not far from the corner where James Plainfield's apartment building stood. Two miles from the suburb where her temporary basement home was. She sighed, pulled still-damp socks from their perch on a heating duct, and stuffed her freezing feet into them, then laced up the combat boots. She could always put the wallet outside for the night so she could get some sleep; but what if someone else found it? It would suffer agonies; few people understood nonhuman things the way she did, and fewer still went along with the wishes of inanimate objects.

Anyway, there was a church on the way to downtown, and she always liked to see a piece of the midnight service, when a whole bunch of people got all excited about a baby being born, believing for a little while that a thing like that could actually change the world. If she spent enough time searching this guy out, maybe she'd get to church this year.

She slipped out through the kitchen, suggesting that the back door lock itself behind her. Then she headed downtown, trying to avoid the dirty slush piles on the sidewalk.

"Hey," said the bartender as she slipped into the Time-Out. "You got ID, kid?"

Matt shrugged. "I didn't come in to order anything." She wasn't sure how old she was, but she knew it was more than twenty-one. Her close-cut hair, mid-range voice, and slight, sexless figure led people to mistake her for a teenage boy, a notion she usually encouraged. No one had formally identified her since her senior year of high school, years and years ago. "I just came to find a James Plainfield. He here?"

A man seated at the bar looked up. He was dressed in a dark suit, but his tie was emerald green, and his brown hair was a little longer than business-length. He didn't look like his driver's license picture, but then, who did? "Whatcha want?" he said.

"Wanted to give you your wallet. I found it in the street."

"Wha?" He leaned forward, squinting at her.

She walked to the bar and set his wallet in front of him, then turned to go.

"Hey!" he said, grabbing her arm. She decided maybe architecture built up muscles more than she had suspected. "You pick my pocket, you little thief?"

"Sure, that's why I searched you out to return your wallet. Put it in your pocket, Bud. The other pocket. I think you got a hole in your regular wallet pocket. The wallet doesn't like being out in the open."

His eyes narrowed. "Just a second," he said, keeping his grip on her arm. With his free hand he opened the wallet and checked the bulging currency compartment, then looked at the credit cards. His eyebrows rose. He released her. "Thanks, kid. Sorry. I'd really be in trouble without this."

"Yeah, that's what it said."

"What do you mean?"

She shrugged, giving him a narrow grin and stuffing her hands deep into her pockets. He studied her, looking at the soaked shoulders of her jacket, glancing down at her battered boots, their laces knotted in places other than the ends.

"Hey," he said softly. "Hey. How long since you ate?"

"Lunch," she said. With all the people shopping, the trash cans in back of downtown restaurants had been full of leftovers after the lunch rush.

He frowned at his watch. "It's after nine. Does your family know where you are?"

"Not lately," she said. She yawned, covering it with her hand. Then she glanced at the wallet. "This the guy?"

—Yes, oh yes, oh yes, oh joy.—

"Good. 'Bye, Bud. Got to be getting home."

"Wait. There's a reward." He pulled out two fifties and handed them to her. "And you let me take you to dinner? And drive you home afterwards? Unless you have your own car."

She folded the fifties, slipped them into the battered leather card case she used as a wallet, and thought about this odd proposition. She squinted at the empty glass on the bar. "Which number are you?" she muttered to it, "and what were you?"

—I cradled an old-fashioned,— said the glass, —and from the taste of his lips, it was not his first.—

"You talking to my drink?" Amusement quirked the corner of his mouth.

Matt smiled, and took a peek at his dreamscape. She couldn't read thoughts, but she could usually see what people were imagining. Not with Plainfield, though. Instead of images, she saw lists and blueprints, the writing on them too small and stylized for her to read.

He said, "Look, there's a restaurant right around the corner. We can walk to it, if you're worried about my driving."

"Okay," she said.

He left some cash on the bar, waved at the bartender, and walked out, leaving Matt to follow.

The restaurant was a greasy spoon; the tables in the booths were topped with red linoleum and the menus bore traces of previous meals. At nine on Christmas Eve, there weren't many people there, but the waitress seemed cheery when she came by with coffee mugs and silverware. Plainfield drank a whole mugful of coffee while Matt was still warming her hands. His eyes were slightly bloodshot.

"So," he said as he set his coffee mug down.

Matt added cream and sugar, lots of it, stirred, then sipped.

"So," said Plainfield again.

"So," Matt said.

"So did you learn all my deep dark secrets from my wallet? You did look through it, right?"

"Had to find out who owned it."

"What else did you find out?"

"You carry a lot of cash. Your credit's good. You're real worried about your car, and you're an architect. There's two women in your life."

"So do we have anything in common?"

"No. I got no cash—'cept what you gave me—no credit, no car, no relationships, and I don't build anything." She studied the menu. She wondered if he liked young boys. This could be a pickup, she supposed, if he was the sort of man who took advantage of chance opportunities.

The waitress came by and Matt ordered a big breakfast, two of everything, eggs, bacon, sausages, pancakes, ham slices, and biscuits in gravy. Christmas Eve dinner. What the hell. She glanced at Plainfield, saw him grimacing. She grinned, and ordered a large orange juice. Plainfield ordered a side of dry wheat toast.

"What do you want with me, anyway?" Matt asked.

He blinked. "I . . . I thought you must be an amazing person, returning a wallet like mine intact, and I wanted to find out more about you."

"Why?"

"You are a kid, aren't you?"

She stared at him, keeping her face blank.

"Sorry," he said. He looked out the window at the night street for a moment, then turned back. "My wife has my daughter this Christmas, and I . . . " He frowned. "You know how when you lose a tooth, your tongue keeps feeling the hollow space?"

"You really don't know anything about me."

"Except that you're down on your luck but still honest. That says a lot to me."

"I'm not your daughter."

He lowered his eyes to stare at his coffee mug. "I know. I know. It's just that Christmas used to be such a big deal. Corey and I, when we first got together, we decided we'd give each other the Christmases we never had as kids, and we built it all up, tree, stockings, turkey, music, cookies, toasting the year behind and the year ahead and each other. Then when we had Linda it was even better; we could plan and buy and wrap and have secrets just for her, and she loved it. Now the apartment's empty and I don't want to go home."

Matt had spent last Christmas in a shelter. She had enjoyed it. Toy drives had supplied presents for all the kids, and food drives had given everybody real food. They had been without so much for so long that they could taste how good everything was. Dreams came true, even if only for one day.

This year . . . She sat for a moment and remembered one of the dreams she'd seen a couple of years ago. A ten-year-old girl thinking about the loving she'd give a baby doll, just the perfect baby doll, if she found it under the tree tomorrow. Matt could almost feel the hugs. Mm. Still as strong a dream as when she had first collected it. Yes! She had them inside her, and they still felt fresh.

Food arrived and Matt ate, dipping her bacon in the egg yolks and the syrup, loving the citrus bite of the orange juice after the sopping, pillowy texture and maple sweetness of the pancakes. It was nice having first choice of something on a restaurant plate.

"Good appetite," said Plainfield. He picked out a grape jelly from an assortment the waitress had brought with Matt's breakfast and slathered some on his dry toast, took a bite, frowned. "Guess I'm not really hungry."

Matt smiled around a mouthful of biscuits and gravy.

"So," Plainfield said when Matt had eaten everything and was back to sipping coffee.

"So," said Matt.

"So would you come home with me?"

She peeked at his dreamscape, found herself frustrated again by graphs instead of pictures. "Exactly what did you have in mind, Bud?"

He blinked, then set his coffee cup down. His pupils flicked wide, staining his gray eyes black. "Oh. That sounds bad. What I really want, I guess, is not to be alone on Christmas, but I don't mean that in a sexual way. Didn't occur to me a kid would hear it like that."

"Hey," said Matt. Could anybody be this naive?

"You could go straight to sleep if that's what you want. What I miss most is just the sense that someone else is in the apartment while I'm falling asleep. I come from a big family, and living alone just doesn't feel right, especially on Christmas."

"Do you know how stupid this is? I could have a disease, I could be the thief of the century, I could smoke in bed and burn your playhouse down. I could just be really annoying."

"I don't care," he said.

She said, "Bud, you're asking to get taken." Desperation like his was something she usually stayed away from.

"Jim. The name's Jim."

"And how am I supposed to know whether you're one of these Dahmer dudes, keep kids' heads in your fridge?" She didn't seriously consider him a risk, but she would have felt better if she could have gotten a fix on his dreams. She had met some real psychos—their dreams gave them away—and when she closed dream-eyes, they looked almost more like everybody else than everybody else did.

He stared down at his coffee mug, his shoulders slumped. "I guess there is no way to know anymore, is there?"

"Oh, what the hell," she said.

He looked at her, a slow smile surfacing. "You mean it?"

"I've done some stupid things in my time. I tell you, though . . . " she began, then touched her lips. She had been about to threaten him. She never threatened people. Relax. Give the guy a Christmas present of the appearance of trust. "Never mind. This was one great dinner. Let's go."

He dropped a big tip on the table, then headed for the cash register. She followed. "You have any . . . luggage or anything?"

"Not with me." She thought of her belongings, stowed safely in the basement two miles away.

"There's a drugstore right next to my building. We could pick up a toothbrush and whatever else you need there."

Smiling, she shook her head in disbelief. "Okay."

The drugstore was only three blocks from the restaurant; they walked. Plainfield bought Matt an expensive boar-bristle toothbrush, asking her what color she wanted. When she told him purple, he found a purple one, then said, "You want a magazine? Go take a look." Shaking her head again, she headed over to the magazine rack and watched him in the shoplifting mirror. He was sneaking around the aisles of the store looking at things. Incredible. He was going to play Santa, and buy her a present. Kee-rist. Maybe she should get him something.

She looked at school supplies, found a pen and pencil set (the best thing she could think of for someone who thought in graphs), wondered how to get them to the cash register without him seeing them. Then she realized there was a cash register at both doors, so she went to the other one.

By the time he finished skulking around she was back studying the magazines. It had been years since she had looked at magazines. There were magazines about wrestlers, about boys on skateboards, about muscle cars, about pumping iron, about house blueprints, men's fashions, skinny women. In the middle of one of the thick women's fashion magazines she found an article about a murder in a small town, and found herself sucked down into the story, another thing she hadn't experienced in a long time. She didn't read often; too many other things to look at.

"You want that one?"

"What? No." She put the magazine back, glanced at the shopping bag he was carrying. It was bulging and bigger than a breadbox. "You must of needed a lot of bathroom stuff," she said.

He nodded. "Ready?"

"Sure."

On the way into his fifth-floor apartment, she leaned against the front door and thought, —Are you friendly?—

—I do my job. I keep Our Things safe inside and keep other harmful things out.—

—I'm not really one of Our Things,— Matt thought. —I have an invitation, though.—

—I understand that.—

—If I need to leave right away, will you let me out, even if Jim doesn't want me to leave?—

The door mulled this over, then said, —All right.—

—Thanks.— She stroked the wood, then turned to look at the apartment.

She had known he had money—those gold cards, that cash. She liked the way it manifested. The air was tinted with faint scents of lemon furniture polish and evergreen. The couch was long but looked comfortable, upholstered in a geometric pattern of soft, intense lavenders, indigos, grays. The round carpet on the hardwood floor was deep and slate blue; the coffee table was old wood, scarred here and there. A black metal spiral plant-stand supported green, healthy philodendrons and rabbit-track marantas. Everything looked lived-in or lived-with.

To the left was a dining nook. A little Christmas tree decorated with white lights, tinsel, and paper angels stood on the dining table.

"I thought Linda was going to come," Plainfield said, looking at the tree. There were presents under it. "Corey didn't tell me until last night that they were going out of state. You like cocoa?"

"Sure," said Matt, thinking about her Christmas Eve dream, cocoa and other peoples' memories.

"Uh—what would you like me to call you?"

"Matt," said Matt.

"Matt," he said, and nodded. "Kitchen's through there." He gestured toward the dining nook. "I make instant cocoa, but it's pretty good."

Matt looked at him a moment, then headed for the kitchen.

"Be there in a sec," said Jim, heading toward a dark hallway to the right.

—Cocoa?— she thought in the kitchen. Honey-pale wooden cupboard doors wore carved wooden handles in the shape of fancy goldfish, with inlaid gem eyes. White tiles with a lavender border covered the counters; white linoleum tiles inset with random squares of sky blue, rose, and violet surfaced the floor. A pale spring green refrigerator stood by the window, and a small green card table sat near it, with three yellow-cushioned chairs around it. Just looking at the room made Matt smile.

—Who are you?— asked the refrigerator as it hummed.

—A visitor.—

—Where's the little-girl-one who stands there and holds my door open and lets my cold out?—

—I don't think she's coming,— Matt said. She wasn't sure if a refrigerator had a time sense, but decided to ask. —How often is she here?—

—Every time Man puts ice cream in my coldest part. There's ice cream there now.—

Ah ha, Matt thought. She went to the stove, found a modern aqua-enameled teakettle. —May I use you to heat water?— she thought at it.

—Yes yes yes!—Its imagination glowed with the pleasurable anticipation of heat and simmer and expansion.

She ran water into it, greeted the stove as she set the teakettle on the gas burner, then asked the kitchen about mugs. A cupboard creaked open. She patted the door and reached inside for two off-white crockery mugs. A drawer opened to offer her spoons. The whole kitchen was giggling to itself. It had never before occurred to the kitchen that it could move things through its own choice.

—Cocoa?— thought Matt. The cupboard above the refrigerator eased open, and she could see jars of instant coffee and a round tin of instant cocoa inside, but it was out of her reach. She glanced at one of the chairs. She could bring it over—

—Hey!— cried the cocoa tin. She looked up to see it balanced on the edge of the refrigerator. She held out her hands and it dropped heavily into them, the cupboard door closing behind it.

"What?" Jim's voice sounded startled behind her.

She turned, clutching the cocoa, wondering what would happen now. Though she couldn't be sure, she got no sense of threat from him at all, and she was still in the heightened state of awareness she thought of as Company Manners. "Cocoa," she said, displaying the tin on her palms as though it were an award.

"Yeah, but—" He looked up at the cupboard, down at her hands. "But—"

The teakettle whistled—a warbling whistle, like a bird call. The burner turned itself off just as Jim glanced toward it. His eyes widened.

—Chill,— Matt thought at the kitchen.

—Want warmth?— A baseboard heater made clicking sounds as its knob turned clockwise and it kicked into action.

—No! I mean, stop acting on your own, please. Do you want to upset Jim?—

—But this is— !— The concept it showed her was delirious joy. —We never knew we could do this!—

Matt sucked on her lower lip. She'd never seen a room respond to her this way. Some things were wide awake when she met them, and leading secret lives when no one was around to see. Other things woke up and discovered they could choose movement when they talked to her, but never before so joyfully or actively.

"What—" Jim said again.

Matt walked over to the counter by the stove, popped the cocoa tin's top with a spoon.

"Uh," said Matt.

"Can you—uh, make things move around without touching them?" His voice was thin.

"No," she said.

He blinked. Looked at the cupboard over the refrigerator, at the burner control, at the baseboard heater. He shook his head. "I'm seeing things?"

"No," said Matt, spooning cocoa into the mugs. She reached for the teakettle, but before she could touch it, a potholder jumped off a hook above the stove, gliding to land on the handle.

"Design flaw in the kettle," Jim said in a hollow voice. "Handle gets hot too."

"Oh. Thanks," she said, gripping the potholder and the kettle and pouring hot water into the mugs. The spoon she had left in one mug lifted itself and started to stir. "Hey," she said, grabbing it.

—Let me. Let me!—

She let it go, feeling fatalistic, and the other spoon lying on the counter rattled against the tiles until she picked it up and put it in the other mug. The sight of both of them stirring in unison was almost hypnotic.

"I've been reading science fiction for years," Jim said, his voice still coming out warped, "maybe to prepare myself for this day. Telekinesis?"

"Huh?" said Matt as she set the teakettle back on the stove and hung up the pot holder.

"You move things with mind power?"

"No," she said.

"But—" The spoons still danced, crushing lumps of cocoa against the sides of the mugs, making a metal and ceramic clatter.

"I'm not doing it. They are."

"What?"

"Your kitchen," she said, "is very happy."

Cupboards clapped and drawers opened and shut. Somehow the sound of it all resembled laughter.

After a moment, Jim said, "I don't understand. I'm starting to think I must be asleep on the couch and I'm dreaming all this."

—Done,— said the spoons. Matt fished them out of the cocoa and rinsed them off.

"Okay," she said to Jim, handing him a mug.

"Okay what?"

"It's only a dream." —Thanks,— she thought to the kitchen, and headed out to the living room.

Jim followed her. She found coasters stacked on a side table and laid a couple on the coffee table, set her cocoa on one, then shrugged out of her coat and sat on the couch.

"It's only a dream?" Jim said, settling beside her.

"If that makes it easier."

He sipped cocoa. "I don't want easy. I want the truth."

"On Christmas Eve?"

He raised his eyebrows. "Are you one of Santa's elves, or something?"

She laughed.

"For an elf, you look like you could use a shower," he said.

"Even for a human I could."

He fished the toothbrush out of his breast pocket and handed it to her. "Magic wand," he said.

"Thanks." She laid it on the table and drank some cocoa. She was so full from dinner that she wasn't hungry anymore, but the chocolate was enticing.

"All those things were really moving around in the kitchen, weren't they?" he said

"Yes," she said.

"Is the kitchen haunted?"

"Kind of."

"I never noticed it before."

She drank more cocoa. Didn't need other peoples' memories at the moment; making one of her own. She wasn't sure yet whether she'd want to keep this one or not.

Jim said, "Can you point to something and make it do what you want?"

"No."

"Just try it. I dare you. Point to that cane and make it dance." He waved toward a tall vase standing by the front door. It held several umbrellas and a wooden cane carved with a serpent twisting along its length.

"That's silly," she said.

"I've always, always wished I could move things around with my mind. It's been my secret dream since I was ten. Please do it."

"But I—" Frustrated, she set her mug on the table, but not before the coaster slid beneath it.

"See, look!" He lifted his mug, put it down somewhere else. His coaster didn't seem to care.

"But I— Oh, what the hell." —Cane? Do you want to dance?—

The cane quivered in the vase. Then it leapt up out of the vase and spun in the air like a propeller. It landed on the welcome mat, did some staggering spirals, flipped, then lay on the ground and rolled back and forth.

"That's so—that's so—"

She looked at him. His face was pale; his eyes sparkled.

"It's doing it because it wants to," she said.

"But it never wanted to before."

"Maybe it did, but it just didn't know it could."

He looked at the cane. It lifted itself and did some flips, then started tapdancing on the hardwood, somewhat muted by its rubber tip. "If everything knew what it could do—" he said. "Does everything *want* to do stuff like this?"

"I don't know," said Matt. "I've never seen things act like your things." She cocked her head and looked at him sideways.

With one loud tap from its head, the cane jumped back into the big vase and settled quietly among the umbrellas.

"I was wondering how you get things to stop," he whispered.

"Me too," she whispered back. "Usually things act mostly like things when I talk to them. They just act thing ways. Doors open, but they do that anyway. You know?"

"Doors open?" he said. His eyebrows rose.

She could almost see his thoughts. So: that's how this kid gets along. Doors open. She met his gaze without wavering. It had been a long time since she'd told anyone about talking to things, and other times she'd revealed it hadn't always worked out well.

"Doors open, and locks unlock," she said.

"Wow," he said.

"So," she said, "second thoughts about having me stay the night?"

"No! This is like the best Christmas wish I ever had, barring having Linda here."

Matt felt something melt in her chest, sending warmth all through her. She laughed.

He stared at her. "You're a girl," he said after a moment.

She grinned at him and set her mug on the coaster. "Could you loan me some soap and towels and stuff? I sure could use a shower now."

"You're a girl?"

"Mmm. How old do you have to be not to be a girl?"

"Eighteen," he said.

"I'm beyond girl."

"You're an elf," he said.

She grinned. "Could I borrow something clean to sleep in?"

He blinked, shook his head. "Linda's got clothes here, in her old room. She's actually a little bigger than you now." He put his mug down and stood up. "I'll show you," he said.

She grabbed her new toothbrush and followed him down the little hall. He opened a linen closet, loaded her arms with a big fluffy towel and a washcloth, then led her into a bedroom.

—Hello,— she thought to the room. It smelled faintly of vanished perfume, a flowery teen scent. All the furniture was soft varnished honey wood. The built-in bed against the far wall had wide dresser drawers below it and a mini-blind-covered window above. A desk held a small portable typewriter; bookshelves cradled staggering rows of paperbacks, and a big wooden dresser with chartreuse drawers supported about twenty stuffed animals in various stages of being loved to pieces. On the wall hung a framed photographic poster of pink ballerina shoes with ribbons; another framed poster showed different kinds of owls. Ice green wall-to-wall deep pile carpet covered the floor.

—You're not the one,— said the room.

—No, I'm not. The one isn't coming tonight. May I stay here instead? I won't hurt anything.—

—You can't have his heart,— said the room.

—All right,— said Matt. This room was not happy like the kitchen.

It relaxed, though.

—Thanks,— Matt thought.

Jim walked to the dresser and opened a drawer. "How do you feel about flannel?" he said, lifting out a nightgown. The drawer slammed shut, almost catching his hand, and successfully gripping the hem of the nightgown. "Hey!" he said.

—*Our* things,— said the room.

Matt thought about the sullen teenager she had seen in the photo in Jim's wallet. Afraid of losing things, holding them tight; Matt had learned instead to let go.

"Maybe you better put that back," she said. "I can rinse out my T-shirt."

Jim touched the drawer and it opened. He dropped the nightgown back in and the drawer snapped shut again. "I've got pajamas you can use. Actually, my girlfriend left some women's things in my closet . . . "

"Pajamas would be good," Matt said.

He showed her the bathroom, which was spacious and handsome and spotless, black, white, and red tile, fluffy white carpet, combination whirlpool tub and shower, and a small stacked washer-dryer combination. "Wait a sec, I'll get you some pajamas. You want to do laundry?"

"Yeah," she said. "That'd be great." She wished she had the rest of her clothes with her, but they were still in the basement of that suburban house, two miles away. Oh well. You did what you could when the opportunity arrived.

He disappeared, returned with red satin pajamas and a black terrycloth robe.

"Thanks," she said, wondering what else he had in his closet. She hadn't figured him for a red satin kind of guy. She took a long hot shower without talking to anything in the bathroom, using soap and shampoo liberally and several times. The soap smelled clean; the shampoo smelled like apples. His pajamas and robe were huge on her. She hitched everything up and bound it with the robe's belt so she could walk without tripping on the pantlegs or the robe's hem. She brushed her teeth, then started a load of laundry, all her layers, except the coat, which she had left in the living room: T-shirt, long johns top and bottom, work shirt, acrylic sweater, jeans, two pair of socks, even the wide Ace bandages she bound her chest with. Leaving the mirror steamed behind her, she emerged, flushed and clean and feeling very tired but contented.

"I can't believe I ever thought you were a boy," Jim said, putting down a magazine and sitting up on the couch. Christmas carols played softly on the stereo. The mugs had disappeared.

"Very useful, that," said Matt.

"Yes," he said. She sat down at the other end of the couch from him. Sleep was waiting to welcome her; she wasn't sure how long she could keep her eyes open.

After a minute he said, "I went in the kitchen and nothing moved."

Matt frowned.

"Was it a dream?"

"Was what a dream?" she asked, before she could stop herself.

"Please," he said, pain bright in his voice.

"Do you want things dancing? Drawers closing on you?"

He stared at her, then relaxed a little. "Yes," he said, "at least tonight I do."

She pulled her knees up to her chest and huddled, bare feet on the couch, all of her deep in the nightclothes he had given her. She thought about it. "What happens is I talk to things," she said. "And things talk back. Like, I asked the kitchen where the cocoa was. Usually a thing would just say, this cupboard over here. In your kitchen, the cupboard opened itself and the cocoa came out. I don't know why that is, or why other people don't seem to do it."

"Like if I said, Hey, sofa, do you wanna dance?" He patted the seat cushions next to him.

—Sofa, do you want to dance?— Matt thought.

The couch laughed and said, —I'm too heavy to get around much. Floor and I like me where I am. I could . . . — And the cushions bounced up and down, bumping Matt and Jim like a trampoline.

Jim grinned and gripped the cushion he was sitting on. The couch stopped after a couple minutes. "But you did that, didn't you?" he said. "My saying it out loud didn't do anything."

"I guess not," Matt said.

"And things actually talk back to you?"

"Yeah," she said.

"Like my wallet."

"It kept whining about how you would die or at least be arrested without it. It really cares about you." She yawned against the back of her hand.

He fished his wallet out of his back pocket and stared at it for a minute, then stroked it, held it between his hands. "This is very weird," he said. "I mean, I keep this in my back pants pocket, and . . . " He flipped his wallet open and closed. He pressed it to his chest. "I have to think about this." He glanced at the clock on the VCR. "Let's go to sleep. It's already Christmas."

Matt squinted at the glowing amber digits. Yep, after midnight.

"Will you be okay in Linda's room?" Jim asked.

"As long as I don't steal your heart," Matt said and yawned again. Her eyes drifted shut.

"Steal my heart?" Jim muttered.

Matt's breathing slowed. She was perfectly comfortable on the couch, which was adjusting its cushions to fit around her and support her; but she felt Jim's arms lift her. She fell asleep before he ever let go.

She woke up and stared at a barred ceiling. —Where is this?— she asked. Then she rolled her head and glanced toward the door, saw the ballerina toe shoes picture, and remembered: Linda. Jim.

The mini-blinds at the window above the bed were angled to aim slitted daylight at the ceiling. Matt could tell it was morning by the quality of the light. She sat up amid a welter of blankets, sheets, and quilt, and stretched. When she reached skyward, the satin pajama sleeves slid down her arms to her shoulders. She wasn't sure she liked being inside such slippery stuff, but she had been comfortable enough while asleep.

She reached up for the mini-blinds' rod and twisted it until she could see out the window. Jim's apartment was on the fifth floor. Across the street stood another apartment building, brick-faced, its windows mostly shuttered with mini-blinds and curtains, keeping its secrets.

She put her hand against the wall below the window. —Building, hello.—

—Hello, Parasite,— said the building, a deeper structure that housed all the apartments, all the rooms in the apartments, all the things in the rooms, all the common areas, and all the secret systems of wiring and plumbing, heating and cooling, the skeleton of board and girders and beams, the skin of stucco and the eyes of glass-lidded windows.

Parasite, thought Matt. Not a promising opening. But the building sounded cheerful. —How are you?— she thought.

—Warm, snug inside,— thought the building. —Freezing outside. Quiet. It won't last.—

—Oh, well, just wanted to say hi,— thought Matt.

—All right,— thought the building. She felt its attention turning away from her.

—Aren't you getting up now?— asked Linda's room. It sounded grumpy. —It's Christmas morning!—

—Oh. Right.— Matt slipped out of bed, pulled the big black robe around her, and ventured out into the hall, heading for the bathroom. Not a creature was stirring. She finished in the bathroom, then crept into the living room to check the clock on the VCR; it was around 7:30 a.m., a little later than her usual waking time. She peeked at the Christmas tree on the table in the dining nook. Its white lights still twinkled, and there were a couple more presents under it.

—Coat?— she thought. It occurred to her that she had never talked to her own clothes before. Too intimate. Her clothes touched her all the time, and she wasn't comfortable talking to things that touched her anywhere but her hands and feet. If her clothes talked back, achieved self-will, could do whatever they wanted—she clutched the lapels of the black robe, keeping it closed around her. She would have to think about this. It wasn't fair to her clothes. —Coat, where are you?— she thought.

A narrow closet door in the hall slid open. Looking in, she saw that Jim had hung her coat on a hanger. She put out a hand and stroked the stained army-drab. Coat had been with her through all kinds of weather, kept her warm and dry as well as it could, hidden her from too close an inspection, carried all kinds of things for her. She felt an upwelling of gratitude. She hugged the coat, pressing her cheek against its breast, breathing its atmosphere of weather, dirt, Matt, and fried chicken (she had carried some foil-wrapped chicken in a pocket yesterday). After a moment, warmth glowed from the coat; its arms slid flat and empty around her shoulders. She closed her eyes and stood for a long moment letting the coat know how much she appreciated it, and hearing from the coat that it liked her. Then she reached into the inside breast pocket and fished out the pen-and-pencil set she had bought the night before. With a final pat on its lapel, she slid out of the coat's embrace.

—Anybody know where I could find some wrapping paper and tape?— she asked the world in general.

The kitchen called to her, and she went in. A low, deep drawer near the refrigerator slid open, offering her a big selection of wrapping paper for all occasions and even some spools of fancy ribbons. Another drawer higher up opened; it held miscellaneous useful objects, including rubber bands, paperclips, pens, chewing gum, scissors, and a tape dispenser.

—Thanks,— she said. She chose a red paper covered with small green Christmas trees, sat at the card table with it and the tape, and wrapped up the writing set after she peeled the price sticker off it. Silver ribbon snaked across the floor and climbed up the table leg, then lifted its end at her and danced, until she laughed and grabbed it. It wound around her package, tied itself, formed a starburst of loops on top. She patted it and it rustled against her hand.

She put everything away and set her present under the tree, then went back to Linda's room and lay on the bed, yawning. The bed tipped up until she fell out.

—It's Christmas morning,— it said crossly as she felt the back of her head; falling, she'd bumped it, and it hurt. —The one never comes back to bed until she's opened her presents!—

—I'm not the one,— Matt thought. —Thanks for the night.— She left the room, got her coat out of the closet, and lay on the couch with her coat spread over her. The couch cradled her, shifting the cushions until her body lay comfortable and embraced. She fell asleep right away.

The smell of coffee woke her. She sighed and peered over at the VCR. It was an hour later. A white porcelain mug of coffee steamed gently on a coaster on the table. She blinked and sat up, saw Jim sitting in a chair nearby. He wore a gray robe over blue pajamas. He smiled at her. "Merry Christmas."

"Merry Christmas," Matt said. She reached for the coffee, sipped. It was full of cream and sugar, the way she'd fixed it in the restaurant the night before. "Room service," she said. "Thanks."

"Elf pick-me-up." He had a mug of his own. He drank. "What are you doing out here?"

"The room and I had a little disagreement. It said it was time for me to wake up and open presents, like Linda, and I hadn't slept long enough for me."

He gazed into the distance. "Linda's always real anxious to get to the gifts," he said slowly. "She used to wake me and Corey up around six. Of course, we always used to hide the presents until Christmas Eve. We used to get a full-sized tree and set it up over there—" he pointed to a space in a corner of the room between bookshelves on one wall and the entertainment center on the other—"and we wouldn't decorate it until after she'd gone to sleep. So it was as if everything was transformed overnight. God, that was great."

"Magic," said Matt, nodding.

Jim smiled. Matt peeked at his dreamscape, and this time she could see the tree in his imagination, tall enough to brush the ceiling, glowing with twinkling colored lights, tinsel, gleaming glass balls, and Keepsake ornaments—little animals, little Santas, little children doing Christmas things with great good cheer—and here and there, old, much-loved ornaments, each different, clearly treasures from his and Corey's pasts. Beneath the tree, mounds of presents in green, gold, red, silver foil wrap, kissed with stick-on bows. Linda, young and not sullen, walking from the hall, her face alight as she looked at the tree, all of her beaming with wonder and anticipation so that for that brief moment she was the perfect creature, excited about the next moment and expecting to be happy.

"Beautiful," Matt murmured.

"What?" Jim blinked at her and the vision vanished.

Matt sat quiet. She sipped coffee.

"Matt?" said Jim.

Matt considered. At last she said, "The way you saw it. Beautiful. Did Corey take the ornaments?"

"Matt," whispered Jim.

"The old ones, and the ones with mice stringing popcorn, and Santa riding a surfboard, and the little angel sleeping on the cloud?"

He stared at her for a long moment. He leaned back, his shoulders slumping. "She took them," he said. "She's the custodial parent. She took our past."

"It's in your brain," Matt said.

He closed his eyes, leaned his head against the seat back. "Can you see inside my brain?"

"Not usually. Just when you're looking out at stuff, like the tree. And Linda. And I'm not sorry I saw those things, because they're great."

He opened his eyes again and peered at her, his head still back. "They are great," he said. "I didn't know I remembered in such detail. Having it in my brain isn't the same as being able to touch it, though."

"Well, of course not." She thought about all the dreams she had seen since she first woke to them years before. Sometimes people imagined worse than the worst: horrible huge monsters, horrible huge wounds and mistakes and shame. Sometimes they imagined beautiful things, a kiss, a sharing, a hundred musicians making music so thick she felt she could walk on it up to the stars, a sunset that painted the whole world the colors of fire, visions of the world very different from what she saw when she looked with her day-eyes. Sometimes they just dreamed things that had happened, or things that would happen, or things they wished would happen. Sometimes people fantasized about things that made her sick; then she was glad that she could close her dream-eyes when she liked.

All the time, people carried visions and wishes and fears with them. Somehow Matt found in that a reason to go on; her life had crystallized out of wandering without destination or purpose into a quest to watch peoples' dreams, and the dreams of things shaped by people. She never reported back to anyone about what she saw, but the hunger to see more never lessened.

She had to know. She wasn't sure what, or why.

"In a way, ideas and memories are stronger than things you can touch," she said. "For one thing, much more portable. And people can't steal them or destroy them—at least, not very easily."

"I could lose them. I'm always afraid that I'm losing memories. Like a slow leak. Others come along and displace them."

"How many do you need?"

He frowned at her.

She set down her coffee and rubbed her eyes. "I guess I'm asking myself: how many do I need? I always feel like I need more of them. I'm not even sure how to use the ones I've got. I just keep collecting."

"Like you have mine now?"

"My seeing it didn't take it away from you, though."

"No," he said. He straightened. "Actually it looked a lot clearer. I don't usually think in pictures."

"Mostly graphs and blueprints," Matt said.

He tilted his head and looked at her.

"And small print I can't read."

"Good," he said. After a moment's silence, he said, "I would rather you didn't look at what I'm thinking."

"Okay," she said. For the first time it occurred to her that what she did was spy on people. It hadn't mattered much; she almost never talked to people she dreamwatched, so it was an invasion they would never know about. "I do it to survive," she said.

"Dahmer dudes," he said, and nodded.

"Right. But I won't do it to you anymore."

"Thanks. How about a pixie dust breakfast?"

"Huh?"

"Does the kitchen know how to cook?"

She laughed and they went to the kitchen, where he produced cheese omelets, sprinkling red paprika and green parsley on them in honor of Christmas. He had to open the fridge, turn on the stove, fetch the fry-pan himself, but drawers opened for Matt as she set the table, offering her silver and napkins, and a pitcher jumped out of a cupboard when she got frozen orange juice concentrate out of the freezer, its top opening to eat the concentrate and the cans of water. She had never before met such a cooperative and happy room. Her own grin lighted her from inside.

Jim's plates were eggshell-white ceramic with a pastel geometric border. He slid the omelets onto them and brought breakfast to the table. She poured orange juice into square red glass tumblers, fetched more coffee from the coffeemaker's half-full pot, and sat down at the green table.

"I'm so glad you're here," Jim said.

"Me too," said Matt.

"Makes a much better Christmas than me quietly moping and maybe drinking all day."

Matt smiled and ate a bite of omelet. Hot fluffy egg, cheese, spices greeted her mouth. "Great," she said after she swallowed.

Jim finished his omelet one bite behind Matt. She sat back, hands folded on her stomach, and grinned at him until he smiled back.

"Presents," she said.

"That was my line. Also I wanted to say having you here is the best present I can think of, because all my life I've wanted to see things move without being touched. It makes me so happy I don't have words for it."

"Did you design this kitchen?"

He glanced around, smiled. "Yeah. I don't do many interiors, but I chose everything in here, since I like to cook. Corey did the living room and our bedroom."

"This kitchen moves more than any other place I've ever been. I think it was almost ready to move all by itself. I bet your buildings would like to take a walk. I wonder if they're happy. I bet they are."

He sat back and beamed at her. Then he reached for his coffee mug and it slid into his hand. His eyes widened. "Matt . . . "

She shook her head.

"Gosh. You *are* an elf." He sipped coffee, held the mug in front of him, staring at it. He stroked his fingers along its smooth glaze. He looked up at Matt. "It's beautiful," he said.

"Yeah," she said. "Everything is."

For a long time they stared at each other, their breathing slow and deep. At last he put the mug down, but then curled his fingers around it as though he couldn't bear to let go.

"Everything?" he said.

"Mmm," she said. For a moment she thought of ugly dreams, and sad dreams, and wondered if she believed what she had just said. Some things hurt so much she couldn't look at them for long. Still, she wanted to see them all. Without every part, the balance was missing. Jim's image of a Christmas Linda was intensified by how much he missed her. Cocoa tasted much better on a really cold day, and a hug after a nightmare could save a life . . .

After a moment, she said, "I got you something." She stood up. He stood up too, and followed her into the dining nook. She picked up the parcel she had wrapped that morning and offered it to him. "I had to, uh, borrow the paper."

"How could you get me anything?" he said, perplexed. "These are for you." He handed her three packages. "I didn't know what to get you." He shrugged.

"Dinner, cocoa, conversation, a shower, laundry, a place to sleep, coffee, breakfast," she said. She grinned and took her packages to the couch, where she shoved her coat over and sat next to it. "Thanks," she said.

He joined her.

She opened the first present, uncovered a card with five die-cast metal micro-cars attached, all painted skateboard colors: hot rods with working wheels. Delighted, she freed them from their plastic and set them on the coffee table, where they growled and raced with each other and acted like demented traffic without ever going over the edge.

Jim sat gripping his present, watching the cars with fierce concentration. "I got them for the teenage boy," he said in a hushed voice after a moment. Two of the cars seemed to like each other; they moved in parallel courses, looping and reversing. One of the others parked. The two remaining were locked bumper to bumper, growling at each other, neither giving an inch.

Matt laughed. "They're great! They can live in my pocket." She patted her coat. "Open yours."

He touched the ribbon on his package and it shimmered with activity, then dropped off the package and slithered from his lap to the couch, where it lifted one end as if watching. Eyebrows up, he slid a fingernail under the paper, pulled off the wrapping. He grinned at the pen and pencil, which were coated with hologram diffraction grating in magenta and teal, gold and silver. "The office isn't going to know what hit it," he said. "Thanks."

"I bought 'em for the architect with a green tie. Not a whole lot of selection in that store."

"Yeah," he said, tucking them into the pocket of his robe. "Go on." He gestured toward the other two presents.

She opened the first one and found a purple knit hat. The second held a pair of black leather gloves. She slid her hands into them; they fit, and the inner lining felt soft against her palms. "Thanks," she said, her voice a little tight, her heart warm and hurt, knowing he had bought them for the homeless person. She smiled and leaned her cheek against the back of her gloved hand. "Best presents I've gotten in years."

"Me too," he said, holding out a hand to the silver ribbon. It reached up and coiled around his wrist. He breathed deep and stroked the ribbon. "God!"

Matt tucked the hat and gloves into a coat pocket, patted the coat, held out a hand to the little cars. They raced over and climbed up onto her palm. "Look," she said, turning over her coat. "Here's your new garage." She laid the coat open and lifted the inner breast pocket so darkness gaped. The cars popped wheelies off her hand and zipped into the cave. One peeked out again, then vanished. She laughed. She had laughed more in the last twelve hours than she had in a whole month.

The phone rang, and Matt jumped. Jim picked up a sleek curved tan thing from a table beside the couch and said, "Merry Christmas" into it.

Then, "Oh, hi, Corey!"

Hugging her coat to her, Matt stood up. She could go in the other room and change while he talked to his ex-wife. Jim patted the couch and smiled at her and she sat down again, curious, as ever, about the details of other peoples' lives.

"Nope. I'm not drunk. I'm not hung over. I'm fine. Missing Linda, that's all . . . okay, thanks."

He waited a moment, his eyes staring at distance, one hand holding the phone to his ear and the other stroking the silver ribbon around the phone-hand's wrist. "Hi, Hon. Merry Christmas! You having fun?"

A moment.

"I miss you too. Don't worry, your presents are waiting. When you get home we can have a mini-Christmas. I hope you're someplace with snow in it. I know how much you like that . . . oh, you are? Great! Snow angels, of course. What'd your mom get for you?"

Matt thought about family Christmases, other peoples' and then, at last, one of her own—she hadn't visited her own memories in a long, long time. Her older sister Pammy sneaking into her room before dawn, holding out a tiny wrapped parcel. "Don't tell anybody, Mattie. This is just for you," Pammy had said, and crept into bed beside her and kissed her. Matt opened the package and found inside it a heart-shaped locket. Inside, a picture of her as a baby, and a picture of Pammy. Matt had seen the locket before—Pammy had been wearing it ever since their mother gave it to her on her tenth birthday, four years earlier. Only, originally, it had had pictures of Mom and Dad in it.

"I'll never tell," Matt had whispered, pressing the locket against her heart.

"It's supposed to keep you safe," Pammy said, her voice low and tight. "That's what Mom told me. It didn't work for me but maybe it will for you. Anyway, I just want you to know . . . you have my heart."

And Matt had cried the kind of crying you do without sound but with tears, and she hadn't even known why, not until several years later.

"That's great," Jim said, smiling, his eyes misty. "That's great, Honey. Will you sing one for me when you get home? Yeah, I know it will feel funny to sing a carol after Christmas is over, but we're doing a little time warp, remember? Saving a piece of Christmas for later . . .

"Me? I thought I was going to miss you so much I wasn't going to have any fun, but I found a friend, and she gave me a couple presents. No, not Josie! She's at her folks'. I know you don't like it if she's here when you come, so we set it up before I knew you weren't . . . " He glanced at Matt and frowned, shrugged. "No, this is a kid. Actually, an elf."

He smiled again. "I wish you could have been here. She made the kitchen dance and the couch dance. I gave her these little cars, because I thought she was a boy, and she made them run all over the coffee table even though they don't have motors in them. I think she works for Santa Claus."

Matt slipped her hand into a coat pocket and touched the hat he had given her. It was soft like cashmere. Maybe *he* worked for Santa Claus. It had been a long time since she had had a Christmas of her own instead of borrowing other peoples', and this was the first one she could remember where she was actually really happy.

"You're too old to believe in Santa?" he said. He sighed. "I thought I was, too, but I'm not anymore." He listened, then laughed. "Okay, call me silly if you like. I'm glad you're having a good Christmas. I love you. I'll see you when you get back." He laid the phone down with a faint click.

Matt grinned at him. She liked thinking of herself as an elf and an agent of Christmas. Better than thinking she must be some kind of charity project for Jim, the way she had been at first.

Stranger still to realize she was having a no-peek Christmas, alone in her own head.

She thought of families, and, at long last, of her sister Pammy. How many years had it been? She didn't even know if Pam were still alive, still married to her first husband, if she had kids . . .

"Can I use that?" she said. He handed the phone to her. She dialed information.

"What city?"

"Seattle," she said. "Do you have a listing for Pam Sternbach?"

There was a number. She dialed it.

"Merry Christmas," said a voice she had not heard since she had lived at home, half a life ago.

"Pam?"

"Mattie! Mattie? Omigod, I thought you were dead! Where are you? What have you been doing? Omigod! Are you all right?"

For a moment she felt very strange, fever and chills shifting back and forth through her. She had reached out to her past and now it was touching her back. She had put so much distance between it and herself. She had walked it away, stamped it into a thousand streets, shed the skin of it a thousand times, overlaid it with new thoughts and other lives and memories until she had thousands to choose from. What was she doing?

"Mattie?"

"I'm fine," she said. "How are you?"

"How am I? Good God, Mattie! Where have you been all these years?"

"Pretty much everywhere." She reached into the coat's breast pocket and fished out one of the little cars, watched it race back and forth across her palm. She was connecting to her past, but she hadn't lost her present doing it. She drew in a deep breath, let it out in a huge sigh, smiled at Jim, and snuggled down to talk.

❉   ❉   ❉

Sarban (John William Wall) was, in 1939, appointed Second Secretary to the British legation in Jedda, Saudi Arabia. As in the story, the very small European community tried to maintain holiday customs such as caroling as mummers. The Yolka (Russian for "spruce tree") the White Russian exile Masseyev mentions was a New Year tree—the Russian equivalent of a Christmas tree—a tradition dating back to a 1699 decree by Peter the Great that New Year was to be celebrated on January 1. Russian Yolka and New Year's celebrations were banned in 1916 during the first World War as a German tradition. The Soviets continued the ban until politician Pavel Postyshev published a plea in Pravda *in 1935 to reinstate Yolka and New Year celebrations.*

A Christmas Story
❄
Sarban

I will tell you a Christmas story. I will tell it as Alexander Andreievitch Masseyev told it me in his little house outside the walls of Jedda years ago one hot, damp Christmas Eve.

It was the custom among the few English people in Jedda in those days to make up a carol-singing party on Christmas Eve. For a week before, the three or four of us who had voices they were not ashamed of, and the one or two who had neither voice nor shame, practiced to the accompaniment of an old piano in the one British mercantile house in the place: an instrument whose vocal cords had not stood the excessive humidity of that climate any better than those of some of the singers. Then, on Christmas Eve, the party gathered at our house where we dined and, with a lingering memory of Yuletide mummers in England, arrayed ourselves in such bits of fancy dress or comic finery as we could lay our hands on; made false whiskers out of cotton-wool or a wisp of tow, blackened our faces, reddened our noses with lipstick supplied by the Vice-Consul's wife, put our jackets on inside-out and sprinkled over our shoulders "frost" out of a little packet bought by someone ages ago at home and kept by some miracle of sentimental pertinacity through years of exile on that desert shore.

I am no singer, but I always had a part in these proceedings. It was to carry the lantern.

Our Sudanese house-boys served us with more admiration than amusement on their faces, and the little knot of our Arab neighbors, who always gathered about our door to watch us set out, whatever the occasion, gave not the slightest sign of recognizing anything more comic than usual in our appearance. We made our round of the European houses in our Ford station-wagon; I holding my lantern on its pole outside the vehicle and only by luck avoiding shattering it against the wall as the First Secretary cut the corners of the narrow lanes. Fortunately, except for our neighbors, who never seemed to go to bed at all (or, at least, didn't go to bed to sleep), the True-Believers of Jedda kept early hours, and by nine or ten at night the dark sandy lanes were deserted but for pariah dogs and families of goats settled with weary wheezings to doze the still, close night away. Poor Jedda goats! whose pasture and byre were the odorous alleys; pathetic mothers of frustrated offspring, with those brassieres which seemed at first sight such an astonishing refinement of Grundyism, but which turned out to be merely an economic safeguard—girdles not of chastity but husbandry; with your frugal diet of old newspapers and ends of straw rope, to whom the finding of an unwanted (or unguarded) panama hat was like a breakfast of 'Id ul Futr; how many a curse and kick in the ribs have you earned from a night-ambling Frank for couching in that precise pit of darkness where the feeble rays of one paraffin lamp expire and those of the next are not yet born!

From the façades of the crazy, coral-built houses that hem the lanes project *roshans*—bow-windows of decaying wooden lattice-work—and on the plastered tops of these bow-windows the moonlight falls so clear and white this Christmas Eve that to the after-dinner eye it seems that snow has fallen.

Our first call was always at the Minister's. There, in the paneled hall which, but for its bareness, might have been in England, we used to range ourselves and, in comparatively good order, deliver our repertoire while the Minister, in his study above, turned down the wireless for a few minutes and his Lady and family listened from the staircase. We always gave the meteorological data of Good King Wenceslaus with feeling, perhaps more conscious than at other times of our prickly heat and the sweat trickling down inside our shirts. Then the Minister's Lady descended to congratulate us, kind-heartedly, on our singing and, spontaneously, on our disguises, while the mustachioed Sudani butler brought wassail on a tray. After our own Minister, we used to go to the American Legation and then to the Dutch Chargé d'Affaires where, also, loyalty to tradition had its traditional reward in the Red Sea equivalent of the wassail-bowl. That used to be about as far as our organization was capable of maintaining a good custom with coherence. A touch of the strayed reveler used to creep in after that. But, while most of the party had still not lost their papers of words and while two or three were still agreed on the tune of any one carol, the Vice-Consul's wife used to insist on our going out to the Masseyev's. We were all always agreed that we wanted to go there; the argument used to be about the order it should take in our round of calls, for at this stage, the length of our stay at any particular house was unpredictable. However, the Vice-Consul's wife always won. So, letting in the clutch with a jerk, the First Secretary would roar round by the town wall and out of the Medina Gate and along the tire-beaten track to the hut-suburb of Baghdadia.

Years and years ago, before even the Vice-Consul came to Jedda, Alexander Andreievitch Masseyev, sometime a lieutenant in the Tzarist Navy, exiled by the October Revolution, had ended a pilgrimage through the Middle East by accepting the post of instructor to the Arabian Air Force.

When I knew him, he and his wife, Lydia, lived in a little white-walled house with a tiny courtyard before it between the straggling suburb and the sea a mile northwards from the Medina Gate.

There, then, we arrive this Christmas Eve. We are expected, but pretend not to be. We shush each other a good deal, and everybody shushes the Vice-Consul, and after the Vice-Consul's wife, being in conspiracy with Lydia, has caused the courtyard door to be opened we tip-toe in and range ourselves round, or some of us, upon a flower-bed the size of a pocket handkerchief, and let fly with "Christians Awake"; then, after a lot of fierce "all-togethering," render "Hark the Herald Angels Sing," and, as a concession to the Vice-Consul, who thought that was what we were singing to begin with, "Good King Wenceslaus" once more. Alexander Andreievitch and Lydia appear in their lighted doorway, smiling, not quite understanding, but smiling because this is something Christian with a faint affinity to white winters far away. With loud "Merry Christmases" we crowd into their little sitting-room, while Lydia exclaims at our daubed visages and disarray, and chatters in a mixture of broken French and English, and Alexander Andreievitch, beaming all over his broad face, brings out bottles and glasses and tumbles his six words of English out at us. He and the Vice-Consul understand each other in what they call Arabic—but it would puzzle an Arab.

Lydia has made a cake. The Vice-Consul's wife has brought a bottle of wine for a present; we have produced a bottle of whisky, and the Vice-

Consul is discovered to have brought a bottle of rum on general principles. There are little dishes of salted almonds and olives, slices of well-matured sausage, and even bits of ham procured from Yanni, the Cypriot grocer in the Suq (at a price that would make the Black Market look like a bargain counter). It is hot in the little room; burnt cork and lipstick trickle down the plump face of Bartholomew, our sole representative of British Commerce; the First Secretary props open the door and fans himself; but Moslem Arabia is shut out beyond the courtyard walls: we are but fifty miles from Mecca and the desert between us and Bethlehem is ten times as wide, but we settle ourselves on the few chairs or the floor and, every Christian glass being filled, sing "God rest you Merry, Gentlemen!"

On the wall there is a faded photograph of some prospect in St Petersburg, and there hang from a nail a prismatic compass and an aneroid barometer in stout though worn leather cases, once the property of the Imperial Navy, which Alexander Andreievitch has saved from the wreck and managed to preserve through all these years. Alexander Andreievitch is a short, squarely built man with short, iron-gray hair and a broad, deeply-lined face that does not often smile. His heart is not so good now as it once was. He no longer flies in the two or three temperamental old Wapiti aircraft that constitute the Arabian Air Force. His job now consists mainly in trying to keep the saleable stores of the Air Force from seeping away into the Suq; in endeavouring to explain to the Nejdi camel-rider who commands the Force that the principles of aerial navigation are not explicit in the Quran, and in petitioning the Minister of War for arrears of pay. He has never announced any notable advance in any of these directions.

I sit near Alexander Andreievitch and pledge him in Russian, at which he smiles, then, with an exclamation as if suddenly remembering something, gets up and fumbles in a little cupboard in the wall. He brings out a strange-looking bottle which he proudly shows me. The label is one I have not seen within a thousand miles of Jedda. Then I remember that some months ago Alexander Andreievitch went to Baghdad.

There, by a lucky chance, he has lighted on a bottle of Zubrovka, smuggled down, I expect, from Tehran or Tabriz. I am the only one in our party who knows what it is. The others prefer whisky or rum. Alexander Andreievitch sets out two little glasses and fills them. Back go our heads: *do dna!* We perform this exercise a good many times while the others are sipping at their longer glasses. Alexander Andreievitch smiles frequently now and talks all the time, in Russian.

The label of the bottle has always interested me. My Russian is not so copious that I can see the connection between the name Zubrovka and the picture of the European Bison which seems to be the Trade Mark. So Alexander Andreievitch explains and adds a word to my vocabulary. "*Da . . .* ", he says, with a melancholy drawing-out of the syllable. "They are all gone now. There were a few in the deep forest of Lithuania until the Revolution. The Tzar preserved them." He sighs. I too remember, when I was a little boy, I saw an old, high-withered, ungainly beast with matted hair hanging on it like worn door-mats leaning against the rails of an enclosure in Regent's Park: a huge, tired, solitary beast hanging its heavy head with half-closed eyes, while a grubby fist thrust monkey-nuts under its muzzle and cockney voices wondered what it was.

"Did you ever see one?" I ask Alexander Andreievitch. He shakes his head so sadly and looks so full of the irrevocable past that I am led to see a symbolic correspondence between him and the Zubor, between them both and Imperial Russia, and the weight of what's gone beyond recall lies heavily on my spirit until we have lowered the level of the Zubrovka below the Bison's feet. Then we cheer up a little and I suggest: "Perhaps . . . Who knows? Russia is very wide . . . There are untrodden forests still . . . "

Very gravely Alexander Andreievitch nods his head. "*Da, v Rossii . . .* Yes, there are rare things in Russia. I have seen—listen, Meester—will you believe I have seen something, oh! far away beyond the forests, something that was not a Zubor?"

"No? What then?"

"No. Not a bison, not a reindeer, not an elk. I was a hunter when I was a boy. I know all those things. Once, it was in 1917, I was on board a cruiser, the *Knyaz Nicolai*, and we were ordered to Archangel. From there we cruised eastward in the Arctic Ocean to the mouth of the Yenessei River. It was summer, naturally. Why we went there no one knew. It was 1917. Some of us thought our orders were to go through the Behring Straits to Japan. We were young. We joked about going ashore in Siberia to chop firewood when the coal ran out, the same as the troops did on the railway. That shore in summer looks just the same as these Hejaz mountains, brown and bare. The *Knyaz Nicolai* carried a sea-plane, an English machine. That was a very new idea then. The English had thought of doing it. We Russians did it. We made experimental flights in the fine weather up there in the Arctic Ocean. The pilot was my old friend Igor Palyashkin. I was his observer. It was a revolutionary idea. I think the Russians were the first who practised it, though the English no doubt thought of it.

"Well, there was a little station near the mouth of the Yenessei River, far, far away from anywhere. A few Russians kept the station and collected furs from the natives; there was also an officer of the Imperial Navy. He did not collect furs. He just drank. The *Knyaz Nicolai* was ordered to call at this station—it was called *Kamyenaya Gora*—and deliver some provisions. We approached, but the winter that year began early. Already, when the sea should have been open for another month, ice was forming. We met fields of ice that stretched as far as the eye could see; thin ice, you understand, which the cruiser could break through. But it was dangerous, for in one day or so of sudden hard weather that thin ice will become solid and lock you in immovably; then it begins to squeeze. The *Knyaz Nicolai* did not reach *Kamyenaya Gora*. We returned to open water, but because we were so near our captain decided to send the sea-plane with a message. It was something that had never been done before. We were to circle the station, drop our message and return and be picked up on the open water.

"We made our calculations, Igor Palyashkin and I, and we took off. It was very fine weather; the last, still, clear days of the Arctic summer. We could not see far; the circle of our vision was bounded by a blue wall, but beneath us we saw the sea quite clearly, without waves, for it was covered with a thin skin of ice, but moving gently as if it breathed; and a little further on we saw the land, brown with streaks of snow. We flew a long way over the land. It is a mournful land, and empty! Ah, emptier far than any you have seen even between here and the Persian Gulf. We flew so far over the land that I thought our calculations must be wrong, but we found that little station, Igor Palyashkin and I! It was the first aeroplane they had ever seen, those people, I think. We saw them running out. We went very low and I waved and dropped the message, then we headed back for the cruiser again. We were the first men who had ever flown in the Arctic Circle, Igor Palyashkin and I."

Alexander Andreievitch refills our little glasses. Bartholomew and the Vice-Consul are singing "Good King Wenceslaus" again, but merely, I gather, to settle an argument about something. The Second Secretary is leaning against the wall behind the door. He appears to be asleep.

"*Da*," says Alexander Andreievitch, as he sets down his glass on the tray, speaking softly to the Bison. "They shot him afterwards, the Bolsheviki. But we were the first, Igor Palyashkin and I." He shakes his head and I wait.

"You understand," he says, "our calculations were not quite right. We saw the land, oh! land on every side. Brown land with streaks of snow, and when we came low we saw the forests of little gray bushes and the mournful marshes, all the wide taiga on every side. But we did not see the sea. And then the blue wall which had been all round us between the sky and the sea turned gray and came very close, and soon we could see nothing at all but gray mist unless we flew very, very low. So we came down very close to the land, just over the tops of little fir trees and gray bushes and over the surface of desolate pools, black and glinting like steel. Up above there was no sun and no sky, and on every side there was only the mournful gray taiga.

"Then, soon, Igor Palyashkin turned and looked at me and I knew that we had no more petrol left. He signed with his arm that he was going to land, and we went down, swiftly, to the drab gray marsh; we touched the tops of the little bushes and then a blackness like steel spread before us and the floats of the machine sent up fountains of water and sheets of white ice. We came to a stop with the nose of our machine in the bushes at the edge of the marsh and we climbed out unhurt. He was a good pilot, Igor Palyashkin.

"We had our map and the compass and we made fresh calculations and set off to walk to Kamyenaya Gora. But the night came down, so we stopped and lit a fire. It took a long time to light that fire. The little willow bushes would not burn very well and before we had got it going well enough to put some moss on to make a smoke we were being tortured by millions of mosquitoes. We had our iron rations: enough for one meal. We ate those, then wrapped our heads in our coats and lay on the wet ground in the smoke of the fire. But still the mosquitoes got at us. *Bozhe moi!* How they bit. 'I wish it would freeze!' Igor Palyashkin said. 'It would kill us but it would kill these damned mosquitoes first.'

"When it was light we began to walk, but you cannot walk very well in the taiga. Everywhere in summer the ground is soft; the little bushes grow in the marsh and you cannot push your way through them when you are up to your waist in water and mud. And the mosquitoes never left off biting. We kept at it for two days. The second and third nights we could not even light a fire, because there was nowhere dry to light it and the matches had got wet, too. It was miserably cold and we had no food, but Igor Palyashkin was cheerful. He had his revolver. 'I shall shoot a reindeer,' he said. I said there were no reindeer in the marshes. 'Well, then, a wolf. No? a fox, a hare, a rat. What matters it? I shall shoot the first thing I see and we shall eat it raw. And if God sends us nothing else to shoot I will shoot you and then myself, so we shall not die a hard death.'

'Igor Sergeievitch,' I said, 'shoot me now, for there is nothing alive in all this cursed taiga but the mosquitoes and we.'

"But I was wrong. On the third day we came to some dry ground where some fir trees grew. Oh! little fir trees like Christmas trees, but we were so glad to see them and to stop wading through the marsh that we clasped hands, Igor Palyashkin and I, and danced round one of them and sang the children's song about the Yolka.

"Beyond that dry ground was a broad river, so broad we could just see the other bank like a brown bar under the gray gloom of the sky. The river was full of spongy, water-logged ice so that it did not flow or ripple, but stood still while we, standing on the low bank by the little fir trees, we, you understand, seemed to move backwards. It was so quiet! There was no bird or animal moving in all the world; even the mosquitoes had left us. It was so quiet that we could hear the sap creeping down the little fir trees into the ground and we knew, Igor Palyashkin and I, that that night the Lord Frost would come to the taiga and bind the river and snap the boughs and freeze us like stones to the earth. It was so quiet that we could hear the Frost coming from far away and Igor Palyashkin pulled out his revolver and shot six times into the north. He was not afraid of God, Igor Palyashkin.

"Then, between the fir trees, stepping softly in their skin boots and holding their bows in front of them, came six little men dressed all in skins; six Samoyed hunters. They took us to a little hut they had built among the fir trees and gave us meat to eat. We ate and ate until we were sick. Then we lay down on some skins in the hut and heard the frost come walking through the dark, cracking the trees as he passed. It was too cold to sleep, but because they had a handful of fire in the middle of the hut and we cowered round it, eight men huddled close together, we did not freeze. They gave us some more meat and this time we kept it down and crouched over that little heap of embers all night, Igor Palyashkin and I and the six Samoyed hunters. Not a word of Russian had they and not a word of their tongue had we. Ah! If we had had a bottle of Zubrovka that night—one glass, even!

The Vice-Consul's wife is on her feet, drawing out a long farewell to Lydia; the First Secretary is holding open the door, still fanning himself; the Second Secretary is on the floor behind the door leaning his back against the wall: he has been asleep for the last ten minutes. But the Vice-Consul has begun another argument with Bartholomew. "What's your hurry?" he says. "There's half a bottle of rum left yet. Time enough for the next folks!" So his wife and the First Secretary sit down again. "Another little glass!" says Alexander Andreievitch to me. "It's still early." And he tilts the Bison.

"In the morning light we set out," says Alexander Andreievitch. "We said *Kamyenaya Gora* very loud to the Samoyeds to make them understand where we wanted to go. So they picked up their bows and arrows and one of them took up an old, old gun, so old and so heavy it had a fork attached to the barrel to support it by, and they beckoned to us to go with them. But Igor Palyashkin was eating some more of the meat, and in the morning light he was looking closely at what he was eating. It was a large piece of meat, purplish, like beef, you understand, but there was a piece of skin on it, and on the skin some hair, and that hair was long and woolly and reddish in color, not like the hair of any cow or ox in Russia or Siberia. 'What is this meat?' says Igor Palyashkin. I looked at it closely, too, and tasted it again, and because my hunger was appeased now I could taste it properly. It had a strong, high flavor; it was more than half rotten. I wondered how I could have brought my snout near it the night before. It was not cooked, you understand, just warmed in the ashes. It stank of age and the earth. I had heard that in summer when the Samoyeds kill a beast they bury what they cannot eat by digging down a little way until they come to the frozen earth which never thaws and there they lay their meat and cover it with earth and it will keep all summer through: or keep well enough for them. Dear God! It smelt like a gravedigger's boots!

"'This meat! This meat!' cries Igor Palyashkin, as he grips the oldest Samoyed by the stiff skin sleeve. 'The Devil take you! *Ot kuda eto myaso?* From where, man, where?'

"'Myaso! myaso!' bellows Igor Palyashkin, seeing they do not understand. He points to the rotten gobbet of flesh with the long red wool on it and roars 'Myaso!' until the little old fellow looks frightened and they all put their heads together and mutter, and it seems they're wondering what to do to calm this ferocious Russian. Then they point away down the river and smile timidly and beckon to us to go with them again.

"'Kamyenaya Gora!' we said again and again to the little hunters as they led us through the brittle gray trees. They nodded their heads and smiled. God knows whether they understood that Russian name, but they knew that we were Russians and they would lead us to the nearest Christian men. It had grown bitter cold! The black sky was no higher than the fir treetops and so solid you bent your head, like going into a hut. An icy mist stood among the little trees like a palisade round us, not two arms' length from us. When we spoke our words rang sonorous as if they reverberated from solid walls all round us. They gave us the skins we had slept on to wrap round us, and we waddled among those little men, Igor Palyashkin and I, like bears on their hind legs.

"We walked all day in single file with the Samoyed hunters, and in the afternoon we came again to the wide marshes. But now the frost had bound them, and we walked over them, sometimes on black ice that bent like thin planks under us, sometimes on frozen mud that squeaked and whined when our boots pressed it, and we broke the brittle willow twigs like stubble on a reaped field. Not a living thing but ourselves did we see and not a sound of anything with a soul came through the cold mist to us.

"But towards evening, towards the early evening, a whisper woke far away on the marshes and came to us, and the mist thinned and a keen wind cut our cheeks. The Samoyeds stopped and looked at each other and snuffed the wind. We too knew what that wind was. It was the snow-wind.

"Far and wide we could see now over the immense, sad taiga: a level, lonely waste of drab brown and faded gray, every particle of life in it stilled by that one terrible grip of the Lord Frost and its dead body stabbed through and through by the bayonets of the snow-wind. When the wind ceased we knew that the winding-sheet would fall from the black sky. The mist, you understand, had not gone entirely, it had thinned to a ghost of mist that rode upon the wind and still half-veiled the lifeless world. There was neither light nor dark, but a mixture of both, as if the night to come were powder blown about us by the freezing wind. The wind cut us to the bone, but it did not rustle the bushes: they were frozen stiff as stone. We could see far and wide, we could see to the world's end, for there was nothing in all the world but that cancelled light, that drab brown earth and that drab gray scrub, as dead as a dead man's hair.

"We did not know, Igor Palyashkin and I, where we were going. We did not look at our compass or at our map. We bent our heads and stumbled through the dead world after the six little hunters. I did not think I should ever see Kamyenaya Gora; I did not think I should ever see Petersburg or any Christian house again. I thought I should die there where there was nothing but grayness and cold. I was young; I should have wept, but it was too cold to cry.

"But the little Samoyeds knew where we were going, and before the gray light was all gone they brought us where something with definite form was visible in that limitless murk. On one side we saw the broad river, immobile under its ice, but blinking pale and hard in that fugitive landscape; and before us, across the level of the marsh we saw a low dark brown cliff of earth caving above the river, its overhang that might have fallen in the brief thaw of summer arrested now and secured for all the long winter by the hand of the frost. About us on that immense and mournful level the thin gray bushes grew sparser but taller. They seemed like columns of smoke that had been drifting up to mingle with the low gray sky and had been frozen, they also, only a little more solid and more defined than the gray atmosphere. The brown mud that stretched so far on every side was wrinkled as it had shrunk in the grip of the frost and in all the wrinkles lay white veins and threads of ice.

"Just as we came in sight of the river and that low bank of earth, the snow-wind dropped. Igor Palyashkin and I, we looked at one another; our lips were so numb with cold we could not speak. The Samoyeds muttered together and their breath hung in little thick white clouds before them. In a few minutes it would begin to snow and not even a Samoyed hunter would then find his way across the waste when the white flurries filled all the air. The oldest hunter gazed round, up at the heavy sky, round at the spectral bushes, down at the glazed and shrunken earth and finally out at that distant low bank that just broke the endless level. Then he stared at us and his dark face, all seamed and wrinkled, was like the frozen mud of the taiga, and the moisture was frozen white in the wrinkles of his skin as it was in the furrows of the marsh. He smiled and the thick hoar-frost on his lip stirred and the skin of ice cracked over his cheeks. Then he pointed to the far-off bank by the river and in his thin, frozen voice croaked, 'Myaso!'

"Igor Palyashkin struggled to shout and managed a hoarse whisper: 'Devil take him! Tartar son of a bitch! What's he mean, meat?' I wanted to say, 'He means we shall be meat if we don't get to some shelter before it snows,' but I do not think my lips could follow my tongue.

"The Samoyeds led us off at a quicker pace towards the little cliff. Nearer the river the ground was not frozen so solid and sometimes it would not bear our weight, but wheezed and creaked and then gave way with a sucking sound. But the hunters glided over, picking out the harder places for us, and we, plunging and ploughing along, managed somehow to follow them. The sky hardened above us, the light thickened round us, the bushes seemed to thaw into smoke once more and waver and dissolve into the twilight. Then we reached the overhanging bank of earth and crouched under its frozen arch of clods. I squatted with my back to the bank, looking out into the dismal waste where all was now a dance of shadows with neither earth nor ice nor bushes any longer clearly to be distinguished from each other. Behind me I heard Igor Palyashkin making a strange noise: curses and laughter were clashing among the ice at his lips. I turned to look. He was kicking at the frozen earth. In the bank, sticking out where summer landslips had exposed them, and in the stiffened debris all round us, were huge yellow bones; whole mighty limbs, fleshy organs frozen hard as pottery, glassy hunks of purple flesh with the hide on them and rigid locks of wool like rusty iron.

"We asked with our eyes what devil's graveyard had we got into? Igor Palyashkin kicked at some of the carrion he had devoured with such appetite that morning. The little old hunter nodded: 'Myaso, myaso!' he croaked, and champed his jaws and creased his stiff cheeks a little more. Igor Palyashkin wrenched at a long bone sticking up like a fence-post and I verily believe he would have clubbed the old fellow over the skull with it if he could have got it loose.

"Suddenly, one of them made a fierce hissing noise. The six Samoyeds all on the instant became as still as the frozen clods around us. Igor Palyashkin and I, we too shrank down against the earth; what we could hear then stilled us like an intenser frost, and I felt cold to the middle of my heart. Through the dead and awful silence of that pause before the snow we heard something coming across the blind waste towards us. All day in that dead world nothing had moved but ourselves; now, out there where the shadows advanced and retreated and the pallid gloom baffled our sight, something was coming with oh! such labour and such pain, foundering and fighting onwards through the half-solid marsh. In that absolute stillness of the frozen air we heard it when it was far away; it came so slowly and it took so long, and we dare not do anything but listen and strain our eyes into the darkening mist. In what shape of living beast could such purpose and such terrible strength be embodied? A creature mightier than any God has made to be seen by man was dragging itself through the morass. We heard the crunch of the surface ice, then the whining strain of frozen mud as the enormous bulk we could not picture bore slowly down on it; then a deep gasping sound as the marsh yielded beneath a weight its frost-bonds could not bear. Then plungings of such violence and such a sound of agonized straining and moaning as constricted my heart; and, after that awful struggle, a long sucking and loud explosion of release as the beast prevailed and the marsh gave up its hold. Battle after battle, each more desperate than the last, that dreadful fight went on; we listened with such intentness that we suffered the agony of every yard of the creature's struggle towards our little bank of earth. But as it drew nearer the pauses between its down-sinkings and its tremendous efforts to burst free grew longer, as if that inconceivable strength and tenacity of purpose were failing. In those pauses we heard the most dreadful sound of all: the beast crying with pain and the terror of death. Dear Lord God! I think no Christian men but we, Igor Palyashkin and I, have ever heard a voice like that. I know that no voice on all this earth could have answered that brute soul moaning in the mist of the lonely taiga that evening before the snow. That beast was alone in all the world.

"So near it came before it sank for ever! So near! Just beyond the baffling curtain of the gloom where the gray bushes were woven with the sullen twilight—even to there, where another last fearful effort would have brought it to the harder earth and to those gigantic bones about us, it struggled before it cried its last long cry. The Samoyeds cowered behind us and hid their heads in the flaps of their skin coats and tried to shrink into the bare earth. Igor Palyashkin felt his empty revolver, then folded his arms on his breast. He did not fear God, and he was prepared to face the Devil. As for me, what made my heart sink so was the pain in that wild voice; the pain, and the drear, drear loneliness. *Bozhe moi!* I am a christened man and that was a brute soul come out of the wild forest; but it was drowning there on the dead Arctic edge of the world where there was neither forest nor field, land nor water, sun nor snow, but only an interminable chaos of cold between day and night, and there was no ear in all the world or in all time to understand its pain. Something that time had forgotten was drowning there, alone, in the gulfs of the freezing dark."

"Jimmy!" roars the First Secretary, exasperated by my failure to heed his repeated summonses. The Vice-Consul is on his feet at last; even Bartholomew is on his—though rocking slightly. I rise. Alexander Andreievitch inverts the Bison over my glass and picks up his own. "*Da* . . ." he says, emitting the word on a long sigh, and turning the glass slowly in his hand. "I saw it. A moment only; but I saw it. A moment between the brown mud and the gray bushes. Then the snow came, sudden and thick, and nothing else was seen but the white swirls of the snow. Still the great head was above the morass, the head and the shoulders, robed with long red-brown wool; the great head and something upraised like a pliant arm and the long, long curling teeth sweeping out in front like sleigh-runners. Then the snow came."

"Alexander!" cries Lydia. "Open the yard door!"

We stumble and jostle out into the little courtyard. The Red Sea night wraps its damp heat round us like a wet sheet hot from the wash-copper. We trip over the sill of Alexander Andreievitch's narrow door; we block the entrance of the courtyard; we rouse the Masseyevs' turkeys to emulation with our clamorous good-nights. Alexander Andreievitch treads on a flower pot and kicks the fragments with violence against the house wall. "*Chort vozmi!*" he swears at it, but comes back to shake my hand. "*Da . . .* We saw it, Igor Palyashkin and I. Afterwards it was the Revolution."

Someone has started up the Ford station wagon. I have lost my lantern. I invariably do at about this point in the proceedings. "Jimmy!" squeaks the Vice-Consul's wife. "What's that star up there?" The Second Secretary is surprisingly wide awake. He sings in basso profundo:

"They looked up and saw a bright star
Shining i-in the heavens beyo-ond them far . . . "

❋   ❋   ❋

Watching Frank Capra's film It's a Wonderful Life *has become a Christmas tradition for many—but it did not attain its status as a now-beloved and inspirational classic until decades after its initial release on December 30, 1946. Capra himself did not consider it to be a Christmas story. But during the 1970s and 1980s, it became a staple of seasonal television programming. The film uses the sf/f tropes of parallel/alternative/infinite realities—embodied in the powers of a guardian angel—to show George Bailey, the protagonist of* It's a Wonderful Life, *what his world would have been like without him, Here, Robert Reed expands broadly on that idea.*

A Woman's Best Friend
❄
Robert Reed

The gangly man was running up the street, his long legs pushing through the fresh unplowed snow. He was a stranger; or at least that was her initial impression. In ways that Mary couldn't quite define, he acted both lost and at home. His face and manner were confused, yet he nonetheless seemed to navigate as if he recognized some portion of his surroundings. From a distance, his features seemed pleasantly anonymous, his face revealing little of itself except for a bony, perpetually boyish composition. Then a streetlamp caught him squarely, and he looked so earnest and desperate, and so sweetly silly, that she found herself laughing, however impolite that was.

Hearing the laughter, the man turned toward her, and when their eyes joined, he flinched and gasped.

She thought of the tiny pistol riding inside her coat pocket: A fine piece of machinery marketed under the name, "A Woman's Best Friend."

The stranger called to her.

"Mary," he said with a miserable, aching voice.

Did she know this man? Perhaps, but there was a simpler explanation. People of every persuasion passed by her desk every day, and her name was no secret. He might have seen her face on several occasions, and he certainly wasn't the kind of fellow that she would have noticed in passing. Unless of course he was doing some nasty business in the back of the room—behaviors that simply weren't allowed inside a public library.

As a precaution, Mary slipped her hand around the pistol's grip.

"Who are you?" she asked.

"Don't you know me?" he sputtered.

Not at all, no. Not his voice, not his face. She shook her head and rephrased her question. "What do I call you?"

"George."

Which happened to be just about her least favorite name. With a reprimanding tone, she pointed out, "It's wicked-cold out here, George. Don't you think you should hurry home?"

"I lost my home," he offered.

His coat was peculiarly tailored, but it appeared both warm and in good repair. And despite his disheveled appearance, he was too healthy and smooth-tongued to be a common drunk. "What you need to do, George . . . right now, turn around and go back to Main Street. There's two fine relief houses down there that will take you in, without questions, and they'll take care of you—"

"Don't you know what night this is?" he interrupted.

She had to think for a moment. "Tuesday," she answered.

"The date," he insisted. "What's the date?"

"December 24th—"

"It's Christmas Eve," he interrupted.

Mary sighed, and then she nodded. Pulling her empty hand out of the gun pocket, she smiled at the mysterious visitor, asking, "By any chance, George . . . is there an angel in this story of yours?"

A gust of wind could have blown the man off his feet. "You know about the angel?" he blubbered.

"Not from personal experience. But I think I know what he is, and I can make a guess or two about what he's been up to."

"Up to?"

She said, "George," with a loud, dismissive tone. "I'm sorry to have to tell you this. But there's no such thing as a genuine angel."

"Except I saw him."

"You saw someone. Where was he?"

"On the bridge outside town," he offered. "He fell into the river, and I jumped in after him and dragged him to shore."

The man was sopping wet, she noted. "But now what were you doing out on the bridge, George?"

He hesitated. "Nothing," he replied with an ashamed, insistent tone.

"The angel jumped in, and you saved him?"

"Yes."

That sounded absurd. "What did your angel look like, George?"

"Like an old man."

"Then how do you know he was an angel?"

"He said he was."

"And after you rescued him . . . what happened? Wait, no. Let me guess. Did your angel make noise about earning an aura or his halo—?"

"His wings."

"Really? And you believed that story?"

George gulped.

"And what did this wingless man promise you, George."

"To show me . . . "

"What?"

"How the world would be if I'd never been born."

She couldn't help but laugh again. Really, this man seemed so sweet and so terribly lost. She was curious, even intrigued. Not that the stranger was her type, of course. But then again, this was a remarkable situation, and maybe if she gave him a chance . . .

"All right, George. I'm going to help you."

He seemed cautiously thrilled to hear it.

"Come home with me," she instructed him. And then she turned back toward the old limestone building that occupied most of a city block.

"To the library?" he sputtered.

"My apartment's inside," she mentioned.

"You live inside the library?"

"Because I'm the head librarian. That's one of the benefits of my job: The city supplies me with a small home. But it's warm and comfortable, with enough room for three cats and one man-sized bed."

Her companion stood motionless, knee-deep in snow.

"What's wrong now, George?"

"I don't," he muttered.

"You don't what?"

"Go into the homes of young women," he muttered.

"I'm very sorry to disappoint, but I'm not that young." For just an instant, she considered sending him to a facility better equipped for this kind of emergency. And in countless realms, she surely did just that. But on this world, at this particular instant, she said, "You need to understand something, George. You are dead. You have just killed yourself. By jumping off a bridge, apparently. And now that that's over with, darling, it's high time you lived a little."

■ ■ ■

Reverence has its patterns, its genius and predictable clichés. Many realms throw their passions into houses of worship—splendid, soothing buildings where the wide-eyed faithful can kneel together, bowing deeply while repeating prayers that were ancient when their ignorant bodies were just so many quadrillion atoms strewn across their gullible world. But if a world was blessed with true knowledge, and if there were no churches or mosques, temples or synagogues, the resident craftsmen and crafty benefactors often threw their hands and fortunes into places of learning. And that was why a small town public library wore the same flourishes and ornate marvels common to the greatest cathedrals.

George hesitated on the polished marble stairs, gazing up at the detailed mosaic above the darkened front door.

"What is this place?" he whispered.

She said, "My library," for the last time.

George was tall enough to touch the bottom rows of cultured, brightly colored diamond tiles, first with gloves on and then bare fingers.

"Who are these people? They look like old Greeks."

"And Persians. And Indians. And Chinese too." She offered names that almost certainly meant nothing to him. But she had always enjoyed playing the role of expert, and when the twenty great men and women had been identified, she added, "These are the Founders."

"Founders of what?"

"Of the Rational Order," she replied. "The Order is responsible for twenty-three hundred years of peace and growth."

George blinked, saying nothing.

She removed her right glove and touched the crystal door. It recognized her flesh, but only after determining that her companion was unarmed did the door slowly, majestically swing open for both of them.

"I can answer most questions," she promised.

Like an obedient puppy, George followed after her.

Sensing her return, the library awakened. Light filled the ground floor. Slick white obelisks and gray columns stood among the colorful, rather chaotic furnishings. Chairs that would conform to any rump waited to serve. Clean, disinfected readers were stacked neatly on each black desk. Even two hours after closing, the smell of the day's patrons hung in the air—a musky, honest odor composed of perfumes and liquor, high intentions and small dreams.

"This is a library?"

"It is," she assured.

"But where are the books?"

Her desk stood beside the main aisle—a wide, clean, and overly fancy piece of cultivated teak and gold trimmings. Her full name was prominently displayed. She picked up the reader that she had been using at day's end, and George examined the nameplate before remarking, "You never married?"

She nearly laughed. But "No" was a truthful enough answer, and that was all she offered for now.

Again he returned to the missing books.

"But our collection is here," she promised, compiling a list of titles from a tiny portion of the holdings. "You see, George . . . in this world, we have better ways to store books than writing on expensive old parchment."

"Parchment?"

"Or wood pulp. Or plastic. Or flexible glass sheets."

His eyes jumped about the screen. He would probably be able to read the words, at least taken singly. But the subject and cumulative oddness had to leave him miserably confused.

"This town isn't a large community," she mentioned. "But I like to think that we have a modest, thorough collection." Mary smiled for a moment, relishing her chance to boast. "Anyone is free to walk through our door and print a copy of any title in our catalog. But I'll warn you: If we made paper books of every volume, and even if each book was small enough to place in those long hands of yours, George . . . well, this library isn't big enough to hold our entire collection. To do that, we'd have to push these walls out a little farther than the orbit of Neptune."

The news left the poor man numb. A few labored breaths gave him just enough strength to fix his gaze once again on the reader, and with a dry, sorry little voice, he asked, "Is this Heaven?"

"As much as any place is," she replied.

George was sharp. Confused, but perceptive. He seemed to understand some of the implications in her explanation. With a careful voice, he read aloud, " 'Endless Avenues. A thorough study of the universe as a single quantum phenomena.' "

"Your home earth," she began. "It happens to be one of many."

"How many?"

"Think of endless worlds. On and on and on. Imagine numbers reaching out past the stars and back again. Creation without ends, and for that matter, without any true beginning either."

Poor George stared across the enormous room, voicing the single word, "No."

"Every microscopic event in this world splits the universe in endless ways, George. The process is essential and it is inevitable, it happens easily and effortlessly, and nothing about existence is as lovely or perfect as this endless reinvention of reality."

The reader made a sharp pop when he dropped it on the floor. "How do you know this?" he asked.

"Centuries of careful, unsentimental scientific exploration," she replied.

He sighed, his long frame leaning into her desk.

"My earth is rather more advanced than yours," she continued. "We have come to understand our universe and how to manipulate it. Everyone benefits, but the richest of us have the power to pass to our neighboring worlds and then back again."

Once more, he said, "No."

She touched him for the first time—a fond, reassuring pat delivered high on his back, the coat still wet from the river. "It takes special machinery and quite a lot of energy to travel through the multiverse," she admitted. "Tying the natural laws into a useful knot . . . it's the kind of hobby that only certain kinds of people gravitate towards."

Poor George wanted to lie down. But he had enough poise, or at least the pride, to straighten his back before saying, "My angel."

"Yes?"

"He was just a man?"

She laughed quietly, briefly. Then with a sharp voice, she warned, "My world embraces quite a few amazing ideas, George. But there's no such notion as 'just a man.' Or 'just a woman,' for that matter. Each of us is a magnificent example of what the infinite cosmos offers."

This particular man sighed and stared at his companion. Then with his own sharpness, he confessed, "You look just like my wife."

"Which is one reason why your angel chose this world, I suspect."

"And your voice is exactly the same. Except nothing that you're telling me makes any sense."

About that, she offered no comment.

Instead she gave him another hard pat. "There's a private elevator in the back," she told her new friend. "And first thing, we need to get you out of those cold clothes."

■ ■ ■

Once his coat and shoes were removed, she set them inside the conditioning chamber to be cleaned and dried. But George insisted wearing every other article on his body, including the soaked trousers and the black socks that squished when he walked.

She stomped the snow off her tall boots and removed her coat. Then before hanging up the coat up, she slipped the little pistol from its pocket and tucked it into the silk satchel riding on her hip.

He didn't seem to notice. For the moment, George's attention was fixed on the single-room apartment. "I expected a little place," he muttered.

"Isn't this?"

"No, this is enormous." Her ordinary furnishings seemed to impress the man, hands stroking the dyed leather and cultured wood. Artwork hung on the walls and in the open air—examples of genius pulled from a multitude of vibrant, living earths—and he gave the nearest sculptures a quick study. Then he drifted over to the antique dresser, lifting one after another of the framed portraits of her family and dearest friends.

She followed, saying nothing.

"Who are these two?" he asked.

"My parents."

George said, "What?"

"I take it those aren't your wife's parents."

"No."

She quoted the ancient phrase, " 'The same ingredients pulled from different shelves.' "

George turned to look at her, and he gave a start. His eyes dipped. He was suddenly like a young boy caught doing something wicked. It took a few moments to collect his wits.

"My DNA is probably not identical to your wife's," she assured. "Not base-pair for base-pair, at least."

He wanted to look at her, but a peculiar shyness was weighing down on him.

She said, "George," with a reprimanding tone.

He didn't react.

"You know this body," she pointed out. "If you are telling the truth, that is. On this other world, you married to somebody like me. Correct?"

That helped. The eyes lifted, and his courage. With more than a hint of disapproval, he said, "When I found you . . ."

"Yes?"

"Where were you going?"

"To a pleasant little nightclub, as it happens."

His hand and her smiling parents pointed at her now. "Dressed like that?"

"Yes."

"You don't have . . . "

"What, George?"

"Underwear," he managed. "Where is your underwear?"

Every world had its prudes. But why had that anonymous 'angel' sent her one of the extras?

George quietly asked, "What were you going to do . . . at this club . . . ?"

"Drink a little," she admitted. "And dance until I collapsed."

George dropped his gaze again.

"You were married to this body," she reminded him. "I can't believe you didn't know it quite well by now."

He nodded. But then it seemed important to mention, "We have children."

"Good."

"Your figure . . . my wife's . . . well, you're quite a bit thinner than she is now . . . "

"Than she was," Mary said.

His eyes jumped up.

"In your old world, you are a drowned corpse," she said. "You must have had your reasons, George. And you can tell me all about them, if you want. But I don't care why you decided to throw yourself off that bridge. Your reasons really don't matter to me."

"My family . . . " he began.

"They'll get by, and they won't."

He shook his head sorrowfully.

"Every response on their part is inevitable, George. And neither of us can imagine all of the ramifications."

"I abandoned them," he whispered.

"And on countless other earths, you didn't. You didn't make the blunders that put you up on that bridge, or you pushed through your little troubles. You married a different woman. You married ten other women. Or you fell deeply in love with a handsome boy named Felix, and the two of you moved to Mars and were married on the summit of the First Sister's volcano, and you and your soul mate quickly adopted a hundred Martian babies—little golden aliens who called both of you Pappy and built a palace for you out of frozen piss and their own worshipful blood."

George very much wanted to collapse. But the nearest seat was the round and spacious bed.

He wouldn't let himself approach it.

But she did. She sat on the edge and let her dress ride high, proving if he dared look that she was indeed wearing underwear after all.

"This club you were going to . . . ?"

"Yes, George?"

"What else happened there? If you don't mind my asking."

Jealousy sounded the same on every earth. But she did her best to deflect his emotions, laughing for a moment or two before quietly asking, "Did your Mary ever enjoy sex?"

Despite himself, George smiled.

"Well, I guess that's something she and I have in common."

"And you have me in common too," he mentioned.

"Now we do, yes."

Then this out-of-place man surprised her. He was stared at her bare knees and the breasts behind the sheer fabric. But the voice was in control, lucid and calm, when he inquired, "What about that tiny gun? The one you took out of your coat and put in your purse?"

"You saw that?"

"Yes."

She laughed, thrilled by the unexpected.

Pulling open the satchel, she showed the weapon to her guest. "Every earth has its sterling qualities, and each has its bad features too. My home can seem a little harsh at times. Maybe you noticed the rough souls along Main Street. Crime and public drunkenness are the reasons why quite a few good citizens carry weapons wherever they go."

"That's terrible," he muttered.

"I've never fired this gun at any person, by the way."

"But would you?"

"Absolutely."

"To kill?" he blubbered.

"On other earths, that's what I am doing now. Shooting bad men and the worst women. And I'm glad to do it."

"How can you think that?"

"Easily, George." She passed the gun between her hands. "Remember when I told you that our richest citizens can travel from earth to earth? To a lesser degree, that freedom belongs to everyone, everywhere. It was the same on your home world too, although you didn't understand it at the time."

"I don't understand it now," he admitted.

"You are here, George. You are here because an angelic individual took the effort to duplicate you—cell for cell, experience for experience. Then your wingless benefactor set you down on a world where he believed that you would survive, or even thrive." With her finger off the trigger, she tapped the pistol against her own temple. "Death is a matter of degree, George. This gun can't go off, unless the twin safeties fail. But I guarantee you that right now, somebody exactly like me is shooting herself in the head. Her brains are raining all over you. Yet she doesn't entirely die."

"No?"

"Of course not." She lowered the gun, nodding wistfully. "We have too many drinkers on this world, and with that comes a fairly high suicide rate. Which is only reasonable. Since we understand that anybody can escape this world at any time, just like you fled your home—leap off the bridge, hope for paradise, but remaining open-minded enough to accept a little less."

George finally settled on edge of the bed, close enough to touch her but his hands primly folded on his long lap. "What are you telling me?" he asked. "That people kill themselves just to change worlds?"

"Is there a better reason than that?"

He thought hard about the possibilities. "This angel that saved me. He isn't the only one, I take it."

"They come from endless earths, some far more powerful than ours. There's no way to count all of them."

"And do they always save the dead?"

"Oh, they hardly ever do that," she admitted. "It is a genuine one-in-a-trillion-trillion-trillion occurrence. But if an infinite number of Georges jump off the bridge, then even that one-in-almost-never incident is inevitable. In fact, that tiny unlikely fraction is itself an infinite number."

He shook his head numbly.

She leaned back on her elbows. "Most of these benefactors . . . your angel, for instance . . . throw those that they've saved onto earths that feel comfortable with refugees like you. My world, for instance."

"This happens often?"

"Not exactly often. But I know of half a dozen incidents this year, and that's just in our district."

George looked down at his cold wet socks.

"Unlike God," she promised, "quantum magic is at work everywhere."

"Do you understand all the science, Mary?"

She sat up again. "I'm a librarian, not a high-physics priestess."

That pleased him. She watched his smile, and then at last she noticed that her guest was beginning to shiver.

"You're cold, George."

"I guess I am."

"Take off those awful socks."

He did as instructed. Then laughing amiably, he admitted, "There. Now you sound exactly like my wife."

They were both laughing when something large suddenly moved beneath the big bed.

George felt the vibration, and alarmed, he stared at Mary.

"My cats," she offered. "They're usually shy around strangers."

"But that felt . . . " He lifted his bare feet. "Big."

"Kitties," she sang. "Sweeties."

Three long bodies crawled into the open, stretching while eyeing the newcomer from a safe distance.

"What kinds of cats are those?" George whispered.

"Rex is the miniature cougar," she explained. "Hex is the snow leopard. And Missie is half pygmy tiger, half griffon."

With awe in his voice, George said, "Shit."

"I take that to mean you didn't have cats like this on your earth?"

"Not close to this," he agreed.

She sat back again, sinking into the mattress.

And again, this man surprised her. "You mentioned Mars."

"I guess I did. Why?"

"On my earth, we thought that there could be some kind of simple life on that world."

"You didn't know for certain?"

He shook his head. "But a few minutes ago, you mentioned something about Martians. Are they real, or did you just make them up?"

"They're real somewhere, George."

He frowned.

Then she laughed, explaining, "Yes, my Mars is home to some very ancient life forms. Tiny golden aliens that drink nothing but peroxides. And my Venus is covered with airborne jungles and an ocean that doesn't boil because of the enormous air pressure. And Sisyphus is covered with beautiful forests of living ice—"

"What world's that?"

"Between Mars and Jupiter," she mentioned.

George blinked, took a big breath and burst out laughing.

That was when Mary told her blouse to fall open.

He stared at her, and the laughter stopped. But he was still smiling, looking shamelessly happy, begging her, "But first, Mary . . . would you please put your gun away? Someplace safe. After everything I've been through, I don't want even the tiniest chance of something going wrong now.

❉   ❉   ❉

In some ancient traditions, the winter battle between the light and the dark called for human sacrifice. During the festival of Fröblot, which occurred at the winter solstice every ninth year, Swedish kings made human sacrifices. There is also evidence for a "Lord of Misrule" who, for the period of the Roman Saturnalia, had the power to command anyone to do anything. At the end of his "reign" he was killed on the altar of Saturn. In James Stoddard's story, young Eric faces the possibility of a terrible sacrifice and witnesses a bloody holiday battle.

Christmas at Hostage Canyon
❄
James Stoddard

For hours the family rolled like tumbleweeds through the flat expanse of West Texas, past pumpjacks and pastureland, fields of winter wheat and empty reaches of harvested cotton. Now, with a sudden turn, they descended into darkness.

"Hey, we're goin' down!" Eric yelled.

"I told you where they live," his mother said from the front seat. "Remember us talking about the Caprock Escarpment?"

"Oh. Right." After driving through one of the largest tablelands in the country, they were entering a canyon at the edge of the plateau, one of a series of ravines marking the Caprock boundary.

"What's this canyon called?" Eric asked.

"She already told you that, dummy," his brother Daniel said beside him in the backseat. "Hostage Canyon, 'cause this is where the Apaches met to ransom their captives back to their families."

"Don't call your brother a dummy," their father ordered, dimming the car lights. "You guys look around. They really decorate for Christmas here."

The sedan made its way along the steep incline and curved around a boulder-strewn hill. Along the headlight beams, Eric glimpsed mesquite, cactus, and yucca.

As they rounded the bend, Eric gaped as a fairy valley opened before them. Houses, decorated with lights of every color, huddled around a small lake. Electric stars hung over garages; bulbs covered pines in Christmas-tree splendor. Shepherds and Smurfs, wise men and snowmen, mangers and Power Rangers stood on the lawns. Banners proclaimed the season. The lights shimmered off the water, and in the darkness it was hard to tell which was real and which, reflection.

"Look at that!" Eric shouted, pointing at a mechanical Santa waving from a row boat in a front yard.

"Don't yell in my ear!" his brother warned.

"Sorry." In a departure from his usual good humor, Daniel had recently joined the vagabonds drifting along the borders of teenage moodiness. Though Eric never consciously expressed the thought, his brother's faltering desertion from childhood left him uneasy.

As the car wound its way around the lake, they encountered other vehicles going both directions, creeping along to see the lights. Their Ford slowed to a crawl. More cars came up behind them and it became a parade. Inflatable choirs on the lawns generated music, providing both band and audience. Eric lowered the window and shouted, "Merry Christmas, everybody!"

"It's too cold to have the window down," Daniel complained.

"Better roll it up," their mother said. "You might catch a chill."

"Bunch of Scrooges," Eric said, annoyed at his brother's treason.

"He's right," Dad said. "Leave it down, son. We're here for Christmas."

Eric was wise enough not to look at Daniel. With a four-year age difference between them, he had learned long ago not to celebrate his triumphs.

They passed a plywood display running the length of the roof of a Colonial—Santa in his sleigh pulled by the reindeer.

"There's Rudolph," Eric said.

A man walking his German Shepherd passed beside the car, his breath a cloud in the cold.

"Merry Christmas!" Eric called.

"Merry Christmas to you, son," the stranger replied, smiling, all the lights making his face clearly visible.

"Nice people," Eric said.

They were forced to stop a few minutes later, as all the drivers paused to observe a particularly festive house, its roof a sea of bulbs, its seven pine trees crowded with twinkling lamps, its Chinese elm and desert willow dipped from trunk to tips in illumination. Eric bounced in his seat in anticipation of drawing next to it.

"Calm down, can't you?" Daniel said.

Eric cut his efforts in half to suggest compliance. He glanced beside the car. Beneath the shadows of a row of oaks sat a figure on the curb, face shining dead-white. Eric studied the creature, thinking it must be a mannequin. To his shock, the figure stood and stepped into the street, a man with a long, thin head and sneering elven features. His face shone with a zombie light. Was it a mask? Some kind of paint?

The creature looked at Eric with pale, piercing eyes that made the boy shudder. There was something animal about him, like an elf gone bad.

The stranger leapt into the air in a fluid movement, twisting his body in a way that seemed physically impossible. He pirouetted, rising over the ground like a ballerina. His clothes were blood red and the dark green of stagnant water.

Inserting a finger of each hand into the corners of his mouth, the elf stuck out his tongue, pulling his mouth wide and then wider, impossibly wide, hideously wide, until his whole face was contorted beyond anything Eric thought imaginable.

"Death," the elf said, looking right at Eric, his voice high and grating.

For an instant, under that dreadful gaze, Eric froze. The elf reached a clawed hand toward him. With a shout, the boy pushed the button to raise the window.

The glass went up; the car moved forward. The elf ran a hand against the rear window, cutting long scratches in the glass with two-inch fingernails.

"Did you see that guy?" Eric yelled.

But his parents were talking and pointing out lights, while Christmas music droned from the car speakers. Daniel ignored him.

"What is it, honey?" his mother finally asked.

"That man! See him?"

Eric turned to where the elf had been, but he was gone. He vainly searched the shadows beneath the trees.

"I don't see anyone," Mom said.

Eric kept his eye on the back window until they reached their aunt and uncle's house.

Aunt Laura and Uncle Gregg lived in a sprawling Victorian on the south lake shore. Eric's uncle, full of stories, loved to play chess and checkers; his aunt did crossword puzzles and read romance novels. They didn't have any children, which Eric thought a shame.

Everyone stayed up late the first night, talking and drinking hot cider around the burning logs of the ornate fireplace. Eric's parents brought the presents out of the trunk of the car and placed them beneath the

Christmas tree, a real pine bedecked in golden bulbs with a ceramic angel atop the highest branch. The brisk aroma of the needles tickled Eric's nose.

At bedtime, Eric was led to his room upstairs, which had an ebony dresser and queen-size bed. The blinds covering the long picture window were closed.

"There's a flashlight on the nightstand if you need one," Aunt Laura said, "or I have a nightlight if you want."

"I'm too old for nightlights," Eric asserted a little uncertainly, glancing at the shadows crowding the corners of the high ceiling.

He was tired but unwilling to turn loose of the day, so he played with the flashlight a while, casting the beam to different parts of the ceiling, illuminating the portrait of a sailing boat, and the carved faces of monks and angels on the antique dresser.

Downstairs, the grandfather clock struck midnight, the sound humming through the walls of the house. He counted the long, slow strokes of the witching hour.

With the sounding of the last chime, he heard a snarl outside, a high throaty cry like a child in pain. His whole body tensed. He shone the light at the window, then remembered cats sometimes made such noises. Despite that reassurance, he lay in bed, the covers around him in the winter chill, waiting. When the noise came again, he rose, gripping the flashlight, and crept to the window. Lifting one slat of the blinds, he peeked out.

His room overlooked the backyard, which sloped down to the water's edge. A canoe and kayak were moored to his aunt and uncle's narrow dock. It was a moonless night, but the lights from the far shore illuminated a figure dancing across the frost-kissed lawn, the elf Eric had seen on the street, his face shining dead-white.

The creature spun in a circle, leapt high into the air, somersaulted across the grass, came upright, did a handstand, pushed himself up by his arms, and landed on his feet. He slid toward the water without moving his legs, like a skater on ice. Turning, he danced backward, then rushed forward and did a roll that brought him just beneath Eric's window.

Landing on one knee, arms outspread as if awaiting applause, he leered up at the boy. His lips were crimson. Even at this distance, Eric could see the hunger in the glistening glare.

The elf dropped one arm to his side, pointed straight at Eric, and with a voice clearly audible through the glass, cried, "Death on Christmas Eve!"

Eric gasped. The elf sprinted back toward the lake, bounded forward, and vanished. For a moment, Eric searched, thinking he must have leapt into the water, but the surface remained undisturbed.

Grasping his flashlight, Eric bolted down the hall toward his parents' room.

"Just a bad dream," his father said, helping Eric back under the covers. "Too many Christmas treats late at night. Happens to the best of us."

"It wasn't a dream, Dad. I promise it wasn't. I saw him in the street and I saw him again. He was like a big elf, but evil!"

From the glow of the hall light, Eric rested beneath the study of his father's thoughtful eyes. Eric's dad was one of those parents who believed his children.

"I'll talk to your uncle in the morning about it. It's probably some local prankster in makeup. But look, we're on the second floor. You saw how high the windows are. No one can possibly climb up here, and Laura and Gregg have a security system, so your elf couldn't get in without the alarm sounding. Go to sleep and we'll figure this out tomorrow. I'll sit by your bed a minute."

Under his father's scrutiny, Eric drifted off to sleep.

By the next morning, the incident seemed more dream than reality. Having placed it in his father's hands, Eric dismissed it, for it was Christmas Eve, and there were games to play and pies and candy to eat, and a light snow that started at noon.

"A white Christmas after all," said his uncle.

That night they drove around and looked at Christmas lights again, though Daniel didn't really want to go. Only then did Eric remember the elf. He found himself searching the shadows, looking for the creature, but they covered the route along the canyon without any sign of him.

"You're awfully quiet," his mother said. "Aren't you enjoying the lights?"

"He's afraid of ghosts," Daniel said.

"Am not!" Eric grimaced, feeling betrayed. His brother must have heard him last night and ferreted out the story from Dad.

"Maybe they'll let you have a nightlight tonight," Daniel said. "Just don't get any ideas about sleeping with me."

Eric hunkered down. Older brothers have all the power.

Home again, they played dominoes on the kitchen table.

"What do you think Santa's going to bring you, Eric?" Uncle Gregg asked.

Eric smiled and looked innocent. On the Christmas Eve of his sixth year, when he and his brother were going to bed, Daniel had casually said, "You do know Mom and Dad are just pretending when they say there's a Santa Claus, don't you?"

"Yes," Eric had replied, his voice quavering slightly. Idolizing his big brother, who sometimes teased but never lied to him, Eric, not without a period of mourning, thereafter realigned his theology.

Still, adults had to be placated in this planet-wide game of pretend, so Eric said to his uncle, "I want Santa to bring me a baseball bat and a *Monster Hero* video game."

"Are you sure you've been good enough for that?" Gregg asked, in feigned surprise.

"He's a pretty good boy," Mom said. "But who knows what Santa will do?"

Having found where his mother kept the unwrapped presents two weeks before, Eric had a fairly accurate picture of the intentions of the Claus organization.

Once upstairs in bed that night, Eric turned on the flashlight and shone it around the room. He sighed. He would never go to sleep; the night would last forever, and it was going to be seven centuries before his parents let him get up to open presents.

With images of *Monster Hero* dancing in his head, he drifted off sooner than he would have thought possible.

The chiming of the grandfather clock roused him. He counted the beats—eight, nine, ten, eleven, twelve. It was only midnight. Hours to go before morning. He groaned and rolled over. Dumb old clock! If it hadn't woke him . . .

A crash came from downstairs, the splintering of wood, the breaking of glass. Eric sat up in bed. Remembering the dark elf, he lay back down and pulled the covers close. Maybe something had fallen downstairs. Maybe the Christmas tree had toppled over. Any minute, he expected to hear his dad's feet padding down the hall to check. He strained to listen, but there was only the screeching of metal on wood floors, the thuds of falling objects.

What if his dad went downstairs and the elf was there? Would even his father, a veteran of Desert Storm, be able to stop him? Dad always kept a gun at the house, but he didn't have one here.

For an instant, Eric lay frozen, afraid of what would happen next. Afraid for his father. Afraid for everybody. Death on Christmas Eve, the elf had said. His parents slept with the door closed. Maybe they couldn't hear the noise.

When Eric was five, Daniel had accused him of being afraid of the dark, a brutal denunciation since it happened to be true. Ashamed and angry, Eric had refused to turn on the light any time he walked into his bedroom, stepping fists swinging into the blackness to wallop the waiting monsters. So he had beaten the dark, mastered it, brought it to leash. But lying in bed listening to the chaos downstairs, he knew his conquest had only been temporary.

He got up, grasping his flashlight, but not turning it on. It was a black night; no moon peeked through the blinds. He stepped into the hall, the floorboards creaking beneath his feet despite his feather-light efforts.

Daniel's room was closest to his, but he passed it by, going straight to his parents' door. He reached for the knob, but it wavered and eluded him—surely a trick of the dark. He snapped on the flashlight and tried again. The knob bulged inward, avoiding him. He tried to knock, but the wood danced away from his fist. He called, softly at first, but with increasing volume. He waited a lifetime, but no one came.

Eric!

He jumped. A voice ethereal as mist beckoned from below.

Eric!

He rushed back to Daniel's door and ran straight at it, straining to reach the knob. It receded, ten yards, twenty, thirty, the door frame stretching like rubber. He halted and found himself standing in the hall before the closed door.

Eric! Come down!

The voice, an insistent humming in his head, sounded louder now.

He clenched his fist and gripped the flashlight. He passed Laura and Gregg's room without even trying the door. There was no one to help him and it wasn't fair! He was the youngest, the littlest, and it wasn't right for the elf to pick on him, for him to be punished just because he was the one who had seen the creature.

As his hand touched the newel post at the top of the stairs, a dim glow rose from below. The sounds of violence ceased.

He crept down the steps, shaking with dread. At the bottom lay the remains of the outside door, splintered wood and broken glass sprawled across the kitchen floor. As he descended, step by step, looking over the banister rail, more of the living room came into view. The fireplace was lit, soft patter of flickering flames.

Heart pounding, he reached the bottom. He had to step over the shattered door, avoiding nails and diamond-glistening glass to reach the living room carpet. A silverware drawer lay upended onto the coffee table. Slashes crisscrossed his uncle's recliner, leaving strips of hanging cloth. Torn presents were scattered around the room; the baseball bat Eric had asked for lay in the middle of the floor, half-covered by the Christmas stockings from the mantel.

Eric sucked in his breath to keep from screaming.

The elf stood by the front window, behind the Christmas tree, peering out from between the branches, razor nose crinkled, mouth gaping a grin, like a kid playing a game of hide and seek.

With deliberate slowness, he stepped from behind the tree, raised one hand toward the boy, and displayed the decapitated body of the Christmas angel.

"Come to me, little one," the elf commanded, beckoning with his other hand. His eyes twinkled like broken glass.

"Who are you?" Eric demanded. He tried to sound brave, but his voice came timorous and thin. "This isn't your house. What do you want?"

The elf laughed. "Such cheek! Such courage in the face of disaster. I am an ancient nemesis of your people, locked out of your world centuries ago. Tonight that will change. This very evening, your blood will permanently secure the passage between my dimension and your own."

"I called the police," Eric said. "They'll be here any minute. You better go."

"You called no one," the elf sneered. "Do you think I can't overcome your childish technology? You haven't any idea. What fun I shall have, playing with you poor mortals."

Eric stood shaking, wanting to run, to flee through the broken door into the cold night. He glanced into the darkness of the yard.

"Don't bother," the elf said. "Even if you chose to desert your family, you couldn't leave the grounds any more than you could enter your parents' room."

The elf stepped forward, backing Eric against the wall. "Do you know what night it is, little one?"

"Ch . . . Christmas Eve," Eric stammered.

"That's right. It is also three days after the Winter Solstice, the longest and darkest night of the year. There are principles and dominions of which you know nothing, Eric, powers which humans can neither imagine nor cope with, creatures too terrible for mortal understanding."

The elf glanced at the fireplace. "There are awful places in the world, places with dreadful names. Auschwitz, the Colosseum of Rome, the Solovki Gulag. Wherever your pitiful human lives have been cheapened, wherever the darkness of human hearts manifests itself, the barrier between my dimension and yours is weakened. This is Hostage Canyon, a minor outpost in your long history of atrocities. I began crossing over on the night of the solstice, but it takes three days to fully manifest."

The elf glanced at the fireplace again. "It is a shame to slay one so young." The creature's long fingernails gleamed like knives in the firelight. "Let's at least have a bit more light, so I can do the job efficiently."

Leaving the boy pressed against the golden wallpaper, the elf threw a heavy log in the fireplace. The flames blazed, making the shadow of the Christmas tree dance.

"Much better." The elf returned to Eric. This close, Eric could smell him, an oily odor, sickeningly sweet. While the child watched in petrified terror, his breath coming in strangled gasps, the elf touched the tip of his fingernail to Eric's throat.

"A single slice and it's done."

Eric howled, shouting for his father and big brother, but his yells echoed uselessly around the room. He fell into quiet sobbing.

"Are we done?" the elf asked. "Good. I like to work without distractions."

Eric closed his eyes, waiting for the terrible pain. The grandfather clock ticked away, second by second, while he anticipated the first cruel cut. The elf's fingernail tapped against his throat. His whole body shook.

The moments passed; the stroke did not come. The creature abruptly withdrew his hand. Eric's eyes fluttered open. The elf looked at him thoughtfully.

"I don't want to do this, you know. So young! Such a tragedy! It's necessary, but I don't like it."

He put his hand to his cheek in thought. "There is another way. It isn't often done, but it could be, in a special case. I could use a substitute instead of you. Someone else. Would you like that?"

Tears running down his face, Eric nodded, too frightened even to speak.

"Hmm," the elf said. "Who would serve? Let me think. Who could I possibly use?"

The creature closed his gleaming eyes in concentration. He opened them and snapped his fingers and said with a smile, "I have it. Your brother will suffice."

A short cry escaped Eric's lips.

"Now understand me, little one. I would be quick. Just slip up to his room and do the deed. He wouldn't know it was coming. It wouldn't be like you, standing here awaiting the blow. He wouldn't feel a thing. A pillow over the face and he's gone. And your parents would never know. Natural causes, they'd think it was. And Daniel would go to heaven to be with the angels."

"Please don't take my brother," Eric said, shaking his head.

The elf glanced at the ornamental bells on the Christmas tree. "Now let's not be irrational. It has to be one of you; you haven't any choice in that. But let's think about it. Your brother has had a lot longer to live. And he hasn't always been kind to you, has he? Oh, I know he isn't one to hit you, but isn't he always bossing you around, telling you how to act, as if you're supposed to be as old as he? And lately he's been distant. Listening to loud music, ignoring you. Talking to his friends on his cell. You've admired him, it's true. You've looked up to him. But you know in your heart you'll never live up to what he is. He's stronger than you, smarter than you. All your life you'll stand in his shadow. I can take care of that right now. You say the word and I'll slip right upstairs. It'll be so much easier."

Eric's tears abruptly ceased as he realized the elf was asking permission to kill Daniel.

"There isn't any other way, Eric. One of you has to go. There are rules you know nothing about. And think of your mother. Hasn't she always told you how precious you are, how special? Don't you know in your heart you're the most important one to her? She'll miss Daniel, of course, but not like she'd miss you. The grief might kill her. Kill her dead."

Eric thought. Though his mother never actually said she loved him more than Daniel, he was sure she thought him extra-special. Wasn't he the compliant boy, her good little man? If there wasn't any choice, if one of them had to die . . .

"I can see by your look you're coming around to my way of thinking," the elf said. "Come now, Eric, let me finish my job. For your mother's sake. It's the right thing to do."

Eric faltered, for in mentioning what was right, the elf had stirred something within him. Eric's parents always told him to do what was right. His mother insisted on it. His dad said a man was measured by it. It was like the heroes in books, like Captain America in the comics. Cap didn't let someone else die in his place. Besides, when the older kids in school tried to pick on him, didn't Daniel stand up for him? Shouldn't he do the same for his brother?"

A log in the fireplace popped and the elf started and whirled toward the sound, his whole body twitching.

He's afraid of something, Eric realized. As powerful as he is, he's afraid.

For the first time, Eric found his courage, as if he were again swinging his fists in the blackness of his bedroom, facing the darkness. He had to stall until he figured out what the monster feared.

"I need to think about it," he said.

"No need to think, and no time for it, either," the elf said smoothly. "You know what you should do." He brought his hand back toward Eric's throat. "Death is dark, Eric, filled with darkness. Unending darkness. Darkness forever and ever."

"You said Daniel would go to heaven."

The elf's eyes blackened, but immediately grew softer. "That's Daniel. Big brothers are different. If you decide to let me take you instead—why, that would be like suicide. And suicide is bad, Eric. Everyone knows that."

"I don't know how that works. Can you explain it?"

The elf shook his head. "No, I can't, Eric. There isn't time. Your time is up. Your brother or you? Which is it?"

Eric felt the sharp edge of the fingernail against his neck, pressing, cutting.

With a sound of collapsing air, the fire went out, plunging the room into darkness.

"No!" the elf shouted out of the blackness. "It was nearly done!"

A figure stood beside the mantle, a tall shadow in the ebony. Broad. Powerful. Eric choked back a cry, thinking it must be something awful, perhaps something even worse, if the elf feared it. Perhaps the monster's terrible Master.

There was light. A single shaft at first, rising to a silver glow. Eric blinked against the brilliance, and when he could see again, he discovered the newcomer had drawn a long sword, a blade capturing every stray illumination in the room: starlight from the windows, lamplight from the houses across the lake, the shine from the refrigerator panel in the kitchen, focusing it into a dazzling radiance.

The figure was a man with ruddy cheeks and an ivory beard, broad-shouldered, easily a head taller than Eric's father. He wore a red suit with white fur fringes, and his eyes were as piercing as the sword he carried.

But the creature had drawn a weapon too, an ebony blade darker than darkness.

Eric had only one thought. There is a Santa Claus and the elf is going to kill him.

But this wasn't the Santa of the old stories, with a belly that shook like a bowlful of jelly. He was big, but there was nothing fat about him, and his suit wasn't felt, but crimson body armor polished to an exquisite sheen. Not Santa Claus at all; Saint Nicholas come to slay dragons.

Without a word, Santa darted forward, his speed belying his size, inserting himself between Eric and the elf, his blade a wall protecting the boy.

They struck swords. The fighting was furious, swifter than Eric believed possible. The elf attacked with savage desperation, and Santa parried, blow after blow, incredible impacts so deafening Eric clutched his hands to his ears. The noise boomed through the house, rattling the walls, sending pictures clattering to the floor.

Back the elf drove Santa, until he pressed him against the wall. Eric's hopes fell. It looked as if it would be over before it began.

With a savage roar, St. Nick began his counteroffensive, his face a gray grim mask, his eyes merciless and terrible. Two of his blows nearly beat through the elf's defenses, sending the creature stumbling back. Santa was on the attack.

They destroyed the living room, splitting the coffee table like a tomato, sweeping the lamps aside, slicing hunks out of the couch. The Christmas tree fell; ornaments and Christmas presents rolled and bounced across the carpet.

Back and forth they fought, grunting with their efforts, neither speaking as they dueled. Eric did not understand what it was about; he only knew his family's lives depended on the outcome.

Santa took a bad stroke to his side, and though his armor held, the blow slowed him. The elf closed. For an instant, they fought face to face, blade to blade, one arm locked against the other. The elf pushed with all his strength, and Santa slipped and fell.

The dark blade whirred above Claus's head. Santa's own sword was down, caught beneath his enemy's booted foot. A triumphant grin lit the elf's blood-red lips, the exultant anticipation of victory.

The baseball bat Eric had wanted for Christmas lay at the elf's feet. The creature kicked it away as he repositioned his foot for the final blow, rolling it to where the boy stood.

Without thinking, without a plan, without considering the power he was up against, Eric snatched the bat, pulled it to his shoulder like Daniel had taught him, and swung with all his might. It was a good, solid blow against the elf's back, a solid thump.

The elf swept his blade backward, a streak of darkness, and Eric was holding the bat-handle while the rest of the bat clattered against a wall. For an instant, he thought his fingers had gone with it, but they were all still there. His eyes passed across a label taped to the handle: *To my little brother. From Daniel.*

Puny as the effort had been, it was enough. Santa freed his sword and blocked the elf's stroke. Claus scrambled to his feet, striking right and left, moving the blade in a dance of death, while the light from his weapon grew to brilliant intensity. Unable to recover from the change in fortune, the elf parried poorly. Santa's blade tore through the creature's upper body.

The elf's eyes widened in shock. He gave a whistling gasp, a shrill whine ending in abrupt silence. Then the monster was gone, vanished in smoke and steam, leaving only an oily stain on the carpet.

Eric and Santa stood facing one another in the ruined room, the warrior bent, hands to knees, panting for breath from his exertions. Eric looked into those fierce blue eyes, as terrible and frightening as the elf's, and burst into tears.

For an instant Santa merely stared, until Eric was certain the warrior would turn his wrath on him. But Claus's dreadful glare abruptly softened.

"Here, now," he said in a deep voice, between gasps. "What's this? And after fighting so well? It was a blow well-struck. I owe this victory to you, Eric."

Still breathing hard, Santa knelt at eye-level and placed a hand on the boy's shoulder. Eric started, but the powerful grip rested gentle as a child holding a sparrow.

The light from the warrior's blade was waning, but before it failed completely, Claus glanced around, and with a wave of his gloved hand, caused the candles on the mantel to emit a soft flame.

"Better," he said. "You have seen enough of darkness this night. Enough darkness for a lifetime."

At this bit of magic, wonder replaced Eric's fear. "Are you really Santa? I didn't think you were real."

"Perhaps it were best if you still believed so," Claus said. "Such horror as you have witnessed is not for little boys. Yes, I am Father Christmas, Saint Nicholas, Hoteiosho, Papa Noel—Santa Claus."

"Do you have a sleigh, with reindeer and everything? Is there really a Rudolph?"

"I sometimes use a sleigh pulled by reindeer, but Rudolph is a legend. Reindeer noses cannot glow, you see." Santa gave him a wink. "I was an ordinary man once, Eric, but was chosen long ago—the why and how need not concern you. When the forces of darkness seek to enter our dimension, it is my task to prevent them. The struggle is fierce and continuous. The moment the elf appeared I knew of him, but he was little more than a phantom until this evening, when he attempted a permanent transition into this world through a blood-sacrifice. I was nearly too late—other powers sought to prevent my coming."

"He wanted to hurt Daniel."

"Daniel was always the target. In the land mortals call Faerie—though it is far, far more, both darker and brighter—there are rules to such encounters. The elf could only strike through the youngest sibling. He couldn't have killed you—he deceived you about that. He wanted to destroy both you and Daniel, your brother through death, you through guilt and remorse. Such is the way of these folk. But you resisted, Eric. You were willing to sacrifice your own life for Daniel's, and that gave me both time to reach you and power to aid you. Your tiny resistance was all I needed to break through. The lit fireplace was but the elf's foolish attempt to create a further barrier against me."

"He said I'd never be as good as Daniel."

"The elf spoke many lies, some close to the truth because those are the most deceptive," Santa said. "I, who am far-sighted, tell you this, Eric, you will not be the high school quarterback, the football star your brother will become. You will not possess his easy athletic ability. Your heart is turned toward books and contemplation. And you will always be the little brother to him, even when you are old, so that sometimes you will long for him to treat you as an equal. But you will be special as he is special, and you will love one another though you have nothing in common save the odd fact of growing up in the same house. And it will have to be enough."

Eric looked into the wise, thoughtful eyes. "You're nothing like the stories."

"No, I suppose not. My task is battle. I am the Defender against the darkest of all nights. No doubt it makes me grim."

"Do you really bring presents?"

Santa laughed, a deep, pleasant rumble. "The gifts are a legend from long ago. All year long I gather my strength for this night. But there are more than presents to be had in this world. There is good done to others. And I think we have exchanged presents tonight."

"Huh? Oh." Eric remembered his manners. "Thank you for saving us."

"And thank you for what you did for me. Not many children can say they saved the life of Santa Claus."

The warrior glanced around the room. "It were best if no evidence remains of this battle." He waved his hand, and all the scattered objects in the room began to move, inching back to their places. The shattered glass of the door quietly reformed, piece by piece. The coffee table and couch began mending themselves. The Christmas tree slowly rose, and the Christmas angel, head intact, returned to the topmost branches.

"By morning all will be as it was," Santa said. "You do understand that no one will ever believe what happened? Best not try to tell them. Especially Daniel."

Eric smiled. "He'd really make fun of me."

"Good night, Eric. Go back to bed. Tomorrow is Christmas, and I must go. There are other evils to defeat before sunrise. I have to do it all in one night, you know."

Santa stepped to the fireplace. He turned, gave Eric a final laugh, and was gone, sliding up the chimney like water.

Under the vigil of the angel at the top of the tree, Eric watched as the living room gradually returned to normalcy. He picked up the bat, now whole, and studied his brother's printed inscription.

Sleigh bells sounded outside. Still clutching the bat, Eric ran to the window. Through the blackness, he caught a glimpse of animals large as bison pulling a mighty wagon into the sky.

"Merry Christmas," Santa's voice rang through the terrible darkness. "Merry Christmas."

❄   ❄   ❄

In The White Goddess *(1948), Robert Graves mentions the archetypes of the Holly King and the Oak King, each representing one half of the year and forever pitted against one another as the seasons turn. Von Jocks adroitly brings the myth of their eternal battle into modern times. The deciduous oak tree was sacred to the Celts, and they believed the evergreen native holly repelled evil spirits and lightning. Botanically, as oaks and other deciduous trees lose their leaves with cold weather, holly remains bright in the barren landscape of winter. When the light of longer days returns, the oak starts growing again. In summer, when oaks are in full leaf, the holly is blooming to produce the berries that will turn red in fall and remain so vibrant with its still-green leaves in winter. Thus when each "king" is at "his" strongest, he is, at the same time, destined to be supplanted.*

The Winter Solstice
❄
Von Jocks

Darkness surrounded the isolated cabin—in more ways than one.

"This," murmured Ivy, watching her breath mist a cold pane of the cabin window, "is *not* what people mean when they call December a season of magic."

Not that the wintery night beyond didn't have a hushed otherworldliness about it. Snow swirled out of the blackness so quietly, Ivy wasn't sure if she heard its tiny, gritty impact against the glass with her ears . . . or with less mundane senses. Magic, *real* magic, worked like that—so subtle it could hardly be differentiated from coincidence, or imagination, or even delusions.

Chenille-sweatered arms braced against the windowsill, narrow chin pillowed on her arms, Ivy stared at her dark-haired, dark-eyed reflection. Sometimes, even the most devoted of witches found that kind of subtlety frustratingly anticlimactic. Maybe that's why so few potential magic users stayed with the discipline. Nowadays, people wanted the kind of instant pyrotechnics only *movie* witches produced.

Ivy wasn't looking for laser beams and levitation—but over the last half-year, especially since the Harvest Moon, she'd become so desperate for a little proof, a little reassurance, that she ached for it, *dreamed* about it. That's why she'd driven out here, by herself, on a day when her friends were preparing to party as only pagans could.

"Magical quest, or fool's errand," she sighed, and in her breath's resulting fog she drew a squeaky, five-pointed star with one finger. " 'Only my hairdresser knows for sure.' "

As the drawing began to weep from its outermost edges, she turned back to the too-cold room and faced her only companion for the Winter's Solstice.

The gray tabby cat stared back, unblinking and unimpressed, from where she lay on the towel Ivy had laid out. She'd darted into the cabin while Ivy carried in her supplies for her night of vigil. Was the cat a visitor from the fairy realm, here to test Ivy's hospitality? A totem animal, arrived to guide her? Perhaps a future familiar . . .

Or maybe, just maybe, she was simply a stray cat, mooching for warmth and a handout. One never *could* tell, with magic . . . unless this night went as Ivy hoped. And she had a long night to get through before she found out.

In any case, the temperatures had been dropping all afternoon. Now that a blizzard had moved in, wind howling in a way that could not sound *less* joyous, the cat would stay.

"My dreams couldn't have arranged for me to do this on the *shortest* night of the year, huh?" Ivy asked now, returning to her nylon camp chair by the rusty-grated fire. Lord and Lady, but it was cold. The flame's warmth seemed to extend only as far as its orange glow. *Oh, the weather outside is frightful . . .*

The cat boosted herself up with her front legs to curl lithely around and chew at the back of one thigh, spread-toed foot high in the air, supremely unimpressed.

Once, Ivy would have laughed at so classic a feline brush-off; now she barely managed a smile. A run of bad luck, from finances to health, had slowly disillusioned her, robbed her of her optimism one disappointment at a time. She'd tried to always do the right thing for so long! But now that she'd reached thirty, with little to show for it, she'd begun to question why. And that wasn't a big leap from questioning all the other intangibles of her life, magic included. Ivy's doctor diagnosed her as clinically depressed. He prescribed antidepressants, which she began to take, and a tranquilizer, which she hadn't touched. As if inspired by her efforts at healing herself, her dreams then gave her even more hopeful instructions—for her magic, anyway. Though almost intangible here on the physical realm, magic could appear *very* dramatic in dreams.

So here Ivy sat, humming Yuletide carols to a stray cat in a dusty, rented cabin. She'd draped the walls with evergreen garlands, like a good little pagan, to symbolize continued life in the midst of winter's cold. The wreath she'd woven, as the storm blew in, represented the turning of the Year Wheel. On the rough-hewn mantle of the fireplace, she'd lit two pillar candles, green for the goddess and red for the god of old. Together, they added a perfume of bayberry and cinnamon to the rich scent of wood smoke and fresh pine. And between them, pillowed on silver-gray silk, lay all her hopes for her sanity, her life path—her magic.

The decorative, double-edged knife had a pewter blade, like a letter opener; it would be used on nothing in this physical realm, and in the astral realm, soft metals worked just fine. Its artist had etched an intricate design of oak-leaves up the blade, to match the carvings of leaves and acorns in its oaken handle. Ivy had never seen so beautiful an athame before buying this one. That she'd dreamed the importance of a ceremonial blade for weeks, with clear instructions for its use, only added to its enchantment. Planning and packing for this witchly version of a vision quest had given her more confidence than she'd felt in months.

This was Yule, after all, the longest night of the year, an ancient holiday from which so many winter traditions evolved. Per her dreams, Ivy intended to spend the night meditating on the true meaning of the Winter Solstice and its returning light. Then—and this, she felt certain, was key—she would take her athame outside to catch the energy of the first rays of the new sun. Somehow, if she did that—and if her dreams really *were* instructions from the astral realm and not side-effects from her serotonin reuptake inhibitor—Ivy would finally gain proof that magic existed, that it worked . . . that it made a difference.

For once and for always, all subtlety aside, she would *know*.

"Okay then—the true meaning of Yule," she said now to the cat, glad to have *someone* to bounce this off of. "Most of the pagans I know equate it with the rebirth of the sun, but some also talk about the myth of the Oak King, who wages heroic battle against the Holly—"

Amidst the storm outside, Ivy heard a thump against the door.

The tabby cat sat up, ready to run. The fire shrank, then stretched. When Ivy turned toward the old cabin's door, away from the fire, her breath misted in the air and warmed her quilted vest to moistness against her cheek.

" . . . King," she finished faintly.

For a long moment, she resisted investigating. How *could* there be anybody out on a night like tonight? But it was too cold to risk being wrong. She stood.

The door opened on its own, dragged an arc across the floor toward her. Wind sliced in, hurling shards of frozen crystal and sending her chair skittering across the floor. It tormented the writhing fire and filled the cabin with an unnerving, otherworldly screech.

"I'm a witch," Ivy reminded herself softly, to maintain calm as she watched the door open further. "A stone in the ancient circle. I can handle whatever this night sends."

She would feel more confidence were it not so dark . . . and if she had more faith in magic, of late.

From the swirling, shadowy white emerged a form of black, tall and broad-shouldered. It filled the doorway for a moment. Then it half-staggered, half-fell through the entrance, crumpling across the cold dirt floor. A glaze of ice that had crusted its heavy coat shattered into dagger-like shards.

Magic or no magic—*this* was real.

Quickly, Ivy waded against the wind to the doorway, past the prone black form. She found temporary shelter behind the door. Bracing on it, she pushed—but Nature pushed back. Her hiking boots slipped from beneath her and she fell to her knees on the frozen floor.

The cat, peeking out from its new shelter behind the woodpile, gave no help.

Ivy dragged herself up and, legs straining, puuushed. Slowly the door retreated from her and finally, blessedly, closed against the wind and the worst of the cold . . . and the darkness.

But not all of it.

She latched the door, leaned on it for support. The chaos outside seemed almost silent in contrast to the indoors only moments before. Then she looked at the fallen stranger.

A sense of unseasonable foreboding stilled her—and not because of any extrasensory abilities. Witches watched the news too. Ivy knew the threat that strangers, especially strange men, could pose. But she could ignore a human being's suffering no more than she could have put the cat out into the cold. She pushed past her hesitance to kneel beside the man.

He wore all black—a long, black wool coat, a black ski cap, a black scarf that cowled his face to obscurity. As Ivy unwound the wrappings, more ice crackled off and she wondered how, or if, he could breathe. When she unveiled his pale, handsome face, she saw that his breath had frozen into a thin, frosty crust over his mouth and nose.

She pressed her hands onto the stranger's high cheeks, leaned forward and breathed on him to melt the frost from his closed eyes and down-turned lips before carefully, tentatively, wiping it away. The cold of his skin repelled her. She checked the pulse in his throat—was it weak? When she pressed cold fingers to her own neck, for a comparison, she decided it was. Desperation shook her hand.

Was he breathing? Did he have any chance of life at all? The cell phone she'd left in her car would not work this far from a transmitter, even if she risked hiking down the hill for it. And even if she did contact emergency services, could an ambulance get here until the storm broke?

Could the police?

"Useless," Ivy muttered. Never had she been so tempted to simply give up. She felt as though an outer presence were urging her pessimism on.

It's the darkness, she thought then. *The darkness wants me to stop.*

Darker magic, the kind that dangerous magicians and creatures that weren't even human practiced, could work in subtle ways too. And this *was* the darkest night of the year . . . in more ways than one.

Was *that* the true meaning of the Winter Solstice?

Fa la la la la.

Ivy shook off that possibility and the apathy it engendered. Tipping the man's head back, she pinched his nose shut. Then she bent and covered his mouth, his cold lips, with hers and breathed for him. *In with the good air . . .*

His eyes opened, strong and sad, depthless and dark.

Ivy drew back, startled.

Arched eyebrows lowered. The stranger's now-damp lips moved, producing only a sigh, and his frown grew fiercer.

Ivy leaned closer, straining.

"You're . . . oak," he whispered, seemingly distressed. Then his eyes fell shut again, dark lashes smudging his high, too-pale cheeks.

Ivy raised fingers to her throat, this time feeling for the pendant she always wore, a branching tree within a circle. To her, the tree represented Yggdrasil, the World Tree of Norse mythology, its roots connecting the earth to the underworld and its branches reaching wide into the realm of the spirit. But . . . Yggdrasil was generally thought to be a yew or an ash tree, not an oak.

Was she hunting for hidden meanings where none existed? Now Ivy couldn't tell if she shivered from the cold or from this man's wan vulnerability, from mundane fears about intruders at night or otherworldly fears less easily defined.

As she'd told the cat, Solstice Night also represented the last stand of the Holly King—the god who, by this time of year, reigned over darkness and even death.

"Well don't use this one in your battle," Ivy hissed from where she crouched over the stranger—hardly a standard holiday prayer. Once again she strained the muscles of her legs, arms and back, this time to drag the prone figure nearer the fire. Since he did not appear to be frostbitten—to her amateur eye, anyway—she chafed his wrists, his face. Trying not to dwell on his dangerously powerful build, she undressed him of his iced, outer layer of clothing so that the fire's warmth would reach him . . .

. . . and she saw that he wore around his neck, on a leather thong, a pentagram overlaid with a tiny, two-headed axe. Despite that he wore the star point up, not point down as Satanists or chic Goths might, Ivy shivered again. These were pagan symbols. Mere coincidence? Or . . . magic?

Her heart drumming louder than a full-moon ritual, she glanced toward the rough fireplace mantle, the fine new athame that must catch the returning sun . . .

She could meditate on the true meaning of the Solstice while fixing something warm for this man to eat—should he regain consciousness—as easily as she could by sitting still. Reassured by his rough but steady breathing and, to be honest, the safety of his continued unconsciousness, Ivy took time for one thing, first. She re-lit the candles that the wind through the open door had blown out. *Then* she turned to her supplies and retrieved a can of stew.

The cat crept out from behind the firewood to investigate this new opportunity.

You're oak, this man had said. Or more likely, of course, *your oak*.

" 'My oak,' " Ivy repeated softly. "Could he have seen my necklace as a symbol of the Oak King?"

The cat, staring expectantly at the can she held, opened and closed her mouth in a silent meow.

"It's an ancient legend of the Winter Solstice," Ivy explained softly, peeling open the pop-top of the can and spooning a little of its contents out for the eager cat before pouring the rest into an aluminum pot. "The forest god has two different aspects—the Oak King and the Holly King. As I remember it, the Oak King stands for light, growth, rebirth. He rules during the waxing year—from Winter Solstice through Midsummer, while the sun gains power. His reign starts tomorrow," she clarified.

Rather, it *would*, if there really were an Oak King . . .

After some consideration, Ivy returned to her backpack for a few more ingredients. "But at Midsummer, the Holly King kills the Oak King in battle. Then *he* rules, through to the Winter Solstice, during the waning year, until the reborn Oak King defeats him again. The world gets lighter, then it gets darker, then it gets lighter, and so on."

And then it gets darker. And so on. Wasn't Midsummer when things had started going wrong in her own life?

Adding her extra ingredients, then stirring, Ivy hung the pot over the fireplace. She felt jittery, overly alert, as if she could *sense* the dark god of withdrawal and death lurking in the shadows . . . or even standing over her unconscious visitor in black.

Black?

Her gaze slid back to the stranger and her heightened awareness saw more than an intruder. His thick, carefully cut hair was dark brown, not black. Although his face seemed taut, somewhat angry—more likely pained, she thought charitably—he couldn't be much older than her. She noted something of a bruised expression in his otherwise regal features.

Leaning closer, she lay her fingers on the smoothness of his cheek, relieved to feel that this man felt warmer now—and still very real. Lord and Lady, but he was handsome. Handsome enough that even *she* noticed. How long had it been since she'd felt physically attracted to anyone . . . ?

His dark eyes slid open again. His gaze wandered, bewildered, and then focused on her, and she reluctantly reclaimed her hand.

"Hello," she said.

He stared at her, then sat up with surprising strength, ignoring her automatic plea to be still. After wincing only once, he examined his hands, then felt his face. Finally, his gaze returned to Ivy.

"How long have I been here?" he demanded in a crisp, authoritative voice.

"Only a short while. You're very lucky."

"That is a matter of opinion. Who are you?"

Her smile felt tighter than it would have been only a minute earlier, but she might as well alleviate his tension—and thus his threat? "Ivy MacDaraich."

"Ivy." His eyes, hardly welcoming in the first place, narrowed with speculation. "How very appropriate."

Like she'd never heard that before, at this time of year. Considering his pentagram, she altered her season's greeting. "Happy Yule."

"For whom?" He spared her a scathing look before rolling to a crouch.

He stood to his full, impressive height, swayed, then steadied himself by force of will. When Ivy moved to help him, he glared at her. Though she still found him attractive, he suddenly became much easier to resist. Score a big zero for Ivy's instincts.

She stood too, then stepped back from the reality of his height over hers. *Regal*, she thought again. Despite that he wore black jeans and a sweater, and modern hiking boots, he could as easily have worn a black cape and armor.

She tried not to picture the Holly King. "You can't go," she said. "There's a terrible storm out."

The man studied her. "Yes," he said, after a moment, then sank into her camp chair without asking. His next words came out so softly, she almost didn't hear. "We were separated in the storm."

We? "Someone else is out there?"

"It's none of your concern." *That*, she heard.

"But they might need help!"

"I have no doubt that my companion is quite safe," he snapped, without a glimmer of concern. His next words came out soft again, as if spoken to himself. "Safer than I."

He was worried about *his* safety? Ivy hesitated before spooning some stew from the pot, into a camp plate, and held it toward him. "Would you like to eat something? It will warm you."

Instead of accepting the food, the stranger folded his arms. She could see the lines of his muscles even through the layers of his clothing. Noting her confused expression, he raised an eyebrow and said, "After you."

He was not, she thought, being polite. He *was* worried about his safety.

A head shorter than him, did she look that dangerous? "Pretty suspicious, aren't you?"

"I have cause to be."

Ah. Without hesitating further, she blew on a spoonful of stew to cool it, then took a bite. Not bad, she thought. For what it was. Since he continued to watch, she took another bite, chewed, and even swallowed, despite her tight throat. "See? Harmless."

When she held the plate to him again he took it and ate greedily, shuddering slightly—from the shock of its warmth against the cold that had held him, Ivy supposed. Despite herself, and his attitude, she softened toward him. He seemed so tense, brittle even, under the weight of his own suspicions. He looked like he could use a good neck rub—*not* that she was offering. But she did move to the other side of the cabin to dig an extra blanket from her pile of supplies for the poor, prickly misanthrope.

She noticed the tabby cat watching her from behind a box of groceries, pupils large and dark, but carefully did nothing to clue the stranger in on its silent, feline presence. Instead she said, over her shoulder, "I noticed that you're wearing a pent. Am I right in assuming that you follow the old ways?"

She turned back—and gasped. Without her hearing him, her visitor had claimed her athame off the mantle and stepped up behind her. Now he loomed over her, the knife too near to her throat.

Its blade might only be pewter . . . but Ivy's throat was only flesh. She swallowed. Hard.

"Yes," said the dark stranger, his voice almost a purr. "And I honor an ancient god."

Pieces clicked into place, subtly—but unavoidably.

"The . . . Holly King?" She couldn't drag her gaze from the blade. So much for subtlety . . .

"Your enemy, this night," he prompted.

"I don't have any enemies." She hoped her breathless words proved true. "Not that I know of."

"You're a Wiccan," he accused—pretty much implying that his own brand of paganism wouldn't follow the comforting beliefs of "Harm None" and "What ye send forth comes back to ye" that her own did. "Yes? One of those love-and-light types, no doubt, who expect nothing but goodness and growth from their magic and their traditions. And you wear the oak."

"It's not an oak, it's a yew. Or an ash. It stands for—" But when he pressed the tip of her athame to her throat, she let her protest fall to silence.

He said, "Do not pretend ignorance about this night."

"You mean about the Oak King and the . . . ?"

"Holly King," he repeated.

This was *not* what she'd assumed her night of meditating on the meaning of Yule would encompass.

"You . . . " She hated to sound crazy—but with a knife to her throat, what did she have to lose? How much *less* subtle did magic have to get? "Are *you* the Holly King?"

And he said, almost a hiss, "Tonight I am."

It was crazy—and yet, damnably, it made sense. Especially on the metaphysical level. The one thing all pagans had in common, be they

Wiccans or Druids, Shamans or Discordians, were the old gods. The Ancient Ones' essence could permeate the pine trees and the snowflakes, the wind and the sky . . . and, sometimes, their followers. Whether viewed as formal pantheons or mere metaphors, pagan gods were as immanent as they were transcendent.

If Zeus could become a swan to have his wicked way with a mortal maiden—if priestesses could "draw down the moon," taking on the essence of a goddess for ritual purposes—then surely the Holly King could co-habit the body of a strong man to . . .

There went that unsteady foreboding again. To what?

"Why?" demanded Ivy, raising her chin slightly to add another millimeter's distance from her ceremonial blade.

"I tire of your pretense," he warned, as casually as if he held women at knifepoint all the time. "To do battle, of course; the same battle that has darkened each winter thoughout millennia. And preferably to win."

"Don't be ridicu—" With the point of the athame, he reminded her to choose her words more carefully. "Magic works *with* nature," she insisted, voice lower. "Not against it. The earth's axis will start to tip back and the sun will gain power starting tomorrow, no matter what happens tonight."

He appeared unimpressed. "That hardly means the *real* light—peace and love, comfort and joy, all those saccharin ideals the Oak King represents—need necessarily return. Not if I prevail."

And that, too, made a horrible sense.

Deal with the knife first, thought Ivy wildly. *Encroaching darkness and despair later.* "Just out of . . . um . . . curiosity. What's any of this got to do with me?"

"You really don't know?" He sounded intrigued, even amused—and still wholly in control of the situation.

"From my take on things, this is between you and Oak King, isn't it?" Maybe the Oak King was the companion he'd been separated from in the storm, the one he'd insisted was safe. She licked her lips. "I don't have any reason to hurt you—I don't *believe* in hurting people. Or gods. And even if I did, I don't have a weapon. So how about you save your strength for the real battle, we call it a truce, and we just get through this night as best we can."

In a smooth movement, the stranger turned and threw her athame into the fireplace. Sparks billowed up around its engraved blade, and the carved hilt immediately began to darken.

"Perhaps," he agreed, turning back to her.

Ivy reached helplessly toward the fire, but she did not dare take a step in that direction. She knew he could stop her.

"That's important to me," she did protest, voice trembling, as she raised her gaze back to this man—this apparent servant of death, of darkness. "It's why I'm here."

"It *was* why you are here," he stressed—and slowly drew a hunting knife from his boot. This blade was obviously of steel, far more deadly than decorative. "Now you are here because of me only. Remember that." And he casually tapped her cheek with the flat of the weapon. The cold of the metal stung. "You are all I have to ward off the boredom of this confinement. But my idea of amusement does not include my death."

Briefly, exhaustion dulled his sharp features, sallowed his cheeks. Then his head snapped straighter, and he glared at Ivy.

She refused to imagine what his idea of amusement *was*. No need to give negative images power by visualizing them. "Would you like some more stew?" she offered instead, her voice a breath away from shaky.

"No." But at least he slid his own knife back into his boot. "I do not want you near the fire."

"But it's *cold*."

He sounded annoyed when he demanded, "What do you expect in December?"

The storm's wail, muffled by the cabin's walls, emphasized their words—and had Ivy wondering, again, if the Oak King were out there. For a moment, she indulged in the fantasy of a golden-haired hero bursting in, defeating the dark stranger and rescuing her. "Let me at least sit closer."

He turned calm, dark eyes to her. She found herself awaiting the inevitable pause before he spoke. "I would rather you not."

"You already know I'm a love-and-light type of witch." One whose greatest hope for true magic was currently smelting in the fireplace, damn it. She told herself that survival was more important than her ritual . . . but she'd been merely surviving for a half year now. She'd hoped for so much more from this holiday. "Don't you trust me?"

"Of course not. And if you were anything but a fool, you would not have trusted me. You would not have left your door unlocked. You would not have turned your back to me." He looked almost sad as he sank again into the camp chair, his hand dangerously near the hilt protruding from his boot.

She knew for sure, then, that the crushed tranquilizer tablets she'd added to the stew were starting to take effect.

"It is annoying to be trusted by fools," he sighed mournfully. Somehow she didn't think that meant he'd approve of the tranquilizer.

"Why?" she challenged. "Do you feel obliged to meet their expectations?"

He shook his head. "No. They are just so terribly boring to defeat. No fight to them."

Think again, holly boy. But she *was* torn. She did not like being bossed around, even by a god, much less held at knifepoint, robbed of her beautiful athame. She did not intend to play the role of victim. But . . . neither did she want to do anybody, even him, actual harm.

Why add more pain and negativity to the universe?

Instead, she settled onto her sleeping bag, wrapping her sweatered arms around her knees. Maybe she could keep him talking until the tranquilizers kicked in, or until the Oak King showed up—whichever came first. "What's your name, anyway? Assuming you have some identity beyond being the Holly King."

"Duncan," he sighed, eyelids beginning to sink. "Duncan Bercilak. But for tonight, you may call me 'My Lord.'"

Like *that* would happen anytime soon! But surprisingly, a wicked gleam in the stranger's dark eyes seemed to acknowledge that. Darkness apparently had a sense of humor.

"Hasn't it occurred to you, Duncan, that your timing with this little apotheosis sucks? The Holly King is supposed to die tonight."

He frowned, seemingly miffed. "Not if I have anything to do with it."

"And you planned to defeat the Oak King by going out in the middle of a blizzard?" insisted Ivy. "No offense, but I don't get it."

"Perhaps you do not *wish* to 'get it,'" Duncan Bercilak assured her. And, she noticed, he took another spoonful of stew. "Perhaps that is wise."

With her athame gone, she needn't worry about meditating on the meaning of Yule anymore—but Ivy shrugged. "Humor me."

"Even though your increased knowledge could increase the menace you pose, and my reasons for killing you?" Reading her blank look, he sneered—albeit sleepily. "I already told you that I am the bad guy, Ivy. Stop trusting me for your answers."

"Yeah, well you're the only one here."

"Am I?"

Did he mean the cat? But no, from the intense way he watched her, he did not. "*Me?*"

"You've *never* heard of the Ivy Girl?"

And, like a burst of magic, she realized she had. But as with most magic, this did not truly come out of nowhere. The term, "Ivy Girl," mixed with the smell of the fireplace and the pine boughs, channeled a memory from her early childhood, her grandfather telling her about English harvest festivals. *"Some country folk bind the last sheaf of grain with an ivy vine,"* Grampa had said, explaining why he called her his Ivy Girl. *"It's their superstition that the grain stands for the fallen king, who dies each autumn, and the ivy stands for a goddess who takes over for him. The holly boy and the ivy girl, they say."*

"You think *I'm* the Ivy Girl?" she demanded. "That I'm here to *bind* you or something?"

He visibly stifled a yawn. "Amusing, isn't it? You see why my hopes for victory are so high this year."

"But what about the Oak King?" His stare clarified things for her. The point of this struggle wasn't whether he fought a king or a woman, Oak or Ivy. The point was that darkness and light met, struggled—and one prevailed. Still . . . "*Me?*"

So much for a god-like blond hero riding to her rescue. She found herself suddenly annoyed with the Oak King for leaving her in this mess—and with the universe for not asking if she was willing to play!

Deal with encroaching darkness and despair first, she reminded herself. *Righteous indignation later.*

But she'd never believed in fighting fire with fire, much less darkness with darkness. "What if I don't *want* to fight you?" she demanded. "What's the penalty for forfeiture?"

"It could be your death," he suggested, far too intrigued, and began to stand from the camp chair. "You *did* accept the benefits happily enough while life was going well for you."

Without any real physical defense, she grabbed her tree pendant for the protection that earth elements—metal and wood—afforded.

Duncan swayed visibly, then braced himself against the mantle. He stared at the plate by his feet, then at her, incredulity mounting. "Damn you! You *did* drug me!"

He kicked the plate at her, but missed in his dizziness. She did not even have to duck.

"I did it even before I knew you were the Holly King, if that helps," she said softly. "I didn't trust you on a mundane level . . . and I thought you could probably use the sleep."

He staggered back, then fell to his knees, his dark, somehow-bruised eyes still fixed on her face. "Damn you . . . " he whispered, his voice almost as hushed as when he'd first tried speaking.

She waited to feel triumph, but all she felt was a sad relief—and the yawn that struggled to escape her, from her own share of the stew. She had not escaped yet.

"What is the penalty for forfeiture if you *don't* kill me?" she asked, with careful calm.

Duncan still stared at her, shocked, even as his eyes struggled to close. He shuddered, and almost against her will, she extended a hand in his direction.

She would not have touched him, but still he winced away.

"I don't intend to hurt you," she insisted, wincing herself from the accusation in his depthless eyes. "I'm one of those love-and-light witches, remember?"

"There is more than one kind of battle," he gasped, crumpling onto the dirt floor, exhausted. "You are my enemy, this night."

She realized, then the full meaning of his bruised expression, and why, even at his worst, he had not completely frightened her.

"You're scared," she said, surprised. "Your darkness isn't anything as simple as evil, is it? It's fear, even withdrawal—you're scared to let me close enough to help you, maybe to let anyone close enough. And it's distrust. And maybe it's the loss of power—if you let me help you, it might change who you are, and who knows *what* you'd be."

His eyes slid shut as the drug overpowered him, and his breathing fell into a soft, steady rhythm.

"You've been weakened by the very things you stand for," she whispered . . . then yawned.

The cat crept out of its corner, sniffed the plate of stew, then turned with annoyance to Ivy and meowed. Loudly. *She* knew better than to eat that stuff.

"You're right," said Ivy. She herself had not eaten as much of the stew, or the drug, as Duncan Bercilak. But she was smaller. She couldn't count on much time before she, too, became useless. So if she meant to do anything significant to protect herself, now was her chance.

"I don't have to kill him, do I?" she asked the cat, now sniffing the unconscious man. Now the cat ignored her.

He'd meant to kill *her*, right? Or had he? He'd passed up on enough chances. In any case, Ivy wasn't sure she *could* do something like that, neither cut his throat with his own dagger—yuck!—nor drag him back into the snow and leave him to the elements. He'd said himself: there was more than one kind of battle.

She would not defeat darkness by giving into it. But neither would she win by waiting passively for the light to return on its own. Not without helping it along.

"The meaning of Yule?" she suggested to the cat, with a wry smile.

The cat moved back to her towel by the fire and curled into the classic feline-at-rest pose, front legs tucked under, tail wrapped neatly around herself. Her eyes narrowed into satisfied slants.

Decided, Ivy kneeled beside Duncan, drew the long, double-edged dagger from his boot, and gingerly moved it to her own backpack. Then, like any good Ivy Girl, she bound the Holly King with strips of cloth that she tore from her sheets, securing both his wrists and ankles.

Warmth radiated off him, despite lying on a near-frozen floor. He had strong legs, chiseled wrists. This was not *only* the Holly King, after all. This was a man named Duncan Bercilak, who had for whatever reason taken on the job.

Pausing to brush brown hair from his troubled face, she wondered how bad *his* year had been, to drive him this far. But she still tied him. And that, she decided, wiping her hands on her jeans, was as pragmatic and mundane as she meant to get tonight.

Then she swayed—and shivered. She wasn't out of danger yet. Exhaustion blurred her vision, and it was so cold out! To stay with this man would be dangerous. So would be trying to leave in the middle of a still-howling blizzard, to hike a good half-mile to her car through the night woods, then to drive while tranquilized.

After a long moment's consideration, she pulled her sleeping bag closer and wrestled Duncan Bercilak's heavy form onto it, off the frozen floor. Then she added her extra blanket and reluctantly lay beside his warmth.

Later on, we'll conspire / As we dream by the fire . . .

It seemed the right thing to do, and not just because she felt so cold.

It seemed the right thing to do in the same, subtle way that magic worked . . .

When she awoke, Ivy felt blessedly warm, curled against Duncan Bercilak's chest. His arms encircled her protectively in his sleep, and the cat—she realized from the vibration of its purr—cuddled against the back of her legs. The winds had fallen silent, marking the end of the long storm. The fire was nearly dead, and only her Coleman lantern and the two pillar candles—one red, one green—lit the cabin. The morning held that hushed magic that had blessed her Christmas mornings as a child, her Yuletide mornings once she recognized herself as a witch.

She hated to leave such peace and warmth for a long, dark, snowy trek to her car.

Then it occurred to her that *Duncan's arms were around her*, despite her having tied his hands! Holding her breath, she slid from his heavy embrace and slowly sat up . . . then sighed with relief to see that he still slept. Somehow in the night his hands had worked free of their bonds. So much for her job as the Ivy Girl.

She found it even harder to believe that he would kill her now than she had before. Did a handsome face blur her judgment so terribly much . . . or were there stronger powers at work here?

The cat stalked away, then sat with its back to her in silent protest at the disruption to her sleep. Bitter air tingled at Ivy's skin, deprived of Duncan's warmth, as though she weren't wearing layered winter clothing. It burned in her lungs and misted her breath as—deciding not to risk waking Duncan by trying to re-tie him—she crept to her supplies and put on her quilted winter coat, her gloves, her scarf. She didn't dare the noise of repacking her supplies—the only belonging she'd considered irreplaceable was her athame, and it, she saw, was a pitted, misshapen thing on the dying embers.

Magic might well exist . . . but so much for her chance at finding proof this year, anyway. On an afterthought, Ivy opened the flap of her half-empty backpack and clucked softly to the gray tabby cat. As if it understood, it trotted over, tried her patience with only a moment of cautious exploration, then crawled into the safety of the bag.

Ivy shouldered the pack, checking its pocket for Duncan's dagger, lest he come after her. When she reached the door, she turned and looked back for a final moment. It really might be best for her physical safety if she killed him, or at least bashed him over the head.

As if she could be sure of not killing him if she bashed him over the head, anyway.

But it would not, she thought, be best for the world, to add even one more act of violence to it. When she got to the closest town, she could do her mundane duty by reporting him as an intruder to the police. Perhaps *they* could keep him from harming anyone else. But she would not empower the darkness by hurting him. It might seem stupid, on the physical level. But on deeper levels, magical levels, it felt surprisingly . . . right. Again.

Impulsively, Ivy blew a kiss at the sleeping man. Then she turned, unlatched the door, and swung it open.

Face to face with an older man, his eyes piggy and small over his purple scarf, she screamed.

Only as the man's voice fell silent in surprise did Ivy realize that he'd been chanting, chanting something that she did not quite understand but which her subconscious did, and it made all the fine hairs on her body stand up. He advanced and she retreated, fumbling the dagger from its pocket in her backpack. Behind her she heard noise—

Duncan's squared hand closed hard around her wrist, made her drop the knife as he pulled her against him, trapped her arms with his hands. Then, to her surprise, Bercilak and the newcomer exchanged familiar glances.

"Silas," said Duncan in his clear, authoritative voice. "I thought perhaps you'd deserted me."

"I searched as quickly as I could Dun—that is, my lord," assured the older man ingratiatingly. Ivy thought he looked guilty. "I searched through the night, despite the storm. You cannot know how frantic I was for your safety."

The man reeked of deceit. More than her fright, Ivy felt amazement that Duncan, who'd seemed intelligent enough, did not see it. Perhaps that was what his distance and apathy had done to this Holly King's instincts.

The stranger, Silas, seemed to sense Ivy's hostility. He searched her face with his piggish eyes. "M'lord," he ventured, "if we might speak for a moment?"

"Granted," said Duncan, as if he truly *were* a king . . . or a god. With a parting glare to Ivy, he set her further into the cabin before releasing her. Then he picked up his dagger and strode out into the darkness of the cold, early morning, his feet crunching in the snow, leaving her alone to contemplate her fate.

Ivy knew she should be afraid . . . but it seemed impossible to fear someone mussed by sleep, someone who had yet to do more to her than threaten and disarm her.

She let the cat out of the backpack. Then she checked her watch—past six a.m. Almost dawn.

"Bring back the light," she said softly, firmly, as she waited. "Bring back the light. Bring back the light . . . "

It felt better than doing nothing.

"My lord," whispered Silas, outside. "I am surprised you've left her alive this long. Dawn is almost upon us . . . "

"And as you can see," noted Duncan, more annoyed by the blind fool than usual, "I still live."

"But she remains a threat. She cannot allow the Solstice to arrive without defeating you. *It is foreordained!* One of you *must* vanquish—"

Duncan glared the older, weaker man into silence. Sadly, it was temporary.

"Ah," said Silas now, more ingratiating than ever. He'd played his role in the Holly King's reign thus far, but . . . "If you do not wish to distress yourself by doing the deed—"

Duncan allowed his face to show his contempt at the assumed insult. "Silas," he corrected. "I am no schoolboy to be softened by a night with a pacifistic white-lighter. You would not deny me my pleasure, would you?"

Silas smiled, obviously relieved by this show of authority. "No, m'lord. I would not."

Duncan sighed. After preparing for this moment for so long, he found himself wishing the danger, the uncertainty, were over. Soon, now. Soon. "I only wish I had time for more creativity . . . but you are right. Daylight presses."

When he strode back into the dugout, the woman named Ivy MacDaraich looked up and smiled at him. *Smiled!* "Are the stars out?" she asked. "Now that the storm's passed, I mean?"

He stared at her, incredulous. He knew the power of the Oak King's representatives as well as anyone, and still she amazed him. How frightened would most pretty young women be, alone in a cabin with him? How many chances had he given her to destroy him? How many excuses to hate him?

How many opportunities to choose darkness at long last?

Curious, unwilling to waste these last few moments, he strode to stand in front of her. Her eyes widened slightly as she stared up at him, more in curiosity than fear even now. Then, as he bent and covered her mouth with his own, she caught her breath with surprise. Touching a tentative hand to his sweatered chest, she kissed him back.

Their kiss deepened. She smelled of wood-smoke, pine, cinnamon and bayberry. Of Yule.

Drawing back from her, Duncan studied her face for a moment longer, resigning himself to what he must do. Her dazed, sated look ought not have made this more difficult.

"You know, one *can* resist the darkness without denying it," he scolded, almost gently, as he raised a hand to her cheek. "One *can* accept it without embracing it. You should not have trusted me."

"I didn't," she reminded him, voice husky with sleep—and something else. "I just refused to *be* you."

He slid his hand downward, found just the right place on her soft throat with his fingers—yes, there. "So you did."

Her green eyes widened, then fluttered shut. In a moment, she'd crumpled as if boneless to the frozen floor.

The cat she'd thought to have hidden from him arched its back and hissed. Duncan ignored it to crouch beside Ivy MacDaraich. He touched her cheek again, touched the tree pendant she wore around her neck on a leather thong.

Then, retrieving his knife from his boot, Duncan slashed it downward toward her throat . . .

He strode into the graying morning, crunching through the snow, and raised an eyebrow at his lackey. "Surely you did not doubt me, Silas?"

"Of course not, m'lord," assured Silas, too quickly.

Duncan looked at the dagger in his hand, contemplating. In a sudden moment, he turned and threw it back into the cabin. With a distinct thud, it buried itself into the opposite wall. He met his companion's surprise with superiority. "We cannot let people think that the Holly King is stingy," he said haughtily. "The next poor wretch who falls upon this place in a snowstorm might be hungry."

Silas stared, startled by the viciousness of Duncan's statement. Then, belatedly, he began to laugh. Amused by the obnoxious man's ignorance, Duncan joined him, and together they hiked downward toward the road and their transportation—and the new year, with its possibilities for change.

In the pocket of his coat, Duncan fingered Ivy's tree-shaped amulet and made plans for the future.

Plans for growth.

Ivy's head hurt. As she became aware of her own existence, sucked deep breaths, the throbbing softened—slightly. Disoriented, she sat up. Dizziness blurred the edges of her sight to a yellow black, and she felt cold . . . so cold.

And . . . alive?

Not that she wasn't grateful, but . . . *why?*

The cat butted its striped head against her hip as Ivy stared out the still-open door. Iron gray expectation was beginning to lighten the winter sky. Perhaps Duncan had left her alive to twist the knife—so to speak. He'd won, hadn't he? He'd not killed her . . . but there was more than one kind of battle. She hadn't "defeated" him, either.

Assuming she'd really been acting in the role of the light, or he in the role of Holly King. Assuming their strange night meant anything on the astral, magic realm at all.

Slowly she stood, shuffled to the doorway and braced herself against the doorjamb. Occasionally, through snow-draped branches on the path far below the cabin, she caught glimpses of the two men descending the hillside. As the sky lightened, Duncan's hair took on an unexpected, burnished tint.

Behind her, in the cabin, the cat yowled.

She'd survived him. He'd kissed her—the most intense kiss she'd ever known, from god or man—and he'd left her feeling more alive than she'd felt in months. Not that she approved of his behavior, of course! But suddenly, the crisp smell of snow and pine and wood smoke seemed to tingle through her with something akin to . . . joy. She'd guarded against the darkness, hadn't given into it. The worst of it had passed, and now she appreciated what she had more than ever.

"Winter Solstice," she whispered, understanding, and smiled as the eastern horizon brightened. Then she frowned. *Damn*, but she'd wanted to do that spell.

If only the son-of-a-bitch hadn't destroyed her athame.

The cat yowled again. When Ivy turned to look, she saw the tabby sitting purposefully beneath something stuck in the wall. Something that had not been there before. Something that caught the waxing light.

What she felt then was still subtle—no pyrotechnics, no levitation. But it also was very real. *True* magic. She crossed the room to take a closer look, to make sure. Slowly, she pulled Duncan Bercilak's hunting knife out of the wooden wall.

He'd *left* it for her?

That was not the sort of thing the Holly King would do, was it? The Holly King tested, challenged, reigned over a world that slowly became barren and cold. He took away. The god who *gave* was the . . .

She remembered how the Duncan Bercilak's hair had glinted in the distance.

When Ivy turned toward the doorway with the knife in her hand, its double-edged blade caught and glowed with the Solstice morning's rising sun.

❄ ❄ ❄

Connie Willis confronts the issues of holiday newsletters, alien invasion, and families . . . all of which, in other hands, might provide fodder for fright rather than the amusement she supplies. Holiday newsletters arose as an extension of sending Christmas cards. Sir Henry Cole commissioned the first commercial cards in 1823 in London, as he was too busy to handwrite all his holiday greetings. Artist John Calcott Horsley designed the cards, which depicted a jolly Victorian family feast with wineglasses raised in an apparent toast to the recipient. Portrayals of charitable acts flanked the center art. The charming scene proved controversial, however, since even the children appeared to be imbibing alcohol. Cards did not catch on immediately, but by 1871 there was an editorial complaint in at least one British newspaper about people trying to outdo one another in the matter of the number of cards sent and received.

Newsletter
❄
Connie Willis

Later examination of weather reports and newspapers showed that it may have started as early as October nineteenth, but the first indication I had that something unusual was going on was at Thanksgiving.

I went to Mom's for dinner (as usual), and was feeding cranberries and cut-up oranges into Mom's old-fashioned meat grinder for the cranberry relish and listening to my sister-in-law Allison talk about her Christmas newsletter (also as usual).

"Which of Cheyenne's accomplishments do you think I should write about first, Nan?" she said, spreading cheese on celery sticks. "Her playing lead snowflake in *The Nutcracker* or her hitting a home run in PeeWee Soccer?"

"I'd list the Nobel Peace Prize first," I murmured, under cover of the crunch of an apple being put through the grinder.

"There just isn't room to put in all the girls' accomplishments," she said, oblivious. "Mitch *insists* I keep it to one page."

"That's because of Aunt Lydia's newsletters," I said. "Eight pages single-spaced."

"I know," she said. "And in that tiny print you can barely read." She waved a celery stick thoughtfully. "That's an idea."

"Eight pages single-spaced?"

"No. I could get the computer to do a smaller font. That way I'd have room for Dakota's Sunshine Scout merit badges. I got the cutest paper for my newsletters this year. Little angels holding bunches of mistletoe."

Christmas newsletters are *very* big in my family, in case you couldn't tell. Everybody—uncles, grandparents, second cousins, my sister Sueann—sends the Xeroxed monstrosities to family, coworkers, old friends from high school, and people they met on their cruise to the Caribbean (which they wrote about at length in their newsletter the year before). Even my Aunt Irene, who writes a handwritten letter on every one of her Christmas cards, sticks a newsletter in with it.

My second cousin Lucille's are the worst, although there are a lot of contenders. Last year hers started:

"Another year has hurried past
And, here I am, asking, 'Where did the time go so fast?'
A trip in February, a bladder operation in July,
Too many activities, not enough time, no matter how hard I try."

At least Allison doesn't put Dakota and Cheyenne's accomplishments into verse.

"I don't think I'm going to send a Christmas newsletter this year," I said.

Allison stopped, cheese-filled knife in hand. "Why not?"

"Because I don't have any news. I don't have a new job, I didn't go on a vacation to the Bahamas, I didn't win any awards. I don't have anything to tell."

"Don't be ridiculous," my mother said, sweeping in carrying a foil-covered casserole dish. "Of course you do, Nan. What about that skydiving class you took?"

"That was last year, Mom," I said. And I had only taken it so I'd have something to write about in my Christmas newsletter.

"Well, then, tell about your social life. Have you met anybody lately at work?"

Mom asks me this every Thanksgiving. Also Christmas, the Fourth of July, and every time I see her.

"There's nobody to meet," I said, grinding cranberries. "Nobody new ever gets hired, because nobody ever quits. Everybody who works there's been there for years. Nobody even gets fired. Bob Hunziger hasn't been to work on time in eight years, and *he's* still there."

"What about . . . what was his name?" Allison said, arranging the celery sticks in a cut-glass dish. "The guy you liked who had just gotten divorced?"

"Gary," I said. "He's still hung up on his ex-wife."

"I thought you said she was a real shrew."

"She is," I said. "Marcie the Menace. She calls him twice a week complaining about how unfair the divorce settlement is, even though she got virtually everything. Last week it was the house. She claimed she'd been too upset by the divorce to get the mortgage refinanced and he owed her twenty thousand dollars because now interest rates have gone up. But it doesn't matter. Gary still keeps hoping they'll get back together. He almost didn't fly to Connecticut to his parents' for Thanksgiving because he thought she might change her mind about a reconciliation."

"You could write about Sueann's new boyfriend," Mom said, sticking marshmallows on the sweet potatoes. "She's bringing him today."

This was as usual, too. Sueann always brings a new boyfriend to Thanksgiving dinner. Last year it was a biker. And no, I don't mean one of those nice guys who wear a beard and black Harley T-shirt on weekends and work as accountants between trips to Sturgis. I mean a Hell's Angel.

My sister Sueann has the worst taste in men of anyone I have ever known. Before the biker, she dated a member of a militia group and, after the ATF arrested him, a bigamist wanted in three states.

"If this boyfriend spits on the floor, I'm leaving," Allison said, counting out silverware. "Have you met him?" she asked Mom.

"No," Mom said, "but Sueann says he used to work where you do, Nan. So *somebody* must quit once in a while."

I racked my brain, trying to think of any criminal types who'd worked in my company. "What's his name?"

"David something," Mom said, and Cheyenne and Dakota raced into the kitchen, screaming, "Aunt Sueann's here, Aunt Sueann's here! Can we eat now?"

Allison leaned over the sink and pulled the curtains back to look out the window.

"What does he look like?" I asked, sprinkling sugar on the cranberry relish.

"Clean-cut," she said, sounding surprised. "Short blond hair, slacks, white shirt, tie."

Oh, no, that meant he was a neo-Nazi. Or married and planning to get a divorce as soon as the kids graduated from college—which would turn out to be in twenty-three years, since he'd just gotten his wife pregnant again.

"Is he handsome?" I asked, sticking a spoon into the cranberry relish.

"No," Allison said, even more surprised. "He's actually kind of ordinary-looking."

I came over to the window to look. He was helping Sueann out of the car. She was dressed up, too, in a dress and a denim slouch hat. "Good heavens," I said. "It's David Carrington. He worked up on fifth in Computing."

"Was he a womanizer?" Allison asked.

"No," I said, bewildered. "He's a very nice guy. He's unmarried, he doesn't drink, and he left to go get a degree in medicine."

"Why didn't *you* ever meet him?" Mom said.

David shook hands with Mitch, regaled Cheyenne and Dakota with a knock-knock joke, and told Mom his favorite kind of sweet potatoes were the ones with the marshmallows on top.

"He must be a serial killer," I whispered to Allison.

"Come on, everybody, let's sit down," Mom said. "Cheyenne and Dakota, you sit here by Grandma. David, you sit here, next to Sueann. Sueann, take off your hat. You know hats aren't allowed at the table."

"Hats for men aren't allowed at the table," Sueann said, patting her denim hat. "Women's hats are." She sat down. "Hats are coming back in style, did you know that? *Cosmopolitan*'s latest issue said this is the Year of the Hat."

"I don't care what it is," Mom said. "Your father would never have allowed hats at the table."

"I'll take it off if you'll turn off the TV," Sueann said, complacently opening out her napkin.

They had reached an impasse. Mom always has the TV on during meals. "I like to have it on in case something happens," she said stubbornly.

"Like what?" Mitch said. "Aliens landing from outer space?"

"For your information, there was a UFO sighting two weeks ago. It was on CNN."

"Everything looks delicious," David said. "Is that homemade cranberry relish? I *love* that. My grandmother used to make it."

He had to be a serial killer.

For half an hour, we concentrated on turkey, stuffing, mashed potatoes, green-bean casserole, scalloped corn casserole, marshmallow-topped sweet potatoes, cranberry relish, pumpkin pie, and the news on CNN.

"Can't you at least turn it down, Mom?" Mitch said. "We can't even hear to talk."

"I want to see the weather in Washington," Mom said. "For your flight."

"You're leaving tonight?" Sueann said. "But you just got here. I haven't even seen Cheyenne and Dakota."

"Mitch has to fly back tonight," Allison said. "But the girls and I are staying till Wednesday."

"I don't see why you can't stay at least until tomorrow," Mom said.

"Don't tell me this is homemade whipped cream on the pumpkin pie," David said. "I haven't had homemade whipped cream in years."

"You used to work in computers, didn't you?" I asked him. "There's a lot of computer crime around these days, isn't there?"

"Computers!" Allison said. "I forgot all the awards Cheyenne won at computer camp." She turned to Mitch. "The newsletter's going to have to be at least two pages. The girls just have too many awards—T-ball, tadpole swimming, Bible-school attendance."

"Do you send Christmas newsletters in your family?" my mother asked David.

He nodded. "I love hearing from everybody."

"You see?" Mom said to me. "People *like* getting newsletters at Christmas."

"I don't have anything against Christmas newsletters," I said. "I just don't think they should be deadly dull. Mary had a root canal, Bootsy seems to be getting over her ringworm, we got new gutters on the house. Why doesn't anyone ever write about anything interesting in their newsletters?"

"Like what?" Sueann said.

"I don't know. An alligator biting their arm off. A meteor falling on their house. A murder. Something interesting to read. Why don't they write about that?"

"Probably because they didn't happen," Sueann said.

"Then they should make something up," I said, "so we don't have to hear about their trip to Nebraska and their gallbladder operation."

"You'd do that?" Allison said, appalled. "You'd make something up?"

"People make things up in their newsletters all the time, and you know it," I said. "Look at the way Aunt Laura and Uncle Phil brag about their vacations and their stock options and their cars. If you're going to lie, they might as well be lies that are interesting for other people to read."

"You have plenty of things to tell without making up lies, Nan," Mom said reprovingly. "Maybe you should do something like your cousin Celia. She writes her newsletter all year long, day by day," she explained to David. "Nan, you might have more news than you think if you kept track of it day by day like Celia. She always has a lot to tell."

Yes, indeed. Her newsletters were nearly as long as Aunt Lydia's. They read like a diary, except she wasn't in junior high, where at least there were pop quizzes and zits and your locker combination to give it a little zing. Celia's newsletters had no zing whatsoever:

"Wed. Jan. 1. Froze to death going out to get the paper. Snow got in the plastic bag thing the paper comes in. Editorial section all wet. Had to dry it out on the radiator. Bran flakes for breakfast. Watched *Good Morning America*.

"Thurs. Jan. 2. Cleaned closets. Cold and cloudy."

"If you'd write a little every day," Mom said, "you'd be surprised at how much you'd have to tell by Christmas."

Sure. With my life, I wouldn't even have to write it every day. I could do Monday's right now. "Mon. Nov. 28. Froze to death on the way to work. Bob Hunziger not in yet. Penny putting up Christmas decorations. Solveig told me she's sure the baby is going to be a boy. Asked me which name I liked, Albuquerque or Dallas. Said hi to Gary, but he was too depressed to talk to me. Thanksgiving reminds him of ex-wife's giblets. Cold and cloudy."

I was wrong. It was snowing, and Solveig's ultrasound had showed the baby was a girl. "What do you think of Trinidad as a name?" she asked me. Penny wasn't putting up Christmas decorations either. She was passing out slips of paper with our Secret Santas' names on them. "The decorations aren't here yet," she said excitedly. "I'm getting something special from a farmer upstate."

"Does it involve feathers?" I asked her. Last year the decorations had been angels with thousands of chicken feathers glued onto cardboard for their wings. We were still picking them out of our computers.

"No," she said happily. "It's a surprise. I love Christmas, don't you?"

"Is Hunziger in?" I asked her, brushing snow out of my hair. Hats always mash my hair down, so I hadn't worn one.

"Are you kidding?" she said. She handed me a Secret Santa slip. "It's the Monday after Thanksgiving. He probably won't be in till sometime Wednesday."

Gary came in, his ears bright red from the cold and a harried expression on his face. His ex-wife must not have wanted a reconciliation.

"Hi, Gary," I said, and turned to hang up my coat without waiting for him to answer.

And he didn't, but when I turned back around, he was still standing there, staring at me. I put a hand up to my hair, wishing I'd worn a hat.

"Can I talk to you a minute?" he said, looking anxiously at Penny.

"Sure," I said, trying not to get my hopes up. He probably wanted to ask me something about the Secret Santas.

He leaned farther over my desk. "Did anything unusual happen to you over Thanksgiving?"

"My sister didn't bring home a biker to Thanksgiving dinner," I said.

He waved that away dismissively. "No, I mean anything odd, peculiar, out of the ordinary."

"That is out of the ordinary."

He leaned even closer. "I flew out to my parents' for Thanksgiving, and on the flight home—you know how people always carry on luggage that won't fit in the overhead compartments and then try to cram it in?"

"Yes," I said, thinking of a bridesmaid's bouquet I had made the mistake of putting in the overhead compartment one time.

"Well, nobody did that on my flight. They didn't carry on hanging bags or enormous shopping bags full of Christmas presents. Some people didn't even have a carry-on. And that isn't all. Our flight was half an hour late, and the flight attendant said, 'Those of you who do not have connecting flights, please remain seated until those with connections have deplaned.' And they did." He looked at me expectantly.

"Maybe everybody was just in the Christmas spirit."

He shook his head. "All four babies on the flight slept the whole way, and the toddler behind me didn't kick the seat."

That was unusual.

"Not only that, the guy next to me was reading *The Way of All Flesh* by Samuel Butler. When's the last time you saw anybody on an airplane reading anything but John Grisham or Danielle Steele? I tell you, there's something funny going on."

"What?" I asked curiously.

"I don't know," he said. "You're sure you haven't noticed anything?"

"Nothing except for my sister. She always dates these losers, but the guy she brought to Thanksgiving was really nice. He even helped with the dishes."

"You didn't notice anything else?"

"No," I said, wishing I had. This was the longest he'd ever talked to me about anything besides his ex-wife. "Maybe it's something in the air at DIA. I have to take my sister-in-law and her little girls to the airport Wednesday. I'll keep an eye out."

He nodded. "Don't say anything about this, okay?" he said, and hurried off to Accounting.

"What was that all about?" Penny asked, coming over.

"His ex-wife," I said. "When do we have to exchange Secret Santa gifts?"

"Every Friday, and Christmas Eve."

I opened up my slip. Good, I'd gotten Hunziger. With luck I wouldn't have to buy any Secret Santa gifts at all.

Tuesday I got Aunt Laura and Uncle Phil's Christmas newsletter. It was in gold ink on cream-colored paper, with large gold bells in the corners. "Joyeux Noel," it began. "That's French for Merry Christmas. We're sending our newsletter out early this year because we're spending Christmas in Cannes to celebrate Phil's promotion to assistant CEO and my wonderful new career! Yes, I'm starting my own business—Laura's Floral Creations—and orders are pouring in! It's already been written up in *House Beautiful*, and you will never guess who called last week—Martha Stewart!" Et cetera.

I didn't see Gary. Or anything unusual, although the waiter who took my lunch order actually got it right for a change. But he got Tonya's (who works up on third) wrong.

"I *told* him tomato and lettuce only," she said, picking pickles off her sandwich. "I heard Gary talked to you yesterday. Did he ask you out?"

"What's that?" I said, pointing to the folder Tonya'd brought with her to change the subject. "The Harbrace file?"

"No," she said. "Do you want my pickles? It's our Christmas schedule. *Never* marry anybody who has kids from a previous marriage. Especially when *you* have kids from a previous marriage. Tom's ex-wife, Janine, my ex-husband, John, and four sets of grandparents all want the kids, and they all want them on Christmas morning. It's like trying to schedule the D-Day invasion."

"At least your husband isn't still hung up on his ex-wife," I said glumly.

"So Gary didn't ask you out, huh?" She bit into her sandwich, frowned, and extracted another pickle. "I'm sure he will. Okay, if we take the kids to Tom's parents at four on Christmas Eve, Janine could pick them up at eight. . . . No, that won't work." She switched her sandwich to her other hand and began erasing. "Janine's not speaking to Tom's parents."

She sighed. "At least John's being reasonable. He called yesterday and said he'd be willing to wait till New Year's to have the kids. I don't know what got into him."

When I got back to work, there was a folded copy of the morning newspaper on my desk.

I opened it up. The headline read CITY HALL CHRISTMAS DISPLAY TO BE TURNED ON, which wasn't unusual. And neither was tomorrow's headline, which would be CITY HALL CHRISTMAS DISPLAY PROTESTED.

Either the Freedom Against Faith people protest the Nativity scene or the fundamentalists protest the elves or the environmental people protest cutting down Christmas trees or all of them protest the whole thing. It happens every year.

I turned to the inside pages. Several articles were circled in red, and there was a note next to them which read "See what I mean? Gary."

I looked at the circled articles. CHRISTMAS SHOPLIFTING DOWN, the first one read. "Mall stores report incidences of shoplifting are down for the first week of the Christmas season. Usually prevalent this time of—"

"What are you doing?" Penny said, looking over my shoulder.

I shut the paper with a rustle. "Nothing," I said. I folded it back up and stuck it into a drawer. "Did you need something?"

"Here," she said, handing me a slip of paper.

"I already got my Secret Santa name," I said.

"This is for Holiday Goodies," she said. "Everybody takes turns bringing in coffee cake or tarts or cake."

I opened up my slip. It read "Friday Dec. 20. Four dozen cookies."

"I saw you and Gary talking yesterday," Penny said. "What about?"

"His ex-wife," I said. "What kind of cookies do you want me to bring?"

"Chocolate chip," she said. "Everybody loves chocolate."

As soon as she was gone, I got the newspaper out again and took it into Hunziger's office to read. LEGISLATURE PASSES BALANCED BUDGET. The other articles read: ESCAPED CONVICT TURNS SELF IN and CHRISTMAS FOOD BANK DONATIONS UP.

I read through them and then threw the paper into the waste-basket. Halfway out the door I thought better of it and took it out, folded it up, and took it back to my desk with me.

While I was putting it into my purse, Hunziger wandered in. "If anybody asks where I am, tell them I'm in the men's room," he said, and wandered out again.

Wednesday afternoon I took the girls and Allison to the airport. She was still fretting over her newsletter.

"Do you think a greeting is absolutely necessary?" she said in the baggage check-in line. "You know, like 'Dear Friends and Family'?"

"Probably not," I said absently. I was watching the people in line ahead of us, trying to spot this unusual behavior Gary had talked about, but so far I hadn't seen any. People were looking at their watches and complaining about the length of the line, the ticket agents were calling, "Next! Next!" to the person at the head of the line, who, after having stood impatiently in line for forty-five minutes waiting for this moment, was now staring blankly into space, and an unattended toddler was methodically pulling the elastic strings off a stack of luggage tags.

"They'll still know it's a Christmas newsletter, won't they?" Allison said. "Even without a greeting at the beginning of it?"

With a border of angels holding bunches of mistletoe, what else could it be? I thought.

"Next!" the ticket agent shouted.

The man in front of us had forgotten his photo ID, the girl in front of us in line for the security check was wearing heavy metal, and on the train out to the concourse a woman stepped on my foot and then glared at me as if it were my fault. Apparently all the nice people had traveled the day Gary came home.

And that was probably what it was—some kind of statistical clump where all the considerate, intelligent people had ended up on the same flight.

I knew they existed. My sister Sueann had had an insurance actuary for a boyfriend once (he was also an embezzler, which is why Sueann was dating him) and he had said events weren't evenly distributed, that there were peaks and valleys. Gary must just have hit a peak.

Which was too bad, I thought, lugging Cheyenne, who had demanded to be carried the minute we got off the train, down the concourse. Because the only reason he had approached me was because he thought there was something strange going on.

"Here's Gate 55," Allison said, setting Dakota down and getting out French-language tapes for the girls. "If I left off the 'Dear Friends and Family,' I'd have room to include Dakota's violin recital. She played 'The Gypsy Dance.'"

She settled the girls in adjoining chairs and put on their headphones. "But Mitch says it's a letter, so it has to have a greeting."

"What if you used something short?" I said. "Like 'Greetings' or something. Then you'd have room to start the letter on the same line."

"Not 'Greetings.'" She made a face. "Uncle Frank started his letter that way last year, and it scared me half to death. I thought Mitch had been *drafted.*"

I had been alarmed when I'd gotten mine, too, but at least it had given me a temporary rush of adrenaline, which was more than Uncle Frank's letters usually did, concerned as they were with prostate problems and disputes over property taxes.

"I suppose I could use 'Holiday Greetings,'" Allison said. "Or 'Christmas Greetings,' but that's almost as long as 'Dear Friends and Family.' If only there were something shorter."

"How about 'hi'?"

"That might work." She got out paper and a pen and started writing. "How do you spell 'outstanding'?"

"O-u-t-s-t-a-n-d-i-n-g," I said absently. I was watching the moving sidewalks in the middle of the concourse. People were standing on the right, like they were supposed to, and walking on the left. No people were standing four abreast or blocking the entire sidewalk with their luggage. No kids were running in the opposite direction of the sidewalk's movement, screaming and running their hands along the rubber railing.

"How do you spell 'fabulous'?" Allison asked.

"Flight 2216 to Spokane is now ready for boarding," the flight attendant at the desk said. "Those passengers traveling with small children or those who require additional time for boarding may now board."

A single olfd lady with a walker stood up and got in line. Allison unhooked the girls' headphones, and we began the ritual of hugging and gathering up belongings.

"We'll see you at Christmas," she said.

"Good luck with your newsletter," I said, handing Dakota her teddy bear, "and don't worry about the heading. It doesn't need one."

They started down the passageway. I stood there, waving, till they were out of sight, and then turned to go.

"We are now ready for regular boarding of rows twenty-five through thirty-three," the flight attendant said, and everybody in the gate area stood up. Nothing unusual here, I thought, and started for the concourse.

"What rows did she call?" a woman in a red beret asked a teenaged boy.

"Twenty-five through thirty-three," he said.

"Oh, I'm Row Fourteen," the woman said, and sat back down.

So did I.

"We are now ready to board rows fifteen through twenty-four," the flight attendant said, and a dozen people looked carefully at their tickets and then stepped back from the door, patiently waiting their turn. One of them pulled a paperback out of her tote bag and began to read. It was *Kidnapped* by Robert Louis Stevenson. Only when the flight attendant said, "We are now boarding all rows," did the rest of them stand up and get in line.

Which didn't prove anything, and neither did the standing on the right of the moving sidewalk. Maybe people were just being nice because it was Christmas.

Don't be ridiculous, I told myself. People aren't nicer at Christmas. They're ruder and pushier and crabbier than ever. You've seen them at the mall, and in line for the post office. They act worse at Christmas than any other time.

"This is your final boarding call for Flight 2216 to Spokane," the flight attendant said to the empty waiting area. She called to me, "Are you flying to Spokane, ma'am?"

"No." I stood up. "I was seeing friends off."

"I just wanted to make sure you didn't miss your flight," she said, and turned to shut the door.

I started for the moving sidewalk, and nearly collided with a young man running for the gate. He raced up to the desk and flung his ticket down.

"I'm sorry, sir," the flight attendant said, leaning slightly away from the young man as if expecting an explosion. "Your flight has already left. I'm really terribly sor—"

"Oh, it's okay," he said. "It serves me right. I didn't allow enough time for parking and everything, that's all. I should have started for the airport earlier."

The flight attendant was tapping busily on the computer. "I'm afraid the only other open flight to Spokane for today isn't until 11:05 this evening."

"Oh, well," he said, smiling. "It'll give me a chance to catch up on my reading." He reached down into his attache case and pulled out a paperback. It was W. Somerset Maugham's *Of Human Bondage*.

"Well?" Gary said as soon as I got back to work Thursday morning. He was standing by my desk, waiting for me.

"There's definitely something going on," I said, and told him about the moving sidewalks and the guy who'd missed his plane. "But what?"

"Is there somewhere we can talk?" he said, looking anxiously around.

"Hunziger's office," I said, "but I don't know if he's in yet."

"He's not," he said, led me into the office, and shut the door behind him.

"Sit down," he said, indicating Hunziger's chair. "Now, I know this is going to sound crazy, but I think all these people have been possessed by some kind of alien intelligence. Have you ever seen *Invasion of the Body Snatchers*?"

"What?" I said.

"*Invasion of the Body Snatchers*," he said. "It's about these parasites from outer space who take over people's bodies and—"

"I *know* what it's about," I said, "and it's *science fiction*. You think the man who missed his plane was some kind of pod-person? You're right," I said, reaching for the doorknob. "I do think you're crazy."

"That's what Donald Sutherland said in *Leech-men from Mars*. Nobody ever believes it's happening, until it's too late."

He pulled a folded newspaper out of his back pocket. "Look at this," he said, waving it in front of me. "Holiday credit-card fraud down twenty percent. Holiday suicides down thirty percent. Charitable giving up sixty percent."

"They're coincidences." I explained about the statistical peaks and valleys. "Look," I said, taking the paper from him and turning to the front page. PEOPLE AGAINST CRUELTY TO OUR FURRY FRIENDS PROTESTS CITY HALL CHRISTMAS DISPLAY. ANIMAL RIGHTS GROUP OBJECTS TO EXPLOITATION OF REINDEER.

"What about your sister?" he said. "You said she only dates losers. Why would she suddenly start dating a nice guy? Why would an escaped convict suddenly turn himself in? Why would people suddenly start reading the classics? Because they've been taken over."

"By aliens from outer space?" I said incredulously. "Did he have a hat?"

"Who?" I said, wondering if he really was crazy. Could his being hung up on his horrible ex-wife have finally made him crack?

"The man who missed his plane," he said. "Was he wearing a hat?"

"I don't remember," I said, and felt suddenly cold. Sueann had worn a hat to Thanksgiving dinner. She'd refused to take it off at the table. And the woman whose ticket said *Row Fourteen* had been wearing a beret.

"What do hats have to do with it?" I asked.

"The man on the plane next to me was wearing a hat. So were most of the other people on the flight. Did you ever see *The Puppet Masters*? The parasites attached themselves to the spinal cord and took over the nervous system," he said. "This morning here at work I counted nineteen people wearing hats. Les Sawtelle, Rodney Jones, Jim Bridgeman—"

"Jim Bridgeman always wears a hat," I said. "It's to hide his bald spot. Besides, he's a computer programmer. All the computer people wear baseball caps."

"DeeDee Crawford," he said. "Vera McDermott, Janet Hall—"

"Women's hats are supposed to be making a comeback," I said.

"George Frazelli, the entire Documentation section—"

"I'm sure there's a logical explanation," I said. "It's been freezing in here all week. There's probably something wrong with the heating system."

"The thermostat's turned down to fifty," he said, "which is something else peculiar. The thermostat's been turned down on all floors."

"Well, that's probably Management. You know how they're always trying to cut costs—"

"They're giving us a Christmas bonus. And they fired Hunziger."

"They fired Hunziger?" I said. Management never fires anybody.

"This morning. That's how I knew he wouldn't be in his office."

"They actually fired Hunziger?"

"And one of the janitors. The one who drank. How do you explain that?"

"I-I don't know," I stammered. "But there has to be some other explanation than aliens. Maybe they took a management course or got the Christmas spirit or their therapists told them to do good deeds or something. Something besides leechmen. Aliens coming from outer space and taking over our brains is impossible!"

"That's what Dana Wynter said in *Invasion of the Body Snatchers*. But it's not impossible. It's happening right here, and we've got to stop it before they take over everybody and we're the only ones left. They—"

There was a knock on the door. "Sorry to bother you, Gary," Carol Zaliski said, leaning in the door, "but you've got an urgent phone call. It's your ex-wife."

"Coming," he said, looking at me. "Think about what I said, okay?" He went out.

I stood looking after him and frowning.

"What was that all about?" Carol said, coming into the office. She was wearing a white fur hat.

"He wanted to know what to buy his Secret Santa person," I said.

Friday Gary wasn't there. "He had to go talk to his ex-wife this morning," Tonya told me at lunch, picking pickles off her sandwich. "He'll be back this afternoon. Marcie's demanding he pay for her therapy. She's seeing this psychiatrist, and she claims Gary's the one who made her crazy, so he should pick up the bill for her Prozac. Why is he still hung up on her?"

"I don't know," I said, scraping mustard off my burger.

"Carol Zaliski said the two of you were talking in Hunziger's office yesterday. What about? Did he ask you out? Nan?"

"Tonya, has Gary talked to you since Thanksgiving? Did he ask you about whether you'd noticed anything unusual happening?"

"He asked me if I'd noticed anything bizarre or abnormal about my family. I told him, in my family bizarre is normal. You won't believe what's happened now. Tom's parents are getting a divorce, which means five sets of parents. Why couldn't they have waited till after Christmas to do this? It's throwing my whole schedule off."

She bit into her sandwich. "I'm sure Gary's going to ask you out. He's probably just working up to it."

If he *was*, he had the strangest line I'd ever heard. Aliens from outer space. Hiding under hats!

Though, now that he'd mentioned it, there were an awful lot of people wearing hats. Nearly all the men in Data Analysis had baseball caps on, Jerrilyn Wells was wearing a wool stocking cap, and Ms. Jacobson's secretary looked like she was dressed for a wedding in a white thing with a veil. But Sueann had said this was the Year of the Hat.

Sueann, who dated only gigolos and Mafia dons. But she had been bound to hit a nice boyfriend sooner or later, she dated so many guys.

And there weren't any signs of alien possession when I tried to get somebody in the steno pool to make some copies for me. "We're busy," Paula Grandy snapped. "It's Christmas, you know!"

I went back to my desk, feeling better. There was an enormous dish made of pinecones on it, filled with candy canes and red and green foil-wrapped chocolate kisses. "Is this part of the Christmas decorations?" I asked Penny.

"No. They aren't ready yet," she said. "This is just a little something to brighten the holidays. I made one for everyone's desk."

I felt even better. I pushed the dish over to one side and started through my mail. There was a green envelope from Allison and Mitch. She must have mailed her newsletters as soon as she got off the plane. I wonder if she decided to forgo the heading or Dakota's Most Improved Practicing Piano Award, I thought, slicing it open with the letter opener.

"Dear Nan," it began, several spaces down from the angels-and-mistletoe border. "Nothing much new this year. We're all okay, though Mitch is worried about downsizing, and I always seem to be running from behind. The girls are growing like weeds and doing okay in school, though Cheyenne's been having some problems with her reading and Dakota's still wetting the bed. Mitch and I decided we've been pushing them too hard, and we're working on trying not to overschedule them for activities and just letting them be normal, average little girls."

I jammed the letter back into the envelope and ran up to fourth to look for Gary.

"All right," I said when I found him. "I believe you. What do we do now?"

We rented movies. Actually, we rented only some of the movies. *Attack of the Soul-Killers* and *Invasion from Betelgeuse* were both checked out.

"Which means somebody else has figured it out, too," Gary said. "If only we knew who."

"We could ask the clerk," I suggested.

He shook his head violently. "We can't do anything to make them suspicious. For all we know, they may have taken them off the shelves themselves, in which case we're on the right track. What else shall we rent?"

"What?" I said blankly.

"So it won't look like we're just renting alien invasion movies."

"Oh," I said, and picked up *Ordinary People* and a black-and-white version of *A Christmas Carol*.

It didn't work. "*The Puppet Masters*," the kid at the rental desk, wearing a blue-and-yellow Blockbuster hat, said inquiringly. "Is that a good movie?"

"I haven't seen it," Gary said nervously.

"We're renting it because it has Donald Sutherland in it," I said. "We're having a Donald Sutherland film festival. *The Puppet Masters, Ordinary People, Invasion of the Body Snatchers*—"

"Is Donald Sutherland in this?" he asked, holding up *A Christmas Carol*."

"He plays Tiny Tim," I said. "It was his first screen appearance."

"You were great in there," Gary said, leading me down to the other end of the mall to Suncoast to buy *Attack of the Soul-Killers*. "You're a very good liar."

"Thanks," I said, pulling my coat closer and looking around the mall.

It was freezing in here, and there were hats everywhere, on people and in window displays, Panamas and porkpies and picture hats.

"We're surrounded. Look at that," he said, nodding in the direction of Santa Claus's North Pole.

"Santa Claus has always worn a hat," I said.

"I meant the line," he said.

He was right. The kids in line were waiting patiently, cheerfully. Not a single one was screaming or announcing she had to go to the bathroom. "I want a Masters of Earth," a little boy in a felt beanie was saying eagerly to his mother.

"Well, we'll ask Santa," the mother said, "but he may not be able to get it for you. All the stores are sold out."

"Okay," he said. "Then I want a wagon."

Suncoast was sold out of *Attack of the Soul-Killers*, but we bought *Invasion from Betelgeuse* and *Infiltrators from Space* and went back to his apartment to screen them.

"Well?" Gary said after we'd watched three of them. "Did you notice how they start slowly and then spread through the population?"

Actually, what I'd noticed was how dumb all the people in these movies were. "The brain-suckers attack when we're asleep," the hero would say, and promptly lie down for a nap. Or the hero's girlfriend would say, "They're on to us. We've got to get out of here. Right now," and then go back to her apartment to pack.

And, just like in every horror movie, they were always splitting up instead of sticking together. And going down dark alleys. They deserved to be turned into pod-people.

"Our first order of business is to pool what we know about the aliens," Gary said. "It's obvious the purpose of the hats is to conceal the parasites' presence from those who haven't been taken over yet," he said, "and that they're attached to the brain."

"Or the spinal column," I said, "like in *The Puppet Masters*."

He shook his head. "If that were the case, they could attach themselves to the neck or the back, which would be much less conspicuous. Why would they take the risk of hiding under hats, which are so noticeable, if they aren't attached to the top of the head?"

"Maybe the hats serve some other purpose."

The phone rang.

"Yes?" Gary answered it. His face lit up and then fell.

His ex-wife, I thought, and started watching *Infiltrators from Space*.

"You've got to believe me," the hero's girlfriend said to the psychiatrist. "There are aliens here among us. They look just like you or me. You have to believe me."

"I do believe you," the psychiatrist said, and raised his finger to point at her. "Ahhhggghhh!" he screeched, his eyes glowing bright green.

"Marcie," Gary said. There was a long pause. "A friend." Longer pause. "No."

The hero's girlfriend ran down a dark alley, wearing high heels. Halfway through, she twisted her ankle and fell.

"You know that isn't true," Gary said.

I fast-forwarded. The hero was in his apartment, on the phone. "Hello, Police Department?" he said. "You have to help me. We've been invaded by aliens who take over your body!"

"We'll be right there, Mr. Daly," the voice on the phone said. "Stay there."

"How do you know my name?" the hero shouted. "I didn't tell you my address."

"We're on our way," the voice said.

"We'll talk about it tomorrow," Gary said, and hung up.

"Sorry," he said, coming over to the couch. "Okay, I downloaded a bunch of stuff about parasites and aliens from the Internet," he said, handing me a sheaf of stapled papers. "We need to discover what it is they're doing to the people they take over, what their weaknesses are, and how we can fight them. We need to know when and where it started," Gary went on, "how and where it's spreading, and what it's doing to people. We need to find out as much as we can about the nature of the aliens so we can figure out a way to eliminate them. How do they communicate with each other? Are they telepathic, like in *Village of the Damned*, or do they use some other form of communication? If they're telepathic, can they read our minds as well as each other's?"

"If they could, wouldn't they know we're on to them?" I said.

The phone rang again.

"It's probably my ex-wife again," he said.

I picked up the remote and flicked on *Infiltrators from Space* again.

Gary answered the phone. "Yes?" he said, and then warily, "How did you get my number?"

The hero slammed down the phone and ran to the window. Dozens of police cars were pulling up, lights flashing.

"Sure," Gary said. He grinned. "No, I won't forget."

He hung up. "That was Penny. She forgot to give me my Holiday Goodies slip. I'm supposed to take in four dozen sugar cookies next Monday." He shook his head wonderingly. "Now, *there's* somebody I'd like to see taken over by the aliens."

He sat down on the couch and started making a list. "Okay, methods of fighting them. Diseases. Poison. Dynamite. Nuclear weapons. What else?"

I didn't answer. I was thinking about what he'd said about wishing Penny would be taken over.

"The problem with all of those solutions is that they kill the people, too," Gary said. What we need is something like the virus they used in *Invasion*. Or the ultrasonic pulses only the aliens could hear in *War with the Slugmen*. If we're going to stop them, we've got to find something that kills the parasite but not the host."

"Do we have to stop them?"

"What?" he said. "Of course we have to stop them. What do you mean?"

"All the aliens in these movies turn people into zombies or monsters," I said. "They shuffle around, attacking people and killing them and trying to take over the world. Nobody's done anything like that. People are standing on the right and walking on the left, the suicide rate's down, my sister's dating a very nice guy. Everybody who's been taken over is nicer, happier, more polite. Maybe the parasites are a good influence, and we shouldn't interfere."

"And maybe that's what they want us to think. What if they're acting nice to trick us, to keep us from trying to stop them? Remember *Attack of the Soul-Killers*? What if it's all an act, and they're only acting nice till the takeover's complete?"

If it was an act, it was a great one. Over the next few days, Solveig, in a red straw hat, announced she was naming her baby Jane, Jim Bridgeman nodded at me in the elevator, my cousin Celia's newsletter/diary was short and funny, and the waiter, sporting a soda-jerk's hat, got both Tonya's and my orders right.

"No pickles!" Tonya said delightedly, picking up her sandwich. "Ow! Can you get carpal tunnel syndrome from wrapping Christmas presents? My hand's been hurting all morning."

She opened her file folder. There was a new diagram inside, a rectangle with names written all around the sides. "Is that your Christmas schedule?" I asked. "No," she said, showing it to me. "It's a seating arrangement for Christmas dinner. It was crazy, running the kids from house to house like that, so we decided to just have everybody at our house."

I took a startled look at her, but she was still hatless.

"I thought Tom's ex-wife couldn't stand his parents."

"Everybody's agreed we all need to get along for the kids' sake. After all, it's Christmas."

I was still staring at her.

She put her hand up to her hair. "Do you like it? It's a wig. Eric got it for me for Christmas. For being such a great mother to the boys through the divorce. I couldn't believe it." She patted her hair. "Isn't it great?"

"They're hiding their aliens under wigs," I told Gary.

"I know," he said. "Paul Gunden got a new toupee. We can't trust anyone." He handed me a folder full of clippings.

Employment rates were up. Thefts of packages from cars, usually prevalent at this time of year, were down. A woman in Minnesota had brought back a library book that was twenty-two years overdue. GROUPS PRAISE CITY HALL CHRISTMAS DISPLAY, one of the clippings read, and the accompanying picture showed the People for a Non-Commercial Christmas, the Holy Spirit Southern Baptists, and the Equal Rights for Ethnics activists holding hands and singing Christmas carols around the crèche.

On the ninth, Mom called. "Have you written your newsletter yet?"

"I've been busy," I said, and waited for her to ask me if I'd met anyone lately at work.

"I got Jackie Peterson's newsletter this morning," she said.

"So did I." The invasion apparently hadn't reached Miami. Jackie's newsletter, which is usually terminally cute, had reached new heights:

"M is for our trip to Mexico
E is for Every place else we'd like to go
R is for the RV that takes us there . . . "

And straight through MERRY CHRISTMAS, A HAPPY NEW YEAR, and both her first and last names.

"I do wish she wouldn't try to put her letters in verse," Mom said. "They never scan."

"Mom," I said. "Are you okay?"

"I'm fine," she said. "My arthritis has been kicking up the last couple of days, but otherwise I've never felt better. I've been thinking, there's no reason for you to send out newsletters if you don't want to."

"Mom," I said, "did Sueann give you a hat for Christmas?"

"Oh, she told you," Mom said. "You know, I don't usually like hats, but I'm going to need one for the wedding, and—"

"Wedding?"

"Oh, didn't she tell you? She and David are getting married right after Christmas. I am so relieved. I thought she was never going to meet anyone decent."

I reported that to Gary. "I know," he said glumly. "I just got a raise."

"I haven't found a single bad effect," I said. "No signs of violence or antisocial behavior. Not even any irritability."

"*There* you are," Penny said crabbily, coming up with a huge poinsettia under each arm. "Can you help me put these on everybody's desks?"

"Are these the Christmas decorations?" I asked.

"No, I'm still waiting on that farmer," she said, handing me one of the poinsettias. "This is just a little something to brighten up everyone's desk." She reached down to move the pinecone dish on Gary's desk. "You didn't eat your candy canes," she said.

"I don't like peppermint."

"Nobody ate their candy canes," she said disgustedly. "They all ate the chocolate kisses and left the candy canes."

"People like chocolate," Gary said, and whispered to me, "*When* is she going to be taken over?"

"Meet me in Hunziger's office right away," I whispered back, and said to Penny, "Where does this poinsettia go?"

"Jim Bridgeman's desk."

I took the poinsettia up to Computing on fifth. Jim was wearing his baseball cap backward. "A little something to brighten your desk," I said, handing it to him, and started back toward the stairs.

"Can I talk to you a minute?" he said, following me out into the stairwell.

"Sure," I said, trying to sound calm. "What about?"

He leaned toward me. "Have you noticed anything unusual going on?"

"You mean the poinsettia?" I said. "Penny does tend to go a little overboard for Christmas, but—"

"No," he said, putting his hand awkwardly to his cap, "people who are acting funny, people who aren't themselves?"

"No," I said, smiling. "I haven't noticed a thing."

I waited for Gary in Hunziger's office for nearly half an hour.

"Sorry I took so long," he said when he finally got there. "My ex-wife called. What were you saying?"

"I was saying that even you have to admit it would be a good thing if Penny was taken over," I said. "What if the parasites aren't evil? What if they're those—what are those parasites that benefit the host called? You know, like the bacteria that help cows produce milk? Or those birds that pick insects off of rhinoceroses?"

"You mean symbiotes?" Gary said.

"Yes," I said eagerly. "What if this is some kind of symbiotic relationship? What if they're raising everyone's IQ or enhancing their emotional maturity, and it's having a good effect on us?"

"Things that sound too good to be true usually are. No," he said, shaking his head. "They're up to something, I know it. And we've got to find out what it is."

On the tenth when I came to work, Penny was putting up the Christmas decorations. They were, as she had promised, something special: wide swags of red velvet ribbons running all around the walls, with red velvet bows and large bunches of mistletoe every few feet. In between were gold calligraphic scrolls reading, "And kiss me 'neath the mistletoe, For Christmas comes but once a year."

"What do you think?" Penny said, climbing down from her step-ladder. "Every floor has a different quotation." She reached into a large cardboard box. "Accounting's is 'Sweetest the kiss that's stolen under the mistletoe.' "

I came over and looked into the box. "Where did you get all the mistletoe?" I asked.

"This apple farmer I know," she said, moving the ladder.

I picked up a big branch of the green leaves and white berries. "It must have cost a fortune." I had bought a sprig of it last year that had cost six dollars.

Penny, climbing the ladder, shook her head. "It didn't cost anything. He was glad to get rid of it." She tied the bunch of mistletoe to the red velvet ribbon. "It's a parasite, you know. It kills the trees."

"Kills the trees?" I said blankly, staring at the white berries.

"Or deforms them," she said. "It steals nutrients from the tree's sap, and the tree gets these swellings and galls and things. The farmer told me all about it."

As soon as I had the chance, I took the material Gary had downloaded on parasites into Hunziger's office and read through it.

Mistletoe caused grotesque swellings wherever its rootlets attached themselves to the tree. Anthracnose caused cracks and then spots of dead bark called cankers. Blight wilted trees' leaves. Witches' broom weakened limbs. Bacteria caused tumor-like growths on the trunk, called galls.

We had been focusing on the mental and psychological effects when we should have been looking at the physical ones. The heightened intelligence, the increase in civility and common sense, must simply be side effects of the parasites' stealing nutrients. And damaging the host.

I stuck the papers back into the file folder, went back to my desk, and called Sueann.

"Sueann, hi," I said. "I'm working on my Christmas newsletter, and I wanted to make sure I spelled David's name right. Is Carrington spelled C-A-R-R or C-E-R-R?"

"C-A-R-R. Oh, Nan, he's so wonderful! So different from the losers I usually date! He's considerate and sensitive and—"

"And how are you?" I said. "Everybody at work's been down with the flu."

"Really?" she said. "No, I'm fine."

What did I do now? I couldn't ask "Are you sure?" without making her suspicious. "C-A-R-R," I said, trying to think of another way to approach the subject.

Sueann saved me the trouble. "You won't believe what he did yesterday. Showed up at work to take me home. He knew my ankles had been hurting, and he brought me a tube of Ben-Gay and a dozen pink roses. He is so thoughtful."

"Your ankles have been hurting?" I said, trying not to sound anxious.

"Like crazy. It's this weather or something. I could hardly walk on them this morning."

I jammed the parasite papers back into the file folder, made sure I hadn't left any on the desk like the hero in *Parasite People from Planet X*, and went up to see Gary.

He was on the phone.

"I've got to talk to you," I whispered.

"I'd like that," he said into the phone, an odd look on his face.

"What is it?" I said. "Have they found out we're on to them?"

"Shh," he said. "You know I do," he said into the phone.

"You don't understand," I said. "I've figured out what it's doing to people."

He held up a finger, motioning me to wait. "Can you hang on a minute?" he said into the phone, and put his hand over the receiver. "I'll meet you in Hunziger's office in five minutes," he said.

"No," I said. "It's not safe. Meet me at the post office."

He nodded, and went back to his conversation, still with that odd look on his face.

I ran back down to second for my purse and went to the post office. I had intended to wait on the corner, but it was crowded with people jockeying to drop money into the Salvation Army Santa Claus's kettle.

I looked down the sidewalk. Where was Gary? I went up the steps and scanned the street. There was no sign of him.

"Merry Christmas!" a man said, half-tipping a fedora and holding the door for me.

"Oh, no, I'm—" I began, and saw Tonya coming down the street. "Thank you," I said, and ducked inside.

It was freezing inside, and the line for the postal clerks wound out into the lobby. I got in it. It would take an hour at least to work my way to the front, which meant I could wait for Gary without looking suspicious.

Except that I was the only one not wearing a hat. Every single person in line had one on, and the clerks behind the counter were wearing mail carriers' caps. And broad smiles.

"Packages going overseas should really have been mailed by November fifteenth," the middle clerk was saying, not at all disgruntledly, to a little Japanese woman in a red cap, "but don't worry, we'll figure out a way to get your presents there on time."

"The line's only about forty-five minutes long," the woman in front of me confided cheerfully. She was wearing a small black hat with a feather and carrying four enormous packages. I wondered if they were full of pods. "Which isn't bad at all, considering it's Christmas."

I nodded, looking toward the door. Where was he?

"Why are you here?" the woman said, smiling.

"What?" I said, whirling back around, my heart pounding.

"What are you here to mail?" she said. "I see you don't have any packages."

"S-stamps," I stammered.

"You can go ahead of me," she said. "If all you're buying is stamps. I've got all these packages to send. You don't want to wait for that."

I *do* want to wait, I thought. "No, that's all right. I'm buying a *lot* of stamps," I said. "I'm buying several sheets. For my Christmas newsletter."

She shook her head, balancing the packages. "Don't be silly. You don't want to wait while they weigh all these." She tapped the man in front of her. "This young lady's only buying stamps," she said. "Why don't we let her go ahead of us?"

"Certainly," the man, who was wearing a Russian karakul hat, said, and bowed slightly, stepping back.

"No, really," I began, but it was too late. The line had parted like the Red Sea.

"Thank you," I said, and walked up to the counter. "Merry Christmas."

The line closed behind me. They know, I thought. They know I was looking up plant parasites. I glanced desperately toward the door.

"Holly and ivy?" the clerk said, beaming at me.

"What?" I said.

"Your stamps." He held up two sheets. "Holly and ivy or Madonna and Child?"

"Holly and ivy," I said weakly. "Three sheets, please." I paid for the sheets, thanked the mob again, and went back out into the freezing-cold lobby. And now what? Pretend I had a box and fiddle with the combination? Where was he?

I went over to the bulletin board, trying not to seem suspicious, and looked at the Wanted posters. They had probably all turned themselves in by now and were being model prisoners. And it really was a pity the parasites were going to have to be stopped, *if* they could be stopped.

It had been easy in the movies (in the movies, that is, in which they had managed to defeat them, which wasn't all that many. Over half the movies had ended with the whole world being turned into glowing green eyes). And in the ones where they did defeat them, there had been an awful lot of explosions and hanging precariously from helicopters. I hoped whatever we came up with didn't involve skydiving.

Or a virus or ultrasonic sound, because even if I knew a doctor or scientist to ask, I couldn't confide in them. "We can't trust anybody," Gary had said, and he was right. We couldn't risk it. There was too much at stake. And we couldn't call the police. "It's all in your imagination, Miss Johnson," they would say. "Stay right there. We're on our way."

We would have to do this on our own. And *where* was Gary? I looked at the Wanted posters some more. I was sure the one in the middle looked like one of Sueann's old boyfriends. He—

"I'm sorry I'm late," Gary said breathlessly. His ears were red from the cold, and his hair was ruffled from running. "I had this phone call and—"

"Come on," I said, and hustled him out of the post office, down the steps, and past the Santa and his mob of donors.

"Keep walking," I said. "You were right about the parasites, but not because they turn people into zombies."

I hurriedly told him about the galls and Tonya's carpal tunnel syndrome. "My sister was infected at Thanksgiving, and now she can hardly walk," I said. "You were right. We've got to stop them."

"But you don't have any proof of this," he said. "It could be arthritis or something, couldn't it?"

I stopped walking. "What?"

"You don't have any proof that it's the aliens that are causing it. It's cold. People's arthritis always acts up when it's cold out. And even if the aliens are causing it, a few aches and pains is a small price to pay for all the benefits. You said yourself—"

I stared at his hair.

"Don't look at me like that," he said. "I haven't been taken over. I've just been thinking about what you said about your sister's engagement and—"

"Who was on the phone?"

He looked uncomfortable. "The thing is—"

"It was your ex-wife," I said. "She's been taken over, and now she's nice, and you want to get back together with her. That's it, isn't it?"

"You know how I've always felt about Marcie," he said guiltily. "She says she never stopped loving me."

When something sounds too good to be true, it probably is, I thought.

"She thinks I should move back in and see if we can't work things out. But that isn't the only reason," he said, grabbing my arm. "I've been looking at all those clippings—dropouts going back to school, escaped convicts turning themselves in—"

"People returning overdue library books," I said.

"Are we willing to be responsible for ruining all that? I think we should think about this before we do anything."

I pulled my arm away from him.

"I just think we should consider all the factors before we decide what to do. Waiting a few days can't hurt."

"You're right," I said, and started walking. "There's a lot we don't know about them."

"I just think we should do a little more research," he said, opening the door of our building.

"You're right," I said, and started up the stairs.

"I'll talk to you tomorrow, okay?" he said when we got to second.

I nodded and went back to my desk and put my head in my hands.

He was willing to let parasites take over the planet so he could get his ex-wife back, but were my motives any better than his? Why had I believed in an alien invasion in the first place, and spent all that time watching science-fiction movies and having huddled conversations? So I could spend time with him.

He was right. A few aches and pains were worth it to have Sueann married to someone nice and postal workers nondisgruntled and passengers remaining seated till those people with connecting flights had deplaned.

"Are you okay?" Tonya said, leaning over my desk.

"I'm fine," I said. "How's your arm?"

"Fine," she said, rotating the elbow to show me. "It must have been a cramp or something."

I didn't know these parasites were like mistletoe. They might cause only temporary aches and pains. Gary was right. We needed to do more research. Waiting a few days couldn't hurt.

The phone rang. "I've been trying to get hold of you," Mom said. "Dakota's in the hospital. They don't know what it is. It's something wrong with her legs. You need to call Allison."

"I will," I said, and hung up the phone.

I logged on to my computer, called up the file I'd been working on, and scrolled halfway through it so it would look like I was away from my desk for just a minute, took off my high heels and changed into my sneakers, stuck the high heels into my desk drawer, grabbed my purse and coat, and took off.

The best place to look for information on how to get rid of the parasites was the library, but the card file was online, and you had to use your library card to get access. The next best was a bookstore. Not the independent on Sixteenth. Their clerks were far too helpful. And knowledgeable.

I went to the Barnes & Noble on Eighth, taking the back way (but no alleys). It was jammed, and there was some kind of book signing going on up front, but nobody paid any attention to me. Even so, I didn't go straight to the gardening section. I wandered casually through the aisles, looking at T-shirts and mugs and stopping to thumb through a copy of *How Irrational Fears Can Ruin Your Life*, gradually working my way back to the gardening section.

They had only two books on parasites: *Common Garden Parasites and Diseases* and *Organic Weed and Pest Control.* I grabbed them both, retreated to the literature section, and began to read.

"Fungicides such as Benomyl and Ferbam are effective against certain rusts," *Common Garden Parasites* said. "Streptomycin is effective against some viruses."

But which was this, if either? "Spraying with Diazinon or Malathion can be effective in most cases. Note: These are dangerous chemicals. Avoid all contact with skin. Do not breathe fumes."

That was out. I put down *Common Garden Parasites* and picked up *Organic Weed and Pest Control.* At least it didn't recommend spraying with deadly chemicals, but what it did recommend wasn't much more useful. Prune affected limbs. Remove and destroy berries. Cover branches with black plastic.

Too often it said simply: Destroy all infected plants. "The main difficulty in the case of parasites is to destroy the parasite without also destroying the host." That sounded more like it. "It is therefore necessary to find a substance that the host can tolerate that is intolerable to the parasite. Some rusts, for instance, cannot tolerate a vinegar and ginger solution, which can be sprayed on the leaves of the host plant. Red mites, which infest honeybees, are allergic to peppermint. Frosting made with oil of peppermint can be fed to the bees. As it permeates the bees' systems, the red mites drop off harmlessly. Other parasites respond variously to spearmint, citrus oil, oil of garlic, and powdered aloe vera."

But which? And how could I find out? Wear a garlic necklace? Stick an orange under Tonya's nose? There was no way to find out without their figuring out what I was doing.

I kept reading. "Some parasites can be destroyed by rendering the environment unfavorable. For moisture-dependent rusts, draining the soil can be beneficial. For temperature-susceptible pests, freezing and/or use of smudge pots can kill the invader. For light-sensitive parasites, exposure to light can kill the parasite."

Temperature-sensitive. I thought about the hats. Were they to hide the parasites or to protect them from the cold? No, that couldn't be it. The temperature in the building had been turned down to freezing for two weeks, and if they needed heat, why hadn't they landed in Florida?

I thought about Jackie Peterson's newsletter. She hadn't been affected. And neither had Uncle Marty whose newsletter had come this morning. Or, rather, Uncle Marty's dog, who ostensibly dictated them. "Woof,

woof!" the newsletter had said. "I'm lying here under a Christmas saguaro out on the desert, chewing on a bone and hoping Santa brings me a nice new flea collar." So they hadn't landed in Arizona or Miami, and none of the newspaper articles Gary had circled had been from Mexico or California. They had all been datelined Minnesota and Michigan and Illinois. Places where it was cold. Cold and cloudy, I thought, thinking of Cousin Celia's Christmas newsletter. Cold and cloudy.

I flipped back through the pages, looking for the reference to light-sensitive parasites.

"It's right back here," a voice said.

I shut the book, jammed it in among Shakespeare's plays, and snatched up a copy of *Hamlet*.

"It's for my daughter," the customer, who was, thankfully, hat-less, said, appearing at the end of the aisle. "That's what she said she wanted for Christmas when I called her. I was so surprised. She hardly ever reads."

The clerk was right behind her, wearing a mobcap with red and green ribbons. "Everybody's reading Shakespeare right now," she said, smiling. "We can hardly keep it on the shelves."

I ducked my head and pretended to read the *Hamlet*. "O villain, villain, smiling, damned villain!" Hamlet said. "I set it down, that one may smile, and smile, and be a villain."

The clerk started along the shelves, looking for the book. "*King Lear, King Lear* . . . let's see."

"Here it is," I said, handing it to her before she reached *Common Garden Parasites*.

"Thank you," she said, smiling. She handed it to the customer. "Have you been to our book signing yet? Darla Sheridan, the fashion designer, is in the store today, signing her new book, *In Your Easter Bonnet*. Hats are coming back, you know."

"Really?" the customer said.

"She's giving away a free hat with every copy of the book," the clerk said.

"Really?" the customer said. "Where, did you say?"

"I'll show you," the clerk said, still smiling, and led the customer away like a lamb to the slaughter.

As soon as they were gone, I pulled out *Organic Gardening* and looked up "light-sensitive" in the index. Page 264. "Pruning branches above the infection and cutting away surrounding leaves to expose the source to sunlight or artificial light will usually kill light-sensitive parasites."

I closed the book and hid it behind the Shakespeare plays, laying it on its side so it wouldn't show, and pulled out *Common Garden Pests*.

"Hi," Gary said, and I nearly dropped the book. "What are you doing here?"

"What are you doing here?" I said, cautiously closing the book. He was looking at the title. I stuck it on the shelf between *Othello* and *The Riddle of Shakespeare's Identity*.

"I realized you were right." He looked cautiously around. "We've got to destroy them."

"I thought you said they were symbiotes, that they were beneficial," I said, watching him warily.

"You think I've been taken over by the aliens, don't you?" he said. He ran his hand through his hair. "See? No hat, no toupee." But in *The Puppet Masters* the parasites had been able to attach themselves anywhere along the spine.

"I thought you said the benefits outweighed a few aches and pains," I said.

"I wanted to believe that," he said ruefully. "I guess what I really wanted to believe was that my ex-wife and I would get back together."

"What changed your mind?" I said, trying not to look at the bookshelf.

"You did," he said. "I realized somewhere along the way what a dope I'd been, mooning over her when you were right there in front of me. I was standing there, listening to her talk about how great it was going to be to get back together, and all of a sudden I realized that I didn't want to, that I'd found somebody nicer, prettier, someone I could trust. And that someone was you, Nan." He smiled at me. "So what have you found out? Something we can use to destroy them?"

I took a long, deep breath, and looked at him, deciding.

"Yes," I said, and pulled out the book. I handed it to him. "The section on bees. It says in here that introducing allergens into the bloodstream of the host can kill the parasite."

"Like in *Infiltrators from Space*."

"Yes." I told him about the red mites and the honeybees. "Oil of wintergreen, citrus oil, garlic, and powdered aloe vera are all used on various pests. So if we can introduce peppermint into the food of the affected people, it—"

"Peppermint?" he said blankly.

"Yes. Remember how Penny said nobody ate any of the candy canes she put out? I think it's because they're allergic to peppermint," I said, watching him.

"Peppermint," he said thoughtfully. "They didn't eat any of the ribbon candy Jan Gundell had on her desk either. I think you've hit it. So how are you going to get them to ingest it? Put it in the water cooler?"

"No," I said. "In cookies. Chocolate chip cookies. Everybody loves chocolate." I pushed the books into place on the shelf and started for the front. "It's my turn to bring Holiday Goodies tomorrow. I'll go to the grocery store and get the cookie ingredients—"

"I'll go with you," he said.

"No," I said. "I need you to buy the oil of peppermint. They should have it at a drugstore or a health food store. Buy the most concentrated form you can get, and make sure you buy it from somebody who hasn't been taken over. I'll meet you back at my apartment, and we'll make the cookies there."

"Great," he said.

"We'd better leave separately," I said. I handed him the *Othello*. "Here. Go buy this. It'll give you a bag to carry the oil of peppermint in."

He nodded and started for the checkout line. I walked out of Barnes & Noble, went down Eighth to the grocery store, ducked out the side door, and went back to the office. I stopped at my desk for a metal ruler, and ran up to fifth. Jim Bridgeman, in his backward baseball cap, glanced up at me and then back down at his keyboard.

I went over to the thermostat.

And this was the moment when everyone surrounded you, pointing and squawking an unearthly screech at you. Or turned and stared at you with their glowing green eyes. I twisted the thermostat dial as far up as it would go, to ninety-five. Nothing happened.

Nobody even looked up from their computers. Jim Bridgeman was typing intently.

I pried the dial and casing off with the metal ruler and stuck them into my coat pocket, bent the metal nub back so it couldn't be moved, and walked back out to the stairwell.

And now, please let it warm up fast enough to work before everybody goes home, I thought, clattering down the stairs to fourth. Let everybody start sweating and take off their hats. Let the aliens be light-sensitive. Let them not be telepathic.

I jammed the thermostats on fourth and third, and clattered down to second. Our thermostat was on the far side, next to Hunziger's office. I grabbed up a stack of memos from my desk, walked purposefully across the floor, dismantled the thermostat, and started back toward the stairs.

"Where do you think you're going?" Solveig said, planting herself firmly in front of me.

"To a meeting," I said, trying not to look as lame and frightened as the hero's girlfriend in the movies always did. She looked down at my sneakers. "Across town."

"You're not going anywhere," she said.

"Why not?" I said weakly.

"Because I've got to show you what I bought Jane for Christmas."

She reached for a shopping bag under her desk. "I know I'm not due till May, but I couldn't resist this," she said, rummaging in the bag. "It is so cute!"

She pulled out a tiny pink bonnet with white daisies on it. "Isn't it adorable?" she said. "It's newborn size. She can wear it home from the hospital. Oh, and I got her the cutest—"

"I lied," I said, and Solveig looked up alertly. "Don't tell anybody, but I completely forgot to buy a Secret Santa gift. Penny'll kill me if she finds out. If anybody asks where I've gone, tell them the ladies' room," I said, and took off down to first.

The thermostat was right by the door. I disabled it and the one in the basement, got my car (looking in the backseat first, unlike the people in the movies) and drove to the courthouse and the hospital and McDonald's, and then called my mother and invited myself to dinner. "I'll bring dessert," I said, drove out to the mall, and hit the bakery, the Gap, the video-rental place, and the theater multiplex on the way.

Mom didn't have the TV on. She did have the hat on that Sueann had given her. "Don't you think it's adorable?" she said.

"I brought cheesecake," I said. "Have you heard from Allison and Mitch? How's Dakota?"

"Worse," she said. "She has these swellings on her knees and ankles. The doctors don't know what's causing them." She took the cheesecake into the kitchen, limping slightly. "I'm so worried."

I turned up the thermostats in the living room and the bedroom and was plugging the space heater in when she brought in the soup. "I got chilled on the way over," I said, turning the space heater up to high. "It's freezing out. I think it's going to snow."

We ate our soup, and Mom told me about Sueann's wedding. "She wants you to be her maid of honor," she said, fanning herself. "Aren't you warm yet?"

"No," I said, rubbing my arms.

"I'll get you a sweater," she said, and went into the bedroom, turning the space heater off as she went.

I turned it back on and went into the living room to build a fire in the fireplace.

"Have you met anyone at work lately?" she called in from the bedroom.

"What?" I said, sitting back on my knees.

She came back in without the sweater. Her hat was gone, and her hair was mussed up, as if something had thrashed around in it. "I hope you're not still refusing to write a Christmas newsletter," she said, going into the kitchen and coming out again with two plates of cheesecake. "Come sit down and eat your dessert," she said.

I did, still watching her warily.

"Making up things!" she said. "What an idea! Aunt Margaret wrote me just the other day to tell me how much she loves hearing from you girls and how interesting your newsletters always are." She cleared the table. "You can stay for a while, can't you? I hate waiting here alone for news about Dakota."

"No, I've got to go," I said, and stood up. "I've got to . . . "

I've got to . . . what? I thought, feeling suddenly overwhelmed. Fly to Spokane? And then, as soon as Dakota was okay, fly back and run wildly around town turning up thermostats until I fell over from exhaustion? And then what? It was when people fell asleep in the movies that the aliens took them over. And there was no way I could stay awake until every parasite was exposed to the light, even if they didn't catch me and turn me into one of them. Even if I didn't turn my ankle.

The phone rang.

"Tell them I'm not here," I said.

"Who?" Mom asked, picking it up. "Oh, dear, I hope it's not Mitch with bad news. Hello?" Pause. "It's Sueann," she said, putting her hand over the receiver, and listened for a long interval. "She broke up with her boyfriend."

"With David?" I said. "Give me the phone."

"I thought you said you weren't here," she said, handing the phone over.

"Sueann?" I said. "Why did you break up with David?"

"Because he's so deadly dull," she said. "He's always calling me and sending me flowers and being nice. He even wants to get married. And tonight at dinner, I just thought, 'Why am I dating him?' and we broke up."

Mom went over and turned on the TV. "In local news," the CNN guy said, "special-interest groups banded together to donate fifteen thousand dollars to City Hall's Christmas display."

"Where were you having dinner?" I asked Sueann. "At McDonald's?"

"No, at this pizza place, which is another thing. All he ever wants is to go to dinner or the movies. We never do anything *interesting*."

"Did you go to a movie tonight?" She might have been in the multiplex at the mall.

"No. I *told* you, I broke up with him."

This made no sense. I hadn't hit any pizza places.

"Weather is next," the guy on CNN said.

"Mom, can you turn that down?" I said. "Sueann, this is important. Tell me what you're wearing."

"Jeans and my blue top and my zodiac necklace. What does that have to do with my breaking up with David?"

"Are you wearing a hat?"

"In our forecast just ahead," the CNN guy said, "great weather for all you people trying to get your Christmas shopping d—"

Mom turned the TV down.

"Mom, turn it back up," I said, motioning wildly.

"No, I'm not wearing a hat," Sueann said. "What does that have to do with whether I broke up with David or not?"

The weather map behind the CNN guy was covered with 62, 65, 70, 68. "Mom," I said.

She fumbled with the remote.

"You won't *believe* what he did the other day," Sueann said, outraged. "Gave me an engagement ring! Can you imag—"

"—unseasonably warm temperatures and lots of sunshine," the weather guy blared out. "Continuing right through Christmas."

"I mean, what was I thinking?" Sueann said.

"Shh," I said. "I'm trying to listen to the weather."

"It's supposed to be nice all next week," Mom said.

It was nice all the next week. Allison called to tell me Dakota was back home. "The doctors don't know what it was, some kind of bug or something, but whatever it was, it's completely gone. She's back taking ice skating and tap-dancing lessons, and next week I'm signing both girls up for Junior Band."

"You did the right thing," Gary said grudgingly. "Marcie told me her knee was really hurting. When she was still talking to me, that is."

"The reconciliation's off, huh?"

"Yeah," he said, "but I haven't given up. The way she acted proves to me that her love for me is still there, if I can only reach it."

All it proved to me was that it took an invasion from outer space to make her seem even marginally human, but I didn't say so.

"I've talked her into going into marriage counseling with me," he said. "You were right not to trust me either. That's the mistake they always make in those body-snatcher movies, trusting people."

Well, yes and no. If I'd trusted Jim Bridgeman, I wouldn't have had to do all those thermostats alone.

"You were the one who turned the heat up at the pizza place where Sueann and her fiance were having dinner," I said after he told me he'd figured out what the aliens' weakness was after seeing me turn up the thermostat on fifth. "You were the one who'd checked out *Attack of the Soul-Killers*."

"I tried to talk to you," he said. "I don't blame you for not trusting me. I should have taken my hat off, but I didn't want you to see my bald spot."

"You can't go by appearances," I said.

By December fifteenth, hat sales were down, the mall was jammed with ill-tempered shoppers, at City Hall an animal-rights group was protesting Santa Claus's wearing fur, and Gary's wife had skipped their first marriage-counseling session and then blamed it on him. It's now four days till Christmas, and things are completely back to normal. Nobody at work's wearing a hat except Jim, Solveig's naming her baby Durango, Hunziger's suing management for firing him, antidepressant sales are up, and my mother called just now to tell me Sueann has a new boyfriend who's a terrorist, and to ask me if I'd sent out my Christmas newsletters yet. And had I met anyone lately at work.

"Yes," I said. "I'm bringing him to Christmas dinner."

Yesterday Betty Holland filed a sexual harassment suit against Nathan Steinberg for kissing her under the mistletoe, and I was nearly run over on my way home from work. But the world has been made safe from cankers, leaf wilt, and galls.

And it makes an interesting Christmas Newsletter.

Whether it's true or not.

Wishing you and yours a very Merry Christmas and a Happy New Year,

Nan Johnson

❄ ❄ ❄

About the Authors

Whether writing noir, historical fiction, urban fantasy, thriller, or traditional mystery, **Dana Cameron** draws from her expertise in archaeology. Her fiction (including several "Fangborn" stories) has won multiple Agatha, Anthony, and Macavity Awards and earned an Edgar Award nomination. The first of three novels set in the Fangborn universe, *Seven Kinds of Hell*, will be published by 47North in early 2013. Dana lives in Massachusetts with her husband and benevolent feline overlords.

Orson Scott Card is the author of the novels *Ender's Game*, *Ender's Shadow*, and *Speaker for the Dead,* which are widely read by adults and younger readers, and are increasingly included in educational curricula. Besides these and other science fiction novels, Card writes contemporary fantasy (*Magic Street, Enchantment, Lost Boys*), biblical novels (*Stone Tables, Rachel and Leah*), the American frontier fantasy series The Tales of Alvin Maker (beginning with *Seventh Son*), poetry (*An Open Book*), and many plays and scripts. Card was born in Washington and grew up in California, Arizona, and Utah. Card currently lives in Greensboro, North Carolina with his wife and youngest child. *Ender's Game* will be released as a major motion picture in 2013.

Harlan Ellison's published works include over 1700 short stories, novellas, screenplays, teleplays, essays, and a wide range of criticism covering literature, film, television, and print media. He was editor and anthologist for two groundbreaking science fiction anthologies, *Dangerous Visions* and *Again, Dangerous Visions*. Ellison has won numerous awards including multiple Hugos, Nebulas, Stokers, and Edgars and Lifetime Achievement awards from the Horror Writers Association, the World Fantasy Convention, and the Eaton Collection of Science Fiction and Fantasy, as well as SFWA's Grand Master Award.

Over the past thirty years, **Nina Kiriki Hoffman** has sold adult and YA novels and more than 250 short stories. Her works have been finalists for the World Fantasy, Mythopoeic, Sturgeon, Philip K. Dick, and Endeavour awards. Her fiction has won her a Stoker and a Nebula Award. A collection of her short stories, *Permeable Borders*, was published in 2012 by Fairwood Press. Nina does production work for *The Magazine of Fantasy & Science Fiction*. She also works with teen writers. She lives in Eugene, Oregon. For a list of Nina's publications, check out: ofearna.us/books/hoffman.html.

Janet Kagan (1946 – 2008) authored two science fictions novels and numerous shorter works of science fiction and fantasy. Some of her stories, which appeared in publications such as *Analog* and *Asimov's Science Fiction*, were gathered in the collection *Mirabile*. In addition to winning the Hugo Award, "The Nutcracker Coup," was also nominated for a Nebula Award.

James Patrick Kelly has had an eclectic writing career. He has written novels, short stories, essays, reviews, poetry, plays and planetarium shows. His fiction has been translated into sixteen languages. He won the Nebula Award for his novella "Burn" and the Hugo Awards for two novelettes: "Think Like A Dinosaur" and "Ten to the Sixteenth to One." He writes a column on the internet for *Asimov's Science Fiction Magazine* and has two podcasts: *Free Reads* and James Patrick Kelly's *StoryPod*. His website is www.jimkelly.net.

Novelist, performer, and public radio personality **Ellen Kushner** may be best known as the longtime host of the national series Sound & Spirit. Her award-winning novels include the "mannerpunk" cult classic *Swordspoint*, and *Thomas the Rhymer*. Kushner's *The Golden Dreydl: A Klezmer "Nutcracker" for Chanukah*, has been produced as a CD (with Shirim Klezmer Orchestra), a picture book, and onstage by New York's Vital Theatre. With Holly Black, she recently co-edited *Welcome to Bordertown*, a revival of the original urban fantasy shared-world series created by Terri Windling. Kushner's audiobook recordings of her three "Riverside" novels were released this year by Neil Gaiman Presents for Audible.com. She lives in New York City, and travels a lot.

Charles de Lint is a full-time writer and musician who presently makes his home in Ottawa, Canada, with his wife MaryAnn Harris. His most recent books are *Under My Skin* (Razorbill Canada, 2012; Amazon.com for the rest of the world) and *Eyes Like Leaves* (Tachyon Press, 2012). His first album *Old Blue Truck* came out in early 2011. For more information about his work, visit his website at www.charlesdelint.com. He's also on Facebook, Twitter, and MySpace.

Robert Reed is the author of more than 200 published stories and a smattering of novels. His novella, "A Billion Eves," won the Hugo in 2007. He is currently at work on a trilogy set in his Marrow/Great Ship universe, due to be published beginning in 2013. Robert lives in Lincoln, Nebraska with his wife and daughter. His website is www.robertreedwriter.com.

M. Rickert is the winner of two World Fantasy Awards, a Shirley Jackson Award, and a Crawford Award. She lives in Wisconsin.

Kristine Kathryn Rusch has written a lot of bestselling, award-winning fiction under a variety of names, including Kristine Grayson, Kris DeLake, Kris Nelscott, and of course, her own name. She's the former editor of *The Magazine of Fantasy & Science Fiction*. Her entire thirty-year backlist is slowly returning to print, courtesy of WMG Publishing. For more information on her work, go to www.kristinekathrynrusch.com.

Sarban was the pen name of British writer and diplomat John William Wall (1910 – 1989). He served the British Foreign Office from 1933 until his retirement in 1977. The majority of his fiction was written during a short period between 1947 and 1951. Three books—*Ringstones (1951)*, *The Sound of His Horn* (1952), and *The Doll Maker* (1953)—were published during his lifetime. *The Sacrifice and Other Stories* (2002) and *Discovery of Heretics: Unseen Writings* (2011), were published posthumously by Tartarus Press in 2002. A biography of Sarban can be found online at homepages.pavilion.co.uk/users/tartarus/wall.html.

Ken Scholes started writing stories at fifteen, but took a long break away from it while logging time as a sailor, soldier, preacher, musician, label gun repairman, retail manager, and nonprofit director. He returned to writing about a dozen years ago, and his acclaimed debut novel *Lamentation* (2009) became the first in a five book series, The Psalms of Isaak, of which *Canticle* (2009) and *Antiphon* (2010) have also been published. He lives near Portland, Oregon with his wife and twin daughters.

James Stoddard's short stories have appeared in SF publications such as *Amazing Stories* and *The Magazine of Fantasy & Science Fiction*. His science fiction story, "The Battle of York," was included in *The Year's Best SF 10*, and his fantasy story, "The First Editions," was included in *The Year's Best Fantasy 9*. His novel, *The High House*, won the Compton Crook Award for best fantasy by a new novelist, and was nominated for several other awards. A sequel, *The False House*, followed. He has recently published a rewrite of William Hope Hodgson's *The Night Land*.

Von Jocks also writes as Yvonne Jocks and Evelyn Vaughn. The tripartite author has published a bunch of novels, the most recent of which is Evelyn Vaughn's *Underground Warrior* (2010). She has also edited (as Evelyn Vaughn) two anthologies, *Words of the Witches* and *Witches Brew*, for Berkley Jove. She has a master's degree from the University of Texas, Arlington (her thesis traced the history of the romance novel), teaches in a community college, and lives between Fort Worth and Dallas, Texas.

Connie Willis is the award-winning author of *Blackout/All Clear*, *To Say Nothing of the Dog*, *Doomsday Book*, and *Bellwether*. She's won six Nebulas and eleven Hugo Awards, and was the first author to have ever won both awards in all four categories. Willis was recently inducted into the Science Fiction Hall of Fame, and is the newest SFWA Grand Master of Science Fiction. She lives in Colorado with her physics-professor husband, a bulldog, and two very bad cats.

Robert Charles Wilson was born in California but has lived most of his life in Canada. His work has won the Hugo Award (for novel *Spin*), the John W. Campbell Memorial Award (for novel *The Chronoliths*), the Theodore Sturgeon Memorial Award (for novelette "The Cartesian Theater"), three Aurora Awards (for novels *Blind Lake* and *Darwinia,* and the short story "The Perseids"), and the Philip K. Dick Award (for novel *Mysterium*). His other novels include *Axis, Vortex, A Hidden Place, Memory Wire, Gypsies, The Divide, A Bridge of Many Years, The Harvest, Bios,* and *Julian Comstock: A Story of 22nd-Century America*. In addition to his novels, he is the author of the short-story collection *The Perseids and Other Stories*.

Gene Wolfe worked as an engineer before becoming editor of trade journal *Plant Engineering*. He retired to write full time in 1984. Long considered to be a premier fantasy author, he is the recipient of the World Fantasy Lifetime Achievement Award, as well as Nebula, World Fantasy, Campbell, Locus, British Fantasy, and British SF Awards. Wolfe has been inducted into the Science Fiction Hall of Fame. His short fiction has been collected over a dozen times, most recently in *The Best of Gene Wolfe* (2009). His latest novel, *Peace,* will be published in December 2012.

Acknowledgments

Special Thanks to Matthew Kressel, Ellen Kushner, Stina Leicht, Lavie Tidhar, and especially Ann VanderMeer for helping with the Great Chanukah Story Hunt.

"The Night Things Changed" by Dana Cameron © 2008 by Dana Cameron. First publication: *Wolfsbane and Mistletoe*, eds. Charlaine Harris & Toni Kellner (Ace, 2008).

"Wise Men" by Orson Scott Card © 2010 by Orson Scott Card. First publication: *Intergalactic Medicine Show,* Issue 20, December 2010.

"Go Toward the Light" by Harlan Ellison © 1994 by The Kilamanjaro Corporation. Reprinted by arrangement with, and permission of, the Author and the Author's agent. Richard Curtis Associates, Inc., New York. All rights reserved. Harlan Ellison is a registered trademark of The Kilamanjaro Corporation. Originally broadcast as a segment of *Chanukah Lights*, a National Public Radio presentation recorded on 15 November 1994. First print publication: *The Magazine of Fantasy & Science Fiction*, January 1996.

"Home for Christmas" by Nina Kiriki Hoffman © 1995 by Mercury Press. First publication: *The Magazine of Fantasy& Science Fiction*, January 1995.

"The Winter Solstice" by Von Jocks © 1995 by Yvonne Jocks. First publication (as written by Evelyn Vaughn): *Witches Brew*, ed. Yvonne Jocks (Berkley, 2002).

"The Nutcracker Coup" by Janet Kagan © by 1992 Janet Kagan. First publication: *Asimov's Science Fiction*, December 1992.

"The Best Christmas Ever" by James Patrick Kelly © 2004 by James Patrick Kelly. First publication: *Sci Fiction*, May 26, 2004.

❄   ❄   ❄